First edition

The Author

When Miles Fish isn't working as a lawyer, he is off hunting for his own adventures. Whether it's scuba diving in sunken Japanese WW2 ships, climbing some of the tallest mountains in the world or exploring ancient Mayan ruins lost to time in the dense jungles of Central America. His passion for exploration and discovery is matched by his hunger for philosophy and the search of wisdom. His best-selling novel, Elliot Hope and the Philosopher's Secret, is the embodiment of this.

Acknowledgement

So many people have helped with the mammoth task of researching, writing, editing, advertising and placing this novel. Although this acknowledgement does not do their contributions and efforts justice, it gives me honour and great pleasure to offer thanks to Stuart Boag, Jessica Morlid, Albert Smith, Hannilee Fish, Ruth Henderson, Irving David, Sean Ferguson, Virginia from the British Museum and Michael Harrison.

With special thanks to Amanda Smith, Chris Ogle, Till Deistel Clare Hagen, Derek Jones, and Judy Casselden for acting as a sounding board and helping me to create, evolve and refine this book.

PROLOGUE

London - Monday 3rd September 1666

The road was filled with floating flakes of orange gold and fallen debris. A woman with torn clothes rushed through Thames Street towards St Paul's Cathedral. Clutching onto her baby. Her grip was so tight her fingernails were digging, making the baby cry. Both gasping for air, but only to further poison themselves with each desperate breath. The smell of toxic smoke was unavoidable. People shouting, crying, screaming while the fire burned, crackled and roared. The great fire at Pudding Lane swept from building to building with immense ferocity. Thousands of people fleeing their homes. Many taking refuge in nearby buildings about to meet the same fate. It was night time, but even the night's shadow was no match for the glow of London's burning homes and shops.

Amongst the chaos was a man in a brown hooded cloak, running towards St Paul's Cathedral on a mission of the greatest importance. The cathedral's solid stone walls stood overwhelmingly tall and proud. To the hooded individual, it was difficult to conceive that such a structure was made from the hands of men, rather than the hands of God. Crows flying away from the fire could see the Cathedral as a long rectangular building. Meticulously designed with a spire in the middle, reaching up for the Heavens.

The hooded man reached the side doors of the Cathedral. He pulled the hood of his cloak forward, keen to ensure his face was concealed from passers-by. He knocked loudly with his right hand, his other trying to conceal a box under his cloak. He didn't like carrying something so valuable to the Order. The damage it could cause in the wrong hands. Regaining his breath, he wiped the sweat from his brow. In the not too distant background, buildings could be heard being pulled down to prevent the ensuing flames from spreading. Controlled gun powder explosions followed by loud crashing noises.

A clang came from the Cathedral door and it started to open. As it did, its weight caused the hinges to make a grating sound. Painful to the ear, like the gritting of teeth. In the doorway stood a priest. Not old, not young. He looked stressed and exhausted.

'We are not taking any more refuge' said the priest, rubbing his eyes and clearly unenthused by the late calling.

The man didn't think the priest would be surprised to see another visitor. He'd heard that with the great fire paving its way through London, many wealthy families had been taking sanctuary there, along with their most valuable possessions.

'Forgive me for the hour of my intrusion and for coming unannounced. My name is Matthew' he said. His voice lowered to a whisper 'I...I am from the Order.'

The priest's eyes widened. He gathered his posture and stood up straight. His face became fully attentive. He extended his hand which Matthew received with a firm grip. As they shook hands, their thumbs tapped the other's hand twice. A particular, but barely noticeable movement. They nodded to each other, acknowledging the other's authenticity.

'It's a relief to see a fellow Brother during this ungodly time. Please come in.'

Matthew entered the Cathedral through the large doors and walked across the main hall. His head gazed around the room. Families were lying on the uncomfortable stone floor, covered in dirt, sweat and soot. The hall way was an elegant Norman design of round arches and patterns surrounding the ceiling. His direction turned to the stained glass windows of angels and saints.

'My mother spoke of these windows to me as a boy, but their fame for beauty preys no justice having now seen them myself. I've never seen anything so magnificent' said Matthew.

'A skill born of arduous practice and immense attention to detail' replied the priest. 'But tell me...I assume the Order did not send you here at this time to see the Cathedral' he said.

Matthew looked around the room. 'No.... they did not. Is there somewhere we can talk in private' asked Matthew, who could feel the eyes of the room fall on him.

The priest opened his hand, palm facing upwards and directed him across the main hall. They walked and talked, passing old statues and paintings until they arrived at Faith Chapel. A large chapel that resonated an echo of their voices. The chapel was made up from, and supported by, a series of pillars, connecting the roof to the floor. A smell of Frankincense permeated the air. Despite the many carefully carved monuments and statues of granite, marble and limestone filled the room, the chapel was so large that it felt almost empty. The priest approached a large altar at the back of the chapel, next to a semi-circular wall of vertical pillars.

'This area is out of bounds to the public. You may speak freely' assured the priest, giving a light smile.

Matthew surveyed the area. No one else was present and so he pulled the cloak back from his head. He was five-ten, early thirties, had brown hair and a medium physique. There was distress in his eyes. Distress and fatigue.

'Our Father tells me you can protect the Order.'

'My child, I have sworn the oath in front of God himself. I'd give my life and everything I own to keep the Order and its brethren safe.'

'Thank you. My instructions are of utmost importance and secrecy' he said anxiously. 'As you may know, the Temple has been breached by the fire. Much of our beloved history has been destroyed and we need to salvage what we can. Our Father has entrusted me to ensure our greatest treasure is kept safe' he said, lifting the box from under his cloak.

The priest stared at the box curiously. As he moved in to touch it, Matthew quickly pulled away nervously and hid it back under his cloak.

'This box contains the only surviving key to the foundation of our Order. As a brother, you know it holds the largest hidden treasure in the civilised world, and with it, a power so great that it should be possessed by no man. Not the people, not the King...not even the Church!'

Matthew felt uneasy about his blasphemous comment, even if it was true. 'I need... sorry, the Order needs you to store it here until the fire has ceased. But whatever you do, it must not get into the wrong hands... the safety of the world depends on it.'

The priest rested one hand on the man's shoulder and with the other, knocked on a wall.

'My brother, these stone walls are solid... no fire can destroy this cathedral' said the priest, offering a small but sincere smile. 'This cathedral was designed to withstand fire. History will tell you, its four predecessors' lives were taken to the ashes by fire and this one will not meet the same fate. Do not worry, I will keep it hidden here until I receive further instructions. On my soul be-it.'

Matthew was beyond relieved that he'd successfully done the job he was entrusted with and that the key was now safe. He held the box out with both hands. The priest took it and, with a gentle pull, released it from Matthew's nervous grip. He wrapped the box in a blanket and held on to it firmly.

'Have faith in God. He will protect us' the priest assured.

The priest put the box down and faced his fellow brother. Matthew attempted to muster a smile, but his fatigue and stress made it difficult.

'Thank you … may your reason guide you well' said Matthew.

The priest held Matthew's hand and closed his eyes. 'I pray to God for mankind.'

He kissed the priest's hand, said good bye and left the Cathedral. On walking away, it was impossible not to notice the fire was closer. The crashing sounds from falling buildings had grown louder than before. The screams, more piercing. It was cold and yet warm. The air was dry. *Still, nothing could penetrate the Cathedral,* he thought. He reached for a cross attached to his necklace, enclosed it in his fist and prayed as he continued walking towards the River Thames.

From the river, Matthew turned around to see the Cathedral. It was now completely surrounded by the fire. It was so bright that the glow distorted his vision. Strong winds pushed the flames over the roof of the Cathedral. The Cathedral was putting up a good fight compared to the adjoining buildings which were now destroyed. At first it seemed that nothing was happening, but to his astonishment, the lead roof began slowly melting, destroying what lay beneath it. Gradually, parts of the roof fell, releasing flames that ripped into the sky from the supporting wooden beams. Matthew's head filled with blasphemous words. The burning Cathedral let out a screech as though it was alive and suffering the pain of being burned to death. The holy structure began collapsing into itself.

The Cathedral was losing the battle against London's great fire.

Fear, panic and disbelief. Matthew knew it was too late to rescue the box. Any attempt would be futile. A gut-wrenching pain ripped through his stomach. Cut by the blade of guilt and the knowledge that the Order's greatest secret and source of power was now gone. A panic attack punched him in the face and his hands began shaking. His cloak was damp with sweat. Unable to focus, unable to stand, unable to breathe. To support himself, he put his hands on the side of the River Thames wall. The exposed river bed lay twenty-five feet below him. He had failed the Order and his brothers. There was no way he could go back to them. Not now. He knew he deserved to go to hell, to be punished for all eternity, and, he knew the quickest way there. He climbed up onto the wall, crossed his hands over his chest, palms towards him. Before doubt could entertain his mind, he quickly leaned back and fell quietly to his death. The low tide of the River Thames took his life, never to be seen again.

St Paul's Cathedral and its secret were lost forever...

1

Kensington, London – Present Day (Thursday)

Teo stepped over the old man's body, keen to avoid treading blood into the already soaked cream carpet. *Footprints are a bitch,* he thought. The police would soon catch his scent if he wasn't careful. But that wasn't his biggest concern. Not right now, at least. He moved quickly from the dining room to search the rest of the large, Tudor-style house.

In the study, he checked the draws of an old mahogany desk. Nothing. The rest of the room was clean. He moved room to room searching the house, top to bottom. The home was turned upside down… torn apart like the old man's neck. Teo stared at a painting of Sir Francis Bacon hanging on the wall. He thought about the philosopher's belief that *knowledge is power*. If only the painting could speak. He'd have the knowledge of where the old man put the map. He looked at several letters on the desk, all addressed to Jonathan Hooke, but none of them gave him any clues.

Teo went back to the dining room to see a ginger cat sitting on top of the body of its lifeless owner. He knelt down and brushed the cat off, who gave a protective hiss, then ran away. Teo searched the old man's pockets and found a business card inside his jacket pocket. "Helen Philips – Curator of Prints and Drawings, British Museum."

Death comes to us all at some point, but people around Teo Brecher tend to have a shorter life expectancy than most. Wherever he went, trouble would find him. Like a deadly disease finds a host - spreading, decaying and destroying. But he was never the host. He was trained to deal with trouble. Ten years in the Israeli Mossad Special Forces gave him an edge. It taught him how to survive, how to notice the smallest detail, and, how to kill.

Teo looked at the dead body, lying on the floor. Arms spread out. Behind his head, the blood formed a misshapen circle, like a dark red halo. Teo's line of work had its messy times, and this was definitely one of them. Not that he had a job anymore. His decisions had turned him to the wrong side of the law. There was no return. There was only the mission, the whole mission and nothing but the mission. Teo pulled out his smartphone and searched the internet for the British Museum's opening times. Helen Philips would be his next visitor. He needed that map and would do anything to get it.

2

British Museum, London – Present Day + 1 (Friday)

Elliot Hope mopped the great hall of Ancient Greek artefacts. Bored. Like Picasso, he made brushing movements on the floor, creating a masterpiece of wet strides. Not that the floor was any cleaner. The remaining dirty marks bore a reflection of his enthusiasm for cleaning. Head slumped, shoulders slumped, spirit slumped. His only solace was that the day's work would be finished in another five hours.

It was a warm day outside, but the air conditioning kept the Museum cool. Tourists walked up and down the great hall, marvelling at the relics on display. Every so often, Elliot would notice a child try and touch a statue or priceless artefact. It was usually soon followed by the telling off by a parent or security guard. This peeked his interest more than this job. Elliot loved the inquisitiveness of children. Always trying to discover what things are made of and why things are the way they are. It reminded him of his younger brother, Toby. Toby would try and get inside anything mechanical. Whether it was their mother's mobile, their father's laptop or Elliot's latest Play Station console. Actually, Elliot didn't like it so much when Toby took apart his Play Station to see what was inside. Elliot was sure Toby would do well as an adult... with the right support at home that is. Elliot missed his brother.

A brunette woman walked towards him, her stride slightly restricted by the hug of her black knee length skirt. Elliot took her for a runner or some other cardio-activity goer, but not today and not in those heels. She was attractive, but too old for him. Her smart appearance made her stand out from the tourists. She was carrying some kind of old document wrapped in plastic tubing. Elliot assumed she must be working for the Museum.

Elliot felt an itch on his face. His hands were dirty from cleaning, so he used the side of his arm to scratch his forehead, slightly ruffling his chestnut hair. The brunette noticed him waving his bent arm up and down like a chicken flapping its wing. She gave him a strange look as she passed him, then entered into one of the study rooms.

He worked his mop along the corridor, passing the historical artefacts. He thought it was ironic that almost none of the valuable treasures in the British Museum were British. Arguably, the largest collection of British relics in the Museum were its employees. Most of the preservation staff were of retirement age and opted for the Museum in lieu of gardening.

Elliot stopped mopping when he reached the study room. The attractive brunette sat at a table, talking to a dodgy-looking man sitting opposite her. The man looked Spanish or Portuguese. Certainly not the type who'd have an interest in the Museum. Shaved head, tribal neck tattoo and an eyebrow piercing. Not typical for an average scholar. Elliot tried not to be prejudiced, and knew he shouldn't always judge a book by its cover. However, there are occasions where a book's cover gives a good indication of its contents, and Elliot, in his abundance of thinking time, couldn't help but wonder what such a man would want with the Museum.

Two kids slid across the hallway floor, making full use of Elliot's half-arsed mopping, each trying to slide further than the other. Elliot turned around to face them. He smiled at their ability to be care-free and in the moment, to treat the world as their playground. Health and safety aside, if he wasn't fussed about keeping his new job, he would have joined them. As if on cue, a woman came over and told them off.

Elliot stood near the exit of the study room. The brunette was still sitting with the skin-head. He noticed that their discussion had turned heated. The man's arms were waving about with enthusiastic aggression. Elliot wasn't great at lip-reading, but could just make out the man swearing as he pointed to the rolled up document. Before he knew it, the skin-head snapped the document out of the brunette's hand, stood up and stormed off towards the exit.

3

British Museum, London – Present Day + 1 (Friday)

The skin-head charged in Elliot's direction like a bull seeing red. The brunette sat there, taken by surprise. He was big like a bull and perhaps just as intimidating. Elliot wanted to do something, but did not like the idea of getting in his way. Still, he hated bullies and had more than his fair share of bruises from standing up to them.

At three feet away, Elliot stuck his mop out just below knee height. The skin-head was running with such force that he didn't have time to stop and tripped over the mop. Unable to regain his balance, he smacked the floor with full momentum. One hand managed to hit the floor first. The other hand held onto the document tightly. If the skin-head looked angry before, he looked even angrier now. His face and bald head started turning purple, as if his body decided his head no longer needed the circulation of blood. Elliot just wanted to run and hide.

'Give me that' Elliot said in an unconfident tone. 'I don't want any trouble.'
The skin-head stood up, brushed himself down and gave an intimidating sneer. 'You got trouble, ya little punk.'

Elliot saw the man reach his right arm back then adjust his waist to enable a full swing. He knew what was coming and quickly stepped out of the way.

The skin-head's fist jolted passed Elliot, hitting thin air and causing him to stumble forward. Before the man had a chance to react, Elliot cracked him over the head with the back of the mop. He fell to the ground, again, but this time the document rolled towards Elliot. Elliot bent down to pick it up. As he stood up, two security guards rushed over to assist. Seeing the tattooed man on the floor, they assumed Elliot was to blame. The larger of the two detained Elliot, whilst the smaller one tried to help the skin-head up.

'Are you ok, sir' asked the smaller security guard.

'No, I aint' he said, cursing. 'This little idiot attacked me for no reason.'

'That's a lie' Elliot shot back. 'He was trying to steal this document...it belongs to the Museum. I saw him take it.'

'That's mine, you idiot! I lent it to the Museum and now I want it back. Check with your boss! While you av a boss that is...I'll make sure you get the sack for this' he said, pointing at Elliot aggressively.

Elliot desperately needed to keep this job. It wasn't much, but he had to prove to his brother's social worker, Angela Bashton, that he was responsible enough to look after his brother, Toby. Angela was in charge of his brother's welfare. She was prickly and didn't warm much to Elliot. But, she did look after Toby's best interests and for that, he was grateful. Working at the British Museum was his last chance of proving to Angela that he can hold down a job and is stable enough to look after Toby.

The taller security officer looked at Elliot and then held onto his arm tightly.

'You need to come with me... this has to be reported to the police.'

The smaller guard turned to the skin-head. 'Sir, we're terribly sorry for the incident. We understand if you want to press charges.'

The man gave a self-satisfied grin and stared at Elliot.

'Wait' said a female voice behind them.

The guards turned around to see the brunette awkwardly running in her heels towards them. As they turned to face her, the skin-head slowly backed away, leaving the document in Elliot's hand.

'This man tried to run off with Museum property' she said, flustered and gaining her breath.

By the time the guards realised Elliot was telling the truth, the man had already sprinted off towards the back entrance of the Museum.

'Thank you, Miss Philips' said the smaller guard, who then turned to Elliot. 'I'll need to report this to the powers that be.'

The taller guard called into his radio for help and they both ran after the assailant, leaving Elliot and the brunette behind. The brunette had deep green eyes, complimented by a light touch of mascara. She didn't need make up, but what she did wear was worn gracefully. She caught her breath, flicked a lock of slightly curled hair away from her face and turned to Elliot.

'Thanks for saving me' said Elliot.

'No, thank you' she said, with a relieved smile.

Elliot was grateful that he had an alibi and wasn't going to get arrested. That would be sure to screw up his promise of looking after Toby. That said, he was anxious about what their boss would say. He'd already been fired from his last job and really needed this one to work.

'I think this is yours, Miss Philips' he said, passing the document to her. 'You must be the curator of prints and drawings.'

'Yes, I am… and thank you. Please, call me Helen. Without your help, we would've lost an important piece of history.' She looked at him curiously. 'How did you know I'm the curator... have they finally put my picture on the Museum's website?'

'No. It was a guess' he said, pleased that his inductive reasoning was correct.

'A guess' she said, looking at him blankly.

'Well, an educated guess. You're wearing heels.'

'So'?

'It means you're not a tour guide. Any experienced tour guide would know that walking around in those things all day would tear your feet apart. This tells me that your job doesn't involve standing around all day.'

'Ok, but that doesn't make me a curator.'

'No, but the pendent on your necklace contains the Latin inscription, "Dictum Muem Pactum." My word is my bond. Clearly, you're an educated woman and the fact that you are holding that old document suggests you work in prints and drawings. To be able to walk around freely with the document also indicates you're a senior employee. Finally, you were addressed by the guards as Miss Philips. This shows a level of respect given to senior staff, most notably curators here.'

She raised her eyebrows, put her hand over her mouth, the smiled again. 'You have a sharp eye. I'm impressed.'

Elliot was pleased with his conclusion, but didn't let it show. He knew that whilst inductive reasoning was sometimes useful, it wasn't always fool-proof. Like when chocolate goes missing from the kitchen cupboard of the family home. Inductive reasoning, and perhaps the culprit, would argue that the mischievous six year-old, Tommy, took it. Evidence would then be sought to support this theory, such as a guilty looking child or empty sweet wrappers near his toys. However, deductive reasoning would instead find evidence to eliminate all other possibilities and suspects, leaving only one possible conclusion. It was the father of the house that raided the cupboard after a drunken night out. Deductive reasoning was more reliable, but not always possible to use.

From an early childhood, Elliot developed a keen eye for detail, noticing everything in his surroundings. It was a gift and a curse. When his parents had been arguing, they would pretend everything was ok, but he knew what was going on. He could feel the pain they felt. He saw it, despite his parents' best efforts to protect him from adult matters. This overexposure to other peoples' suffering from a young age created an anxiety that would eat at him. This led to an overinflated guilt gland, as his mother called it, and a compulsion to help others. A form of co-dependence. Despite his observational skills and supposed brilliant mind, he was now working as a cleaner at the British Museum. A path he did not intend to follow, but one that life took him down nevertheless.

Elliot wondered why the man had tried to steal the document from the Museum. From speaking with him, if he could call it that, it was clear the skin-head was not an educated man. For now, Elliot was more concerned with what would happen to his job once the incident had been reported to his boss.

4

Outside the British Museum, London – Present Day + 1 (Friday)

Teo Brecher waited in the forecourt near the front entrance of the Museum. He kept an eye on the tourists leaving the building to see if any of them were Marco. Even with Marco's distinctive neck tattoo, he couldn't see him anywhere. The British Museum was covered in tourists like a swarm of ants on a picnic, welcomed by the sunny day. An Iranian man stood by two big red telephone booths, cooking flavoured peanuts in a heated stainless steel container. Teo could smell chocolate caramel in the air, advertising itself to the spend-happy visitors.

The front of the Museum reminded him of the ancient Acropolis in Athens, with its large pillars rising out of the ground to support its solid stone triangular roof. He climbed the large set of steps to the building's entrance to get a closer view. Unlike the Acropolis, there were no ancient philosophers discussing matters of national importance. Only tourists, voluntary donation boxes and a pear-shaped security guard.

No sign of Marco, but more importantly, no sign of the map. Teo was so close he could almost taste his end goal. Nothing would stand in his way. He would not stop until he was either dead or possessed the map and the power it could give. Marco was supposed to be saving him the task of getting the map out of the Museum. However, Teo's patience was wearing thin. If Marco didn't come out with the map in ten minutes, he'd go in and get it himself.

A police officer ran passed Teo, up the entrance steps and into the Museum. *The police must have been alerted* he thought and wondered if Marco had failed. Teo felt the gun on the inside of his dark jacket pocket. It was too public to do anything. He'd have to wait for a better opportunity.

5

Inside the British Museum, London – Present Day + 1 (Friday)

Any assaults or accidents at the Museum, had to be reported to Arthur Heartman. The person in charge of hiring and firing. Despite the warm day outside, it was always cold in Arthur's office. The air-conditioning stayed on a low temperature, even during winter. He would tell people that the heat disagreed with his concentration.

Helen Philips sat in his office, giving her account of the events earlier that day. She rubbed her arms to keep warm, but her thin red blouse did little to retain any heat. Arthur sat at his large desk, semi-distracted by recently uploaded Facebook pictures on his computer. After a minute of his bad "multi-tasking", Helen gave a deliberately loud cough. He re-gained focus and turned his attention away from his pc and over to Helen. He sat there, running his fingers around his short thick grey beard… a known sign that he was now paying attention. Elliot waited outside the office like a school kid in trouble.

'I don't think I have much of a choice' said Arthur. 'Getting into a fight is unacceptable… let alone doing it on his first day of work.'

He moved closer to his desk and gave Helen his authoritative "elbows down, hands interlinked and I'm serious" pose. She was used to this look. It put some of her colleagues in their place, but not her. She'd used her charm on more than one occasion to get Arthur to see reason, or where needed for other important decisions, like authorising holidays.

Helen put her hands on his desk and leant forward. 'Arthur, he rescued Museum property. Had it not been for him, a valuable artefact and important part of my work for the exhibition would've been stolen!'

'I hear you. I do. But the Museum's in financial difficulty as it is and we can't afford a court case' he said in a deeper tone, trying unsuccessfully to assert his authority. 'Plus if the papers get involved and saw we allowed violence to occur to a member of the public without consequence, we'd be under scrutiny by the board. Elliot will have to go.'

Helen was usually patient with her boss, but his closed-mindedness was starting to cause agitation.

'With respect, it was not clear whether that guy was actually Mr Hooke, the legal owner of the drawings. This man looked dodgy as ever and was unable to provide evidence of his identity, as is protocol here.'

'I know the protocol' he shot back.

'Sorry. I didn't mean to sound patronising' she said, taking a pause. 'I'm just saying that Elliot helped to protect the Museum and these plans. He should be rewarded, not punished! I'll call Jonathan Hooke. If it's the same person that I spoke with, I'll apologise and hope this will be the end of it. If not, then we'll know that Elliot has just saved an important piece of history and can stay here as a cleaner.'

Arthur leant back in his chair and stared at the white washed ceiling. He drew his two index fingers together, rested them over his mouth and paused for a few seconds. He looked at Elliot through the glass window, then back to Helen and leant forward.

'Helen, you shouldn't be privy to this.'

'Privy to what?'

'Elliot joined us through the St Michael's Fellowship Family Support Scheme. The scheme tries to help broken families.'

Helen had never heard of it. She shrugged her shoulders and looked at Arthur blankly. 'Since when do we take on this kind of thing?'

'We don't. Elliot's parents died a couple of years ago… little brother's in foster care. As a favour, we've agreed with the support group to employ Elliot. The idea is to help him support himself enough to have legal guardianship of his brother. Social services are on board. They may agree to let Elliot have custody if, and only if, he can hold down a steady job. If he can keep a job here, it's a start to build a case to be his brother's legal guardian.'

Helen raised her eyebrows. 'Isn't that more of a reason to not fire him?'

'You'd think so. You need to understand that Elliot has a history of uncontrolled aggression. He's a loose cannon. Fired from his last job for hitting his boss. As I hear from the social worker, he's constantly in trouble and there's little to no chance of him getting to look after his brother.

Arthur picked up a piece of paper. 'Basically…' he said scrunching the paper into a ball and throwing it at a bin across the room. 'He's a walking liability.'

His aim was off and he missed the trash can. Helen picked it up and placed it inside the rubbish bin. She could understand why he wouldn't want to keep such a troublemaker. If it was unlikely this would be an isolated event, it was better to fire him now before more disasters arose. Helen walked up to the chair in front of Arthur and rested her well-manicured hands on its back.

'Fair enough. But, if he's so bad, why did you even hire him in the first place? I didn't think we endorsed charity schemes.'

'You're right, we don't endorse other charities. Normally, that is. We made an exception for this one.'

'Why?'

'As a favour to Elliot Hope's father.'

It finally clicked. Hope. George Hope. He was the head curator at the Museum until he passed away a couple of years ago. Helen knew Elliot's father well. They were close. Perhaps too close.

'George Hope' she said.

Arthur nodded. 'His father was an asset to the Museum. I feel we owed Elliot a chance.' Arthur went back into his "I'm serious" pose. 'And now he's had that chance.'

'I heard he was at university. Why was he given a cleaning post?'

'Kicked out of uni' he said. 'The only suitable job we had available was as a cleaner.'

Helen moved to the front of the chair, sat down and leaned forward onto Arthur's desk. 'I think we should give him a chance.'

'But I thought you understood. We need to get rid of him' said Arthur.

'I do, but on this occasion Elliot was doing the right thing. Plus…' she said, resting her hand on his forearm. 'If Elliot and his brother are what's left of a brilliant academic family, I think we should help them.'

Arthur sat back in his chair, and frowned in confusion at Helen's sudden change of view. 'Even if I didn't want to fire him, he can't continue working here' he said. The trustees of the Museum are strict with their policies. I've checked with legal. Anyone involved in such an assault, cannot work in the Museum unsupervised. We cannot afford to hire a supervisor just so he can keep his job. I'm sorry, but it's out of my hands.'

Helen looked through the window at Elliot. His back was arched forward, arms on his legs with his head slumped. He looked tired and stressed. He raised his head and looked back at her. She looked into his innocent light-blue eyes. Perhaps misguided, but not a bad soul. He didn't look capable of maliciously hurting another. She couldn't imagine him getting into trouble. But, her mum always told her she wore rose tinted glasses and saw the best in everyone. She hated violence, which did concern her. So much so, that she took up defence lessons in martial arts. Ironic. She wasn't a pro, but could defend herself if need be. *Could he be that much trouble.* Helen had a history of looking after the "bird with the broken wing." Her therapist told her this co-dependent behaviour was something she needed to stop for her own wellbeing. However, the idea that he would stay separated from his remaining family if she didn't take responsibility tore a hole in her heart.

'I'll supervise him' she said.

'What'?

'Let me supervise him. I think he'd be useful. If he's anything like his father, he'd be an asset to the Museum. I've spoken with him. He's clever and definitely not being put to his best use by cleaning.'

Arthur scratched his chin. 'I don't know. I don't think it's a good idea.'

'He can only work here under supervision. Those are your words. With the exhibition starting imminently, I need all the help I can get.'

Arthur looked at Elliot again, then back at Helen and frowned. 'Ok, but he's got one chance. I mean it. Any more hiccups, no matter how small, and he's out. I still have to report the assault to the social worker, but I will say there were mitigating circumstances.'

'Noted and thank you. I promise I'll keep him out of trouble' said Helen. 'I'll tell him he's on his last life.'

6

Outside the British Museum, London – Present Day + 1 (Friday)

A final warning. Marco could make no more mistakes. If he valued his life, at least. The last person that made a mistake ended up free-diving at the bottom of a lake. Permanently. Marco's employer was far from impressed, and didn't take failure lightly. It was not too late to recover the plans and Marco was alive. For now. However, his older brother David had to take over. More educated than Marco and with time in mandatory military service, David should prove to be of better use.

David and Marco learned from a young age how to handle themselves. Getting thrown around and hit by their stepfather taught them a lesson. Get beat or do the beating. After a traumatic outburst, they both retaliated resulting in a wheel-chair destined step-father. For David, it was about teaching him a lesson. For Marco, he got enjoyment out of it. The un-nurturing environment didn't change and their dysfunction took them to adulthood. Always in trouble. Apart from military service, David's career took him down the path of organised, and usually very well paid, crime. Marco on the other hand, had less finesse. A careless and volatile thug that took enjoyment out of other people's pain. David was the brain of the two and was always looking after Marco when he got in trouble.

CHAPTER 6

David called the Organisation to see what intel he could get on Helen Philips. For David, it was essential to be equipped with information about his targets, even if it was a straight forward theft. His sources were good at digging for information, especially when it was for dirt. It'd saved his bacon in the past. Once David blackmailed a judge into extraditing a murder suspect, the son of an Iranian billionaire, back to his homeland where he would be under the protection of his father and free from persecution. Not an easy feat, particularly as the son was in police custody and so smuggling him out of the country wasn't possible. David needed leverage. Everyone had a pressure point and for the judge, it was photos of him indulging in a Nazi-esque, homoerotic display of sadomasochism with a group of men. Not the sort of thing a Jewish judge wants disclosed to the public, or to his wife and children.

David needed to know Helen's pressure point. In the meantime, the exhibition of Sir Christopher Wren was due to start in two weeks, and the plans would be on display then. David and Marco now have time to prepare their plans to steal the drawings once on show.

7

Inside the British Museum, London – Present Day + 1 (Friday)

Helen closed Arthur's door and gestured for Elliot to walk with her. Elliot was curious as to his fate, but didn't ask as he knew he'd find out sooner or later. Given his track record, he expected the sack. He stood up and followed her to the strong room where important documents and artefacts were stored for safekeeping. He noticed she was carrying the same document that was nearly stolen. At the end of the corridor, they were greeted by an electric lock and a metal door. Helen swiped her pass and the door clicked open.

'Welcome to the strong-room. Please…take a seat' she said, pointing for him to enter.

Elliot nodded, went inside the room and sat next to a large heavy table that was bolted to the floor. It had several lamps fixed in the middle, with necks that stretched out like the legs of a spider. There were bars on the windows and he felt like he was in a police cell, about to be interrogated. The metal door locked behind him.

'Am I going to be arrested' said Elliot, half joking.

'What? No, of course not.'

'Then why am I here?

Helen filled him in on his new role as her assistant. The pay was the same, but it got him off mopping duties. He didn't understand why she had stuck her neck out for him, but he was relieved and grateful. Not just to have kept his job, but to be doing something that would finally stimulate his mind a little more.

'Why are you helping me?'

She paused, flicked a lock of her brown hair away from her head, then spoke uncomfortably. 'You, erm, saved an important piece of history. Plus you're sharp. My gut tells me you'd be an asset on my team.'

Elliot wasn't convinced. He wasn't used to getting help and was sceptical as to why she would want to do him any favours. The last thing he wanted was to be in her pocket. He sat there in his grey cleaning shirt and grey trousers, looking like a convict. In the caged room, he certainly felt like one. Helen watched him stare at the bars on the window.

'It doesn't have the ambiance of a cosy country-house, but it keeps our history safe' she said.

'I'd still rather be here than mopping the corridors, any day' he said. Elliot looked at the document contained in the transparent tube. 'What is that' he said, pointing.

Helen pulled out the drawings from the tube and gently laid them on the table. They were beat up, light brown and looked like a treasure map from an Indiana Jones film. She flicked a switch on one of the outstretched lamps. They lit up the drawings, revealing numerous slightly faded stencil marks. Elliot examined the document carefully then looked up at Helen. Her lock of curled brown hair was determined to stay in front of her face. She flicked it away again.

'These look hundreds of years old.'

'They're from 1667 to be exact' replied Helen.

'That is old. How do you know…carbon dating' he said, trying to make his showing off sound as natural as possible.

Elliot's father enjoyed bringing his work home. This gave Elliot some knowledge of archaeology, but he was in no way an expert.

'No, the date's at the bottom of the next page' she said, lifting up the first drawing and pointing.

'Ah.'

Elliot laughed under his breath, but felt slightly stupid. He looked at the documents in more detail. The drawings were of a large building with a dome in the middle. *Architect plans?* He recognised the building and the design, but the dome looked slightly different.

'St Paul's Cathedral?'

'The same. We have an exhibition on architectural designs from the sixteen hundreds being launched in a couple of weeks. These plans, and other works by Sir Christopher Wren, are going to be some of the main exhibits and this is what I need your help on.'

'The dome looks thinner on paper' Elliot pointed out.

'You do have an eye for detail, just like your father' she said, then looked away and shifted on her seat. 'The dome's design was altered several times throughout its construction. It is much wider than was originally intended.'

Elliot wasn't particularly into architecture or buildings, but could appreciate St Paul's. It was difficult not to. His parents took him there as a child and he was taken aback by its overwhelming size and beautiful design.

'But why did that dodgy man want them?'

'He didn't say. He claimed to be Jonathan Hooke, a descendent of Sir Christopher Wren's right hand man, Robert Hook. Mr Hook's the legal owner of the plans. They were only recently lent to us by him. When I asked for proof of ID, he refused and, as you saw, tried to run off with them. They are valuable and could be sold in the open market' she said, pausing with her mouth open.

'But?'

She explained that selling the drawings in the open market would require the verification of their authenticity. There are two main types of authentication. The first is a certificate given by a reliable person. The second is by checking the attributes of the drawings compared with other drawings by the same author, e.g. carbon dating, style of drawing etc. In both cases, archaeologists, scholars and Museums will check online at the Serious and Organised Crime Agency to make sure the artefact in question is not the subject of any criminal activity.

'Erm, ok. That's assuming the verifier is honest' said Elliot.

'True' she replied.

Elliot wondered why the tattooed man wanted the drawings, if not to sell them on for financial gain. He scanned through them. They didn't look valuable or important enough to steal. *Perhaps he was the owner of the drawings. Maybe he wanted to sell them on the black market. No. Unlikely,* he thought. Even on the black market the drawings wouldn't fetch much without authentication. He held up the papers closer to him. As he did, a drawing slid on to the floor.

'Be careful' said Helen.

'Sorry' he replied, picking it up.

He laid the drawing back on the table, careful not to cause any tears or marks. The drawing was of the underground crypts. Unlike the others, this one contained a Latin inscription.

'Look at this' he said, holding out his index finger. 'Where it says "Faber est quisque fortunae suae." I'm a little rusty, but I think it says:

"Every man is the architect of his own fortune.
Pythagoras, your beauty finds truth before Faith.
The foundation of greatness and strength lies with Plato's missing element."

'A little rusty...and a little modest' Helen replied, looking at him with her eyebrows raised. 'You're spot on. I've had it translated' she said handing him a piece of paper. 'Sir Christopher Wren was also a philosopher. Our PhD researcher believes this was just a philosophical message taken from his studies of the ancient Greek philosophers.'

Elliot loved Latin. His parents would play games with him in Latin when he was younger. He soon developed a hunger for it in his teens and by the age of 19 he was reading Latin books unaided. He had a thirst for knowledge, but Latin was a hobby that he kept personal to him. Since his parents passed away, he stopped having hobbies. Elliot studied the words.

'"Every man is the architect of his own fortune". Well, Sir Christopher Wren certainly made a fortune from his architecture.'

'Yes he did' Helen said, smiling. 'He designed over 50 of London's churches, making a small fortune for himself.'

The first line seemed relatively straight forward, albeit a tad odd to write on an architect's drawing. It was the next two lines that interested Elliot. They were unusually cryptic. Elliot studied philosophy for his undergraduate degree. Before he was kicked off of the course, that is. Philosophy can be difficult to understand, but these two lines were beyond his comprehension.

'Hey, I don't think this is a typical philosophical statement. I'm not sure what it is. I've studied Aristotle, Pythagoras and Plato both at university and as a hobby. This just doesn't make sense. I think this is some kind of hidden message.'

8

London – Present Day + 1 (Friday)

'Enlighten me' said David, on answering his mobile. For the Organisation to call back so quickly, it meant they had results. As with any of David's assignments, a sacrifice would have to be made between quality, time and cost. On this assignment, quality and time were essential. Obtaining the plans without delay was crucial and so the increase in cost was a necessary sacrifice.

The Organisation were expensive, but worth it. They were the Swiss army knife of private investigators and problem solvers. Highly technical, highly capable and highly illegal. They provided a full service. From tracking people around the globe, hacking into Government databases to attacking the credibility and reputation of their targets. They have one overarching rule. Discretion. No one knows their client base. No one knows who the Organisation really are. David had heard rumours that they were run by an ex-M15 employee and a couple of computer geniuses, but no one knows for sure. Given their work can be both immoral and illegal, discretion was best for the protection of all involved. However, if the authorities did ever start snooping around, all evidence of the Organisation would vanish… disappearing like a snowflake in the Sahara Desert.

David's current employer was a referral from the Organisation. Very dangerous and well connected. It was imperative to keep the client happy. If not for his health, then for the sake of getting more recommendations from the Organisation.

Intel told David that Helen lived in Guildford, Surrey and had no immediate family. Family was always useful leverage, but David would have to make do without it. However, he now had her work timetable, banking information, National Insurance Number, a tap on her mobile phone calls and location. If she used her credit card, he would know about it. *Time to do things properly*.

9

Inside the British Museum, London – Present Day + 1 (Friday)

Helen went to investigate whether the skin-head in the Museum was the true owner of the architect's plans. She called Jonathan Hooke several times, but there was no answer. She had no mobile number for him. Elliot was afraid they'd have to go and visit him at his home. If he turned out to be the same guy in the Museum, he could be in big trouble. He searched the name Jonathan Hooke on the internet. A match came up on Linkedin. He clicked on it and a picture of a silvered haired, wrinkled, kind face appeared.

'Well... that jerk in the Museum was obviously an imposter' she said, putting her hand on Elliot's shoulder. 'I think the Museum has its very own hero.'

Elliot nodded slightly, but said nothing. It was nice, but unusual to get recognition for trying to do the right thing. The way he saw it, he was always getting in trouble for trying to do the right thing. After a while, he just tried to stop caring. The only thing he focused on was looking after his younger brother, Toby. But even that wasn't working. The feeling of helplessness caused him anxiety and he found that the best way for him to deal with it was to focus on work.

The silence was almost awkward. Helen gave him a pursed lip smile. 'Hey, I know. You could be my head assistant. I might even be able to get Arthur to give you a pay rise' she said.

Elliot smiled, but still stayed silent. He still had no idea why she was being so nice. Yes, he helped save an artefact in the Museum, but it didn't warrant a pay rise or promotion on his first day at work. Her kindness did not seem proportionate. He put it down to her just being an overly caring individual. Elliot turned his attention to the translation again.

"Every man is the architect of his own fortune.
Pythagoras, your beauty finds truth before Faith.
The foundation of greatness and strength lies with Plato's missing element."

He stared at the drawings and paced around the table like a detective trying to size up its suspect. He raised his index finger against his mouth as he was deep in thought. Searching the recesses of his brain brought nothing to mind. He was grateful to be working on something more engaging than mopping floors and cleaning the urinals from the bad aim of apparently sober visitors and staff. There was a slight, but noticeable change in his body language. His head was less slumped than before.

'Are there any other inscriptions' he asked, thumbing through the drawings.

Helen shook her head. 'No, just what you see here.'

Whilst searching through the drawings, he saw that someone had defaced one of them with a marker pen. *Idiot.* The drawing was of one of the underground crypts, called Faith Chapel. The pen mark circled a column with the words "pillar V" in writing next to it. Elliot could tell the mark was recent… the ink was thick and unfaded. The fifth pillar, he thought. Then it came to him.

'Look' he said, leaning in on the table and pointing at the message.

'At what?'

'Pythagoras, your beauty finds truth before Faith. Why is the Latin word for faith, "Fides", spelt with a capital F?'

'No idea… it's important?'

'It's a place' replied Elliot, showing her the drawing of Faith Chapel. 'I bet this message has something to do with that underground crypt. What else could it be?'

'Hmmm… not sure. Excellent observational skills though. But…' she said, shrugging her shoulders. 'As I said before, we've had our best look at it. If there was anything relevant, our researchers would've noticed.'

Helen patted Elliot on the back and gave him a patronising smile. Or maybe it was an encouraging one, he wasn't quite sure. He certainly felt patronised. She seemed happy with him, unusually so. Still, she wasn't convinced there was a hidden message on the plans. Either she was being obtuse or just didn't believe that he could spot something her "best" didn't notice.

'Maybe your researchers just didn't pick up on it.'

'Ha, unlikely' she said, combing her fingers through her silky brown hair. 'Ok, let's say you're right, which I doubt you are… no disrespect. What could the statement mean? And what does it have to do with Faith Chapel?'

Elliot had no idea, but was determined to find out. He loved a challenging puzzle. On his birthday, his father would leave presents around the house and give him one clue. Often it would be a secret code or cipher. They were his favourite…the more undecipherable the better. It was kind of like the Mensa's version of an Easter egg hunt. The thought of finding a hidden message on a historical document filled him with excitement. He felt like Indiana Jones…all he needed was a whip, a hat and a short Oriental assistant.

Helen read the last sentence of the message aloud. 'The foundation of greatness and strength lies with Plato's missing element. What's Plato's missing element?'

Elliot moved around the table and stood next to Helen. He rested his hands on the table, both arms straight. Helen observed his movements, smiled and turned her gaze to the documents.

'Plato's missing element' he said. He tapped his finger on the table a few times as he contemplated its meaning. 'I'm not completely sure…' he said, frowning. 'But the "missing element" could be referring to the elements of the world.'

'The elements?'

'In natural philosophy, Plato believed the earth was made of four elements. Fire, earth, air and water' said Elliot.

Elliot spoke with the confidence and authority of a lecturer. Helen watched him take control of his investigation and entertained his thoughts.

'So what's the missing element?'

'There isn't one. It doesn't make sense' Elliot said, scratching his head

'God knows… maybe he's taken the meaning to the grave with him' said Helen.

'Maybe that's it.'

Helen raised one eyebrow. 'You want to check his grave?'

'No. "God knows"!'

Helen looked at him blankly.

'Plato's student, Aristotle, believed there was a fifth element known as the God particle. This isn't the God particle that C.E.R.N in Switzerland has been trying to find with the Hadron Collider. No, Aristotle called the God particle the fifth pillar of creation. You may have heard of it as the aether.'

'Ah, that could add up' said Helen.

'How so?'

'Sir Christopher Wren studied Aristotelian Physics at Oxford University. He'd probably know about the fifth element.'

Elliot nodded. He knew he was probably right, but didn't want to rub it in. He showed Helen the drawing with "pillar V" circled in felt pen.

'The fifth pillar' said Helen.

'Exactly' said Elliot. 'I don't fully understand the message, but it appears something of value to Wren is connected to the fifth pillar in Faith Chapel at St Paul's Cathedral. If you want help on the exhibition, this could be a good place to investigate.'

Elliot's face lit up with excitement. The idea that he had discovered something no one else had gave him a sense of adventure. He wondered what it could be. *Something of historic value?*

Or even better, a treasure hunt?

'I doubt it' said Helen. 'In my 12 years of research for the Museum, X never marks the spot. Still, if you really think there's something of historical importance relating to Wren, it's lunch time and I suppose we could go and check it out now.'

'What if X does mark the spot' replied Elliot.

'There's only one way to find out.'

10

Outside St Paul's Cathedral – Present Day + 1 (Friday)

Elliot and Helen arrived at the rear of the Cathedral from New Change Street. They went through the large open courtyard, passing the landscaped gardens and winding paths. The gardens contained an array of trees, flowers and benches. The smell of red tulips, bluebells and daffodils gave the air a freshness, despite London's busy roads being less than forty meters away. The gardens were well kept. Had it not been for the numerous visitors eating their sandwiches on the benches and concrete steps, Elliot would've forgotten it was lunchtime.

'So, what do you think we'll find' said Helen.

Elliot shrugged his shoulders. 'St Pauls has been built for over three hundred and fifty years. I have no idea that whatever was there, still will be. That is, if there ever was anything in the Cathedral in the first place. Still, it's worth checking out and it's a nice day for an adventure away from the Museum.'

'Yes, it is. The ticket office is just here' Helen said, pointing to the side entrance.

Elliot saw a crowd of people gathering by the entrance. 'Looks like a tour's about to start' he said walking towards the ticket office. 'Let's see if we can jump in on this group instead of waiting for the next one.'

Helen approached the ticket desk. 'Two tickets please.'

An attractive, curly-haired, Indian woman stood behind the ticket desk. She pushed the glasses up from her nose as she raised her head to see Elliot and Helen.

'Certainly. Would you like the complimentary lunch for an additional ten pounds per person' the ticket attendant asked.

Helen shook her head. The attendant gave Elliot a flirtatious smile. He'd changed from his cleaning attire into casual wear. Unfortunately, his top got slightly shrunk in the wash, which meant his blue sleeveless shirt clung to his torso, revealing his toned outline. The attendant didn't seem to mind. The young woman's gaze moved up to his light blue eyes, soft lips and three days' worth of stubble. Helen hadn't noticed his physique before, but the attendant's slightly awkward stare made it difficult not to notice.

'Ahem' Helen coughed.

The attendant turned to Helen. 'That's thirty-two pounds please.'

Helen paid with her credit card and took the tickets.

Unbeknownst to them, they were being followed by David, Marco and Teo. Marco and David kept their distance, making sure Helen and Elliot were not warned by their presence. Teo kept an eye on all of them from even further away. He was highly trained in surveillance and so he didn't need to be as close. Helen and Elliot entered the side of the Cathedral. David continued walking forward... he didn't want to make it obvious that he was following them. Not yet, anyway. As the older brother, David, gave Marco strict instructions not to kill Helen until he had the drawings and anything else they could find. Teo looked inconspicuous in his dark trousers, black shoes and short-sleeve white shirt and went in the Cathedral after them.

11

St Paul's Cathedral – Present Day + 1 (Friday)

Inside the Cathedral, Elliot and Helen were greeted by the breathtaking view of the nave; a long central section of the Cathedral that was covered in renaissance alcoves, an infinity chequered floor and an overwhelmingly magnificent dome, seventy meters above the floor. Elliot felt like he'd been introduced to heaven. A man made one at least. They joined the rest of the group, surrounding a young blonde woman. It was difficult to miss her dressed in an almost luminous orange t-shirt, with the words "Guide" in large print on the front.

'Welcome to St Paul's Cathedral' said the blonde. 'My name is Natalie and I'll be your guide for today. Please do shout if you have any questions during the tour. Well, maybe don't shout. Before we get started, can you make sure you stay with the group at all times. Due to some refurbishments, the Cathedral is out of bounds to the public, except for those who stay with me. If you go astray, the Bishop may have to chase you out with his broomstick.'

A few generous chuckles came from the group. The tour commenced and they slowly worked their way around the Cathedral floor, with its many chapels and crypts - learning about the Cathedral's architecture, history, décor, tombs and its memorials, all the while soaking up the grandeur of the building. After half an hour passed by, Elliot and Helen arrived at the underground crypts; a massive area spanning the floor of the Cathedral. Aptly, it was the same shape as the Holy Cross. The tour guide huddled the group together by some large arches then shushed them to silence.

'This Cathedral has been built five times' said the guide. 'The first three times it was constructed out of wood, but each time it was destroyed by fire. The fourth time it was made of stone and lead and was built to be more robust. Like the Titanic, it was thought to be unbreakable. But in 1666, the Great Fire of London brought the building down to its knees. The only part of the Cathedral to partly survive the Great Fire was this area here, known as Faith Chapel' she said, pointing ahead to a large open room cordoned off with yellow health and safety tape. 'Unfortunately, you'll see it's currently closed for repairs and renovations and so we won't be going inside today.'

Elliot and Helen turned to the Chapel, then faced each other and nodded. The chapel was empty. Elliot knew it was probably the best chance they'd get to investigate the chapel without interruption. It was better to go now, or they might not get another chance before the exhibition took place.

12

Outside St Paul's Cathedral – Present Day + 1 (Friday)

The front of the Cathedral looked like a giant, articulately designed, house of cards. The first level of cards was made up of twelve high-rise columns. The second level had four columns with a triangle block above them. Like a fairy-tale castle, a cone-shaped spire stood at both sides of the pyramid. David waited behind the row of pillars. He ran out of patience and tried to open the nine-meter-tall, very thick front door. It wouldn't budge. He assumed it was closed shut, although it could've been just too heavy to move.

David didn't have much confidence in Marco, but he was family. He knew they had to stick together, especially if Marco was going to survive in the world. Not that it gave him any comfort. Marco was a loose cannon that almost always let his assignments get out of control. Once they'd been hired to scare a witness out of testifying in a billion-dollar oil spill law suit. Marco was supposed to just rough up the witness, but only a bit. However, his thirst for violence and lack of control didn't stop there and ended up paralysing the victim. If David hadn't intervened, the witness would've been killed. It almost screwed up the whole court case and David's reputation with it. He didn't like to admit it, but he knew there was something wrong with his brother. A darker side that did not always see reason.

David wondered how he was getting on inside the cathedral. There was no sign of him and he'd been in there for half an hour.

The Organisation called David with an update. Helen's assistant was a twenty-two year old, dead-beat, no-hoper called Elliot. It was difficult to track his living arrangements as he'd been living off people's couches. No security, no permanent address, no known ties other than his employ at the Museum. Both of his parents were deceased. They found no information on any siblings and the only relative left was an aunt in Suffolk. Elliot's phone records showed that he'd not contacted his aunt in the five years he'd had his mobile phone contract. It was leverage, but not much. David's sources also told him that Helen left the British Museum with a copy of the architect plans. They weren't the originals, although they'd have to do. He pulled back the sleeve of his brown leather jacket and checked the time. *The tour will be finishing soon,* he thought. *Not long now.*

13

Inside St Paul's Cathedral – Present Day + 1 (Friday)

The tour group spent a few minutes taking in the crypt's décor, with its numerous arches forming the ceiling, all connected by supporting square pillars placed around the room. As the group continued on towards the next stage of the tour, Elliot pulled Helen's arm, signalling for her to slow down. She gave a confused look, but did as he said. The guide continued chatting away as Elliot slowed down, reaching the back of the group. He whispered "Now" and pulled her by her arm into one of the bays of a nearby wall. Out of sight. Nobody noticed and the group carried on walking.

'What are you doing… we have to stay with the group' she whispered.

'Trust me.'

Elliot could tell Helen was uncomfortable as she stood awkwardly in the bay. She didn't move. His arm slightly stuck outside of the arch. Helen leant against him gently to prevent them from being seen. They kept out of site until the group gradually moved on. A few minutes passed. Apart from the faint sound of their gentle breath, the room was filled was silence. Elliot popped his head out, looked left, then right and slowly came out of the bay, tiptoeing towards Faith Chapel.

'What the... why am I letting you do this' said Helen. 'Your job's already hanging on a thread! I really don't think this is a good idea. If we get caught, we'll get arrested. You'll be fired from the Museum and who knows what'll happen to me.'

Elliot could see she was getting flustered. He needed to calm her down before someone heard them and they got in trouble.

'It'll be ok. Besides, you can't get arrested for trespassing. It's a civil offence. The worst they'd do is tell us to leave' he said, raising his finger to his lips for her to stay quiet.

Helen looked unimpressed, but followed him anyway.

'We'll be really quick' he whispered. 'We'll check it out and then we'll be on our way before anyone realises we left the tour.'

'It's my job to look after you. You're my responsibility' she huffed.

Elliot lifted the line of yellow health and safety tape in front of the Chapel. 'Ladies first.'

'Thanks... I think.'

Helen bent down, climbed under the line of tape then turned around and held it up for Elliot to climb under. The chapel was as still as a photograph. It was so silent that they could hear the gentle echo of their own footsteps. The room was shaped into a rectangle of columns, standing up like a set of dominos. Each domino was connected to another by artistically designed, golden brown, pearly gates. To dampen the sound of their footsteps, they tiptoed over a red and golden rug covering the length of the chapel and made their way over to a large altar located at the back of the chapel. Helen took out a photocopy of the drawing with the translation and handed it to him. He studied it again; scrolling his index finger to the fifth pillar on the drawing. He looked at Helen, pointed to a pillar in the corner of the crypt and signalled for Helen to walk over. A metal crashing noise came from a stairway behind them. Helen and Elliot's line of sight shot to the exit.

'What was that' asked Helen.

'Quick, hide.'

With haste, Helen hid behind a pillar at the side of the room, and Elliot huddled down behind the altar. A few seconds later, a young priest appeared.

'Hello, is anyone there? Father Arnauld... is that you?'

No response. The priest marched up to the yellow tape and scanned his eyes across the room. He couldn't see anybody. He turned around to walk away, just as Helen's mobile began to vibrate. Helen cursed under her breath. She pressed reject, but it was too late... the priest looked over to the pillar where she was hiding. He could see the pillar had a faint but odd shadow behind it.

The priest bent down to climb under the yellow tape and investigate. Helen closed her eyes and held onto the locket around her neck. As the priest climbed under the tape, a button from his black robe got caught. He turned around, untangled himself from the tape, then walked towards the pillar.

Without raising his head above the altar, all Elliot could see was the white-washed arched ceiling above him. He laid down, rested his head against the floor and looked under the altar. His view was partly obstructed by a large candle stand, but he could just about see the bottom of the priest's legs walking towards Helen's pillar. His heart began racing. As much as he reassured Helen they'd be ok, there was still a risk that his boss, Arthur, would find out and give him the sack.

The priest jumped in front of the pillar. 'Busted!'

Elliot knew they'd been caught. His heart sank and he waited for the priest to call him over. Something touched his foot, making him jump. He kicked out thinking it was a rat or something, then tilted his head towards his feet. He saw Helen was crouching down next to him. He realised she must have stealthily moved from the pillar when the priest turned around to untangle himself. She put her finger against her mouth, telling Elliot to stay silent.

Elliot's mouth could keep quiet, but there was no silence to the pound of his beating heart. He was scared...not for himself, he could handle trouble as he had on many previous occasions. But, he couldn't afford to jeopardise his chances of being reunited with his brother. Losing his job would do just that. He'd made a promise to his brother, Toby, and while his track record hadn't been great, he was desperate to make good on that promise.

Elliot could see the priest's legs turn from the pillar towards the altar and walk in his direction. *Not out of the clear yet.* The priest was just opposite the altar. Close enough to touch. He held his breath, desperate not to make a sound.

'Excuse me, what are you doing' said a deep male voice.

Elliot and Helen looked at each other. *Caught.* Elliot spoke several profanities in his mind. Helen scrunched her face, put her hands on the floor and began to push herself up.

14

Inside St Paul's Cathedral – Present Day + 1 (Friday)

Elliot realised that the voice was slightly deeper than before. He quickly pulled Helen back down to stop her from standing up from behind the altar. She froze mid press-up and mouthed "what" to Elliot. He gestured for her to stay silent.

'I said, what are you doing.'

After a few seconds the priest turned around. 'I was just…' he murmured.

'You were just nothing' interjected the deep male voice. 'The Chapel is out of bounds. It's not safe…you know this. An Act of God may not strike you down for it, but I might!'

'I thought I heard something' said the priest.

'Go and help Thomas with the scriptures upstairs.'

The priest nodded, stepped away from the altar, climbed back under the health and safety tape and left the Chapel. Elliot waited until they were alone again and let out a deep sigh. The Chapel fell silent again.

'Let's get out of here' said Helen.

'In a second… let's take a look at the pillar first' Elliot insisted.

Helen huffed, but did as he said. They tiptoed back to the fifth pillar and inspected it from all angles. There were just some creative indents and sculpted angels. Nothing about Sir Wren. Elliot wondered if they'd hit a dead end. Helen tapped her head…a quirk that Elliot noticed she did when she was thinking sometimes.

'Are you sure this is the right one' asked Helen. 'I can't see anything.'

'According to this drawing.'

The pillar looked the same as all the others. Elliot studied it again, top to bottom. He looked at one of the angels in the middle of the pillar. The angel was slightly different to the rest.

'Hang on' said Elliot.

'What is it?'

'These angels have wings. But this one…' he said pointing to one of the carvings on the pillar, '…this one here's slightly different.'

'It looks the same to me' she said, shrugging her shoulders and giving him a blank look.

'Look closer at the angel's back' he said. 'They appear like wings, but they're not. It's a circle with an additional line around its edge.'

'Er, ok' she said.

'Aristotle's chemical symbol for the God Particle is the circle' Elliot explained.

Helen gave another blank look.

Elliot shrugged his shoulders. 'A hobby.'

They looked closer at the angel. Its left leg was bent, crossed over in front of the right one. The angel held a harp in its left hand and pointed towards the floor with its right one.

'You know the British philosopher, John Lock, believed creative ideas come from seeing and hearing things that already exist in the world. For example, the angel comes from two of our external experiences... the human form and the wings of a bird' said Elliot.

'Or the human form and a circle in this case' added Helen.

'Exactly.'

Helen followed the path of the angel's pointing hand, which led to a floor tile in the shape of the chapel. The tile was covered in a triangle of dots. She walked over to it, knelt down and took a closer look.

'Whatever Sir Wren was trying to tell someone must be under this' she said, touching the tile.

'Maybe, but how can we get underneath. We can't break it. I'm pretty sure it's a criminal offense' said Elliot.

'Yes. But not if we just lift it up. Besides, they're renovating the place... they probably wouldn't notice.'

Elliot walked back to the altar, picked up a large candle stand with a flat base and returned to the tile. Using the stand, he scratched away some of the grout between two tiles. The grout began turning to dust, making a gap between the tiles. He wedged the candle stand in the gap, started to push and then paused.

'This isn't right.'

Helen rested her hand on his shoulder. 'Elliot, I really don't think it's a criminal offense.'

'No, that's not what I mean. I don't think this is the right tile.'

'What do you mean? It must be...why wouldn't it be?'

'The dots in the middle of the tile are in the shape of a triangle.'

'So?'

'The triangle of dots is the symbol for the Pythagorean Brotherhood.'

'The what Brotherhood?'

'The Pythagorean Brotherhood. An ancient group of followers of the philosopher and mathematician, Pythagoras. He did more than just invent a way to work out the length of a triangle. The Brotherhood and Pythagoras believed that everything in the world could be understood and solved with maths to find esoteric truths. They were often persecuted and killed for this belief by tyrannical governments and so had to keep their teachings underground.'

'How do you even know this?'

'Personal interest.'

'OK, but if this is their symbol, then whatever we're looking for must be underneath this tile. This is where the angel is pointing' said Helen.

'That's what I thought at first, but it's not. The Brotherhood would hold secret meetings. Meetings in hidden locations that could only be determined through the use of mathematical codes. The most common one being the Pythagorean Cipher, or as you may know it today as the Polybius Cipher.'

Elliot explained that to work out the location of whatever they were hoping to find, a key word was needed. *The message on the drawings?* He pulled out the photocopy of the drawing, turned it over, drew a five by five square box and listed the Latin alphabet, left to right, working downwards. He then listed the numbers 1 to 5 along the top of the box and down along the left-hand side. He showed the grid to Helen.

	1	2	3	4	5
1	A	B	C	D	E
2	F	G	H	I/J	K
3	L	M	N	O	P
4	Q	R	S	T	U/V
5	X	Y	Z		

'So we need a key-word' asked Helen.

'Yes, but I've got no idea what it could be.'

Elliot's knee was a bit sore from kneeling down. He stood up and suddenly felt an awareness of the space around him. Although the area was deathly silent, he felt as if he was being watched. He stared over at a creepy gothic-looking statue of a demon in the area just outside the Chapel. He thought it'd suit being in a horror movie rather than a cathedral. He turned his head and did a quick scan of the area, but no one was around.

He pulled out the Latin translation again.

"Every man is the architect of his own fortune.
The foundation of greatness and strength lies with Plato's missing element.
Pythagorus, your beauty finds truth before Faith."

Elliot stared up at the ceiling in deep contemplation.

'The foundation of greatness and strength lies with Plato's missing element' said Helen, reading out the translation. 'Maybe it's the fifth pillar.'

'That's too long' he said, rubbing the back of his head.

'But' he said, scribbling on the piece of paper.

'But what' asked Helen.

'Aether, its chemical name. That might work.'

'You know aether is also the Greek word for burnt. That's where the term "Ethiopian" came from. Not particularly PC' she said.

'Charming!'

Elliot wrote down "Aether" on the piece of paper, and for each letter noted the number at the top and left hand side of the square. He then put these numbers together.

'No, this isn't right.' He said.

'What about "Faith"' she asked.

'That could work.'

Elliot wrote down the word "Faith", then put these numbers together.

'No, this isn't correct either.'

Elliot looked back at the drawing. 'Doh, I'm such a donut.'

'Why?'

'The message is in Latin, not English. The Latin for Faith is Fides.'

He went back to his sheet of paper, repeated the process again and came out with a series of numbers.

" F I D E S"

"12, 42, 41, 31, 54"

Elliot jumped to his feet and held on to Helen's arm. 'This is it…'

Elliot explained that the first two numbers were used by the Brotherhood as the co-ordinates for the location of their secret meetings. The other numbers were coded to give a date and time for the meeting.

He cross-referenced the co-ordinates against the markings on the Chapel-shaped tile. Twelve points north, Forty-two points east of the pillar. He flipped over the piece of paper and made two lines on the drawing of the crypt to show the relevant axis. The two lines crossed together in an X shape somewhere near where the altar was placed. He waved Helen to bend down. She knelt down on one knee next to him. Elliot smiled.

'Yes. Look' he said pointing to the "X" on the drawing.

'I guess X can mark the spot.'

15

Inside St Paul's Cathedral – Present Day + 1 (Friday)

Marco had been keeping track of Helen and Elliot whilst they were on the tour, but lost them when they disappeared from the tour group. Teo would have to get the map himself. He could see them from the shadows of the large demonic monument with a perfect view of the chapel. He watched with great interest as they unravelled the cryptic message behind the drawings. Surprised at the progress they were making. Until now, he didn't quite appreciate how capable they were. The Order went to great efforts to ensure the map could only be understood by the most intelligent of philosophers. Teo himself wasn't sure how he'd decipher the map once he'd retrieved it. However, now that Helen has the map, she and Elliot were doing the work for him. For now, at least. He needed to be careful. If they discovered what the map led to, they'd be more of a risk to him alive than dead.

In the meantime, Marco was off searching the rest of the Cathedral to find Elliot and Helen. Teo was happy that Marco wasn't in sight. He would just get in the way and make a mess of things.

Without taking his eye off of them, Teo felt the Rimfire pistol with silencer, resting in a holder against his ribs. He felt its cold smooth handle, then put his arm back down. He would continue watching and take over when the time was right.

16

Inside St Paul's Cathedral – Present Day + 1 (Friday)

Helen used her phone to take a picture of the "X" on the drawing. It made a clicking sound and she quickly looked up and scanned the area in case anyone was around to hear. She surveyed the Chapel to get her bearings and walked back towards the altar. She stopped just in front of it, knelt down and looked down at the rug beneath her. She waived Elliot over.

Elliot was staring at a demonic monument. It made him uneasy, but he wasn't sure why. Little did he know, Teo was behind the statue. He heard a scratching noise behind him and turned around to see Helen trying to get his attention by waiving with one hand and scratching the floor with the other. He ran over as quickly and quietly as possible.

'If your calculations are correct, then whatever we're looking for is beneath us' she said.

Elliot rolled up a section of the rug, got down on his hands and knees then inspected the floor. Helen stood at the side and watched him crawl around like a puppy sniffing for food.

'Ouch' he said, snapping his hand back from the floor.

He looked at his hand to see a sharp cut on his little finger. Blood gently trickled down his skin. Helen handed him a tissue which he wrapped around his finger to soak up the blood. The sight of the red liquid made her feel faint and so she looked down to the floor, away from his bleeding finger. Blood had marked the chipped edge of a stone slab.

Helen pointed to the chipped tile with blood marks on it. 'Look.'

Elliot looked at the edge of the tile. Unlike the other ones, this tile had no grout filling in its edges. It was loose. 'Hand me that candle stand, please.'

'I erm, I don't know about this' said Helen.

'What's wrong' he said, although suspected she had just got cold feet.

'We shouldn't be here. We shouldn't be doing any of this.'

Elliot was fed up with doing nothing, being nothing and having nothing. He wanted something different. A life of his own where it had purpose and fulfilment. This was the first time in over seven years where he'd felt a glimmer of this and was determined to see it through.

'I'm staying here to see what's beneath' he said. 'You go and I'll see you back at the Museum.'

Helen reluctantly handed him the candle stand. 'Well, someone better make sure you don't damage anything. You need my help.'

Elliot put the flat base of the stand in a gap next to the chipped old tile, pushed its neck down and the large stone tile lifted up a little. The gap was not big enough to put his fingers inside to lift. He tried again. He kicked the candle stand harder into the gap and pushed it down with more weight. This time it lifted an inch off the ground...just enough room to wedge something inside.

'It's heavy. Give me a hand.'

Helen held the side of the candle stand down. He let go, bent down and lifted the slab with both hands. The slab began to rise and made a loud gritting sound. Elliot tried to lift as slowly as possible to deaden the noise and avoid any damage. Fortunately, no one was around to hear the commotion. Once raised, he held the stone upright to stop it from smashing back down.

They stood by the gap in the floor and peered down to see what looked like the front of a very old safe. It was made of rusty metal cogs that were covered in Roman numerals.

17

Inside St Paul's Cathedral – Present Day + 1 (Friday)

The tour group were coming to the end of their visit of St Paul's Cathedral. They finished up at the gift shop to look at the books, pictures and souvenirs. The shop was more like a library than a gift shop, and just as silent. The guide did a head count as each visitor walked into the shop. She counted thirty people. *Two people missing.* She counted again, but still came up short.

The guide walked up to the gift shop attendant. 'Barb, did you see two people come out here before me?'

'Sorry Natalie. You're the first. It's been dead in here.'

All people had to be accounted for, or the tour guide would get in trouble. She felt stressed and it brought on that all familiar desire for a drink. She'd been sober for over a year and the urge never left. Natalie looked at her watch. Thirty minutes until her AA meeting was due to start. She hadn't been for the last couple of weeks and was feeling vulnerable. She was keen to go, but couldn't leave with people unaccounted for.

The guide huddled the visitors together and asked about the missing two. No one knew who they were or where they went. The people on the tour just looked at each other and either shook their heads or shrugged their shoulders. She went back to find the two strays, jogging across the Cathedral floor and downstairs to the underground crypts. Natalie would give them a piece of her mind if they made her miss her AA meeting.

18

Inside St Paul's Cathedral – Present Day + 1 (Friday)

Elliot stared at the ancient vault in the ground, as he held the stone slab upright to stop it from falling. The vault had six dials with Roman Numerals, I to IX, underneath each dial. He assumed he needed to put each dial over the right number to unlock the vault. He did a calculation in his head and worked out that there were three hundred and sixty-two thousand, eight hundred and eighty different possible combinations. There was no way he'd be able to open the vault. Not without a code, at least.

'The co-ordinates!'

'What' said Helen.

'Here, hold this' he said, signalling for her to hold the stone slab.

She carefully held the slab, then Elliot pulled out a piece of paper from his pocket. It had the co-ordinates from the Pythagorean Square. He bent down and added the remaining numbers from the code that he'd used to find the location of the vault.

'See, usually the cipher gives a location for the first two digits and date and time for the remainder. But not here. I wondered what the remaining numbers were as they didn't add up to make a date.'

Helen didn't say anything. She just smiled, nodded and let Elliot carry on talking.

'Maybe these are the codes for this vault…it would help to protect whatever's inside if the tile was ever lifted by an unintended stranger.'

'I think that's us' replied Helen.

He moved the dials into place and the vault made a clicking sound. Elliot put his hand under a handle, gave it a firm pull and the vault opened. It was dark inside, two feet deep and covered in dust. He could just make out something inside.

'We found it' he said.

'Found what?'

'I don't know yet.'

'Wow, you really are as clever as your father' she said.

'You knew him well' asked Elliot, looking up at Helen.

Helen looked sad. Her eyes took refuge on the floor. 'He was a great member to the team at the Museum. Everybody loved him.'

Elliot could tell they were close. The very mention of his father changed Helen's mood. It happened on more than one occasion. In a way, it was nice that he got to work with someone who knew the family. He reached his arm into the dark vault and pulled out a wooden container. It was no bigger than a shoebox and covered in dirt. He was so excited he could've climbed the walls.

'Let's see what's inside' he said, desperate to know what secrets were about to be unveiled.

'Not here, not now' she said, taking the box from him and putting it in her bag. 'Let's get out of here first and open it somewhere else.'

Elliot closed the vault, laid down the stone slab and unravelled the rug back on the floor. They both smoothed out the wrinkles in the rug, then quietly made their way out of the Cathedral before anyone noticed.

19

Inside St Paul's Cathedral – Present Day + 1 (Friday)

Natalie, the blonde tour guide, backtracked through the Cathedral to search for the two missing visitors. She was angry that she'd miss her twelve step recovery meeting and was ready to give the strays "what for". Her shoes made a fast tapping noise as she marched along the stone and marble floor, not dissimilar to the trot of a horse. She passed the nave of the Cathedral, down the stairway and back through the crypts.

The guide got closer to Faith Chapel. She could feel that something wasn't right. It was in her skin. A nervous tingling at the back of her neck. It was the same feeling she'd get from watching a horror movie. She dismissed the feeling as childish. The cathedral was a bit eerie when no one was around. The Chapel was just around the corner and she could hear what sounded like the scrapping of stone. *The contractors aren't due to come in until Monday*. She peered around the corner and saw a man standing in the Chapel. The expensive red rug had been pulled back from its place and the man was lifting a floor tile that had been removed from the ground.

'What are you doing' she demanded. 'Stay right there. I'm calling the police.'

The man looked up and turned to face her. He pulled out a dark object from inside his jacket pocket. It didn't take long for her to work out what it was and she looked at him with overwhelming dread. Natalie immediately realised she was in very real and very serious danger. She turned around to run. As she did, she caught the bottom of her heel on the edge of a tile, fell down to the ground and scraped her knees. Desperately, she clawed at the ground to pull herself up then ran as fast as she could towards the stairs. The man chased after her as she ran with all the energy she could muster.

The tour guide was fast, but she had no chance against the speed of a bullet. A few seconds later... bang. She felt a jolt in her back and she leapt forward to the ground. A perfect, cold blooded shot to the back. She lay on the floor like a defenceless animal, hunted on an open safari.

20

Coffee Shop – Present Day + 1 (Friday)

Elliot and Helen went to a quaint café located in one of London's hidden spots. Set in the centre of the bustling West End of London, but down a narrow alley that no tourist would think to investigate. They sat in the corner away from the window and ordered their drinks. Helen asked for a skinny latte and Elliot opted for a hot chocolate with whipped cream and chocolate sprinkles.

'You know, you could easily be a curator at the Museum' said Helen. 'With your intellect, I'm sure you'd get fast tracked.'

'You need a degree for that' said Elliot, staring at his hand as he twiddled.

'Why don't you go back and finish yours?'

Elliot knew why, but wasn't sure if it would prejudice him to share it with his new manager. 'I erm, I can't. They won't have me back. Besides...' he said, changing the subject. 'I need to look after my brother and I can't do that if I'm wasting my time going to university.'

Helen didn't say anything and Elliot assumed, and hoped, she was too polite to ask him to elaborate. Behind him was a wall covered with pictures of modern art for sale. Helen looked at the different types of paintings then turned her attention to Elliot who was wrapping a tissue around his cut finger.

'Are you ok' she asked.

'yep… I just need to apply pressure. My blood doesn't coagulate.'

'Haemophilia?'

'Type A. Small cuts are ok… internal bleeding and deep lacerations can cause problems' said Elliot. 'You know haemophilia only affects the X chromosome. That's why women don't get it. They'd need both of their X chromosomes to carry it. As men only have one X chromosome, the chances of being affected are much greater.'

'I didn't know that.'

Elliot tried to avoid sports injuries more than the average person, especially after the last one. He thought back a few years ago to when it happened. The first and last time he abseiled alone… or ever for that matter. A clear sunny day along the coast of France. A remote, beautiful place, with the nearest village over an hour's drive away. A collection of abseiling medals made him an overconfident climber. An over confidence that was stripped down and turned into a debilitating fear. He remembered the tension in the rope give way with great clarity. At the time, the fall was too quick to think about. But, in his mind's eye, the feeling of dropping played back in slow motion. The wind brushing up against him as he fell nearly thirty feet, crashing to the ground. His mobile smashed to pieces in the fall. The blood seeping from his body, draining him of life. With two broken legs and no way to contact for help, he just lay there, awaiting the Reaper. Never break the golden rule and go alone. Had it not been for a man walking his dog, he would have died for sure. It sent a shiver through his spine. He was lucky to be alive, let alone make a full recovery. The clash of a mug hit the table. Elliot regained focus to see his drink had arrived. A waitress had spilt some of the decorated hot chocolate, leaving a white and brown smudge on the table. The waitress was too rushed off her feet to notice.

'So…what's in the box' Elliot asked.

He was beyond eager to find out what they'd discovered, but tried to play it cool until his new manager was ready. So far Helen had followed him on this adventure, but he didn't want to push his luck.

'Ha, you know with all the drama of trying to run out of the Cathedral unnoticed, I'd almost forgot.'

Helen moved her coffee to the side, picked up her leather hand bag and set it on the table.

'You want to do this here' he said.
'You don't?'
'Good point.'

She pulled out the box from her bag, held it close to her chest, made sure no one was looking, then opened it.

'What the…'
'What is it' said Elliot.
'Huh. It's erm…it's empty!'
'What do you mean?'
'I mean, it's empty' she said, passing him the box.

Elliot did a quick scan of the café to make sure no one was looking. Since the Cathedral, he felt paranoid that someone was watching them. *Paranoia or a heightened sense of awareness,* he wondered. A young couple sat behind him, spending more time eating each other than they were their lunch. Across the side from them sat an old lady in a bobble hat and green cardigan. She attempted to drink a cup of tea, but her hand shook as though she was taking part in an egg and spoon race. She looked at Elliot and smiled. He smiled back, then turned his attention to the box.

'There's an inscription on the back of the lid.'
'What's it say' asked Helen.

'It's Latin:

"The intemperate man shall not quench his thirst for power
The conscious body is not seen with eyes of greed, but only by those who are invisible
The root of evil is gluttony"

Helen got her pen out and wrote down the translation. 'Know what it means?'

'I'm not sure... possibly or possibly not. Intemperance, or overindulgence, was a quality Aristotle discussed in detail in his works on ethics. He believed it's something to avoid for the growth of humanity. In fact, his views on human behaviour have helped to shape the world today. He's not alone though. The Bible and other texts share similar moral values on how people should behave.'

'Ok, but what does it mean?'

'It seems to be suggesting that those seeking personal gain will not find "power."'

Helen frowned. 'Power. What power?'

'Who knows, maybe Wren really did have some hidden treasure' he said. 'The Ancient Greek philosopher, Epicurus, believed that we only need the simple things in life. A roof over our head, food on our plate, friends and family. We can then be happy. He argued that one who is not happy with little, will never be satisfied with a lot. Maybe the statement just means the power of happiness or something.'

'Hmmm' said Helen pursing her lips. 'Maybe.'

Elliot could tell Helen wasn't convinced. He couldn't work out why she was so nice to him and agreed to follow his lead in the Cathedral.

'When you mentioned my dad, George, you became very sad' he said, trying to make eye contact with her.

Helen didn't look at him. 'We were very close friends. He'd helped me a lot and it's tragic what happened to him.'

Elliot couldn't agree any more, although he'd never heard of Helen until he started working at the Museum. His father used to take his friends from work home for dinner and he didn't remember her ever being one of them. He turned his attention to the message on the box. *Why would someone leave such a cryptic message*? He wondered what was stored inside it that was so important it needed to be hidden by Sir Christopher Wren. He wasn't sure, but he had an idea of where to start.

21

St Paul's Cathedral – Present Day + 1 (Friday)

Henry Wrightman had been with the force for too long to remember. He'd seen every type of crime and it was rare for him to be surprised by the violence of others. Like this surprise, the excitement of his job left him a long time ago. Probably about the same time that his wife left him and took the kids. At least he got to keep the incontinent dog. If he wasn't clearing up shit at work, he'd be doing it when he got home. He didn't moan about it, but certainly felt he'd been dealt a bad hand.

Henry received a call out to St Paul's. A homicide and minor criminal damage to the Cathedral. He had to tread carefully since the new government stepped in. A new cabinet with a manifesto that heavily focused on crime rates meant all eyes were on the homicide department. Henry's boss, Claire Nelson, was feeling the heat and so in turn, she shared it with her officers. Everyone was breathing down his neck. No mistakes. Everything had to be done by the book.

He drove his way through the snail pace traffic. London's busy roads made it difficult for him to gain much speed, even with the flashing blue lights. He eventually reached St Pauls and was greeted with a black coffee and a forensic team. He walked into the Cathedral. Henry knew someone that worked there as a tour guide, but had never visited it himself and didn't quite realise how beautiful it was.

'Officer' said Henry, nodding to a lower ranking policeman.

'You must be Henry' said the officer.

'It's detective. What's the status?'

The officer filled him in as they walked through the gift shop and main floor to the underground crypts. Henry soaked in the environment as much as he could. The tidiness of the books and gifts, their order of arrangement, the clothing of the staff, the security cameras overlooking the counter. Apart from the sombre mood of staff, nothing looked out of the ordinary.

'Anything on the vic?'

'A one, dead Miss Szczytkowski. She was shot in the back. No witnesses or security cameras.'

'When was Miss skartowki…'

'Szczytkowski' the officer interjected.

'starkwi.'

'Szczytkowski.'

'Moving on. When was the victim last seen?'

The officer was dressed in full uniform, which was odd given it was such a hot day. Henry could tell the officer was a newbie. They tend to do everything by the book and one of the main rules from the police manual was to always wear a full uniform when on duty. Henry took more of an interpretive approach than a literal one and wore a short-sleeve white shirt, dark trousers and dark shoes.

'She gave a tour of the Cathedral at half twelve. She ended the tour at…'

Henry interjected 'Wait… the victim was a tour guide. What was her first name?'

The officer flicked through his note pad. 'Er, Natalie' he said.

'Was she blonde' asked Henry.

'Yes' said the officer, giving him a *"you know something"* look.

Henry knew the victim alright. He couldn't understand why someone would want to harm her. Not a bad bone in her body. He felt an anger begin to bubble up inside him. *This fracking world,* he thought. He couldn't comprehend why bad things happen to such good people. If there was a God, Henry considered either they were not benevolent or not all powerful.

'Sorry' said Henry. 'You were saying?'

'Yes, the victim ended the tour at the gift shop. The shop worker saw the victim checking something with the group at the end of the tour, then left them to go back into the underground crypts. That was the last anyone saw of her.'

'Do we know what she was asking?'

'No, we're working on it.'

'What do we have' asked Henry.

The officer shook his head. Nothing. This was not going to look good with the people upstairs. There was enough heat on the department. The last thing Henry needed was his boss Claire chewing his ass off.

'What about Natalie?'

The officer looked left then right, keeping his head still.

'What about the victim?!'

'Ah' said the officer. 'The victim was a part time uni student, studying to be an accountant. Her colleagues are not aware of anyone that might want to harm her. We'll send the body to the autopsy lab and should be able to find out more on the type of gun then. My guess from the impact is that the weapon was a pistol. No one heard a gun-shot and so it's likely a silencer was used.'

'A professional hit?'

'It seems that way.'

'You notified ballistics?'

'Not yet.'

'Why hasn't a perimeter been set up' said Henry, frowning as he looked at the crime scene.

'I, uh.'

'Get it done. And why are people coming in through this entrance?'

The officer just shrugged his shoulders. *Rookie.* Causing minimal contamination of a scene was imperative, and a basic part of that requirement was to ensure access to and from the crime scene was along the shortest route.

There was no way that someone ordered a professional hit on Natalie. There had to be something else. Collateral damage, perhaps. Being a homicide detective had its rewarding moments. And its darker ones. But, Detective Henry Wrightman would usually only get involved once someone had already been killed. It was a rare occasion to have the foresight to prevent a murder. It wasn't as if murderers advertised their intentions on Twitter. At the start of his career, not being able to save someone used to eat at his soul. After a while his stomach grew accustomed to it. His body and mind learned to block it out. A self-defence mechanism. For Henry, it was either that or end up in a mental hospital. However, the death of someone he got on well with was not something he could easily suppress. It hurt Henry and as much as he tried to not let it show, it was obvious that something was wrong.

In Faith Chapel, forensics were dressed in white and doing their thing. Although a plastic sheet had been put over the body, the rest of the scene was intact. The large rug had been folded backwards and a stone tile had been removed from its place. It looked as though someone had lifted it then carelessly dropped it, causing it to crack in the middle.

'What do we know' asked Henry.

'Forensics have swept the area, but found nothing.' said the young officer. 'It looks like the victim caught someone messing around in here and the perp didn't want to get caught and so off-ed the vic.'

'You said Natalie was giving a tour. Had everyone on the tour been accounted for?'

'We believe so. According to the ticket office, thirty-two tickets were sold.'

Henry was getting pissed off by the lack of information. An innocent person has just been killed and no one seemed to be taking it seriously. If they were going to solve this case, everyone needed to be more thorough. He recalled seeing a security camera at the gift shop.

'I need to see the video of the gift shop' he said.

The officer gave Henry a confused look. 'But nothing happened there, sir.'

'Just do it! Now.'

The officer ran off, as ordered. Henry looked down at a stone tile, next to the vault in the ground. A small part of it had a slight red mark. *Blood.* He got forensics to take some samples for testing. With any luck, it would be the perpetrator's. As he was kneeling down, the forensic camera flashed a few times. Henry's peripheral caught the shine of something on the floor. He turned his head. The camera flashed again. The light reflected on the small object again. He walked over and bent down. An empty bullet cartridge. It was small enough to have been used in a pistol. There was little point in waiting for forensics to confirm this. He walked back and looked down at the old vault. He had pictures taken, then asked his research team to see what historical information they could find on the Cathedral. If this was a professional hit, no doubt the vault had something to do with the homicide.

Henry went over to the plastic covering lying on the floor. Although deep down he knew it would be his friend, he was praying it was not. He lifted the covering to see the stone cold face of a once beautiful warm friend. His heart grew heavy and his throat tensed up, making it difficult to swallow.

'Can someone do some bloody work around here! Find me that god damn perp!'

22

Coffee Shop – Present Day + 1 (Friday)

Elliot felt his stomach grumble. He looked over at the couple making out and noticed they'd barely eaten their food. One plate looked like spaghetti carbonara. He could smell the flavours and melted cheese waft passed him.

'Let's order lunch.'

Elliot and Helen ordered their food then the waitress rushed off. The coffee shop was busy and Elliot's stomach hoped this didn't mean there'd be a long delay for his food. He brought his attention back to the box to distract him.

"The intemperate man shall not quench his thirst for power
The conscious body is not seen with eyes of greed, but only by those who are invisible
The root of evil is gluttony"

'The conscious body is not seen with eyes of greed, but only by those who are invisible' he said.

'Any ideas' asked Helen.

'The conscious body rings a bell. I mentioned the Pythagorean Brotherhood. It's believed that one of their members, a German man called Christian Rosencruez, set up a society called the Rosicrucian Order in the fourteenth century.

'I've heard of them. Aren't they a part of Freemason teachings?'

'Yes' he said. 'If you ever go to the Grand Lodge in London, you'll see the Rosicrucian Order sits in the temple there.'

'Sir Wren was a Freemason, apparently.'

Elliot nodded, then continued. 'The Rosicrucian Order dedicated their lives to finding secret truths. Philosophical truths too important for the general population to be involved with. Their symbol was the Rosy Cross. A cross with a rose in the middle. The rose represented consciousness. The cross represented the body.'

'The conscious body' said Helen.

'Exactly' said Elliot.

'So the Rosy Cross was in this box' she asked.

Elliot wasn't sure what was in the box, but whatever it was, someone considered it important enough to be kept a secret for centuries and stop it from being found.

'I doubt the Rosy Cross was in the box. Some academics believe it is a reference to Jesus. There are others who believe it's the philosopher's stone. Of course, it's probably just a metaphor for something else.'

'Well, if Jesus did exist, he probably wouldn't fit in this box' said Helen.

Elliot smiled at her attempt to be funny, although he was too hungry to engage in humour. The waitress came over with their food, laid it on the table, this time without spilling anything. Elliot had carbonara and Helen had a salad. She tried to stay away from carbs where she could. Not because she didn't like them and not because she needed to. Healthy eating was a habit. Elliot ate a mouthful of creamy pasta. A strand of it flicked against his mouth as he sucked it up.

'The message appears to be saying that the Rosy Cross can only be found by those who are invisible.'

'Who could it be referring to?'

'I don't know.'

Elliot re-read the Latin message. 'Here, this proves it is referring to the Rosicrucian Order. This is real' he said. 'Look at the last sentence "Radix malorum est Cupiditas."'

'The root of evil is gluttony?'

'Yes' he said. 'Notice how the R and C in the last sentence are capitals. When the Order sent messages they would sign off with "RC", the initials for their symbol, the Rosy Cross. I love this crap' he said.

Helen smiled awkwardly. Elliot realised she was not comfortable with swearing. He decided to make more of an effort to stop it. He knew there were several people who were believed to be part of the Order, but there's no real proof of it. Benjamin Franklin, Sir Isaac Newton...even the philosopher Sir Francis Bacon. But, that didn't help him to understand what was in the box. They finished eating their food and washed it down with another drink. He gave Helen the box to put it in her handbag. As the box tilted slightly, she saw something underneath it and turned it upside down.

'There's a stamp on the bottom' she said, showing it to him.

They both looked at it together. The stamp was an emblem... a shield between two hounds. On top of the shield was a knight's helmet with a crown and eagle. Underneath the shield it said "Nullius in Verba."

'I've never seen this crest before, but the Latin says "take no one's word for it." Where have I heard that before' he asked.

'Isn't it Socrates who said we should always assess a principle of common sense based on our own logic and not just follow the crowd?'

Elliot was impressed that she knew about philosophy. It was a passion for him, but he knew most people were not that interested in it.

'I don't think this emblem relates to Socrates. He never wrote down any of his teachings. We only know about him from the writings of his students, like Plato. Anyway, I highly doubt that he'd have his own crest. This looks like it's from a much later period.'

Elliot finished his hot chocolate. There was a dollop of cream left at the bottom of the cup. He put his finger in, wiped it around and licked it clean. He put on his researching cap, pulled out his smart phone and Googled "Nullius in Verba." Three hundred and four thousand results came up, with the top result being a note from a historical study from a university website. He clicked on the link to see the same crest that was stamped on the box.

'Found something.'

'What's that?'

'The stamp is the crest for the Royal Society. It says here that the Society was formed by a group of philosophers and scientists known as the Invisible College, who themselves were formed out of the Rosicrucian Order.'

'The message says "The conscious body is not seen with eyes of greed, but only by those who are invisible." This must be what they're referring to' said Helen.

'Who are they' he asked.

'I'm not sure yet' said Helen. 'Maybe it's trying to tell us that only the Royal Society can find the Rosy Cross or whatever the "power" is meant to be.'

Elliot shrugged his shoulders and carried on reading. 'It says here that Sir Christopher Wren and his right hand man, Robert Hooke, were members of the Royal Society. What do we know about the owner of the drawings? If he was the one who marked the fifth pillar, he may know what was in this box.'

'His name's Jonathan Hooke. Otherwise' said Helen, shaking her head 'I don't know much about him.'

'Maybe he was related to Robert Hooke.'

'Maybe' she said, pursing her lips in contemplation.

'Do we know where he lives?'

'Somewhere in London I think... the office will have a record.'

'Let's pay him a visit.'

Helen paid the tab and left the café to bring her car around. Elliot checked the time. His Omega read three pm. Elliot didn't have many valuables. He couldn't afford them. His watch was a present from his parents and he never took it off. It stood out from the rest of his attire. He turned his head to the street to keep an eye out for Helen's car. The congestion of London's traffic was heavy, especially for a weekend. Three black cabs queued in-line beside him. All beeping their horns impatiently as the traffic stood still.

Across the road, people from different cultures and walks of life marched up and down the street. London was a hub of diversity, with paint pallet of people from around the world. The locals rushed around, often getting stuck behind the slow tourists. The tourists soaked up the atmosphere, often disturbed by the intolerant locals overtaking them. Elliot looked across the road. He saw a man in a white short-sleeved shirt and dark trousers looking at him. No emotional expression, just a stare. Like a sedated patient with his eyes open. Mediterranean. Not bad looking. A big red double-decker bus, with a brightly coloured advert of a beach holiday on its side, stopped in his view path. When the bus moved on, the man had disappeared. Elliot thought he was seeing things.

Elliot waited for Helen's car and thought about his little brother Toby. He was keen to see him this weekend if he could. It pained him to think Toby was without any of his actual family. He pulled out his phone and called his social worker, Angela Bashton.

'Hello, Angie speaking.'

'Angela, hi, it's Elliot.'

'Elliot, I've been trying to get hold of you.'

'Sorry, I've been busy with this new job at the British Museum. It's going really well.'

'Is it? That's not what I've heard.'

'What do you mean?'

'I spoke with the St Michael's Fellowship. You've assaulted someone... again!'

'It's not like that. I stopped someone from stealing something from the Museum. Ask my boss.'

Angela let out a sigh. 'Elliot, I can't help you if you don't help yourself. You can't honestly expect me to recommend that Toby lives with you when you can't even look after yourself. You leave me with no choice. I will have to raise it as a concern at the next review.'

Elliot knew she was right, even if it hurt like hell. He felt helpless, desperate and incapable. Trying to help others has just got him into more and more trouble. *Why wouldn't she just understand,* he thought. He tried to keep it together. He wanted to stand up for himself, but knew she'd just push back and so decided to go with it.

'I'll improve. I can do this. I promise.'

'Elliot, I want to help you...I do. But...' she said, letting out a deep breath. 'Toby is in a good home with foster parents that look after him. I can't change that unless you're able to provide for him. Emotionally as well as financially.'

They finished the conversation and he put his phone away. He saw Helen driving towards him in her silver BMW three series. *Not bad for a curator.* She pulled up and he jumped in. He had the same look on his face as when he was cleaning in the Museum.

'What's wrong' she asked.

'I'm fine.'

Elliot was far from fine, but he knew there was nothing Helen could do to help him. However, if he could find out what was in the box, maybe he'd have a chance to prove himself. The Museum would give him recognition. Angela would see how capable and responsible he was and then he could be together with his brother. All he needed to do now is go see Jonathan Hooke. He was hoping it would be the answer to his problems.

23

London Police Station – Present Day + 1 (Friday)

Detective Henry Wrightman sat in his office with his feet on his desk. He held a plastic coin in his hand. It had "AA - Three years" indented on each side. Henry held onto it tightly. He felt for Natalie. They weren't close friends, but she helped him with his recovery. Even now he still wanted a drink… the urge never really left him. He just did his best to stay away from temptation.

His pc gave out a ping. Incoming email. He opened a draw in his desk. It had a picture of him and his children. He put the sobriety coin in the draw, then turned his attention to his computer. He opened the email to find a link to the camera feed at the gift shop at St Paul's Cathedral. It covered the day's footage. He forwarded it to the time that the tour ended. There was no volume on the feed. The group left the tour followed by the guide. Natalie was pretty. It was nice to see life in her body on screen, but the realisation of her tragedy soon crept back into his mind. He watched as she went up to different people in the group and asked them something. *What is she asking them?* He watched her leaving the gift shop to go back down towards the crypt. He wished he could shout at her from the video feed not to go back, but there was no way of rewinding time. There was nothing else out of the ordinary. The group bought their gifts from the gift shop and gradually left, one by one.

Henry's door opened. There was no knock, which could only mean it was his boss. In walked Claire Nelson, captain of the homicide team. Always dressed smartly. Although Henry got on well with her, the younger members of staff were scared of Claire. She may be an elegant blonde, but she carried the authority and intimidation of a shotgun. Mess with her and you'd be scraping off chewing gum from underneath tables. That said, she was fair if you did your job properly.

'What happened' she asked.

'Superintended' he said, nodding. 'Someone was shot. We don't know who did it, but we're working on it.'

'Work faster. You know I've got heat from this God damn new Government. Secretary Johnson thinks that just because someone new steps in, solving crime will be easier.'

'We're on it.'

'I hear the victim was your sponsor' she said. 'I'm sorry. I know she's helped you, but you can't make this personal. We need to do this by the book or my arse is on the line.'

He didn't say anything. He didn't need to. He just got his head back down and got to work. Claire left his office and Henry rewound and watched the video feed again. This time he counted the people that entered the gift shop from the tour. He counted thirty. There were thirty-two tickets sold. He rewound it and counted them again, just to double check. There was no doubt. Thirty-Two started the tour, but only thirty people left through the exit with Natalie. Two people were unaccounted for. *That must've been what she was looking for. The killers.*

He walked out of his office to find his partner, James. PC James Catchwell was the nephew of Claire Nelson. A young family man that was assigned to Henry. She wanted to make sure he was looked after properly. Initially, Henry felt like he was put on babysitting duties, but after a while, they became close friends. Henry even became a godfather to one of James' children.

'J, I think we've got something on the cathedral case.'

James' youthful face looked up from his desk. 'What's up.'

James spoke with an enthusiasm that Henry found difficult to relate to. The pressures of the force had not yet worn him down, but then Henry had been doing the job for much longer.

'I need you to get me a list of people who paid for a ticket at the tour. Check for any card payment records or pictures from CCTV. Two people on the tour didn't leave with the rest of the group. I need to know who they are. Do whatever you have to.'

Henry was finally onto something. It was too coincidental that two people go missing from the tour and someone ends up dead. He needed to find them so that he could put this case to bed. He hadn't got a match on the DNA samples taken from the blood on the tile yet, but he suspected it would lead him to the killers who went missing from the tour group in the Cathedral.

24

Kensington, London – Present Day + 1 (Friday)

Elliot stepped out of the car and onto the cobbled drive leading to the house of Jonathan Hooke. The smell of the flowers surrounding the front lawn reminded him of his old family home. Blue Sweet Williams and Jasmine. A happy smell that complimented the house. The sun was shining down as they walked up to the generously sized, detached house. Like many of the other houses on the tree filled road, the top half was of a Tudor design, with white walls and dark timber beams supporting the structure of the building. The front garden was landscaped, although the hedges and grass hadn't been cut in a while.

Helen knocked on the oak coloured door, causing it to open slightly. Something didn't feel right. She rang the doorbell a couple of times. They waited a minute or so. No answer. Elliot stepped in front of Helen, pushed the door further and it slowly opened. He peered into the hallway to see a book shelf emptied on the floor and a broken vase scattered into pieces on the ground.

'Hello…' Elliot said loudly. 'Is anyone here?'

Still no answer.

'We need to call the police' said Helen. 'It looks like there's been a break-in.'

'In a minute' said Elliot. 'If Jonathan's in there, we need to make sure he's ok.'

She gave a hesitant nod. They stepped inside cautiously, slowly and quietly, making their way into the living room. Elliot was in front. The place had been turned inside out. He noticed a laptop and TV in the living room out in the open. It can't have been a burglary or they would've taken the electronic goods. A laptop would be the first thing to go... valuable and easy to carry. All the cupboards were open, their contents laid out on the floor. It was as if a pressurised air-tank had exploded in each cupboard simultaneously, throwing everything outward. The house smelt of gone off meat. Elliot felt slightly nauseous and tried hard not to gag. The smell came from the adjoining dining room. The door was shut. Elliot went to put his hand on the door handle, when he heard a thumping noise come from the ceiling.

'Did you hear that' he whispered, looking at Helen and pointing upwards. 'Someone's in the house.'

He pointed to the stairway. Adrenaline filled his body as he went into fight or flight mode. Elliot grabbed a broom from the cupboard, twisted off its head and carried the stick as a weapon. The house fell silent again.

'What are you doing' she said. 'We have to leave, now.'

Elliot shook his head and slowly made his way towards the stairs. If Jonathan was there, he needed to make sure he was ok. They both began breathing heavily. Helen was almost at the point of hyperventilating. Being equipped with a weapon, he slowly made his way up stairs. Helen followed behind as he held onto the stick tightly with both hands. Helen's foot pressed against a step, half way up, making a sharp creaking sound. She froze, stopped breathing and briefly closed her eyes. Nothing. The coast was clear and they continued slowly upstairs, until they reached the top.

They crept along the landing. Another thump. This time it was louder. Elliot's heart jumped and he went into full fight or flight mode. Helen pointed to the second room on the right, held her finger over her mouth and gestured for him to stay silent. They heard a rustling sound on approaching the door. Elliot held his broom stick high, just behind the door. The rustling noise stopped. His grip tightened as an attempt to try and control the shaking of his hands. He wiped the sweat from his hand on the side of his trouser then opened the door. A cat jumped out at them. They both shot back. Elliot lost his balance and hit his back against the wall of the corridor.

'Jesus' he said, letting out a deep sigh.

The cat ran across the corridor and down the stairs. Elliot held his chest in shock, then calmed down his breathing.

Elliot went into the bedroom first. No one was there. No Jonathan Hooke. Just a double bed, a desk and an en-suite bathroom. Next to the desk was an oil painting of Sir Francis Bacon. In the bottom right corner of the painting was the same printed crest from the secret box they found.

'Look' said Helen.

'The emblem for the Royal Society' said Elliot.

Elliot noticed the painting didn't lie completely flat against the wall. He pressed his face to the wall and could see a handle bar pushing the painting away from the wall. He lifted the painting from its hook and put it down gently to reveal an electronically coded safe.

'Good find, but I'm pretty sure we're now burglars' said Helen.

'Whoever tore this place apart was obviously looking for something. It's clearly no ordinary burglary. First that man tries to steal the drawings in the Museum. Now this? I think someone knows about the hidden messages besides us. If this is an important piece of history, it should be protected or it could be lost forever. It's our job to protect it. We need to get in that safe and store whatever's in there until we find Jonathan Hooke.'

'I don't know' she said.

'Helen, trust me. I promise, we won't get in trouble.'

Whether or not Helen was happy to be there, the safe was securely locked and they had no way of opening it. It had an electric lock with a nine numbered keypad. The screen had enough room for six numbers to be punched in. Elliot calculated that to be about one million different possible combinations for the code. An incorrect number could trigger a security alarm which was the last thing he needed.

Helen looked around the solid mahogany desk with a leather top, opened a few drawers, then pulled out some sticky tape.

'What are you doing?'

'Watch and learn, dear Elliot. Watch and learn.'

Helen bit off three strips of tape and lined them over each other to make a rough rectangle, with each sticky side facing up. She gently pushed the sticky side over the numerical keypad. When she lifted it off, it revealed five oil marks, each in the shape of a finger print and each one more faint than the other. She looked at the fingerprint with the most oil, and put them in order working her way down to the faintest fingerprint. Helen then worked out the numbers in that order, punched them into the safe and it clicked open.

'Where did you learn that' he asked.

'Too many detective movies. I have to admit, I wasn't sure if it would actually work. The natural oil from our skin decreases as it touches the surface. That way, we know the mark with the most oil was the first number to be pressed.'

Helen opened the safe fully and took out its contents. An old publication from the Royal Society and a handmade pinhole camera. She gave a confused look. Elliot was becoming nervous over his presence in a house that he had no permission to be in and which had clearly been broken into. If he was caught by the owner, he would certainly get arrested.

Helen's phone began to vibrate. 'Hello.'

'Helen, it's Arthur, where are you? Why aren't you in the Museum?'

'I'm with Elliot… you know, the cleaner. We've been working on the exhibition and had to take a visit to St Pauls.'

'I know, I've had a visit from the police.'

'What do the police want with us?'

Elliot's heart dropped. How could they know about their discovery? He'd covered up the rug in St Pauls and so there's no way someone could've noticed that they'd taken the box. Being in someone else's house made him panic even more. They needed to get out of there now.

'There's been a murder and you're both wanted for questioning' said Arthur.

'Excuse me?'

'A murder. Yeah, I know. Messed up huh. Obviously you had nothing to do with it. Apparently you were the last to see the tour guide before she died.'

'Jesus, what happened.'

'The police are hoping you could tell them.'

Arthur explained where the tour guide's body was found. Helen said she'd come in and ended the call. Helen turned pale and told Elliot what had happened. Thoughts rushed through his head like speeding cars on a motorway. He just wanted to throw up. *What was so valuable that someone would be prepared to kill for it?* For now, they agreed not to say anything about their visit to the burgled house. It would only make them suspects. Helen took the contents of the safe and put the painting back. They left as quickly as they could without checking the rest of the house and without noticing the dead body in the dining room.

25

London – Portman Place - 4 October 1821

John Rennie Junior came as quick as he could in horse and cart through the cobbled streets of London. He was going so fast he nearly knocked over a couple crossing the street. He just missed them, but the sudden jolt almost caused him to fly off the cart. It was late and the lack of visibility made the journey all the more difficult. The horses were brought to a halt outside Five Portman Place. He climbed off the carriage with the assistance of his driver, ran up the steps and knocked loudly on the door of the large London home. The big red door slowly opened, revealing an old man dressed in a black and white suit like a penguin.

'Mr Rennie, I'm so glad you could make it' said the butler, gesturing for him to enter.

John stepped inside, took off his beige hat and brown jacket. 'Where is he? Has the doctor been yet? I came as soon as I heard.'

'Your father's upstairs. Dr Richards came a few hours ago.'

The butler was dressed impeccably as always. He took John's hat and jacket then walked off quietly. John made his way up the grand spiral stairway and along the corridor passing old family paintings, portraits and ornaments. A testament to the family's wealth. The doctor came out of the master bedroom and into the corridor. He extended his arm and his warmest thoughts to Sir Rennie's son, John. As they shook hands, both men's thumbs tapped the side of the other's twice. They then hugged each other.

'Doctor, thank you for being here. How... how is he?'

'Hello, John' said the doctor in a gentle but somber tone. 'I'm very sorry. Your father's ill and I'm not sure how long he has left in this world. I would make the most of what little time you have together' he said, lowering his eyes to the ground.

'Thank you' said John.

John's eyes welled up. He tried to wipe them clear so his father didn't see him in pain. Hide the pain... that was the Rennie way. John opened the door softly and walked over to the four poster mahogany bed. His father lay there in his weakened state, as frail as a premature newborn entering into the world. Incapable of life without support. The body was but a shadow of the world's greatest engineer it once was. He now lay in this bed, barely able to talk.

'Father, I'm here. It's me, John.'

He sat by the side of the bed. His father looked up at his son with glazed over eyes. Mustering all his remaining energy, he raised his hand. John held it tightly and didn't let go.

'My son' he said.

'Father, don't speak...you need to rest.'

'No' he said, coughing. 'My son. It saddens me to see you in so much pain. I will be with God soon. I've had a good life. Believe me when I say, I am at peace.'

'I'm fine father' said John, wiping a tear from his eyes.

'My son, you are just like your mother. Strong, kind and spirited. You will make a great father. My only regret is that I will not get to see your first born' said Rennie Senior, looking around the room in a semi-dazed state. 'Tell me, how is the bridge coming along?'

His father coughed violently. John feared his lung contractions. They were painful and desperate.

John had been working on his father's engineering design for some years now. Set to be the greatest bridge ever designed. He was hoping to have it finished before his father passed, but there were delays. Some of the materials were supposed to come from Greece, but the Greek war with the Turks had just started and so the materials had to be sourced elsewhere. It led to an inevitable delay.

'My dear John, I need to tell you something. But, before I do, I need you to swear to secrecy.'

'Yes father, anything.'

'Do you swear?'

'Yes, I swear I'll not say a thing.'

Rennie Senior cleared his throat. 'There is a treasure of significance greater than anything on the planet. A wealth so great that no one man should possess it. If found it could lead to a corruption of the world.'

'What is it?'

'Even I'm not allowed to know its true value. I only have the key. It is said that only a pure philosopher who is not tempted by greed can find it. As a member of the Order I am sworn to its secrecy until and only until I appoint a successor' he said coughing again. 'My son, this is a burden that has been in our family for generations. I need you to swear to protect it with your life. Someone from the Order will contact you.'

His son looked at him with pain. 'Father, I promise. As God as my witness, I will do everything I can to protect the key and keep it safe.'

'Can you call Philip in please?'

John walked over to the door and called in the doctor, who came in carrying a briefcase.

'Philip, John knows and has sworn to protect the key' said Sir Rennie.

The doctor approached the bed. 'Has he sworn in blood?'

Rennie Senior gave a frail shake of his head. 'Not yet.'

'Before Sir Rennie Junior is appointed as your successor he must swear in blood' said the doctor.

The doctor took out a small gilded knife with the pattern of the Rosy Cross on it, then held out his hand, and asked for John to give him his arm. John did as requested. The doctor rolled up his sleeve and made a slight cut on John's arm. Blood began to trickle out lightly. A couple of drops fell to the floor. The doctor pulled out a velvet cloth from his briefcase, wrapped it around John's arm and made him say the oath.

'It is done' said the doctor.

He handed John an object covered in cloth that had "Good decisions are based on knowledge and not numbers" written on the fabric. John was curious, but his mind was more focused on his father's health.

'Take this and protect it with your life. No man can ever discover its truth. Hide it if you must, in a place where no one will ever find it, except the Order' said the doctor.

'How am I supposed to do that?'

'You will find a way.'

John let the doctor out then went back upstairs to spend time with his father during his last living moments. When he got back to the master bedroom his father was still. No coughing, no heavy breathing, no sign of life. His father was now at peace. John put his hands over his father's eyes, closed them and said a prayer.

CHAPTER 25

John had made two promises which he was determined to keep. To hide the key to the greatest treasure known to man and to finish his father's construction of the biggest feat in English engineering. London Bridge.

26

British Museum – Present Day + 1 (Friday)

Helen and Elliot went back to the British Museum to store their findings in the strong room for safe keeping. Detective Inspector Henry Wrightman and his partner, James, were already there awaiting their return. Elliot couldn't understand how the police would be on to them. His palms were sweaty and so he rubbed them against his jeans. He felt a sharp pain on his hand and remembered his cut from the stone tile in the Cathedral. *They must my DNA*, he thought. Several profanities swam through his mind. He would be a suspect for sure and had no idea how he could throw the heat off of him. If he came clean, he'd get done for criminal damage, lose his job and chances of ever being able to look after his little brother. If he said nothing, he risked being suspected for murder. His options weren't great.

The policemen sat in the café located in a large open area of the Museum, drinking a hot cup of coffee. The open plan atrium was like a giant greenhouse, except the glass windows were fifty metres high and not fully transparent. As a result, it kept the sun out, but they were still warm. They saw the officers sitting there and walked over.

'Miss Philips' said Henry, standing up from his seat.

'Please, call me Helen' she said, extending her arm.

'I'm Detective Wrightman. You can call me Detective' he said, keeping his arms by his side.

PC Catchwell jumped in to cut the awkward social tension that Henry was so good at creating. 'Hi, I'm PC James Catchwell. You call me anything you want...as long as it's polite' he said, reaching for her hand that was left there unshaken by Henry.

Helen smiled at PC Catchwell. If the concept of good cop, bad cop actually existed, he was definitely the good one. And the more attractive one. He had youth on his side. That, a strong physique and a beautiful face. The detective on the other hand was older, with brown and grey hair. He dressed smartly for an officer of the law.

'This is my associate, Elliot Hope.'

'Oh yes, the cleaner' said Henry, moving his wide eyed stare to Elliot.

What a prick, Elliot thought. 'Nice to meet you both' he said, with a deliberately fake smile.

Henry put his worn wrinkled hands on the table and lowered himself into the seat. His well-fed waist pressed up against the side of the table. He was of a medium height. Elliot could tell the detective knew how to handle himself, even if he didn't pay close attention to his weight. They all followed suit and sat down with him. Henry skipped any pleasantries.

'You were at St Paul's Cathedral earlier today.'

'That's right' replied Helen.

Elliot gave a nervous twitch. Helen looked down to see him rubbing the sweat from his hand against his trouser.

'What were you doing there' asked Henry.

'The Museum's holding an exhibition in the next few weeks. We were preparing for it' she said as clearly and as calmly as she could.

'Yes, but what were you doing there' Henry asserted.

Elliot could tell the older detective did not like Helen's response. He was sure this meant they knew him and Helen were guilty. Elliot wanted to run, hide, climb over the wall like Spiderman. Anything to get away from his current situation.

PC Catchwell interjected. 'What my colleague wants to know is, what specifically were you doing at the Cathedral?'

Helen looked at Elliot, almost as if she was trying to tell what he was thinking. It was obvious that he was uncomfortable. He just hoped the police didn't pick up on his body language.

'Part of the exhibition is on Sir Christopher Wren' she said. 'We went on a tour for research. Elliot is now helping me and I thought it would be useful for both of us to see the Cathedral first hand' said Helen.

'When did you last see Natalie' demanded Henry.

'Who?'

'The tour guide' PC Catchwell said.

'When we were on the tour' said Elliot.

Henry looked at Elliot, then at Helen, scratched his stubbly chin, took in a deep breath of air through his mouth and let it out through his nose.

'Mr Hope, our police records show that you have a history of violence and criminal damage' said Henry. 'Does a leopard ever change its spots?'

'Er, excuse me' said Helen. 'What does that have to do with anything?'

'We have evidence that you left the tour group and the victim went back to find you. What were you doing, and what happened to the victim' said Henry, looking at Elliot.

Elliot noticed Henry's eyes searching for the truth in their body language.

It made him nervous. His body tightened as though he was undergoing the effects of rigor mortis. His throat swelled up and he wasn't sure that he'd be able to speak. He prayed the detective hadn't noticed his increase in discomfort.

'I had a migraine and so had to leave. We went back the way we came' Helen answered.

Henry raised his eyebrows. 'Why didn't you say anything to the group.'

'I was in too much pain...I just needed to get out of there. I didn't see the tour guide after we left the group.'

Elliot could tell that Henry was unconvinced. *Why did Helen lie?* He was waiting for them to arrest him. *Any second now. Maybe they just want a confession first to save on paperwork for later.*

'Ok... for now' said Henry. We may need to call you in for questioning shortly. In the meantime, don't go far.'

'If you remember anything that stood out or which you think could help, please do call us' said PC Catchwell, handing her his card. 'Thank you for your time.'

James Catchwell and Henry Wrightman left the café. Elliot felt a deep relief and he could tell that Helen did too. It was as if someone had turned on a tap to let out all the adrenaline for the day from their bodies. Helen looked at him. He felt drained and rubbed his eyes.

'That was close' she said. 'Time to go home. We can continue where we left off tomorrow.'

Although he was tired, his mind raced. Why did Helen lie to the police? What was so important about the contents of the safe that was worth killing over? Who is after the plans and the contents from St Paul's? He was grateful the day was over and prayed that the police would leave them alone.

27

Outside the British Museum – Present Day + 1 (Friday)

Henry left the Museum and jumped a bit too quickly into James' patrol car, which was like a magnifying glass to the sun's rays. The seats were hot. Henry felt like his behind was being cooked.

'Put the air-con on' said Henry.

'Please' said James.

Henry cursed. 'Please' he said, rolling his eyes

Henry was in no mood for being nice. He knew that Elliot and Helen had something to do with the loss of his friend, even if they didn't fit the MO. He just needed to dig until the forensic results came through. He decided to check whether his research team had found anything. If they dug up something of historical importance linked to the vault, it could help his case.

'Can you calm down please' said James. 'What's wrong?'

Henry looked at his partner's face and frowned. James' youthful skin had not been subject to the wear and tear of the job like Henry. Not yet, at least.

'James, do me a favour. Get out of this job while you can. It's no place for a family man to work. It'll just get to you eventually.'

'Is it the Cathedral murder? You've been acting funny ever since this case started. What's going on?'

'I knew the vic.'

'Natalie?'

'Yes, she's from the AA group' he said, looking down at the floor. 'My sponsor.'

Henry felt guilty for revealing her anonymity. The number one rule of recovery. Not that it would make much of a difference now. He felt for her. Henry's drinking was the cause of destruction to his marriage. With Natalie's help, he'd managed to get sober, worked the steps and was even a sponsor himself. It was a slow progress, but as of last month he was even allowed to see his children. Not that they wanted to see him now. The damage was done and repairing a hole that big was not going to be easy.

'I tell you what, Lilly's been asking to see you for a while and I know the boys would love a visit from their God father. Why don't you come over for dinner tonight?'

'I don't know. I'm not sure I'd be good company' replied Henry.

James put his hand on Henry's shoulder. 'Come over. It'll be good for you. It's gotta be better than staying in that unkempt apartment you call home. Besides, Lilly's making casserole.'

Henry needed to get his mind off the murder and maybe this would help. He hadn't been doing much of his godfather duties and it would be good to see James' family. Seeing his godson gave him a warm feeling that reminded him of his own family, which he sorely missed.

28

Outside the British Museum – Present Day + 1 (Friday)

David sat in his non-descript car outside the Museum with Marco in the passenger seat. They watched as Detective Wrightman and PC Catchwell returned to their white and blue vehicle. David needed to understand what they knew. If Helen and Elliot told them about their findings it'd make David's job more difficult. Not impossible, just more difficult. He didn't like to use the word impossible, even when it was true. The last thing he needed were the pigs to slow him down or screw up his assignment. After a few minutes the officers pulled away from the Museum and drove off. He made a note of their registration plate. He sent it to the Organisation to put a tap on their phones and radio. If they had information, David would find out about it.

Marco sat there, holding a photo of Helen with his left hand and with his flick-knife, scratched several lines over her face.

'She's pretty' said Marco.

David was repulsed by the way his brother behaved. If he wasn't family, he would've sacked him off a long time ago. Or worse.

'For God's sake... stay focused' said David, snatching the photo from

Marco's hand. 'You're not to touch either of them unless I say so...I'm not saving your arse again.'

'I aint doin nothing' Marco replied.

'Keep it that way.'

David gripped onto the steering wheel tightly like a stress ball. He knew his brother was a loose cannon around women.

The Museum was closing. David kept his eye on the front entrance whilst his back-up kept their eyes on the rear entrance. Most of the tourists had left and the employees were now starting to vacate. He saw Helen and Elliot leaving from the front. They had no bags with them. Whatever they'd found must be stored in the Museum.

'We'll have to break in... but not today' said David.

David didn't appreciate that the cleaner would be so involved. Another person to deal with complicates matters, but only slightly. He'd ask the Organisation to see what pressure points Elliot had. In the meantime, they had to find a way to break into the Museum, but, there was no point breaking in until they knew where the map was kept. David needed more information first.

29

London – Present Day + 1 (Friday)

It had been an unusual day for Elliot. Eventful and exciting, but he was glad it was over. *Back to normality tomorrow,* he thought and hoped. He made his way home by train on the London Underground. The grey train with red sliding doors was packed as the day's commuters made their sweaty travels home in the unventilated mechanical snake. A pregnant woman carrying a baby got on at Kings Cross St Pancras Station. There were no seats available. All filled with suits and tourists. The heavily pregnant person hobbled next to the seat designated for the pregnant, disabled or elderly. She stood there looking down at a well-fed, male suit reading the Financial Times. The paper was so big that each time he turned a page he had to open the large pages out into the personal space of the faces near him. The neighbouring passengers were too British to say anything. The pregnant lady coughed and the suit looked up, smiled then carried on reading. Elliot thought that either the man didn't clock she was pregnant, or he was an arsehole. Either way, Elliot stood up and gave the woman his seat. In his mind, he cursed the suit for not helping. *Three days of chronic diarrhoea.* Elliot would always give up his seat if someone was old, disabled or pregnant. It made him feel better inside, but only if he didn't tell anyone about it. He believed that an altruistic act is not altruism if it is done to seek praise or approval.

Elliot got off the train, made his way up the escalators and walked home passing several council estates that looked post-apocalyptic. He missed his brother. It had been at least two months since he'd seen him. Elliot pulled out his phone and decided to give him a call. The dial tone rang a few times before being answered.

'Sandra, hi, it's Elliot.'

'Elliot, I erm wasn't expecting your call. We're just about to have dinner.'

'Sorry. Is Toby there' he said.

Ordinarily he'd just call back another time, but after today's events he was desperate to hear his brother's voice. He needed family. He felt all alone in the world and Toby was the only remaining bloodline on this planet.

'Yes, but he'll have to be quick' she said.

He could hear Sandra calling out for Toby, followed by small thumps on some steps.

'He's just coming. I hear you have a new job working at the Museum.'

'Yeah, it's going well' he said, although he wasn't sure if that was the truth.

'That's great news. I hope this one works out for you.'

'Thanks Sandra.'

She handed Toby the phone. 'Uh, hello' said a young voice.

'Hey bud, how's it going?'

'Elliot! I miss yew.'

'I miss you too little bro. I love you very much and will see you as soon as I can. I'm getting things sorted. How's school?'

'S'ok. We had running today. I came second, got a medal... Sandra put it on the fridge.'

'Well done, Tobe's. I'm very proud of you' he said. 'As soon as I clear some things up, I'll take you to Lego land. I promise.'

Elliot struggled. As much as it was comforting to speak with his little brother, it brought back all the pain. A reminder that both of their parents were dead and they were all that's left. A wound that never healed. He wanted to be strong for Toby. He had to be. But, it didn't stop him from feeling upset. His breathes were short and he could feel his eyes becoming teary.

'I've a… I've gotta go now Tobe's, but I will come and visit really soon.'

'Ok.'

'See ya bud. Take care.'

'Bye ya. Love you El.'

Elliot got home and did his usual routine. Shower, tea and movie. His housemate was out on a date and so he had a free reign of the sub-mediocre apartment. Elliot had been sleeping on different friends' couches after he was kicked out of university. It was nice to finally have a room, albeit a small one, to himself. Tomorrow would hopefully be calmer. He went to bed earlier than usual and fell asleep instantly.

30

Helen's Office – Present Day + 2 (Saturday)

Although the sun had not yet woken, the trains and workers of London did their best to get out of bed. Elliot was one of those workers. Tired, but awake. His main motivation for the day was to investigate the contents of Jonathan Hooke's safe. He hoped that the burgled house and the incident in St Pauls were just coincidental. He wasn't convinced. Someone was after the Rosy Cross, not that he knew what it really was. Elliot took comfort that it was unlikely the murderer or anyone else would know him and Helen had stumbled across the map.

He arrived at the British Museum and, as instructed, went straight to Helen's office. It was a small room without natural light, but well-lit by halogen bulbs. Helen sat behind a desk more suited to an office junior than a curator. She had a hot chocolate waiting for him, with cream and chocolate sprinkles. He dodged the wall-length, tall book shelf protruding towards the door that nearly jabbed him in the waist and sat down in a cheap plastic chair. He noticed a book on the shelf, written by H Philips.

'Morning Elliot, here you go' she said, handing him the hot chocolate.

'Thank you.' He smiled and took a sip. 'This is the same drink from the café yesterday.'

Helen shrugged her shoulders. 'I knew you liked it.'

'Thank you very much' he said. He was touched, but thought the sentiment was disproportionately friendly. 'Have you been in long?'

'An hour or so. I'm no good at sleeping... came in early. You sleep ok after yesterday's madness?'

Elliot nodded. He never had any trouble with sleeping. If anything it was the opposite. He could sleep anywhere. Literally. As a kid, his parents found him asleep in a cupboard after a drawn out game of hide and seek. Whilst getting to sleep was not a problem, if he didn't get his sleep he could barely function. Elliot saw a small statue of Anubis, the Egyptian Pharaoh on the shelf to his right. It looked like a half dog, half human sitting on a raised platform. He had one as a kid and it made him smile.

'You have an Anubis' he said, pointing.

'Yeah, collector's edition. A present from an old flame. He went away, but I liked it too much to get rid of it.'

'What happened?'

Helen looked at him, then down at the shelf in her room. She put her mouth into a kissing position then moved her pouted lips to the side of her face.

'It turned out he was in a relationship.'

Elliot liked to actively listen. At least, that's what he called it. Others called him out as being argumentative. That was not his intention. He'd often probe with questions that would come across as challenging to the speaker's viewpoint or was just an uncomfortable question. Something he picked up from his studies in philosophy, but a boundary he needed to work on.

'Do you know that for sure' asked Elliot.

'Uh, yes. Yes I do.'

Infidelity had caused so much destruction in Elliot's life. He'd experienced its negative impact on his family. A pain that he wished he didn't know. It made him feel warmer to Helen, although he wasn't sure why. Maybe it was the hurt they had in common. Perhaps she was not that different to him, after all.

'Painful huh' he said.

Helen nodded, then paused for a few seconds. 'You ever have a girlfriend cheat on you?'

'No' he said shaking his head. 'No, but my father did.'

Helen paused. 'What happened?'

Elliot felt uncomfortable. He wasn't used to sharing feelings unless they were on the surface. These feelings about his parents had been buried deep for a couple of years now. Suppressed as part of his coping mechanism.

'Not much to say. My mum found a pair of knickers in my dad's work bag with a love note. They had a big, and I mean big, argument over it. It was horrible, especially for Toby. Of course my father denied everything, then drove off. That's when the crash happened. I never did get the chance to tell him how angry I was. Anyway, that's all there is to it' he said, dismissively.

He kept his eyes on the floor, hoping it was enough of an explanation to stop him from exposing his vulnerability. Sure he'd had counselling after his dad died, and again when his mother stopped fighting her struggle with cancer. But, he'd never forgiven his dad for the damage he caused to the family. A poison in his body, visible in his face when he talked about it.

Elliot's body went into stonewalling mode. He froze. He eventually took the courage to look up at Helen. She was tearful, but trying to hold it back. She wiped the sleeve of her suit jacket against her face.

'Urgh, my eyes...must be the hay-fever' she said.

Elliot knew it wasn't hay-fever. Either, she cared deeply about his dad, or she was very empathetic. He changed the subject.

'What's this' he said pulling out a book from the shelf. "The History of History."

'Oh that. It's my book…if I ever get it published I'll bite off my right arm. Sent it to several agents, but so far no one's offered any interest.'

'I'm sure you'll get there' he said, putting the book back on the shelf, next to a book on the architecture of Sir Wren. 'Let's look at that stuff we found in the safe. Have you studied it yet?'

'Yes actually, looked this morning. According to my research, this contraption is a pinhole camera' she said, picking it up from her desk and passing it to him. 'The first one's believed to have been invented by Aristotle.'

Elliot found it odd that there were so many connections with philosophers. Were all of these philosophers part of the Pythagorean Brotherhood or the Rosicrucian Order? What were they hiding? He picked up the contraption and examined it. The pinhole camera was a black, light-proof box with a small hole in one side. It didn't look overly technical or well crafted.

'What's it do?'

'It's a simple camera…no lens. It was first used by philosophers and astronomists to observe the solar eclipse and examine the laws of projection.'

Elliot held the camera so that the pin-hole faced the light of the window. As the light shone through the tiny hole, the reflection of the window, window frame and tree projected onto the back of the box. The projection was upside down and inside out. The tree looked like it was floating in mid-air with the branches facing down, rather than up.

'But what does this have to do with the publication from Hooke's safe, the box or the architect drawings' said Elliot.

'I'm not sure. But, I do think it has something to do with what we're looking for.'

Elliot picked up the Royal Society magazine. The publication date was 1960. It was in unnaturally good condition for its age.

'Have you read this' he asked.

'Yeah. Nothing that refers to what we've found so far, but feel free to have a look.'

Helen needed to continue her preparations for the upcoming exhibition, and so she left Elliot with the task of piecing their findings together. He went through everything they knew. That Sir Christopher Wren was a Freemason, member of the Royal Society and possibly the Rosicrucian Order. He had left puzzles that only a philosopher would know. *But why and leading to what,* Elliot wondered. The message in the box seemed to indicate that a treasure or power can only be found by the group of philosopher's known as the Invisible College. Even with his passion for philosophy, there was still so much unanswered. What perplexed and scared him most of all was the possibility that someone was prepared to kill for it.

He picked up the publication, thumbed through its pages and stopped when he reached a book mark. The pages contained an article with a picture of London Bridge, taken from a boat on the Thames. It didn't look like the London Bridge he knew. It was much older and made of stone. It had some sort of concrete anchor protruding from a middle arch. It looked familiar, but he couldn't think why. He picked up the camera, put the page against the light and faced the camera towards the page. As he did, the picture of London Bridge turned upside down and inside out. He squinted at the anchor in the middle of the bridge. It wasn't an anchor. It was a cross with a rose in the middle.

CHAPTER 30

'Helen, the Rosy Cross.'

She stopped reading and looked up from her desk. 'What?'

'I've found something.'

'You've found the Rosy Cross, the missing contents from the box?'

'I'm not sure what it is, but I've found something.'

He showed her the inverted image. 'Whatever we're looking for, should be at London Bridge' said Elliot. 'It's too much of a coincidence otherwise. Let's go check it out.'

'Elliot, there's uh. There's one problem. That's the old London Bridge.'

'So this one's no longer there?'

'Correct.'

Elliot's excitement fell to the ground with a thud. They'd hit a dead end. 'So that's the end of it then?'

'Not quite' said Helen.

'How so?'

'In 1971, the American philanthropist, R P McCulloch, attempted to buy Tower Bridge. You know... the pretty one with the platform that raises up. Unfortunately for him and for us, the American got it wrong and ended up buying London Bridge. The philanthropist had it transported, piece by piece, to Arizona.'

'So the Rosy Cross could still be there.'

Helen nodded, but there was no way that Elliot could afford a flight to Arizona. Not on his salary. The Museum was not going to foot the bill.

'You know... the Museum loans historical artefacts and treasures to Museums all over the world. Let me check with Arthur Heartman to see whether there are any scheduled flights going that way. I'll explain we're onto something big for the Museum. In a way, it's kind of true.'

Elliot never underestimated the power of a strong woman, but he wasn't convinced Arthur would authorise and pay for a low level employee, hired as a cleaner, to go on an international trip. Especially as only yesterday he was called up for assaulting a visitor at the Museum. Still, he left it with Helen to see if she could work her magic.

31

Arthur Heartman's Office – Present Day + 2 (Saturday)

Arthur's office was as cold as usual. Helen remembered to bring her suit jacket this time, even then it was still chilly. She wondered how Arthur managed to avoid getting hypothermia.

'I can't give permission for you and the cleaner to go off to another country' said Arthur, shaking his head disapprovingly then leaning back into his chair. 'Elliot's only been here one day and you have the exhibition starting in two weeks!'

Helen wasn't expecting it to be easy. It wasn't like she was asking to have an extra thirty minutes for lunch. She was beyond intrigued over the new discovery. She also felt responsible for Elliot and wanted to encourage him after all he'd been through. Desperate to help appease his pain. Whether it was maternal instinct or just co-dependence, she wasn't sure.

'Arthur, you don't understand' she said, taking in a full breath. 'We've found something. Something big and I'm almost certain it will help with the exhibition. All I'm saying is we go there, check it out then come straight back.'

Arthur brought his hands together to make his "I'm serious" triangle pose. Helen could tell he was contemplating the idea from his pose. Either that or he was trying to find a way to let her down so that she couldn't object. She knew he didn't like defeat and when he ever did eventually concede to her charm, he'd often try and make it sound as if other factors were at play. Anything to avoid admitting the other person was right.

'I'm sorry, but we just don't have the budget. As you know, we rely on the public for funding. Donations are low as they are and I just can't justify it to the Board.'

Helen looked at the paperwork on his desk. Amongst the organised chaos of letters, there were some loan proformas for the transfer of artefacts from the Museum to other museums. The Museum had agreements to lend and borrow treasures and they had to be carefully accounted for, insured and transported.

'What about a cargo plane to America' she asked.

'What?'

'You must have a transfer with an American museum coming up soon.'

Arthur tapped his index finger against his closed lips. 'We do have a shipment going to the Natural History Museum in Las Vegas tomorrow. I suppose you could get on the same flight. But, you'll have to make your way from there. Elliot can't go though. He'll have to stay here.'

'Arthur. The clues found were so well hidden. Not even our best researcher discovered them. The only reason we've come this far is because of Elliot. He may have been employed as a cleaner, but he's very clever. Beyond clever. Anyway, the point is I need him with me. He has to come.'

Arthur let the air hang with an almost awkward silence. He just sat there, playing with his beard and looking at her. It was as if he was waiting for Helen to back down and renege from her request.

'Technically, Elliot can't stay here unsupervised. Thinking about it, legally he'll have to come with you' said Arthur. 'However, do not let your feelings for his father cloud your judgement. He's a messed up kid and if you're not careful, he will get you in trouble.'

Like clockwork, thought Helen, although she wasn't expecting the insult. Now to break the good news to Elliot. If the police asked about their whereabouts, Arthur could just update them. Besides, they'd be back in no time and no one would notice.

32

London – Present Day + 3 (Sunday)

The next morning, Elliot packed as quickly as he could, gathering a few t-shirts, shorts and trousers. He had one smart top and brought that in his case. He was pleasantly surprised that the Las Vegas Natural History Museum was doing an exhibition on Pharaoh Akhatan and as luck would have it, the British Museum had a large collection of artefacts that they wanted to borrow. If it wasn't for the cargo of artefacts going to America, he'd have no way of getting to America. Before then, he was pretty sure they'd met a dead end.

They had lunch before making their way to the airport. Helen picked a Paleo restaurant nearby. It was filled with slim and toned individuals, many of whom were wearing lycra and running gear. If it hadn't been for the absence of exercise equipment, Elliot could've mistaken the place for a gym.

Helen had swapped her heels for pumps, but her clothes were still classically smart. Elliot wore his usual travel attire of a white t-shirt, chinos and blue boat-shoes. They sat next to a couple that looked like they were about to try out for a weightlifting competition. Elliot had eggs benedict on a bed of spinach and mushrooms and Helen had the chicken salad. Elliot went through a phase of only liking orange food in his childhood. Chips, beans, pizza, onion rings. Not anymore. A sharply dressed, olive skinned man approached them while they were eating.

'Excuse me, Miss Philips' said the man.

The man took Helen off-guard. She looked up to see a pair of dark brown, deep set eyes and short black hair. There was a slight scar under his chin, but otherwise he had a handsome face.

'Sorry, do I know you?'

'No, not yet. My name's Edward Sanchez and I work with the police. I've been investigating the crime that happened yesterday in St Pauls.'

'Are you working with Detective Wrightman?'

'No. I'm from a separate department.'

His tie was perfectly set in the middle by a tie-pin, groomed hair, sharp suit and white shirt without a crease. Elliot recognised his face, but couldn't think where he'd seen him.

'How can I help? I've told everything I know to the police' she said.

'It's to do with the contents of the vault in St Paul's. We saw you on camera' he said.

Elliot's heart sank and he began to tense up. He looked at Helen for guidance, but she looked just as distressed.

'Don't worry Miss. I have no interest in pursuing you, or your companion here. I just need to know what you found.'

Elliot and Helen knew they'd been busted. At least the camera would absolve them from being suspects to the tour guide's death. They had no choice...they had to come clean. Helen told the man about the drawings, the box, the pin-hole, their hidden meaning and even that they believed it led to some kind of great treasure.

For Elliot, it didn't feel right… there was something wrong. The man presented himself without any proof of ID and knew everything Detective Wrightman didn't. Something was fishy. Then it hit him. He knew where he'd seen the man before.

'So whatever you're looking for is at London Bridge' said the man.

Elliot stepped in. 'That's right. Not far from Borough Market.'

Helen gave Elliot a funny look, but let him take the lead.

'The message indicates that the Rosy Cross, or whatever it really is, is located on the side of the Bridge.'

'Ok, thank you. The vault and the murder are linked. I'd strongly advise you stay out of this. I'll handle things from here' said the man, with a tone that made it sound more like a warning than advice.

Edward Sanchez left the restaurant and went on his way. Helen didn't speak until he was completely out of site.

'What was that about' she asked.

'I don't trust him.'

'We didn't have much of a choice. Elliot, he's the police. '

'No, he's not. I've seen him before. Yesterday outside the café, near Soho. It doesn't add up.

'What do you mean?'

'He didn't show us any ID and knew everything that Detective Wrightman didn't. If there was a camera in St Pauls, why didn't the police speak to us about it earlier? They'd know we had nothing to do with the murder. I remember looking in Faith Chapel and unless it was well hidden, there was no camera. Also, did you see the way he was dressed? Not a thing out of place. There is no way he was with the police.'

'You don't know that for sure.'

'Call Detective Wrightman and ask if he knows Edward Sanchez. If I'm wrong, at least we can clear it up.'

'And if you're right?'

'Then it means we're being followed' he said.

The thought of them being followed made Elliot fearful. A murder, a break in and now this. *How could anyone know they were at the vault?* Someone knew they were involved more than they should be. Helen called the police station to speak with Detective Wrightman, but he wasn't there so she spoke with PC James Catchwell instead. James confirmed their fears. She explained how Edward Sanchez had followed them, pretended to be with the police and was going to London Bridge. She left out all the information she told Edward Sanchez about the hidden messages. James agreed to send someone to investigate.

Teo Brecher had enough information for now and no longer needed to follow Elliot and Helen. He knew that London Bridge, being in the Square Mile, would be relatively quiet if not dead on a Sunday. All the city workers were there Monday to Friday, but not today. The bankers, lawyers and accountants would be resting in their comfortable homes so there was less chance of him being noticed. He made his way to London Bridge, unaware that the police would soon be there.

33

Cargo Flight – Present Day + 3 (Sunday)

The cargo flight took off from London's Heathrow airport. A little bumpy to start, but low turbulence for the rest of the journey. Elliot and Helen sat in the passenger section of the plane. Despite Elliot's best efforts to rationalise his fear of flying, it was something he'd not been able to overcome. When he wasn't using his hands, they'd automatically revert to the arms of his chair where they'd grip on firmly. Outside the plane was a sea of grey clouds, darkened by the night's sky.

Seven hours into the flight, a stewardess came over and offered them drinks. She looked as if she'd used a whole can of spray-on tan and was not dissimilar to an overgrown dolled-up Umpalumpa. Elliot wondered whether he'd ever seen anyone so orange. She smiled at them revealing several wrinkles. Elliot stretched out his legs as much as the seat in front would let him.

'We're half way there' he said, yawning.

'It's gone quicker than expected' said Helen, catching Elliot's infectious yawn and moving her hands over her mouth.

'Not quick enough' said Elliot.

Elliot's palms were sweaty from holding onto the sides of his seat for so long. The orange woman handed over their drinks, then went off with her trolley to serve other people. Elliot pulled the ring on his coke can and the spray of gas rushed out of it. He found the sound it made satisfying. He took a big gulp, put the reading light on and kicked his shoes off. Helen turned to face him, opened her mouth to speak, then closed it again.

'What's wrong' he asked.

She looked down, left then right and scratched her arm nervously.

'I was just wondering. Why did you beat up your previous boss? You don't seem the type.'

An awkward question, but he was happy Helen didn't think it was like him. He was used to people rejecting him and he was starting to believe he was a bad person. Elliot shrugged his shoulders.

'A few wrong turns and people write you off' said Elliot. 'I may have gone a bit over the top, but he deserved it.'

'What happened?'

'My uh' he said, looking out through the window at the clouds, keen to avoid eye contact. 'My manager at the time, James... tall man, short temper. He started fooling around with one of the cleaners, Cassandra. I called her Cassy. A sweet woman from the Philippines. Her visa expired, but the office turned a blind eye as she did a good job. Plus she was sleeping with the manager. James was already married and had his own family. He didn't want the affair to get out. Cassy unintentionally fell pregnant... when he found out, he went ape.'

'I bet he did'

Elliot fiddled with his empty coke can. 'One night he got drunk and decided Cassy would have an abortion. His persuasiveness turned nasty and when she refused, he beat her. She lost the baby. Cassy came from poverty and the baby would've been a way for her to stay in the country.'

'I'm sorry. Did she go to the police?'

'She couldn't.'

'Why?!'

'James said that if she told anyone, he'd report her to the immigration authorities. There was nothing she could do. Her visa had expired and she'd be kicked out the country.'

'And so you beat him up' she said.

Elliot nodded. 'Cassy was in the kitchen at work, balling her eyes out. When I saw the bruises, I put two and two together and she eventually confided in me. The arsehole. I hate bullies. She was unable to do anything about it. Completely helpless. One day, James was in the office flirting with another colleague and trying, as he often did, to assert his masculinity by putting other people in the office down. He made a careless comment about me being parentless. It was tactless, socially awkward, but nothing major. Then he decided to start taking the piss out of Cassy for taking so much time off for the miscarriage.'

Helen's hands clenched slightly.

'I lost it… gave him a black eye. I don't like fighting, but he deserved it. I just saw red… couldn't help myself.'

Elliot didn't dare look up, for fear of seeing her judgement, but after a few seconds he felt her hand on his shoulder.

'He know why you did it?'

'Nope. He thinks it was over the comment he made about my parents. I'm not gonna lie, I was a little sore about my parents then anyway, but it was a good cover.'

Elliot was lying. He was more than a little sore. The death of his parents ruptured any stability he'd known.

'If the truth came out, Cassandra would be sent home. I didn't have much choice. It was the only thing I could do.'

Elliot explained it was at this point the social worker, Angela Bashton, intervened and started causing trouble for him. At first he found she was reluctant to help, and treated him like some hopeless kid, pent up with anger that he needed to release. After a while she began to defrost. She expressed that with some guidance and support he'd be able to look after his younger brother. But not yet, he still had to work through his own stability. For now, Toby was better off with his foster carers.

'I can understand why you did it. I'd certainly want to hit him if I were in your shoes' said Helen. 'You've been through so much, it's hard to believe you're still functioning.'

Elliot didn't feel like he was functioning. After losing his parents, he lost interest in interacting with others. He became a recluse, wouldn't go out, stopped looking after himself. After a while, he developed a coping mechanism of suppressing anything that hurt. It wasn't healthy, but it worked for now and enabled him to be around people. At first, he thought he was rationalising the pain. Using logic as a way of working around the hurt. But, he wasn't. The suppressed pain was kept in a place that would eventually build up and implode if not dealt with. He raised his eyebrows and shrugged his shoulders.

'Listen Elliot, I need to tell you something.'

It was Helen's turn to let her eyes take refuge on the floor. The aeroplane shook due to turbulence and it took Elliot's attention. The seatbelt sign lit up on after a few seconds. He buckled in as fast as he could, then held onto the arms of his seat until the aeroplane calmed down.

'That was unpleasant' he said, slowly releasing his grip. 'Oh yeah, what were you going to say?'

'I was going... to say' said Helen, slowly exhaling her breath for a few seconds. 'I was going to say that, I uh, think we should be very careful now the police know who we are. No law breaking. We play this by the book.'

Elliot nodded, but knew there was something else, but decided to leave it. She would tell him in her own time.

'I wonder what we'll find at London Bridge' said Elliot.

Helen raised one hand palm upwards and tilted her head back. 'Not sure. Whatever it is, we know that many people have tried desperately to keep it secret, and someone is desperate to get it. It's clearly valuable...but whether it's of intrinsic, historical or sentimental value...I don't know.'

'Either way, it should be a good find for the Museum. Imagine if it was the wealth of Sir Christopher Wren. By today's standards, he'd be a millionaire.'

The idea of having ten thousand pounds overwhelmed Elliot, let alone being a millionaire. He'd be sorted for life. He could get a house, look after Toby and re-unite his family.

'That'd be nice' she said. 'Well we know it has something to do with great power and the Rosy Cross.'

'You think it's the body of Christ or the philosopher's stone?'

'Ha, no chance. I'm sure it's a metaphor for something else.'

Elliot agreed with her, but his quench for answers could not be satisfied quick enough. He was desperate to see what they'd find at London Bridge. He also wondered whether PC Catchwell had found the intimidating man impersonating a police officer.

34

London Bridge – Present Day + 2 (Saturday)

The summer evening cooled as the sun finished working its nine to five. The wind offered a gentle breeze through the city streets. With the exception of the waves of the River Thames and a few pigeons, the area was almost still. The jungle of concrete buildings were empty, but for a few cleaners. Coffee shops were all closed. With not a tree in sight, there were no leaves for the gentle wind to dance with. The lawyers, bankers and accountants retreated from the skyscrapers to their cosy homes until the new week commenced. Unlike the rest of London on a Saturday evening, the Square Mile slept.

At the top end of London Bridge was an eclectic gathering of old and new buildings. Tall corporate offices with old churches in between. A reflection of England's organic growth since time immemorial. The Church St Magnus the Martyr, sat next to London Bridge. It was dwarfed between two large offices, both occupied by a prestigious law firm. The church was dated and in need of repair. PC James Catchwell walked through the church grounds and made his way to the north side of the river. He climbed down a flight of steps that took him on a pathway running along the water's edge and under London Bridge. It was dark and eerie. Apart from a couple of rats, no one was in sight. He pulled out his torch and shone it down a further set of concrete steps that led to the Thames water.

The soft waves of the river hit the bottom of the steps with a steady tempo. It was almost calming had it not been surrounded by darkness, empty beer cans and used syringes. Near the steps, James could swear he saw a shadow move. *Probably just some junky or kids mucking about.* Still, he'd received a credible tip-off and was obliged to check it out.

James made his way down the second set of steps. He was careful not to slip on the floor, which was wet from the river waves. The visibility was poor at the bottom and he could just make out where the steps finished. At the last step, he shone his torch around, but there was no one to be found. Just more used syringe needles and plastic bottles on the floor around him.

Behind the slimy concrete steps was a round tunnel leading to an underground sewer. It was gated shut. Again, there was nobody in site. He heard a car rush over the bridge and it caused him to look back up the damp dark stairway. He shone his torch upstairs out of instinct, but there was nothing to see. He was giving himself the creeps. There was nothing here so he decided to head back upstairs.

As James started climbing the steps, he heard the crack of a glass syringe being stepped on behind him. Before he could turn around, he felt a sharp pain travel through his back. It felt wet and warm. He jolted forward and felt another pain charge through his back. He fell to the ground and began to shake. A dark figure walked in front of him, put a knife away before making his way up the steps. James' lungs were filling up with blood. Unable to call out for help, he lay there in a growing pool of his own blood.

35

Lake Havasu, Arizona – Present Day + 4 (Monday)

Elliot woke up early. The jetlag was messing with his body-clock. He couldn't go back to sleep so got dressed and went to the hotel lobby to get a drink. It was a medium sized hotel with moderate facilities. Not that Elliot was planning to use any of them. He took the lift downstairs, walked through the corridor to see Helen sitting on a sofa in the foyer. She was wide awake and reading. Helen wasn't wearing make-up, although she didn't need it. He rubbed his eyes, sat down next to her and put his feet on the coffee table.

'Morning' he said, yawning and stretching his arms.

'Good morning...feet off the table.'

Elliot was too tired to pay attention to what he was doing, but quickly took his feet of the table. It was his usual morning routine at home and his subconscious hadn't registered that he was in a new morning environment.

'Coffee?'

'A hot chocolate would be good' he said, smiling.

'I'm beginning to think you might have a chocolate addiction.'

'Any worse than coffee?'

'No...no, I guess not.'

Helen smiled and went off to order him a hot chocolate from the twenty-four-hour bar, then came back and sat down. Elliot looked at her reading book sitting on the coffee table. It was titled "The History of Economics and the Slave Trade."

'Bit of light reading' he said, half-pointing at the book.

'Technically I'm still working. This is not a holiday for me.'

'Sounds depressing.'

'It's actually pretty interesting. Though yes, bits do require a strong stomach.'

Elliot was not a morning person, and the idea of reading right now was the last thing on his mind. He needed at least another thirty minutes before he left the land of the zombies.

'Did you know that almost every country that engaged the slave trade prospered in its economy? Yep, the Ancient Greeks, Egyptians, Turkish, Romans, England and obviously USA.'

Elliot couldn't be arsed to think, but didn't want to appear rude. 'But wasn't it the southern states of America that wanted to keep the slave trade? Their economy wasn't as strong as the northern states, who wanted it abolished.'

'Yes, but the people in the northern states had a higher wage and benefited from better technology. It meant that they could use machinery to output their produce quicker. You know, like cotton, corn and flour. The southern states had a lower average salary and less technology. Many produce was collected and made by hand instead of machinery. For them to keep up, they needed more man power and so the slave trade was more attractive to them.'

'As much as I love ancient philosophy, even Aristotle believed the slave trade was a good thing. So did Plato. In fact, the reason the Ancient Greeks advanced as much as they did, is largely because all their chores were carried out by slaves. It's nuts.'

Elliot didn't want to think about the atrocities. His stomach rumbled. 'I'm hungry. The breakfast room's just opened. Let's eat.'

They had breakfast, then went to walk it off, leaving the cosy hotel and making their way towards Lake Havasu. The sun had not yet fully developed, but the morning was still bright. The air was cool and wind free. The lake was surrounded by yachts and sail boats. Some of them were travelling to their next destination, but most of them were just there floating, gently rocking left to right. Houses, condos and commercial buildings were surrounded by trees dotted around the lake. Some of the buildings benefited from a view of the mountains in the distance. London Bridge stood there, cutting through the middle of the waters. The bridge had been taken piece by piece from London to Arizona and the reconstruction looked exactly the same as the picture they'd seen. Elliot and Helen walked towards it.

'Can I ask you something' asked Helen.

'You just did' he said. He sometimes forgot he was an adult and his inner child loved to play. 'Sure, what's up.'

'Your dad, George. He had money. You didn't need to work as a cleaner, but you did anyway.'

'Actually, I did need to.'

Elliot explained how before his parents were married his father wrote a will in favour of Elliot's auntie. After getting married, his dad forgot to change the will. When George passed away all of his assets were inherited by Elliot's aunt. Greed took over and despite a small claim for dependency by his mum and Toby, the aunt kept everything. She did not care much for George's wife and cared less for Elliot and Toby.

'That's horrible' said Helen, shaking her head. 'I'm sure I've heard of some law relating to that.'

'Yeah well, we've had a high street lawyer have a look at it and it seems pretty solid.'

'I'll speak with my friend when we get back. I'm sure something happened in similar circumstances, but I can't remember what.'

Elliot was grateful, but not hopeful. He knew that he could only rely on himself in this world. No one else to bring him to financial security except himself. He fantasized that they'd find some treasure left by Sir Christopher Wren which could give him a deposit on a house. Not that he could afford the mortgage payments. It didn't stop him from dreaming.

'Fingers crossed that whatever we're seeking, is still there' he said.

'Me too. There's only one way to find out.'

They walked over the bridge, stood in the middle and peered over the edge. He could just about see a stone feature protruding out from the middle leg of the bridge and Elliot assumed it was the upside down Rosy Cross. The drop below reminded Elliot of his abseiling accident and he began to feel light headed and nervous. There were too many people around to climb down there now. They'd be seen. Besides, they didn't have the right equipment and it'd be too dangerous. They agreed to come back at night, when they were fully equipped and less likely to get caught.

36

London – Present Day + 4 (Monday)

David was feeling the pressure from his employer. He wasn't afraid for himself, although he knew he should be. He feared for his brother, Marco. It had been three days and neither of them had results. With Helen's phone switched off and no records of her credit and debit cards being used, they had no way of tracking her and no way of knowing what she was up to next. She hadn't been at the Museum or her home for a couple of days. David had no idea whether the map was still in the British Museum and so he decided to call in the help. A short, but stocky man called Abrafo Jenkins and a nasty piece of work known as Rav Manek. Neither of them had been professionally trained, but both were useful in a fight.

Abrafo and Rav were introduced to David through the Organisation. As much as Abrafo and Rav argued, they'd been dragged through hell in Chechnya together. Both prisoners marked for death for fighting on the wrong side in guerrilla tactics. Apart from the internal side effects, the only evidence of their suffering was in the shape of an identification number tattooed on their arms. A sign that they were not entitled to human rights, but instead allocated a ticket number to meet their reaper. Their bond was not one of mutual affection, but one of dysfunction and trauma.

Abrafo lost a bet on a boxing match a week ago and needed the money… again. He wasn't good with money, but was very good with his hands. Growing up in a rough area gave him a choice; be the predator or the prey. His bulky stature helped. Small fights on the childhood estate soon evolved into robbery, burglary and even kidnapping. His questionable morals were directed by his upbringing, rather than by than his desire to do harm. However, after Chechnya his moral compass had been stuck next to a trauma magnet and was all over the place.

Rav, on the other hand, took enjoyment out of inflicting pain. He was slim and didn't look intimidating. His psychotic personality made up for it. He'd get the job done, but was a troublemaker that needed babysitting. Naturally, Marco and Rav saw eye to eye. If there was an Oxford dictionary for hired thugs, Rav would be found under "Liability." David wouldn't normally choose him, but Marco insisted. A few years back, Rav helped muddy some evidence pinpointing Marco in a rape case. To this day, Marco assures David that he didn't do it. David says he believes him, but doesn't. Not really. The tampered evidence got Marco off the charge and, much to David's disagreement, Rav became a close friend of Marco's since.

Abrafo and Rav were brought up to speed and the Organisation was doing all it could to track Helen and Elliot. Soon they'd show up on the radar. Just one slip. A phone call, payment on a card or email. When they did, David would be on them like a shoe on a bug.

37

Lake Havasu, Arizona – Present Day + 4 (Monday)

Helen and Elliot waited on the middle of London Bridge as the moon glistened on the waters behind them. The engine-boats were as motionless as the gentle waves on which they rocked. It was gone one in the morning and there was no one in sight. Helen dangled over the edge, peered down and then shuffled along until they were aligned with the Rosy Cross. Seeing her so close to the edge with nothing to hold onto made Elliot feel nauseous. His back and stomach tensed with anxiety and it reminded him of his past accident. Helen pulled out a rope from her bag and started to unravel it.

'What are you doing' asked Elliot.

'What do you think' she replied. 'How else are we going to get down there? Here' she said, passing him one end of the rope. 'Tie this to that lamppost…and make sure it's tight enough to take my weight.'

'I can't let you do this.'

'Elliot, we don't have much of a choice. Unless you want to do it?'

Elliot looked at the floor and shook his head. As much as he didn't want Helen to climb down, he was too afraid to do it himself. His hands were shaking as though he'd just had five cups of coffee. He wanted to tell her about his experience, but was so afraid of climbing he decided it was best to stay silent. He tied the rope in a triple knot around the lamppost and pulled on it with all his weight. It didn't budge.

'Ok, it's done.'

'Thanks. Now keep an eye out for anyone.'

Helen sat her bum on the waist height, stone wall and dangled her legs over the edge, one after the other. Her baggy blue jogging bottoms created a friction against the stone, making it more difficult to turn around onto her front. She found a groove on the outer edge of the bridge, wedged her feet in, loosened the rope from around her waist and slowly leant back.

Helen's journey down the middle of the stone wall was a slow one. Her legs were strong enough to handle the climb, but her arms were shaking a little. Her breaths were getting heavier as she descended. The Rosy Cross was only a few drops down.

'Helen, are you ok? Anything I can do' Elliot whispered.

'I'm ok. New pair of arms, maybe?'

She looked at the upside-down cross. It was definitely not an anchor. The bridge was moved to Lake Havasu in 1968, taken apart piece by piece and then re-constructed. It was possible that the treasure had been taken during the move and could be anywhere.

'I'm getting tired. I have no idea how I'm going to get back up.'

Helen pulled out her mag-light and turned it on.

Elliot leant over the edge, several metres above and saw the bright light. 'Helen, you'd better put that away in case someone sees us.'

She put the torch in her bag, leaving her in almost complete darkness.

There was nothing obvious that stood out. She ran her hands over the cross to feel her way around. The Rosy Cross was smooth and solid. As her hands reached near the top of the cross there were a series of light bumps on one of the bricks. *Brail?* It was not brail, but a triangle made up of bumps.

'The Pythagorean Brotherhood' she whispered under breath.

'What did you say?'

'I think I've found something' she said.

'What is it?'

'Hang on' she said, out of breath.

Helen retrieved a knife from her satchel, scrapped around the brick with the triangle and the grout around it came off easily, leaving the brick was loose. She pulled it out with relative ease, revealing a dark hole, too dark to see inside. Helen's legs were shaking from the overexertion. She stopped and stared at the black hole.

'This is horrible' she said, slowly putting her hand inside. 'If I find a rat or a spider I will scream.'

She felt around and grabbed onto something firm, but soft. It definitely wasn't a rat or a spider. She pulled it out.

'What the…' she said, looking at something covered in a cloth. Helen opened the cloth to see an old clay mug. Carefully, she put it in her satchel, moved the bag so it was around her back and put the brick back in its place.

'Ok, I've got something' she said taking in a deep breath. 'I'm coming back up.'

Helen's legs were noticeably shaking. She tried pulling herself up, but it wasn't working.

'Help' she said.

'What's wrong?'

'Nothing major, but I'm stuck. I can't climb back up. Try and pull me up.'

Elliot went into panic mode. He put one foot against the wall, knee bent and held onto the rope with both hands. He pushed his leg straight and pulled with his hands at the same time. She moved up a bit, but not enough. The friction of the rope against the stone was making it difficult. Helen put her feet up higher against the wall and held on. Elliot re-adjusted his position, moving his hands along the rope so that the part of it tied to the lamppost was now slack. He tugged at the rope with all his strength and Helen lifted up by another foot. Slow, but steady progress. Elliot re-adjusted himself again and pulled. As he pulled, his hand suddenly slipped. The rope ran through his fingers, burning the skin as it yanked with great thrust. Helen fell back down and crashed against the wall of the bridge with a thud. Elliot looked over to see her dangling there. She was not moving and must've bashed her head against the wall. The rope, taught by her weight, was tangled against her neck and cutting off her air supply. With the risk of strangulation, he needed to act fast before any lack of oxygen gave her brain damage, or worse, killed her.

Elliot cursed a whirlwind of expletives as he panicked for her safety. 'I'm so sorry.'

Helen was too dazed to speak or move. He had to move quickly. Elliot's hands were shaking. Adrenaline pumped through his veins.

Whilst his fear was all consuming, he had no choice. He tied a second rope to the lamppost, made his way to the edge of the bridge, climbed over and abseiled down before his mind had a chance to second guess itself. He reached Helen within seconds, but she was barely conscious and choking. He quickly untangled the rope from around her neck so that she could breathe. As her airway opened, she gasped for air.

'You'll be ok' he said.

Helen gave an incoherent mumble. Elliot was worried that she might be concussed. He moved her so that her legs were facing the wall.

'Urgh, where am I.'

'Don't worry. I'm getting you out of here.'

He was so focused on getting Helen to safety that his fear of heights had to take a back seat. Helen was beginning to come around, but was still murmuring. Elliot managed to tie her rope to his. He positioned himself in the usual climbing position and lifted up, using the strength of his legs to pull them both up. Each time he would pull, raise his legs and arms up, re-adjust himself and pull again. She was light for a person, but still heavy to carry up against a wall. Gradually, they both moved up, one pull at a time. His arms and legs were aching, shaking and losing control. The lactic acid was building up in his body and painful.

As they reached the top, Elliot managed to put his feet in the grooves of the bridge's wall. He then held onto the side and pushed himself up and body forward. One leg over, then the other. He lay there on the floor and caught his breath, not that he had time to recover. Helen was still dangling there. He quickly got up, held onto the rope that attached him to Helen, took a big breath, then pulled with all his might. Helen was now at touching distance. He quickly grabbed her arm before she had the chance to fall back down. He pulled her up and held under her arms and around her chest, then tugged her towards him and onto path of the bridge. He fell back on the floor and Helen collapsed on top of him. Elliot quickly put her in the recovery position.

'Helen' he said, shaking her. 'Helen!'

Helen lay there, slowly moving her head left to right in a daze. 'Argh, my head. Not sure what happened there.'

She held her head where it had been hit on the bridge. Blood was seeping out.

'I'm so sorry… lost my grip and you fell back. It's my fault' said Elliot.

'No, I couldn't get back up…you saved me. Thank you.'

'I couldn't leave you there. We need to get out of here, before someone comes.'

38

Lake Havasu - Present Day + 3 (Sunday)

Back in the hotel, Elliot brought a bag of ice and some snacks to Helen's room. On opening her door, he found her sitting at the end of the bed with a cold, wet flannel on her head.

'Here' he said, taking the flannel and wrapping it around some ice. 'Try this.'

'Thanks.'

As she applied the icy cold flannel to her head, she took in an audible deep breath.

'Are you ok?'

'I feel like I've been used as a piñata, but I'll be alright. Thanks for saving me. I'd be in a much worse position if it wasn't for you.'

Elliot didn't feel like he should be thanked. Quite the opposite. He felt immensely guilty for letting her climb down the bridge. Deep down he knew it would've been easier and safer for him to do it. Fear held him back. A fear which almost led to Helen's demise. He wouldn't let it happen again.

Helen's room was nicer than Elliot's. Only slightly bigger, but it had a beautiful view of the lake, a sofa, kitchenette and HD wide screen TV. The TV was on. A picture of the Nazi swastika on the screen caught his attention. A documentary on the Holocaust. A Jewish historian was arguing that the New Testament led to the continued persecution of the Jews over the years, including an attempt at their total annihilation. By blaming the Jews for the death of Jesus. Elliot wasn't convinced it was the only reason that Jews had been persecuted, but he couldn't deny it may've had some impact. To what extent, he had no idea. After all, it was the Church in Roman times and during the Medieval Period that crushed other beliefs. Destroying all other schools of philosophy. Universities, their books and millennia of ideas, burnt to the ashes. Not to mention the countless non-Christians put to death for not believing. Historically, there had been a lethal dose of anti-Semitism. Elliot was less worried about that now. Due to input from Christian philosophers, the Church had evolved to become kind, more tolerant and accepting of others. Thanks to Saint Thomas Acquinas, people were considered to be capable of both good and evil, rather than some people being good and others being bad. A concept that most people today adopt without realising its origin.

Helen walked over to Elliot.

'I'm starving' she said, rustling through his shopping bag. 'What the...'

'Twinkies. I've seen them on American films and it's been on my bucket list to try one.'

'You know, I don't think they're very good for you.'

He shrugged his shoulders. Helen pulled out a sandwich from the plastic bag, sat back down, put the ice on her head and nibbled at the crust. Elliot found the documentary depressing and so turned over to the news. CNN reporting a scientific breakthrough by haematologists. Scientists have discovered a pattern within human blood that shows certain blood types are more susceptible to viruses and disabilities. With this information, it could help eradicate disease and disability. It was positive news, but Elliot's brain didn't have the capacity to deal with much and so he turned the TV off. Helen picked up her satchel from the side of her bed, pulled out the cloth covered object from the bridge and put it on her lap.

'What is it' he said, looking down at the old brown cylinder shaped object.

Elliot picked it up and took a closer look. It was a cup... a very old one. It had a long phallic piece of clay inside, rising from its base. At the bottom of the phallic piece were a few holes. Ancient Greek writing was inscribed along the side.

'I don't think this would make a good cup, it has holes in it' said Elliot. 'What's it for?'

'I don't know, but I know someone who will.'

Helen phoned her colleague, Virginia Smithson at the British Museum. It was 9am in London and so Virginia was already at work, slugging away. She got the details for the esteemed professor of Ancient Greek history, Christopher Seacrest. He was based in Washington DC, which was kind of en-route home, but definitely worth the stop. He'd know what to make of the cup.

39

London – Present Day + 5 (Tuesday)

Back at the station, Henry sat in his office waiting for the DNA results of the blood sample taken from the stone tile in St Pauls. He'd managed to finish a medium difficulty Sudoku puzzle. He was now stuck on the hard one and had been for a while. He brushed his pencil across his short grey moustache as he tried fruitlessly to solve it. He needed another clue before he could move forward. Wasting time, but it was a good distraction from the fact that he was getting nowhere on the St Paul's investigation. It caused him pain to know that his sponsor was dead. The person who got him off alcohol. He felt shaky. It would be so easy to touch the bottle. A temptation that he was struggling with in his emotional state.

A police officer knocked on the door, walked into Henry's office and placed some pictures on his desk. Henry looked up to see the slaughtered body of an old man. His frail body lay on the floor, surrounded by a pool of blood as if someone had just poured two litres of red emulsion on the ground and left it to dry. His neck was cut wide open. Judging by the cleanness of the cut, it was more likely to be a calm and calculated attack than a crime of passion. Most knifings in the heat of the moment, like provocation, were messy. But not this one. Someone was trained and knew exactly what they were doing.

'What's this' asked Henry.

'A new murder enquiry. Namely, one Jonathan Hooke, murdered in his own home. There are no witnesses to the murder. That've come forward at least.'

Henry put down his pencil then leaned forward and rested his arms on his desk. 'Any leads?'

'Sort of' said the officer. 'We checked his phone records. He'd made several calls to the British Museum.'

'Really?'

The officer nodded. The officer was aware of Henry's case involving the employees at the British Museum.

'Also, I checked with the neighbours. Apparently, Mr Hooke generally kept to himself and didn't have many visitors. One neighbour, who insists she was not being nosey, said she saw a woman and young man hanging outside the property.'

'Did you get their description?'

'I did. They match your suspects, Helen Philips and Elliot Hope. The chief thinks these might be related to your St Paul's murder and wants you to take it forward. Only one thing doesn't match. The estimated time of death was several hours before Helen and Elliot's visit.

Henry needed to speak with Helen and Elliot, now. Whilst he didn't believe they fit the profile of murderers, they knew something. Their body language ran wild when they were questioned and whatever they're hiding must be linked to these murders.

'Find Jonathan Hooke's surviving family and tell them the news. And God, whatever you do, don't reveal any of the gritty details or let his family into the house until all evidence and the body have been cleared. I don't want it to be any more traumatic for the family than it needs to be.'

'Will do, sir.'

'Where is James?'

'PC Catchwell…not seen him for a couple of days' said the officer shrugging his shoulders.

'Call his house and find out where he is. I need him here now. And get me Helen Philips and Elliot Hope!'

40

London – Present Day + 5 (Tuesday)

David stood by a bar in the Blind Beggar, a refurbished pub in the dodgy East End of London. Famous for a shooting by the notorious gangsters, the Kray twins. Marco was obsessed with the Krays. David encouraged his interest in history, but Marco only liked the brutal gang related elements. The public house was smaller than it looked from the outside and covered in pictures of the Krays. David ordered another water for himself and a beer for the others. Abrafo went to the washroom, while Marco showed Rav where Ronnie Kray shot and killed his rival gang member, George Cornell. David wasn't interested in the Krays. He was focusing on how to get the map for his employer and hoping that Helen and Elliot would soon slip up. The lack of progress for such a seemingly simple task was making him nervous. He prayed it wouldn't impact on his health or future business. Reputation. Takes a lifetime to build and less than a day to destroy. David saw Marco and Rav coming back to the bar to get their drinks.

'Ronnie Kray even bought his mum a pub' said Marco, picking up his cold beer, taking a refreshing gulp then clearing his throat. 'The Krays were actually pretty nice guys.'

'I know wot ya mean' replied Rav.

Rav pulled out a pack of cigarettes, sparked one up and blew smoke over the bar. Smoking indoors had been banned for a while now and the timid bar tender, who was clearly not the manager, decided that passive smoking was better for his health than to say anything. A stocky builder stood at the bar next to them, having a pint of lager. He coughed a couple of times, hinting that the smoke was getting in his face, but Rav paid no attention. The builder tapped Rav on the shoulder.

'Excuse me' he said. 'Jew mind not smoking in my face...I'm trying to ave a drink.'

Rav turned around and stared at the man, looking up then down. He was a good foot taller than Rav, had a broader chest and bigger arms.

'Sure' Rav said, then took a large puff on his cigarette, blew it in the builder's face and flicked his fag in the man's beer. 'Now fuck off, before someone gets stabbed.'

The builder may've been bigger than him, but Rav's psychotic temper was enough of a deterrent. Rav did not abide by the normal rules of social convention. Any fight would not be played fairly. The builder just picked up his car keys from the bar and left the pub.

David's mobile vibrated. It was the Organisation. He stepped outside to take the call. Teo Brecher was on the case and had been in contact with Helen, but so far, didn't have the map. However, the Organisation had now managed to trace a call at the British Museum to Helen in Arizona. David learnt that Helen had requested details for Christopher Seacrest, a professor of history, specialising in Ancient Greece. *Crap,* he thought. David wondered if they knew what they were onto. If they didn't, they were certainly close. He couldn't deny that Helen and Elliot were saving their employer the trouble of deciphering the map. However, if they knew what they were looking for, they'd almost certainly alert the authorities which would ruin his plan. They had to be stopped, now. The Organisation booked a flight for David and Marco, and would organise some muscle to meet them there.

Abrafo came out of the washroom. He was stocky, had Mediterranean skin and a round bald head that seemed to have no neck. He was the same height as Rav, but much wider. Rav's leg was sticking out and Abrafo accidentally trod on his new white trainers.

'Sorry' said Abrafo.

'Ah' said Rav, swearing. 'Watch me Nike Air's. They aint cheap.'

'Bite me, you skinny piece of crap -.'

David interjected. 'Both of you pack it bloody in. I need you focused. Helen's got something very important to our employer and we have to get it. No matter what. He's already on the case, but wants extra help. Marco and me will go to Washington and pay a visit to the National Geographic Museum. Unless we're one hundred percent sure we've got everything, they're not to be killed. Otherwise, once we have what we need I'll leave it to you on how to treat them. But Marco.'

'What' he said, in a curt tone.

'Don't do anything that could get you caught. Abrafo and Rav will stay here in case Helen and Elliot come back to London. No doubt the police will do everything they can to contact Helen, and we have to beat them to it.'

41

National Geographic Museum, Washington – Present Day + 5 (Tuesday)

Elliot and Helen arrived at one thousand and forty-five, Seventeenth Street, Washington DC. The National Geographic Museum was much more modern than the British Museum. It was a smart, state of the art and practically shaped, rectangular building. The weather was cooler than in Arizona, but the sun was still shining. They walked into the large reception and made their way to a slim receptionist in a red suit jacket and matching skirt. She was on the phone, whilst staring up at the high-rise ceiling. She looked down to see Elliot, smiled, then finished her call.

'Hello, how can I help' she said, staring at Elliot.

Helen leaned in to the reception counter. 'I'm here to see Christopher Seacrest. I have an appointment.'

'Who can I say is here' she said, picking up the phone again.

'Helen Philips…'

'And Elliot Hope' he said, smiling back and offering a handshake.

'I love your accent' said the receptionist, continuing to stare at Elliot as she ran her hand through her golden hair.

Elliot was happy for the attention, but a little embarrassed as he was sure Helen had picked up on it. The body language was obvious. The receptionist, whose face was turning red, picked up the phone and punched a few numbers in.

'Hello, Helen Philips here for Christopher. Thanks' she said, then hung up the phone.

'Mr Seacrest will be with you in 10 minutes.'

They waited in the lobby and sat on a cheap but comfortable sofa next to an obscurely shaped glass sculpture. The bright colours from the display opposite him caught his attention. It was an exhibition called "The lost Ancient Greek temple of Artemis – myth or just forgotten." The display had Christopher Seacrest as the head curator for the project. On the right-hand side of the display was a picture of a large statue of Zeus. Behind that was a Greek temple taking up the majority of the display. It pricked Elliot's interest and after they had finished here, he'd see if Helen wanted to go and visit the exhibition.

Elliot wished his brother was with him. Toby loved museums, especially the natural history museum. Toby wanted to be a dinosaur when he grew up. Elliot tried to be supportive and said if he studied hard, he could do anything. Maybe not a dinosaur, but he'd let Toby make his own discoveries on that when he was old enough.

A slim man walked up to them. Elliot thought he looked in his late forties, or late fifties. Clean shaven, wide blue eyes and grey hair.

'Miss Philips…nice to meet you. I'm Chris Seacrest' he said, holding out his hand.

'Nice to meet you too' she said, giving a firm hand-shake. 'This is my associate, Elliot Hope.'

'Elliot' he said. He nodded, then shook Elliot's hand with one hand and held the other on top. A very warm welcome.

'Thank you for seeing us on such short notice' said Helen.

'Pleasure. Ancient Greece is my passion. When you said you might have a new discovery, I was very interested to see what you were talking about. Please come. I'll take you to our strong room.'

Elliot followed the steps of Chris' loafers down the corridor, until they reached two lifts and a set of stairs.

Chris pointed to the lift. 'Fifth floor. I'll meet you there.'

'You not joining us' said Helen.

'Lifts and tight spaces don't agree with me' said Chris, shuddering as he looked at the lift. 'I'll take the stairs.'

The strong room was similar to the one in the British Museum, except this one had no windows and the vault was set behind a further door, rather than being a locked cabinet. There were machines in the room, which looked like they belonged in a hospital.

'Please' he said, gesturing for them to take a seat.

Helen and Elliot sat down together, as if they were about to interview Chris for a new job. Helen lifted her bag onto the table, pulled out the ancient cup and placed it on the table.

'We found this and were wondering what you could tell us about it' she said.

Chris picked it up and carefully examined it. 'Goodness.'

'What is it' asked Helen.

'This is a Pythagorean cup. Used in Ancient Greece to stop soldiers from consuming all their rations during warfare. It was designed to prevent greed, although I'm not sure how effective it was. You'd fill up the cup. If you tried to fill it to the top, the mechanism in the middle would make the liquid, usually wine, leak out.'

'Is it valuable' said Elliot.

'If it's authentic, yes. My guess is that it could fetch half a million at Sotheby's.'

Elliot's eyes lit up. Half a million or even half of that would turn everything around. He'd go back to uni, look after Toby and get a house. Maybe even a hot tub.

'But, I'm not sure whether this is genuine. I can ask our guys to do a couple of tests if you like. It shouldn't take more than a day.'

Elliot frowned. 'It must be real. No one would go to all this trouble over a fake cup.'

'What trouble?'

'Helen interjected. 'Thank you. That'd be great! There's an inscription on the side. I think it's Ancient Greek. Are you able to translate it?'

Chris nodded. He read the inscription engraved on the cup, squinting as he read the faded writing. He got a pen and paper and wrote it down in English, crossed bits out, then re-worded it and handed the translation to Helen, who read it out aloud.

"The only thing that cannot be doubted. Reason allows our lady to resonate life from the tree of philosophy of God's palm."

Helen looked at her assistant. 'Elliot?'

Elliot thought for a moment, then scratched his head. 'Not sure. The only thing that cannot be doubted is cogito ergo sum.'

'I think therefore I am' said Chris.

'Exactly' said Elliot. 'The philosopher, Descartes, questioned how he could know for certain that the world he saw around him existed. Our eyes can be deceptive, as can our senses. For example, to you this chair may appear yellow, but at night or to someone else, it may be seen as brown. It reminds me of the film, the Matrix. People's minds are trapped inside a giant artificially intelligent computer. The human population are kept under the illusion that the virtual world they're plugged into is real. How do we know that this table and the world around us aren't just programmed into our minds or that we are a figment of someone else's imagination created for the enjoyment of others?'

'We don't, but I'm pretty sure we're all here now' said Helen.

'I agree on both counts. Descartes cut back everything he wasn't sure of and started with the one thing he knew for sure.'

'Which is' she asked.

'I think, therefore my mind is real. Or as Descartes put it, I think therefore I am.'

Chris shook his head. 'That doesn't work. If authentic, this cup would precede the date Descartes was around. It must be a fake.'

Elliot hoped that they hadn't been chasing after a fake piece of history. It's value would be much less, if not worthless. *If it was fake, why would someone go to such lengths to hide it?*

'You think it's a replica and not from the Ancient Greek period' asked Elliot.

'We'll soon find out for sure' replied Chris, picking up the cup. 'I'll take this to our researchers...they'll carry out some non-intrusive tests.'

Chris left Helen and Elliot in the strong room. They'd been travelling and filled with so much adrenaline over the last few hectic days, Elliot needed to rest. He looked forward to going back to his hotel room and lying in bed. He decided to be productive while Chris was in the lab, and researched the second paragraph of the translated message on Google. He read over it again.

"Reason allows our lady to resonate life from the tree of philosophy of God's palm."

He googled a combination of "our lady", "Descartes", the "tree of philosophy" and "God's palm." It brought back numerous results, including links on the bells of Notre Dame, Lady Liberty, philosophy and biblical sites. He scanned the search results, trying to find the most likely connections. Descartes was a French philosopher who had a big love of God and frequently visited the Notre Dame. There was a bell called Our Lady. That seemed to be the most likely probability. However, the philosophy tree was Descartes explanation of philosophy with its various branches. In Loire, France, there's a hollowed out tree with the Notre Dame chapel inside. The bells in Notre Dame Cathedral was Elliot's first bet. The hollowed out tree sounded too obscure and had no known connection with Descartes. In any case, whatever they were looking for seemed to be in France.

42

Washington – Present Day + 5 (Tuesday)

Chris returned to the room with the Pythagorean Cup, after carrying out his investigations. Elliot immediately noticed that there was something wrong with his face and body language. It wasn't half as friendly as before and colour had gone from his cheeks. Chris locked the door behind him, then walked up to the table where they were sitting and stood, towering over them.

'What the hell have you got me into?'

Helen looked at him blankly. 'What do you mean?'

'Don't play dumb. I just received a call from the police in London. You're both wanted in connection with the murder of two people. What on Earth is going on?'

If they wanted Chris' support, they'd have to come clean. Elliot looked at Helen for approval and she nodded. Elliot pulled out a copy of the inscription from the architect plans of St Paul's Cathedral and the messages from the box they found. He showed them to Chris and explained everything they knew and everything that had happened. Their work on the exhibition, the attempted robbery in the British Museum, the philosophical puzzles and clues and that they were being followed. Elliot knew about the murder inside St Paul's, but had no idea that there was a second victim.

Chris stood there in silence as he absorbed the information. He took in a deep breath. 'Ok.'

Elliot was expecting a little more than OK, but it was a lot to take in. 'Ok?'

'No, it's bloody not ok! I'm supposed to assist in your immediate deportation back to England.'

'Chris' said Helen, giving him a semi-puppy dog look. 'We've done nothing wrong. Please help us and we'll happily go back home where we can prove our innocence. I promise.'

After much persuasion, Chris reluctantly agreed to help them on the cup, but solely on the condition that they went back home afterwards. Chris read the translated messages, spending more time on the first one than the second. He held it close to his face. Either he had bad eye sight or was hoping that bringing it closer would trigger something in his mind.

Chris leaned forward into the table. 'Alexander the Great was a student of Aristotle who himself was taught by Plato. As I'm sure you know, Plato was a student of Socrates, the founding father of philosophy. Between the four of them, they created a wealth of knowledge that has developed the way the western world thinks, breaths and sleeps. Aristotle himself was the founder of psychology, physics and biology.'

'Yes' said Helen. 'But what does that have to do with the Rosy Cross or Sir Wren's treasure?'

'I don't think it's talking about Christopher Wren's treasure.'

'You don't' said Elliot.

'No' said Chris. 'I could be wrong, but I think this is talking about the undiscovered treasure of Alexander the Great. This is speculation based on the unfounded gibberings of a few scholars. Until now, there were no reliable sources backing this up.'

'Really' said Helen. 'Well, the people following us believe in it. How big are we talking about?'

'Yes, enough to kill for it' said Elliot.

Chris explained how Alexander the Great conquered ninety percent of the known world by the age of twenty-five, without losing a single battle. Legend suggests that his reign was due to his strong counsel and a powerful weapon known as the Philosopher's Stone. Created by his teacher and alchemist, Aristotle, it's said to be a tool that can be used to create, destroy and change any elements within the periodic table. Alexander the Great used it to conquer his enemies, seizing the entire wealth of the known world. Gold, silver, diamonds, jewels, trinkets, jade, medallions and anything else of intrinsic value. They seized valuables of his bloody campaign across country after country. Enough treasure to fill a football pitch. All of it, safely stored in a place that could not be found without knowing its exact hiding place. Only Alexander the Great was believed to know its location. His slaves that hid the treasure were said to be buried alive to stop anyone from finding it. There was one disagreeing scholar who believed Alexander's heralds left a map to the treasure. A complicated map that could only be deciphered by understanding the most testing of philosophical puzzles. One where only a worthy ruler could interpret it.

'You know Plato believed that only philosophers should be kings' said Elliot. 'If Alexander the Great was influenced by the great three, it would explain why he left philosophical clues. It would ensure that only a philosopher could find the treasure. If it's as big as you suggest, the person who discovers it would have enough money to rule.'

Helen cut in. 'I'm surprised I haven't heard of this treasure before.'

Chris looked up and right as he searched the recesses of his memory. 'The Rosicrucian Order and the Pythagorean Brotherhood believed that some truths were too important for public knowledge. Esoteric truths that needed to be kept secret. These secrets were passed on by word of mouth and most of them never saw the light of day. It was dangerous to ever put it in writing. The sources I have are unreliable and the information you've shown me is the first proof confirming that the treasure is real. Either that, or it is a very convincing imitation.'

'Thank you for that' said Helen. 'I'll call the police shortly and let them know that we'll be on our way home.'

'Once you've cleared things with the police, I'd very much like to assist you. If that's ok' said Chris.

'Delightful' said Helen nodding. 'But what about your exhibition?'

Chris pulled his head back, as if to say "are you joking." 'Helen, I've spent over a decade trying to find the lost Temple of Artemis, with no solid evidence and just speculation. But you... you have found a real link to one of the world's greatest pieces of history. I'm not convinced the Philosopher's Stone is real, but the treasure must be. If I can help, I'd be honoured. Besides, my team can cover me.'

Elliot was beyond excited. Once they returned to England and sorted out the misunderstanding with the police, they could carry on with the hunt. Their starting point, France. Elliot could become an archaeologist, a historian, a normal person with a stable job. More than a stable job. He could be a king. No, maybe not a king, but he could look after his brother and be depended on. No more orders, no more scraping by and no more trouble. They decided to go for lunch to celebrate, before heading back to London.

43

Washington – Present Day + 5 (Tuesday)

Helen and Elliot walked with Chris down Sixteenth Street, towards Capitol Hill. They passed a large jungle of museums, offices and residential blocks. The White House, with its distinctive dome, could be seen in the distant background. Slightly hidden by an array of leafy trees. The high rise buildings protected them from all, but a gentle breeze. Elliot could feel his stomach rumbling. He hadn't eaten since breakfast and was starting to feel weak and irritable. There were no restaurants in sight.

'I'm starving' he said.

'There are nice places to eat on Seventeenth Street' said Chris. He stopped, turned around and pointed to Swan Street just behind them. 'There's a good restaurant just around the corner from here.'

Elliot looked where Chris was pointing to see three men walking towards them. Their eyes were fixed on Helen and on noticing Elliot staring back, they stopped walking and just stood still. He recognised one of them from somewhere, but couldn't think where. Then it hit him. *The tattooed man from the British Museum.*

'Helen, we need to get out of here... now!'

'What's wrong?'

'We're being followed...your six o'clock.'

She turned to see Marco. He had a taller man with him, David, and another who was out of shape, but looked rough. Marco put his hand inside his jacket to pull out something. Before she had a chance to see what it was, she turned and ran as fast as she could. Chris and Elliot sprinted behind her... the adrenaline rushed through their bodies and before they knew it, they were darting off like hunted antelopes in the Serengeti.

They ran down Sixteenth Street. Helen saw a path between two buildings on her right, which led to Seventeenth Street. She dashed into the alley. Elliot and Chris followed. Elliot looked back to see Marco and David getting closer. The podgy guy was lagging behind. Elliot jumped into the alley so that they were out of sight and carried on running. They reached the other side of the alley. Helen stopped and turned to Elliot.

'We've got a better chance if we split up. Meet me back at the hotel in an hour' she said, then sprinted off.

'Be careful' said Elliot, running in the other direction.

Elliot ran off by himself, heading north up Seventeenth. Helen and Chris headed south towards a parade of shops. David and Marco split up. Marco kept on Elliot's trail while David followed Helen and Chris.

44

Washington – Present Day + 5 (Tuesday)

Helen and Chris weaved their way, as fast as they could, through the parade of shops which were swarming with tourists and workers on their lunch break. They tried to avoid bumping into people without great success. Helen almost knocked over a man working at a coffee street-stand. One guy shouted at her as she bumped into him. David could see Helen between the tourists and was able to catch them up if he was quick.

'This way' said Chris, pointing towards a book store.

'No, there'll be no way out. We'll get caught.'

'Helen, just trust me' he said, grabbing her hand and pulling her towards the store.

They ran over to the book store, swung open the door and darted inside. There was no one around, other than the shop keeper, who was paying attention to his mobile and listening to his I-pod. He didn't notice them come in. Chris and Helen made their way to the back of the shop.

Outside, David ran as fast as he could to the shop. He looked around, but couldn't see them. David turned to an old man on the floor that was being helped up by a pregnant lady. He was saying something disgruntled and pointing to the book store. David turned his gaze to the shop to see its door was closing.

'Bingo' said David.

At the back of the shop, Chris stood between two book shelves which stood parallel. One against the rear wall and one freestanding. He appeared to be looking for something.

'What are you doing? We're stuck. Oh my God… we're done for' said Helen.

Chris scanned the bookshelf against the wall, raising his finger from left to right where the books were organised alphabetically. The shelf and its books were old, tatty, and would be better suited to a gothic home than a small bookshop.

'During the 1920's alcohol prohibition, several hidden bars were set up and kept secret from the authorities' said Chris. 'This was one of them.'

Chris' hand stopped when it reached an old book titled "Sobriety." He pulled it back, and the bookshelf made a clicking sound. Chris pulled the shelf to the left and it began to slide revealing a passageway. They crept inside and closed the shelf quietly.

David burst through the shop door and ran around the shop with his gun out. The shop keeper didn't notice and carried on playing with his mobile whilst listening to his music. He searched between each bookshelf working his way from the front to the back. His pray were nowhere to be seen. David stood by the old bookshelf at the rear of the store and called Marco. Helen and Chris stood in the hidden passage behind the old book shelf. Chris scratched his face, which made a quiet sound. Helen touched his hand to get his attention, then held her finger over her mouth, gesturing for him to stay silent. They could hear David talking on the phone on the other side of the book shelf. Helen leant her ear closer so she could hear him.

'Marco…what's happening?' He paused. 'Good. Whatever you do, don't kill him unless we've got everything we need. I'm coming to get you. Stay where you are.'

45

Washington – Present Day + 5 (Tuesday)

'Don't move or I'll kill you' said Marco, holding Elliot down with the right cheek of his face against the path. 'Actually, do move and then I can gut you like a fish.'

He pressed his knife against Elliot's neck, under his chin. A dab of blood seeped out on the blade. Elliot froze with fear, lying bruised on the ground. He was tempted to retaliate, but with the knife so close to his neck, it wasn't worth the risk. He felt the grit of the floor against his cheek as he was pushed into the ground. It hurt. In the distance he could see Marco's companions pacing towards them. Elliot was relieved. This could only mean that Helen and Chris had escaped.

'What are you doing' said David, as he approached them.

'Staying ere, like you said' replied Marco, looking up from the floor.

'I said no more crap. I'm fed up of clearing up your crap. Get off him.'

David grabbed Marco by the back of his shirt and yanked him away. Marco jerked backwards, off of Elliot and fell over.

'Piss off, David' said Marco, standing up.

David punched Marco in the face. 'No, you bloody piss off. Now he knows my name.'

Marco's face twisted to the side as he reacted to the punch, although he managed to keep his footing. He rubbed his face and bald head, and staggered a few feet. David bent down and lifted Elliot off the ground. His face was bruised and hair, ruffled, but there was no permanent damage. The podgy one stayed out of the way, not wanting to get involved. Elliot's eyes glazed over. He was red in the face.

'I'm sorry for my brother. If you do as we say, you'll not be harmed' said David.

Elliot brushed himself off and stood up straight. After two people had been murdered, he knew they couldn't be trusted to keep their word. He needed to be focused if he was going to survive this. His body was pumped with so much adrenaline that he could hardly think.

'Wha, what do you want' said Elliot, looking across the path to an open area, considering whether he could make a run for it.

David pulled out a gun from inside his pocket. 'Don't even think about it. You know what we want.'

'The cup?'

'The cup and everything else you've found. They don't belong to you. They belong to my boss.'

'I don't have them with me.'

'If you want to live, you'll get them.'

46

Washington – Present Day + 5 (Tuesday)

Helen and Chris got back to the hotel room, but there was no sign of Elliot. The bed had been made, presumably by the cleaners. None of his stuff had been moved since this morning and so it was unlikely that he'd been back. Having just overheard David talk about killing him, she feared the worst. They had him. The person she was responsible for. Helen couldn't believe how much pain she had unintentionally inflicted on him. A gut wrenching guilt cut through her insides like a carving knife.

If these were the same men who were responsible for the two murders, then they were all in big trouble. Someone knew about Alexander the Great's hidden wealth and Helen and Elliot were not the only ones seeking it.

Helen checked the time. It had been over an hour since they'd split up from each other. All she could think of was Elliot's safety. She picked up the bedroom phone and dialled reception to see if they had seen him come back. The receptionist didn't know. Chris sat on a chair next to a small bedside table and Helen sat on the bed, holding her hands over her face.

'What do we do' said Helen.

'Call the police. We have to.'

'If we do, they might hurt him.'

'Do we have much choice? We don't even know if he is alive.'

Chris was right. Helen couldn't do this alone and needed to be transparent with the police. It had got too far. She went to get the phone. It suddenly rang, making her jump. Helen and Chris looked at each other and a massive surge of hope ran through her body. *Elliot.* She jumped over the bed and picked up the phone.

'Elliot, thank God you're safe' said Helen.

A deep male voice spoke. 'No, he's not safe and neither are you, unless you do exactly what I say.'

'Is Elliot hurt? What have you done with him?'

'He's fine…for now.'

'I'll do whatever you want…just don't harm him!'

'We want the Pythagorean Cup, the message from the drawings and the box.'

'OK, how do I contact you?'

'Meet us by Lafayette Square in one hour. You and your granddad must come alone. When you're here, call this number.'

'We'll be there.'

'No fishy business. If you're late, I'll kill him. If you call the police, I'll kill him. If you try anything funny, I'll kill him.'

The man hung up. His last words sent a chill through Helen's spine. She could tell from his unwavering tone that he was serious. Deadly serious. Helen told Chris exactly what happened and they both deliberated in fear for their missing friend and colleague.

'I'll go, you stay here' said Helen.

'No, we have to call the police' said Chris, picking up the phone.

'No way' she said, cursing and snatching the phone from his hand. 'If we involve the police, they'll kill him.'

'How could they know if we did' asked Chris.

'Only my boss knows we're here. If those men can track us here, is it worth the risk?'

Chris shook his head. 'Ok, but I can't let you do it alone. Did you even speak with Elliot?'

'No' she replied.

'Then we still don't know if he is alive.'

The thought made Helen want to be sick. She had to believe he was still alive. She couldn't cope with the idea of Elliot being killed.

'No, he is alive. They need leverage and we've got ours.'

Helen knew David had no intention of keeping his word. Once he had the cup, there would be nothing to stop him from killing Elliot, Chris and Helen. They needed a plan. Something to guarantee the exchange of the cup and map, but in a way that would keep them all safe. They couldn't involve the police. Helen had no idea what she could do, but she had to think fast.

47

Washington – Present Day + 6 (Wednesday)

It was half three in the afternoon. Thirty minutes before they were due to swap the map and cup for Elliot. The sun's heat was beating down on Helen and Chris, which only added to their discomfort and stress. The streets were busy with tourists, locals and office workers. Helen took some comfort that the exchange would be in broad daylight, but it would not stop them from being tracked down afterwards. A small cloud covered the sun allowing Helen to see window cleaners on a high-rise, fifteen floor building that faced the White House. After her abseiling accident, the idea of climbing at any height made her shudder.

Helen and Chris had collected the Cup and map from the National Geographic Museum, then put them in a brown satchel which Helen held onto tightly.

'I don't feel safe' she said.

'No. Me neither' said Chris. 'Unfortunately, this is the best we can do. We've got a better chance of success if we keep public.'

Helen continued to watch the window cleaners on the building, moving up and down on a platform attached to ropes on a pulley system. As the platform went down, the rope dangling to the side went up. It gave her an idea. She spoke with the window cleaners, then called David and said to meet at the top of the building. In the meantime, Helen and Chris kept out of site and away from the rooftop of the office block. Twenty minutes went by. Nothing. Suddenly, Helen's phone rang.

'Are you there' she asked.

'We're here, but you're not. I said no funny business. Your friend is gonna die.'

'No, wait! We're here too. Go to the edge of the roof facing the White House. Look down. You'll see a platform with rope. You put Elliot on the platform and lower him down. At the same time, I'll tie my satchel with the map and cup to the bottom of the rope. As Elliot comes down, the cup will go up. Everyone wins.'

'I said we had to meet in person.'

'Think of this as a safety precaution. You said no one will be harmed and so this shouldn't be an issue.'

There was a pause for ten seconds. Helen prayed they'd agree to her proposal. She didn't want to risk Elliot's life, but it was the most logical conclusion to ensure the safety of all of them.

'Ok' said David. 'Put the map and cup on the rope.'

Helen went to attach the bag to the rope. She tried to look up, but the sun was blinding. She tied a part of the rope to the satchel.

'Wait! I want to see the contents first.'

Helen held her mobile between her head and neck, then opened up the satchel. She pulled out the cup and the drawings as proof, waved them above her head, then put them back in the bag.

'Fine' said David, hanging up the phone.

Helen's nervous system was going crazy. She had no idea whether they would actually let Elliot go or try something underhand. It wouldn't surprise her if they did. Her neck was aching from looking up, but the overwhelming fear dampened the pain. She could see something happening on the roof top. A few seconds later, Elliot appeared, dangling over the edge.

48

Washington – Present Day + 6 (Wednesday)

Elliot carefully, but quickly, held onto the edge of the roof top, climbed over and onto the window cleaning platform. He didn't dare to look back down. His first foot pressed against its wooden base. His weight caused the platform to bend slightly and make a heart jumping creaking sound. There were metal support beams underneath it, but it didn't stop him from being terrified. He put his second foot over the edge and onto the platform. *Nearly there.* He tried to focus on his breathing to keep him calm. It helped, but only just. Elliot moved one hand at a time onto the support rail. The base was still wet with soapy residue from the window cleaners. It was slippery. His hands gripped even tighter to the sides. His knuckles were beginning to turn white.

Using the pulley system, Elliot slowly made his way down the side of the building. As he went down, the satchel made its way up. He couldn't look up because of the blinding sun, but staring down only escalated his fear of heights. He decided to face the wall of the office, which was mostly made of concrete and tall mirrored glass showing a reflection of the large open area around him.

A third of the way down, he was beginning to feel a bit relieved. David and Marco were not in touching distance. Elliot looked across to the cloudless sky, then mustered the courage to peer down at the big drop below. He felt dizzy and so quickly turned back to face the building and closed his eyes tightly.

At two thirds of the way down, he was now five stories high. The bag was nearly with David and Marco. Elliot was close, but the distance below was still too far down for him to feel safe. The platform began shaking. He looked up to see David pulling up the rope carrying the satchel and the podgy henchman moving his arm back and forward on one of the ropes that supported the platform. *Cutting the rope?*

'Holy crap!'

Elliot searched around, but apart from a few decorative crevasses on the building's edge, there was nothing for him to hold onto. Not safely, and not unless he could jump two stories down and five meters across to an open window. Even in long jump at school, he'd be lucky if he could clear three meters. There was no way he could make it now. Plus, with the two story fall to the window, the chances are he'd break his leg…or worse, his neck.

The platform jolted as a rope holding a corner of the structure became slack. The platform swung, hitting the concrete wall with a thud. It felt as though the floor was about to give way. A second later, a supporting rope fell down, slapping against a lamppost before hitting the floor in a swirling motion. The rope coiled like a snake as it landed on the ground. Elliot lost his footing on the slippery floor and fell back onto the window cleaner's platform. One hand lost its grip from the metal bar, nearly causing him to fall over the edge. He just managed to hold on for his dear life with the other hand. He carried on with the pulley system as fast as he could.

The platform continued shaking as the next rope was being cut. Elliot had to move quickly, but there wasn't much he could do. He was freaking out. *Climb down the fallen rope?* He looked down to see it had reached the floor. After the recent event at London Bridge, he had gained a little confidence in his climbing ability, but he was still afraid. He had two choices. Die, or climb. He quickly climbed over the rail, holding on so tightly it restricted his movement. His legs dangled over the edge. One passerby saw what was going on and screamed. It was shortly followed by a crowd on the ground all looking up in horror.

Helen and Chris looked up in despair to see him dangling from the platform. Elliot went to move one hand from the guard rail to the fallen rope. Before his hand reached it, another rope went limp, causing the left side of the platform to swing with great force. It sent Elliot whooshing forward, pulling his grip from the rail. As gravity started to drag him down, he grabbed onto the rope below, sending him swinging like a monkey in a jungle. The rope was coarse and burnt his hand. He hung there, helpless. Like a mouse being dropped by its tail into a snake's cage. Moving left to right, keen to do anything but fall to the ground.

'No' Helen shouted.

Another woman screamed from the ground, alerting more people, who then looked up in disbelief. David and Marco kept their faces away from the site of people on the ground, but the overweight henchman was still leaning over, continuing to cut the remaining rope. Elliot could feel the vibration.

Elliot cursed in his mind. Too far to jump down, too little time to climb. The lactic acid was building up in his arms. Aching to the point that he was unable to hold on for much longer. His left arm shook. He glanced over to the window on his right. He was still five meters away, but much lower than before. With all his energy, he swung back and forth. It only moved slightly, but with each new thrust forward the momentum grew. The window was closer, but still two metres away at nearly full swing.

Chris could see from the ground what Elliot was trying to do. He ran into the building, looked at the escalator, which showed it was on the fourteenth floor. He couldn't wait and so ran up the steps, making his way to an office on the south side of the building. He burst through the office doors, scouted for an open window, and ran through the reception area.

A receptionist stood up as he ran into the room. 'Sir, do you have an appoint...'

Chris darted through the reception before the receptionist could finish her sentence. The open window was between two desks, where workers were on the phone, keeping themselves to themselves. He heard a loud female scream. It was Helen from outside. His heart sank. He looked out the window... Elliot was still clinging on. Just. He was down to one rope left. Chris hung out of the window, held onto the side of the wall with one arm and spread his other arm out the window.

'Swing to me' shouted Chris. 'I'll grab you.'

'I can't.'

'You can. You can do this. You have to do this.'

Elliot tried swinging again, back and forth, back and forth, then felt the vibrations travel through the last rope. Elliot freaked. He knew the inevitable was upon him. Panic spread through his body like an electric shock. He wanted to let go, just so that he had some semblance of control over the lasting moments of his life. He knew it was not rational.

Helen looked up to see the henchman leaning over the edge, ferociously moving his knife back and forward as he cut the rope. 'Come on!'

Suddenly, a large figure came tumbling down. The henchman appeared to have lost his footing and fell over the edge. He fell from such a height that it took a good three seconds for him to come crashing down onto the pavement, just missing Elliot. There was no way he could've survived.

Elliot was still swinging from the platform. The rope had already been cut into, and he could feel it unwinding at the top. It was only moments before the platform would crash to the ground. He swung as hard as he could and with his last swing, held out his hand, touched Chris' finger tips, then swung back again.

'One more time...you, you can do this' said Chris.

Elliot swung back, moved his legs into position like an acrobat and swung forward as hard as he could. He wasn't sure where the energy came from, but he pelted forward with a burst of force which carried him further than before. He approached Chris, re-adjusted the grip of his left hand, held out his right and grabbed onto him. Elliot let go of the platform rail, but Chris' grip was not tight enough and he could feel himself slipping. He tried to use his other hand to grab onto the window ledge, but it was no use. He fell down with his arms sticking out.

After a couple of meters of falling, he hit the top of a tall lamppost with a thud, hooking one arm over to stop him from falling further. He groaned in agony as he cracked his side. He grabbed on with his other hand. He was breathing heavily and was not far from having a panic attack. It was either that or a heart attack. Like a koala, he hugged onto the lamppost and slid down, burning the inside of his legs until he reached the ground. He'd never before been so grateful or satisfied to be on the floor. Helen ran up to him and hugged him tightly.

'We'd better go' he said. 'We're not in the clear yet.'

'Those men are still inside' said Helen. 'I've not seen them come out yet.'

The doors of the building burst open and Chris came running out. Helen flagged down a cab, they all jumped in and made their way off as quick as they could. Now Marco and David had the map and the cup. Any luck of finding the treasure was now in the control of a criminal.

49

Washington – Present Day + 6 (Wednesday)

The taxi took them away from danger, moving passed the White House and east, along one of the main roads. There was heavy traffic. Each time the car stopped, Elliot feared David would catch up with them, but so far he was nowhere in sight. Elliot didn't know how they'd managed to find him and Helen, but they obviously had some kind of tech that helped. Chris tried to get the taxi to go down a back road to avoid traffic and the risk of being seen. The driver refused as he didn't want to chance getting his car scratched by the narrow metal barriers. Elliot was losing patience and just wanted to push the driver to the side and take over the steering wheel. Not that he was a good driver. At all. He passed his test, but hadn't really driven since then.

'We need to get our stuff' said Helen.

'We can't, those men might be there' said Elliot. 'They just tried to kill me!'

'Don't worry, I thought about that already. Chris and I took everything to a different location, just in case.'

'Just here please' Chris said to the cabbie.

The taxi stopped abruptly and a car close behind them beeped its horn in frustration. It made Elliot jump, but after what had just happened, he was pretty jumpy anyway. Chris paid the fare, while the others hopped out next to a large grassy area on one side of the road and a group of buildings on the other. Beyond the grass, they could see Lincoln's Memorial. Elliot had seen the memorial in plenty of movies and always wanted to visit it in person. It had been on his bucket list since he was twelve. He didn't quite appreciate how big it would be in reality.

'Wait here' said Chris, running across the road and into a nearby building.

Within a few minutes, Chris walked back out of the building carrying Helen and Elliot's stuff. He carefully crossed the road. They walked towards Lincoln's Memorial, over the winding paths and passing the grassy fields. Elliot climbed a large set of steps and reached the pillars with a giant statue of Abraham Lincoln looking deep in thought. The pillars fronting the statue made it look as though Abe was in a prison. He thought it was ironic given that he was the man that set America free. His legs were tired, but not as much as his arms. All that hanging around like a monkey would give him muscle ache for at least a few days. He sat down on a step in front of Abe and rested his legs. Chris pulled out a can of sugar filled fizzy orange and handed it to Elliot.

'Here, this should help.'

'Thanks', said Elliot, although he didn't really feel like drinking. 'What do we do now?'

'They've got everything…' said Helen.

Chris interjected. 'Not everything.'

'What do you mean' asked Elliot.

Chris pulled out a picture. It was a cat scan of the Pythagorean cup.

'We scanned it to determine its age…and you're right. It's not from the Ancient Greek period. I forgot to give this to you in the rush of everything.'

'Thanks, but I don't think it matters too much now.'

'Maybe, maybe not' said Chris. 'I found something unusual inside the

Cup. Look.'

Chris showed them a copy of the scans. There was a picture on the outside with the Ancient Greek message. However, the scan on the inside revealed Latin numerals which read:

"1 2:7, 4:11, 20:17, 12:10"

'Does this mean anything to you' asked Helen, looking at Elliot, then back to Chris.

'Not to me' said Elliot, shaking his head.

'Nope, me neither. I'm afraid I have no idea. It rings no bells with the Ancient Greek world.'

Elliot thought back over everything they'd found. The Rosy Cross, the treasure, the philosophy tree, the secret Brotherhood and the Rosicrucian Order. He looked back at the message on the cup.

'What does this message mean again' asked Elliot.

Chris took the picture from him and read it aloud. 'The only thing that cannot be doubted. Reason allows our lady to resonate life from the tree of philosophy of God's palm.'

Elliot searched the recesses of his brain. *What could these numbers mean? A location? A code to a vault? A mathematical equation left by the Pythagorean Brotherhood?* No, the numbers seemed too obscure to fit any of those ideas. *Think, think, think.* Reason allowed our lady to resonate life from the tree of philosopher from God's Palm. *The hand of God?* No, that didn't fit. *Unless...*

'Of course. It's so obvious' he said.

'Uh, is it. What is' said Chris, scratching his head.

'God's palm' he said, tapping at the numbers on the scan. 'It's not the hand of God, but passages in the bible. Get it?'

'No' said Helen, raising her eyebrows.

'God's PALM. P A L M. It's referring to passages in the bible. You know, Peter, Acts, Luke and Mark!'

Helen looked at Chris and smiled. 'He's good, huh.'

Chris nodded. 'Not bad.'

'We need a copy of the bible' said Elliot.

Chris stood up and brushed himself off. 'I know just where we can find one.'

50

Washington – Present Day + 6 (Wednesday)

The great Library of Congress was busy for a weekday. Filled with tourists and students. Helen, Chris and Elliot walked through the main marble-laid hallway. It was a wide open space with numerous passages leading to God knows where. Elliot looked at a plastic stand with a map on it and searched for religious studies.

'This way' he said, pointing down one of the corridors.

They made their way to a study room, surrounded by books. Shelves stacked from floor to ceiling. Several large wooden steps led to some of the higher shelves. The steps looked fixed in place, but it was possible they were movable. Helen and Chris grabbed a seat by the only desk that wasn't already taken and Elliot went off to find a copy of the bible. He found a section on Christianity in the back rows of the room. He scanned along the shelf until he found a leather-bound copy, pulled it out, dusted it off then brought it back to the others. He dropped it on the desk making a noticeable bang. He didn't realise it would be so loud and promptly sat down to camouflage himself among his friends. Several people looked up and one of them said "shhhh."

He opened the front cover of the old, slightly torn book. He worked his way through each passage. Gods P A L M. He looked at the scan from the cup again. 12:7, 4:11, 20:17, 12:10. He turned the pages until he reached Peter and scrolled his finger along the pages until he found 12:7. It referred to a "chief corner stone that came about from our Lord." *What is someone trying to tell us*? He did the same process again. Looked up Acts, then passage 4:11. Again, it referred to a chief cornerstone that came about from our Lord. The passages in Luke and Matthew also referred to the chief stone.

'Guys, I think this is referring to the philosopher's stone.'

Helen raised her eyebrows. 'You think that's what the Rosicrucian Order were trying to tell us?'

'Not us, but someone' he said, tapping his finger against his clean shaven cheek. 'The Rosy Cross...of course! Good old internet.'

'You're not making any sense' she said.

'Yeah' said Chris. 'I'm not following.'

Elliot stood up, spread out his arms on the desk, and put his palms flat down on its surface. 'Chris, you said that scholars believe Alexander the Great conquered the known world with the Philosopher's Stone.'

'Two scholars' he replied.

'OK, two scholars. Still. I believe all these cryptic clues about power and the Rosy Cross are referring to the stone. I looked on the web a few days ago. It was believed that the Rosy Cross is another name for the body of Christ or the philosopher's stone. It's obviously not going to be Christ. Maybe it is the stone, and maybe this is why we're being chased.'

'You're suggesting there's a better chance of the philosopher's stone existing than there is Christ' said Chris.

At the risk of offending anyone, Elliot didn't want to get into a religious debate. 'I know it sounds nuts. Maybe it's a metaphor for something else. Whatever it is, someone has gone to great lengths to conceal it in plain sight. Come on, it's even in the Bible!' If someone's prepared to kill for it, we should at least entertain the idea.'

Chris agreed and went off to find books on alchemy or anything that might refer to the philosopher's stone. One of the librarians wasn't helpful and just pointed him to a Harry Potter book. After a few minutes, he returned with a big red book headed Alchemy and Chemistry, Science of the Ancient Greeks. It was a copy of a very old book and had photocopies of the original Ancient Greek text with translations and illustrations next to them. He spent over an hour reading passages on the philosopher's stone. Alchemists including Aristotle, had spent centuries carrying out experiments to try and create a power that could be used to turn lead into gold, preserve life and, if one so desired, cause death and destruction. The act of creating the stone was called Magnum Opus.

Chris paid particular attention to the original Ancient Greek text by Aristotle, with the translation next to it. The translation said that Aristotle created something similar to the stone, although his experiments were lost during Alexander the Great's reign. Chris stretched his arms, yawned, then rest his hands on the table and leaned in. He read the original text, then frowned. He read it again.

'Hang on.'

'What is it' whispered Elliot.

'This translation doesn't correspond with the original text.'

'How so' asked Helen, leaning in.

'The author of this book didn't interpret it properly. An easy mistake to make... some Ancient Greek words are very similar to others. Look here' he said, pointing. 'The translation says Aristotle was close to creating the stone and made something like it. However...' said Chris, moving his index finger to the Ancient Greek symbol, "ὁμός." 'This is Kione, the Ancient Greek text used in the Hellenistic period. It means "same."'

Chris got out a pen and paper then wrote down the Ancient Greek word " ὅμοιος." He put it next to a copy of the original text, "ὁμός."

'See, these words are close, but not identical' said Chris. 'The first word means the same. The second, which is what the author has written down, means "similar."'

'Sorry' said Helen. 'What are you saying?'

Elliot leaned in. 'He's saying that Aristotle didn't create something similar to the philosopher's stone. He created the philosopher's stone.'

'Spot on' said Chris.

Chris went on to say that all evidence of the stone was lost during Alexander the Great's reign. When Alexander died, any whisper of the stone died with him. Elliot still found it difficult to believe that such a stone exists. With today's advances in science, someone would've re-created it already. If it was possible, that is. However, he couldn't get his head around the fact that highly trained people were prepared to kill to get the map and the cup. Most explorers and treasure hunters do not carry the criminal intent David displayed.

'I think the stone, or whatever it is, will be with the treasure' said Elliot. 'That must be what these people following us were after. Who knows what they intend to do with it!'

'I don't know, but I wouldn't like to find out' said Helen. 'These men… they're dangerous.'

'We have to get there before they beat us to it' said Elliot.

'No' said Chris. 'You need to go to the police, as agreed!'

'We can't' said Elliot. 'Not yet. By the time we go to England and report everything to the police, it'll be too late! We cannot take that risk.'

'I have to be honest' said Helen. 'I'm in agreement with Elliot. Let's find the treasure and the stone, then report everything to the police.'

Chris didn't agree, although stopped pushing the point. 'So where to next then?'

'Based on the message on the Pythagorean Cup, my guess… France' said Elliot.

51

London – Present Day + 7 (Thursday)

Detective Henry Wrightman bit into his baguette with ham and brie that he made at home, then sat back into the chair behind his desk. He was making solid progress on the St Paul's case, but there were many unanswered questions and he still hadn't spoken with Helen Philips or Elliot Hope. He looked at his mobile. Missed call and a voicemail. The number was 001202 862 8638. *America?* He pressed the voicemail button and raised the phone to his ear.

'Detective Wrightman…it's Helen, Helen Philips from the British Museum. I hear you've been trying to get hold of me and that there's been another murder. Elliot and I are onto something big. We're being followed. We're innocent, although I think the murder in St Paul's may be connected. I'm in Washington, but making my way back to London. I'm not sure it's safe to talk over the phone, but will fill you in on my return.'

Henry knew Helen and Elliot were in Washington DC. His research team were able to track them down. He was surprised that Chris Seacrest had not helped him, despite his agreement to help. The threat of being charged for aiding and abetting potential suspects is usually a strong motivator to assist the police. A warrant was not always necessary to get what he needed. Henry knew they were up to something, he just didn't know what yet. *Why phone me if she's guilty.* Unless she was trying to bide time to enable her to do something. *Maybe, escape to a country that had no treaty with the UK?* Mexico, Guatemala, Chile were all possibilities and easier to get to from America than England.

Henry's hard-ass boss, Claire Nelson, came into his office. Something was wrong. Usually, she'd wear her poker face and it was impossible to tell what mood she was in. Today, she looked like she was about to burst into tears. That or erupt abuse at him like an angry volcano. Either way, he knew something bad had happened.

'Henry' she said in a soft tone.

'Can it wait' he said, hoping it would avoid the abuse she was about to hurl at him. 'Me and James are in the middle of an investigation and I'm onto a lead.'

'It's about James. He um. I uh...' she said, taking a deep breath to calm herself down.

'What is it? What's wrong? Where is he?'

'James was found dead earlier today... underneath London Bridge. A couple of stoners found him.'

Henry didn't believe it at first. He can't just die. He's a good cop. No, an excellent one. He felt sick. His job taught him to suppress any discomfort and it was easier to do when the victims were unknown to him. He still cared, just hid it well. But his partner, James Catchwell. His colleague, friend and father to his God child. Henry's face turned white. He felt all the energy being drained from his body, as though a part of James' life was a part of his. He wanted to hit something. Cause some pain, somewhere. Anything that would take some of the focus from what he was feeling.

Henry gulped, before shaking his head. 'How'd it happen?'

'Hoping you could tell me.'

'What do you mean?'

'He was stabbed after responding to a call given to you. Why didn't you back him up?! You let him go by himself! I deliberately left my nephew in your care.'

'Call. What call? If a call was directed for me, it hasn't reached me, I swear!'

Claire stayed silent and looked down. She was never afraid to speak her mind. It was one of her great, and sometimes frustrating, qualities. Henry realised that James was trying to help him whilst Henry was away on the investigation. Henry hated himself. If he'd gone and checked it out, PC James Catchwell, husband, father of a new born and friend to many, would be breathing and present.

'Who made the call?'

'Helen Philips.'

Henry was angry. Angry for not bringing in Helen and Elliot when he had the chance. Angry for not arresting them there and then. And Angry that, because of Helen and Elliot's actions, whether they were murderers or not, he has just lost a close friend and partner.

'Has Lilly been told?'

Lilly was James' wife. She was beautiful and despite her fear of the inherent dangers, she was supportive of James' career. She wanted him to quit, but never discouraged him from his goals. Henry wished she'd encouraged him to leave. Maybe then, he'd still be alive.

'No, not yet' replied Claire. 'I've got no idea how I break this to my family'

'I'll do it. I owe it to them and I want to be there to give whatever support Lilly needs.'

'You did not kill James, but God damn you've got to find his killer. I mean it. Whoever did this has to pay.'

Whilst Henry knew logically it wasn't his fault, he still wore the guilt like a hair-shirt with razors and wires attached. He let James die, even if it wasn't deliberate. Henry should have taken the call, not James. Claire had entrusted him to look after her nephew and he screwed it up. Someone needed and deserved to pay for James' death. Now more than ever, he needed to speak with Elliot Hope and Helen Philips. Even if he had to go to Washington to get them himself.

'Detective…you do whatever you have to, to bring this sick bastard to justice.'

'Bastards' he corrected, under his breath.

The captain walked out of the office and took the rest of the day off. Henry was alone. He stared at the picture of his son on his desk and couldn't imagine leaving his child alone in this world. He would be there for Lilly and James' young baby. He looked at his computer, jiggled his mouse and the screen came alive. There were a few emails. One selling Viagra, another about an old case. The last email was from his research team. He clicked it open. Helen Philips, Elliot Hope and one other had booked a flight to Paris. Helen hadn't mentioned this in her voicemail. She clearly had something to hide. Three murders and they were all pointing at Helen and Elliot. Time to issue a warrant for their arrest. *Enough. This is enough.*

Henry shouted from his office to the receptionist and smashed his clenched hand against his desk. 'Get me a God damn flight to Paris. Now!'

52

London – Present Day + 7 (Thursday)

Rav and Abrafo waited in the safe-house until they received instructions from David. It was in a neglected area in the east end of London, where crime and poverty were rife. Arguably, it was an un-safe house. There were no restaurants. The high street was dominated with obesity inducing take away shops and pro-addiction gambling retailers. The apartment itself was a small two bed flat, but one of the bedrooms had been used to store their moderately sized arson of guns, knives and anything else illegal. Abrafo, being the bigger of the two, got the spare bedroom. Rav reluctantly, and without choice, got the couch.

They sat in the kitchen of the old dilapidated flat, keen to get a move on so they could be paid. Abrafo was eating a bacon and egg sandwich. One of his favourite hobbies.

'That shit's bad for your health' said Rav, taking a large puff of his cigarette.

Abrafo put down his yolk-dripping sandwich and looked up at Rav to see him breathe out a waft of carcinogenic smoke. 'You're an idiot.'

Rav stood up and leaned against the table. Abrafo had no problem in squaring up to him and pushed his chair back then also stood up. The tension between them had always been there and it was only a matter of time before a fight would ensue. Abrafo's phone vibrated heavily against the table and they both looked down. It was David. They both sat back down and Abrafo answered the phone.

'What's up?'

'We've got the map and the cup. Helen and Elliot escaped. You need to get to Paris, quickly. I believe what we're looking for is in the Notre Dame Cathedral. Pack light and go now. Me and Marco will join you over there.'

'Got it.'

'Oh, and be careful. It wouldn't surprise me if they took copies of the map and cup so you may have company.'

'They're still alive?'

'For now' replied David. 'I believe they know what we're after, which means they probably know where to look next, too. Be alert. They are not stupid. If you see them, you know what to do.'

Abrafo went online and booked their flights. There were lots of seats available as it was a week day and exam time for schools. He booked their tickets, but made sure him and Rav were not sitting next to each other.

'Oh no' said Abrafo. 'They don't have seats together. Sorry Rav.'

Rav shrugged his shoulders and lit up another cigarette. They packed their stuff, but left their arson. Bringing weapons through customs was a bad idea. They'd have to get new ones over there. The Organisation would take care of that, for an additional fee of course. Abrafo sent a text to David so that he could call ahead and make the necessary arrangements. Half an hour later, Rav and Abrafo were ready to leave and would be in Paris later that evening.

53

France – Present Day + 8 (Friday)

Elliot had a smooth landing at Paris' Charles de Gaulle airport. It was 8am and a little chilly outside, but Helen and Chris had dressed appropriately. Elliot, with his lighter packing had little choice but to wear his skinny jeans and short sleeve t-shirt. He was tired after a sleepless journey and couldn't wait to jump into a bed. They made their way to baggage reclaim, stopping off at the restroom so Helen could relieve herself. The airplane facilities were less than hygienic and so she decided to wait. Elliot liked baggage reclaim. For no reason other than the fact that his inner child enjoyed watching the conveyer move around while he imagined all the fun he could have sitting on top. Not that he ever tried.

Elliot switched his mobile on as they were now in France and so cheaper European international receiving and calling rates applied. Having alienated himself over the last year, there were no messages from friends, although he did have a missed call from the social worker, Angela Bashton. Elliot wasn't due to check-in with Angela until this Saturday. If anything was wrong with Toby, he needed to know. He pressed call-back and it rang a few times, but went through to voicemail. He didn't leave a message. *Maybe she was in bed.* It was fairly early, after all.

They grabbed their bags and waited in the airport café. Chris went off to get a cab. Elliot sat in a cold metal chair, then turned to face Helen. She looked jetlagged and deep in thought as she stared at the floor. She was holding a pendent that was around her neck. Her right hand gripped around it and kept it close to her mouth, as if she was about to kiss it. Elliot noticed the pendent a few days ago. It had the Latin words "Dictum Muem Pactum" scribed on it. He knew it meant "my word is my bond" and suspected it had a deeper meaning from the way she held it.

'Was that a present from someone' he asked.

Helen pulled the pendent away from her lips and looked at it. 'Kind of… it was a present to myself. A reminder that I can trust myself, even if I can't trust others' she said, letting it fall back around her neck. 'Having it around me gives me strength. I know it sounds stupid.'

'Not stupid' replied Elliot. 'We all seek comfort and strength from something. Family, friends, religion. It's sad, but not stupid.'

'How so?'

'Sad. You know… that you have difficulty trusting people.'

Elliot realised he was being hypocritical. If he couldn't trust his own father, there was little hope he'd be able to trust the rest of the world. It was a dysfunctional lesson that had been entrenched into the building blocks of his upbringing.

'Believe me, if you knew what I'd been through, you'd understand' said Helen.

'Try me' said Elliot.

Elliot and Helen looked around to see if anyone was being nosey, but no one was close enough to listen.

'Bad choices with men, I guess. Sometimes I think I'm never going to meet a guy that doesn't jerk me around. I did meet a nice guy. Once.'

'What happened?'

Helen looked up at Elliot. She shook her head, but didn't say anything. He felt for her. Whilst she seemed strong and stable to an outsider, she was just as messed up as everyone else in the world. It was becoming apparent that her strength came from having to overcome adversity. It is often in the face of hitting rock bottom that we choose to rise up. For some people, traumatic experiences chew them up and spit them out. Left to live dysfunctional lives without growth, happiness or recovery. For others, including Helen, adversity can be a catalyst to pump determination through their veins. To overcome, step up and achieve the unachievable. Elliot wasn't yet sure which category he was in, but so far his path had been a shaky one.

'I was engaged once' said Helen, looking back down at the floor. 'University romance. Full of passion and naivety. It lasted for seven years and I thought he was the one… at least until I fell pregnant.'

'You have a kid' asked Elliot, surprised that she hadn't mentioned it before.

'No, I'm afraid not… I think.'

'Did you get married?'

'Ha. No… thankfully. Six months after finding out we were having a baby, he decides he's not ready to have a baby and walks out. A few months later I find out he was having an affair behind my back. Not ideal, but I …'

Helen stopped speaking as an old couple walked towards them. They went behind Elliot and sat a few tables away. Elliot waited until they were out of ear-shot.

'What did you do' asked Elliot.

'I uh, I couldn't eat, was barely earning a salary, couldn't afford the rent, let alone bring up a baby by myself! The stress became too much. I have no idea if my body was reacting to the stress, but a month later, the baby died and didn't go to term. I still have the scar. Not surprisingly, I suffered with depression… thought my life was at an end.'

'I'm sorry' said Elliot. He wanted to put his hand on Helen's shoulder to give her comfort, but given she was his boss and mentor, it felt a bit awkward. 'Must've been tough. I thought you said your ex was nice.'

'What Darren? No, he was a jerk. After that, I was single for four years. I eventually found someone, but he...' she said, pausing.

'He?'

'He uh, he went away.'

Elliot found it odd that Helen was happy to talk about her miscarriage and cheating fiancé, but didn't want to talk about the nice person in her life. Rather than digging he decided it was more respectful to let it be. In any case, he could relate to the pain as his father was unfaithful with his mother and decided to leave them.

'After my...' said Elliot, coughing to clear his throat. 'After my dad had an argument with my mother over his affair, he drove off. That was the night he died in a car crash' he said, playing with the handle on his luggage case. 'You know the ambulance came, but... it was too late to save him. He'd lost too much blood. The thing that hurts the most...'

Elliot paused. A ball built up in his throat, making it difficult to swallow or talk.

'What was it' asked Helen, in a soft tone.

'Just before he died, he spoke with the paramedic. He told them and... uh, I quote "I love someone else and cannot be with her. Tell my family I was trying to do the right thing"' he said, letting a tear fall from his eye. 'Even on his God damn death bed the cheating son of a bitch cared more for someone else than his own family.'

Helen's eyes welled up and she put her arm around him. 'I'm sorry.'

Elliot wiped the tear from his face. 'It's ok... not your fault.'

After a short silence, Elliot saw Chris coming back. He gestured for them to follow him. Elliot had assumed he'd found a taxi cab. He turned his focus back on their trail. They needed to find the philosopher's stone before David and Marco did. He didn't completely believe in the philosopher's stone, but these dangerous men did and he couldn't take the risk of more people being killed. Or... of it getting into the wrong hands. Not to mention all the treasure that would go on the black market.

An old yellow car pulled up. The cab driver was a short Indian man who didn't speak French or English. His head was only just taller than the steering wheel and Elliot wondered if it was safer for him to take the wheel. Chris hopped in the front. Elliot and Helen sat in the back. Elliot tried to explain the name of their hotel several times, but his efforts were wasted. Chris pulled out a map, leant across and showed the driver. It triggered some form of verbal acknowledgement, not that Elliot understood what he was saying. The cabbie then drove off towards their hotel.

54

France – Present Day + 8 (Friday)

Teo got off the train that went from London Kings Cross International to Paris Gare du Nord. It was busy due to the school holidays. Teo didn't mind a crowd. Easier to get lost. He needed to stay hidden until he found the stone. Then he'd make those bastards pay.

Teo made his way to border control. He pulled out his passport and stared at his photo. He was eight years younger back then and didn't have the noticeable scar on his neck that he did now. It was a clean slice. A painful reminder of the suffering that had been inflicted on his family. Border control looked tired and barely paid any attention to Teo so he quickly walked through. He travelled light. Always did. It was easier that way.

He walked away from the Gare du Nord entrance and stopped next to a sheltered bus stop to protect him from the wind, as he put away his passport. There were three people waiting for the bus. Teo opened up a small leather folder containing two other passports, bank cards, a wad of cash and a photograph of a woman and two young children. He put the passport carefully in its place, ensuring there was half a centimetre gap between the sides of the passport and the folder. Teo was meticulous in every area of his life. Whether it was from the way he dressed, organised himself or killed.

Teo stopped and stared at the photo of his family, pulled it out and held onto it. He felt pain and anger. He looked up at the bus shelter, saw his reflection on the Perspex holding an advert in place. A surge of anger shot through his body and he punched the advert hard, causing it to crack in half. Two of the three people waiting at the bus stop rushed away. The third person was listening to his mp three player and didn't notice the commotion.

Teo would do anything to get the stone. He didn't care who he had to take care of. Although David and his men had the map and Pythagorean Cup, he didn't have the same faith in them as he did in Helen and Elliot. Between Elliot and Helen, they'd managed to uncover clues that had been hidden for centuries. Clues specifically designed to be virtually impossible to decipher. He decided to keep tabs on them, just in case. He'd tracked them to a hotel in Paris. It was obvious that they kept copies of the map and cup, otherwise they wouldn't be in France. He would take them, but not yet. They were still doing his job for him. Without realising it, of course. Once he had the stone, then he would change the course of history.

55

France – Present Day + 8 (Friday)

After freshening up at the hotel, Elliot and the others ate at a French fish restaurant in the heart of Paris. Elliot was clean shaven and wore his only smart shirt and a pair of navy chinos. He even managed to style his chestnut hair, something he hadn't done for a long time. He didn't like most fish, but loved the grilled scallops and clam minestrone. Helen ate salmon pasta and took tiny inadequate nibbles. He wondered if he'd ever seen anyone eat so slow. He kept looking around the restaurant and out of the window. There was no sign of David and Marco. After what had happened, he wasn't about to let his guard down, even if David did now have the map and no longer needed him or Helen.

Elliot thought back on what they'd discovered so far. The secret society of philosopher's known as the Rosicrucian Order, and before that, the Pythagorean Brotherhood, kept a weapon used by Alexander the Great, safe and hidden. Somewhere, the accumulated wealth of Alexander the Great was hidden and only a worthy individual, a philosopher king, would be able to find its whereabouts. The inscription on the Pythagorean Cup indicated that they needed to investigate the main bell in the Notre Dame Cathedral. Elliot suspected it would just lead to another clue. It was unlikely that a mountain of treasure could be kept in the Cathedral tower without being noticed. The thought had crossed his mind as to whether there was really any treasure in the first place or whether the whole thing was a hoax.

Chris had a contact that was able to organise a private visit at the Notre Dame Cathedral and so after dinner they made their way there. Elliot and the others walked through the Fourth Arrondissement of Paris, reaching the Ile de la Cite. From the road, he could see the Notre Dame Cathedral. A paragon of Gothic French architecture, monuments and stained glass windows. It was huge. From the western front, it stood like a giant sandcastle with two rectangular turrets sat on top at both sides. A circular stained glass window, as big as a bus, was symmetrically placed in the middle. A security personnel of gargoyles and religious statues covered its rooftops.

The sun was on its way out, but the evening wasn't cold. Tourists hung outside the Cathedral, taking romantic photos and selfies with their cell phones and selfie sticks. Chris knocked on the Cathedral's side entrance. There was no answer, so he sent a text to the number his contact gave him. A few minutes passed and the door eventually opened. There stood a dark haired, olive skinned, member of the clergy in the doorway, wearing a robe and out of place new white running trainers. The clergyman gave a smile that almost looked like a sneer. He nodded and gestured for them to come in.

'Thanks for letting us visit after hours' said Chris. 'We'd just like to visit the South Tower if that's ok. We won't be long. If you have other things to do, please don't let us keep you.'

The less than talkative clergyman nodded again and let them do their thing. Elliot walked down the nave of the Cathedral with Helen and Chris following behind. The lampposts from outside bounced light through a large circular stained glass window in the middle of the western wall, creating a sombre setting. Elliot noticed the clergyman kept on peeking over. Pretending to mind his own business. Trying to stay far enough out of sight, but doing a bad job of it. Elliot didn't mind. He could tell the guy was just a nosy member of the cloth. They climbed up a mountain of old concrete steps and went across a walkway that overlooked Paris and the serene moonlit river Seine. At the south tower, they climbed up another set of steps that were old and creaky until he eventually reached the head of the tower, their final destination. It looked as though it hadn't been touched for centuries. Covered in old rotten wood. A heaven for damp proofing-surveyors. In the middle of the seemingly haunted tower was a massive bell, as big as a small car.

'Our lady' said Elliot, walking up to the bell.

It was too dark to see any noticeable signs or markings. Elliot took out his smart-phone and flicked on the flashlight app before scanning the bell. Helen pulled out a mag-light that she bought in Arizona and helped to search for clues. The light from their torches Waltzed around the bell, revealing a smooth-surfaced, pattern-free, chunk of metal. Parts of the bell had turned light green due to a chemical reaction with the air that took place over centuries. Apart from a couple of lines running around the bell, nothing stood out. But then, so far, nothing stood out on any of their discoveries. Elliot reluctantly peeped his head inside the bell, conscious of avoiding any spider webs. Again, there was nothing apart from a few scratches on the metal. There was no treasure and certainly no clue.

'Any ideas' said Helen.

'Nope, none' replied Elliot.

'The website said this is the tower where our lady would be' said Chris.

'It doesn't make sense' said Elliot. 'It must be here!'

They took some photos of the bell on their phones as Helen directed her mag-light. The photos may come in handy later, although Elliot had no idea how to move forward. They'd reached a dead end. Elliot pulled out his phone and searched the internet to see if he could find anything on the bell.

'Crap...Guys...'

'What is it' asked Helen.

'Erm, it says here that Our Lady, also known as Marie Bell used to be here, but was destroyed during the French Revolution in the late seventeen hundreds. The only one to survive was the Emmanuelle Bell, which has taken its place. How did we not spot this?'

'Destroyed? Damn. No idea. So what do we do now' said Chris.

'I don't know. Without the bell, we're stuck.'

'On the positive side, if we can't find it those men can't either' said Elliot.

They made their way back down the rickety steps to leave the building. As Elliot reached a corner, he saw the shadow of the clergyman walking up the stairs towards him. There was a sudden cracking noise and the sound of a short burst of air. The clergyman fell forward into Elliot's sight, landing on his side with his face up. His right arm reached out to Elliot as a desperate plea for help. Elliot could see blood seeping from his chest. His eyes seemed to scream at Elliot to run. Another burst of air travelled across the stairway as the clergy man was shot dead

Dread force-fed its way through Elliot's body. Before he could see who was at the bottom of the stairs, they all ran back up towards the tower to hide. Elliot was petrified and could control neither his thoughts nor the violent shaking of his hands. He could hear the creak of the old wooden steps as someone made their way up the tower and, with no other way out, he knew they were trapped. Chris hid as best he could, but his panic stricken breathing wasn't helping to stay silent. Elliot hid in the shadows of a dark corner. The figure, unrecognisable due to the lack of light, walked up the last set of stairs. Elliot saw the outline of the man's face, but couldn't identify him. He was wearing a hat and carrying an object in his hand. Given what had just happened to the poor clergyman, it was obvious that it was no water-pistol. Elliot had two choices. Wait and see what happens, or take action. The passive approach didn't work out so well for the clergyman. He'd have to take action.

The man reached the final step and slowly put one foot in front of the other. Cautious and alert. This was a cold calculated killer. Helen attempted to hide behind an old metal crate, but the side of her leg could still be seen. If Elliot could see her from the other side of the tower, it wouldn't be hard for the murderer to see her. Elliot couldn't sneak up on the man. His footsteps would alert the killer. Elliot would have to run and charge at him with full speed… there was no other way. Elliot didn't like his options, but then he really didn't have any. Be killed or take a chance and potentially be killed.

Elliot counted to three in his head then ran as fast as he could. One big stride, two, three. He crashed into the man knocking him off his feet. The dark figure landed on his back. Elliot jumped on top of him and tried to pin the man to the ground. A struggle ensued as Elliot desperately tried to disarm him, but it was no use. The guy was much stronger and was far more experienced in a fight. A gun shot went off in the struggle, followed by a powerful punch to Elliot's face. He rolled over in agony. The man quickly stood up and raised his gun.

'Unless you want your friend to die, you have five seconds to come out' said the man, pointing the gun at Elliot.

Elliot held his face, dizzy from the punch. He sat up and tried to gain focus. His jaw hurt like hell, but it wasn't broken. He looked up at the dark figure and could now make out his face.

'Officer Edward Sanchez? You're not a police officer.'

'Shut up' said Teo. 'Five….Four….Three'…he clicked his gun back and kept it aimed at Elliot's face. 'Two.'

Helen rushed out from behind the metal cage and a second later, Chris also came out. They made their way over to Elliot. Chris stood in front of them both.

'Don't try to be a hero. This is not Hollywood and I will not hesitate to kill each and every one of you.'

'We're innocent' said Helen. 'We didn't kill anyone.'

'You don't say' he said, gesturing with his gun for them to move over so they were all together. 'You've been a little too successful for your own good. I was going to leave you be, but not now. It's too dangerous.'

Helen and Chris helped Elliot from the floor, before he brushed himself off. His face was red from the punch. He gave Teo an evil stare.

'You can glare at me like that all you want, but it means nothing. You've got heart kid, but I've got the gun and you'll do as I say.'

Elliot didn't appreciate the condescending tone, but he was not going to argue and at that moment he certainly felt like a kid. He wanted to cower. Unable to do or say anything that would make a difference.

'Where's the stone?'

'What stone' asked Helen.

'Don't play dumb. The philosopher's stone.'

'We don't know' said Elliot, semi-surprised that he was more interested in the philosopher's stone than the greatest treasure known to mankind. 'We came here to find it, but hit a dead end.'

'Don't lie to me' said Teo, raising his gun back at Elliot.

Elliot needed to keep the status quo if they were going to survive. If Teo believed they were no longer of any use, there was no real reason to keep them alive.

'We came to the wrong place... I got it wrong.'

'What jew mean?!'

'We should've gone to Loire.'

Teo walked up to them. 'Start talking.'

'I thought the Rosy Cross was here, but I should've realised' Elliot said, pausing. He could feel his hands shaking even more than before. 'The erm... the Cup. The Pythagorean Cup' said Elliot, trying to pull out his phone and reading the message. It said:

"The only thing that cannot be doubted. Reason allows our lady to resonate life to the tree of philosophy from God's palm."

'The philosophy tree was referring to an actual tree. Not a metaphorical expression. Our lady means the chapel inside the tree. In Loire Valley, there is a giant hollowed out tree that was struck by lightning. The Notre Dame Chapel is actually inside the tree. Descartes used to go there in his younger years.'

'You're lying.'

'No, he's right' said Chris. 'This place was our first bet, but we've found nothing. I don't know why I didn't think of it before. We've been trying to find the hidden meaning behind the secret messages so much that we ignored its literal meaning.'

'Exactly' said Elliot. 'God's palm. The Rosy Cross must be in God's palm. Or, to be more specific, the palm in which he exposed himself to the world...through Jesus.'

'I bet the stone can be found by looking at the hand of Jesus on the cross at Loire's Notre Dame Chapel' said Helen.

'How do I know you're not telling the truth' said Teo.

'You don't, but you have a gun and I'm not going to risk my life or anyone else's over some stone' said Elliot.

'If you're lying, I will come back and I won't be so amenable.'

Teo took them into a passageway at the back of the tower, to a small, closed off, stone-walled room. As Elliot was pushed into the damp and cold room, the darkness became even darker. The light from the moon and lampposts outside faded away. There were no windows and the only exit was the one they'd come from. Elliot could just about make out the outlines of Helen, Chris and Officer Sanchez or whoever he really was. He bumped into a bucket and mop. *We're in a storage room,* he thought.

'What are you doing? I told you everything I know' said Elliot.

'Insurance. I'll know where to find you if you're lying' Teo replied.

'Please' said Helen. 'We won't tell anyone we saw you. Just let us go.'

'Shut up' said Teo. 'Once I've got what I want, you'll want to disappear if you know what's good for you.'

'You mean you'll make us disappear' said Helen.

Teo didn't reply. He pulled out some plastic cable-ties and tied their arms behind their backs, zipping their hands together, one person at a time. He then tied their feet together. Chris, Helen and Elliot lay there, in the dark, defenceless and unable to move. Flopping about like fish out of water. Teo shut the solid wood door. Elliot heard a bolting sound as the door was locked from the outside. Teo's footsteps faded until they could no longer be heard. He was gone, but there was no light, no help and no escape.

'Are you guys ok' said Elliot, breathing heavily.

'I'd be better if I was on a beach in Barbados' said Helen, wriggling around and trying to break herself free.

'Next time we'll go to the Caribbean.'

'Can we go to Antigua' said Chris. 'I went to Barbados last year.'

'Sure…' said Helen. 'If we can get out of here.'

The cable-ties were tight and restricted Elliot's circulation. He struggled, rocking left and right to try and break free, but it was no use. The binding was too strong. The more he moved, the more the cable-ties cut into his skin.

'Why didn't you tell him the next clue was destroyed' asked Helen. 'Descartes never went to Loire... he used to come here. You said it yourself.'

'I had to' said Elliot.

'Well, he's going to be pissed when he gets there and realises we've lied to him. He's going to come back and kill us. We're sitting ducks.'

'I know' said Elliot. 'But, if I told him it was destroyed, he'd no longer need us. We'd be dead already. You saw what he did to that poor guy on the stairs.'

'Ok' said Chris. 'So it may have bought us some time, but no one's going to come here until morning to notice we're here and save us. That police man, or whoever he was, will be back by then.

'Great. So we're waiting to be killed' said Helen.

56

France – Present Day + 8 (Friday)

Henry was so hungry he could kill for something to eat. The only food on his flight to Paris was the pre-packaged, sub-par standard, allegedly "fresh", culinary excellence offered on your typical budget airline. He grabbed something to eat at the airport instead of resorting to the tempting alternative of eating his own arm. Apart from his boss, no one else knew he was in France. As a result, there was no way of getting the cost of the flight paid for and so business class on a scheduled flight was not an option. He was outside his jurisdiction and had to keep a low profile. Despite this, Claire Nelson was determined to find the killer of her nephew and Henry's partner. She'd put Henry in contact with an old friend who was high up in the French police.

Henry arrived at Préfet de police on Place Louis Lépine and sat in the waiting room. The base of the French police headquarters was a large, old building that looked like the barracks for the royal guard back in London. The main difference was that it was next to the river Seine and surrounded by officers with blue hats instead of the giant black fluffy ones worn by the queen's guards. Henry never understood the flamboyance of those hats and thought they looked more like the top of a cotton bud than a hat of any practical use. *At least they wouldn't have to get earmuffs in winter.* Henry's attention came back to focus when he was greeted by a short officer. Too small to be a street officer and so Henry assumed he was probably an office bod.

'Bon soir, Monsieur Wrightman' said the vertically challenged man.

'Hello, yes, that is me' he said, standing up and extending his hand.

'Le inspector is ear and expecting you' he said, in a strong French accent, pronouncing every couple of words with a hawking sound. 'Please, follow me.'

Henry had hardly slept and was tired. The pain of losing his partner and the pressure to solve the case only made it worse. He couldn't be arsed to pretend to be nice, but if he wanted help, he had to make an effort and play by the French authority's rules. After all, they were kind enough to assist him in his endeavours. Henry followed the officer through the building. It was night time, but the building was busy enough to be mistaken for being daytime.

A tall policeman with a slightly crooked nose, oiled back, black hair and stubble marched a handcuffed criminal through the corridor, where Henry was walking. The arrested man was shouting in French. Henry had no idea what he was saying, but he assumed it wasn't polite.

'Inspecteur, voici le Detective Wrightman' said the short officer to the tall policeman.

'Ah, Detective. Pleasure to meet you' said the inspector.

'Good to meet you too' said Henry.

The inspector turned to the officer and pointed to the arrested man. 'Renoir, emmenez cet homme en cellule quatre'

The shorter officer took the handcuffed man down the corridor and into a prison cell. The criminal continued shouting, but it seemed common place in this building, and no one except Henry appeared to notice. The inspector signalled for Henry to follow him into his office which was just off the corridor. Henry obliged. His office was not much larger than Henry's office in London. The wall adjoining the corridor was covered in windows. Covered up by cheap, faux-wood, window blinds. Henry sat in an overused chair that was in keeping with the rest of the room. He sat up straight and faced the inspector.

'Thank you for your hospitality' said Henry.

'But, of course, Detective.'

Henry's eyes followed the inspector as he walked behind his desk. The inspector sat down in his comfy chair, lent back then raised and rested his left foot on his right knee.

'A criminal is still a criminal, whether the crime was here or in Engerland' he said. 'Besides, a police officer was killed and we haff to stick together.'

'Thank you. It is appreciated.'

Henry told the inspector everything he knew. The murder of his sponsor in St Pauls, the death and burglary of Jonathan Hooke and, of course, the tragic death of his partner and friend, PC James Catchwell. He showed the inspector pictures of both Helen and Elliot. He also showed him a picture of someone who is believed to be with them. Christopher Seacrest.

'Detective. I will give these to my team' he said, holding photos of the suspects. 'We will do whatever we can to help.'

Henry's mobile rang. It was Louise Allen, his chief researcher on the case. She didn't know why he was in France and he wanted to keep it that way. Not that he didn't trust her. But it allowed plausible deniability if an enquiry was made. Louise had new information. There was a DNA match on the blood found on the stone in St Paul's Cathedral. It was Elliot Hope's blood. He finally had solid evidence that linked Elliot to the murder. Proof that he was involved. He wasn't one hundred percent sure before, but now there was no question about it. He couldn't work out their motive, but for now he just needed to find Elliot and Helen. Henry was grateful for all the help he could get and with the inspector's assistance, he was hopeful they'd catch Elliot and Helen.

57

London – Present Day + 8 (Friday)

David and Marco arrived back in the UK after a ten hour, turbulent flight. Jetlagged and looking like zombies, they were ready to count sheep. They were not allowed to rest. Not yet. Work had to be done. David turned on his mobile to see if there'd been any developments. There were a few messages, but none were from Rav or Abrafo. He called Rav to see if he'd found anything at the Notre Dame Cathedral. The phone rang. The dial tone was international and David knew Rav was still in Paris. There was no answer. So he sent a text. "Where are you?" No doubt Rav and Abrafo would check in soon.

David scrolled through his messages. One was from an undisclosed number and just said "update." He knew that meant the Organisation had new information. He called them to get up to speed. Helen used her card in a restaurant on the Seventh Arrondissement, she was last seen on CCTV going into the Notre Dame Cathedral and she'd not yet come out. *Maybe Elliot and Helen had already been care taken of.* His employer did say he'd take care of it himself, after all.

The Organisation had further intel on Elliot. They'd made a mistake. His family were not all deceased. He had a younger brother, Toby, that hadn't come up on his records as he was registered to foster parents that lived not too far away. It was only when the foster parents made an application to court, that the public records were brought to their attention. It was unheard of for the Organisation to make a mistake. Mistakes do not happen. As recompense, they agreed to provide a couple of highly trained mercenaries to assist with his endeavours. David could use the extra muscle.

'Wad they say' said Marco.

'They've found something' said David.

'What's that?'

'Leverage.'

58

France – Present Day + 8 (Friday)

Back in the dark locked storage room, Elliot and the others wiggled around desperately. After ten minutes of trying, it was clear her strength alone was not enough to break the plastic restraints binding their hands and legs together. Helen manoeuvred her body across the floor and managed to reach Elliot. It was difficult to see. Elliot could feel her face and lips moving around his hands, which tickled slightly.

'What are you doing?'

'I'm trying to break us free. Stay still' she said.

He felt her mouth move to the binding on his wrists, then start nibbling against the plastic.

'Ouch' he said, as she bit his skin.

'Oops, sorry' she said, then continued biting at the binding, trying to break him free. 'Elliot are you ok?'

'Yep. Ish.'

'Why are you wet' she said, feeling the dampness on his clothes. 'My God, you've been shot!'

Elliot knew if he said something it would've created more stress. More stress meant less concentration. 'When Teo's gun went off, it just caught the side of me. I'll be ok… we just need to get out of here.'

Helen remembered that Elliot suffered from Haemophilia. If they didn't stop the bleeding, his blood wouldn't coagulate and he could bleed to death. Helen couldn't see how big or deep the wound was. If it was bad, he could die in a matter of minutes. She hoped they had longer, but it would not surprise her if Elliot was down playing its severity in order to try and keep her calm. She was already panicked at the thought that Teo was probably on his way back to kill them. She tried to keep calm and tried biting his restraints again. This time even harder. A crunching sound came from her mouth, followed by a sharp pain as she chipped a tooth.

Chris was moving around and panting as he tried to break free, but his efforts were just as useless as the others. If they didn't escape soon, they were all going to die, starting with Elliot.

59

Loire Valley, France – Present Day + 8 (Friday)

It was pitch black by the time Teo's car pulled up to the chapel. An old hollow tree, which looked as old as time, with a chapel inside. Its overgrown branches were supported by poles and wires, keeping them from falling to the ground. The tree was over twelve hundred years old and had survived the Hundred Years War with the English, The Black Death, the Reformation and the Revolution. It had seen more than the surrounding buildings and it didn't surprise Teo that the stone would be hidden here. It was nicknamed the Tree of Reason, which he thought was fitting.

There were houses nearby, although none of the lights were on. At two am, there was no one around in sight. Teo opened the glove compartment, pulled out his pistol and a torch then grabbed a crowbar from the boot of his car.

He sneaked over to the tree, being careful to keep the crunching sound of the gravel under his feet to a minimum. The chapel looked like more of a Disney tower than a chapel. A spire reached out from the top of the humongous tree trunk, with a spiral wooden staircase . Not surprisingly, the front door was locked shut. Teo wedged the crowbar in the side of the door and applied pressure. Wedging the door open would make less noise than kicking it down. He pushed hard and the wood surrounding the lock gradually cracked apart until the door opened. He looked around. Still, no one about.

Inside the tree was a tiny chapel, barely big enough for five people. He shone his torch around. It was minimalist in decor. Two benches, a tiny altar and large cross with a statue of Jesus pinned against it.

"The hand of God" he said under his breath.

Teo kept his torch fixed on the cross, as he walked over to it. He bumped into a low height bench which toppled over and made a loud bang. He froze like a statue for a few seconds, and turned off his torch. After a minute of silence, the coast was clear so he made his way over to the cross and examined it. There were no noticeable marks or signs. The plastic statue of Jesus didn't even look that old. Both palms were open and not concealing anything. He realised he'd been duped. *Elliot.* He jumped back in his car and sped as fast as he could back to the Notre Dame Cathedral to deal with Elliot and the others.

60

France – Present Day + 8 (Friday)

It had been hours since Teo left Elliot locked in the Cathedral. By now, he will have realised Elliot gave him the wrong information so they could escape. He'd be back any second. The side of Elliot's back wouldn't stop seeping blood. He was beginning to feel weak, nauseous and slightly dizzy. He needed help soon. Elliot heard the faint sound of distant footsteps.

'Crap' said Chris, desperately trying to free himself. 'He's back.'

The footsteps grew louder and louder until they were just behind the door. Chris hid in the corner of the room, laid on his back and raised his legs up so he could kick Teo when he came through the door. Elliot looked around the room to get his bearings, but it was too dark. The bolt of the door made a clang and it opened slowly, letting in a small amount of light, just enough to see the shadow of a man moving into the room. Before the dark figure had a chance to do anything, Chris kicked his legs out, causing the shadow to lose his footing.

'What the' said the dark figure, falling to the floor.

Helen and Chris leaped onto him with all their weight.

'Get off me!'

The dark figure started shaking violently, spasming out of control. It wasn't Teo. He was much shorter and plump around the waist.

'Quick, get off. It's not him' said Helen.

'Who is it' asked Elliot.

'I don't know' said Helen, trying to look at his face. It was too dark to see. 'It's someone else.'

Elliot leant his back against the side of the room, pushed his legs into the floor and pressed his hands against the wall. He pushed out to raise his body, letting out groan as he hit his wound, but continued until he was upright and on his feet. He hopped out of the storage room and into the bell tower to find something sharp. There were no tools around to cut himself free. The area was almost bare. He thought about trying to escape whilst tied up, but climbing down the stairs would be difficult. He looked over to the large old and rusty metal cage where Helen hid previously. It was the size of a refrigerator and stood in the corner of the bell tower. He hopped over to it. With each movement, the weight of his body jolted against his bullet wound, making it painful to move.

He reached the rusty old cage and aligned himself so that the plastic cable met with a rusty metal corner. He scored the plastic, moving it up and down, up and down, careful not to let it cut his hands. It took a few minutes, but the plastic eventually broke, releasing his wrists. He turned around and bent a length of the rusted metal back and forth until it snapped off, then used it to cut his legs free. He rushed over to help the others.

Once free, they helped carry the man through to the bell tower. As his face came into the light, they saw an older man, late fifties and coming to the end of an epileptic fit. His hair looked brown in the light, but there was a slight tinge to it. Not a brunette, but ginger.

'We need to get him out of here before that guy comes back for us' said Chris.

'Agreed' replied Elliot. 'Help me carry him downstairs.'

They struggled to carry the man down the narrow stairway and over the clergyman's lifeless body. Elliot and Helen both trod in blood that had drained out onto some of the steps. Elliot slipped on the lubricated floor, but managed to regain his balance. It made him gag. Chris followed behind, held onto the hand rail and jumped over the bloodied steps. They made their way out of the Cathedral and away from the area, before Teo came back.

61

France – Present Day + 8 (Friday)

Elliot and Helen helped the ginger, middle-aged man into a late night coffee shop and sat him down. It was brightly lit. Too bright for Elliot's eyes, which hadn't yet adjusted from the darkness of the Notre Dame. Apart from a mid-thirties couple sitting in the corner and a shop worker behind the till, the shop was empty. The only sound was from the spray of steam into a jug of milk as the shop worker made a café latte. The smell of coffee made Elliot crave a cup to wake him up. Elliot went to clean up his gunshot wound. It wasn't deep or particularly wide, but there was a gentle flow of blood trickling out of his body. He grabbed a wad of tissue from the bathroom and held it firmly against his lower back. The tissue helped to stop the flow, but he'd need to get help eventually.

Elliot pulled out his mobile to check the time. Three am. He had missed calls and a voicemail. It was the social worker again. She was the last person he needed to deal with now. However, if it meant getting to see Toby, it was not a message he could avoid. He clicked on his voicemails and reluctantly forced the phone to his ear.

'Elliot! What the hell is going on' said Angela. 'There's a warrant out for your arrest! I'm being hounded by the police for your whereabouts. What the bloody hell have you done? I'm very worried. I want to help you. I really do. But this… this just can't go on. Can you honestly say it'd be in Toby's best interests to allow him to live the life you lead? I've spoken with your boss. If you get charged by the police, you won't have a job.' There was a pause. 'Toby's foster parents have made an application to court for adoption' she said in a softer tone. 'I'm sorry, but if they get it, they'll have complete parental control over him. Please just… just stay out of trouble and call me tomorrow.'

Toby's foster parents didn't like Elliot all that much. At all, in fact. He knew that once they'd adopted Toby, he'd have no chance of reuniting the last of his family together. If he gets a criminal record, he'd be lucky if they'd even let him see Toby, let alone live with him. He wanted to call her back and scream and shout. Not that it would've helped. In any case, it was too late at night to call her. They'd have to speak tomorrow. He felt himself burning up and just wanted to smash something to release his anger. Or have someone kick him to the ground. Anything that would take his focus away from the pain of losing his brother. He felt completely and utterly helpless. It triggered the memory of the loss of his parents. He went to the bathroom, wet his face and took in several large slow breaths to calm him down.

A few minutes later, Elliot grabbed a glass of water and walked back over to Helen and the rest who were sitting down at a small coffee table. He handed the water to the ginger-nut who was beginning to come round.

'Wa, what happened' said the man.

'It looks like you had an epileptic fit… that and you saved our bacon' said Helen.

The man rubbed his chin and had a look of confusion. 'I do suffer from epilepsy. Thanks for your help. What do you mean, saved you?'

The ginger-nut was not in brilliant shape. His face had a semi-double chin and crow's feet to the sides of his baggy eyes. Clean shaven. Helen explained to him about the kidnapping and that if he hadn't unlocked the door when he did, they would probably be dead by now. The man looked horrified by it all and sat down as he took in the information.

'Can I ask' said Elliot. 'Who are you and what were you doing there?'

The man looked at them, sized them up and made a quirky twitch of his nose as if he was trying to scratch it without using his hands.

'My name is Jean-Claude Aspinel' said the man. He paused, looked around the room, then back to the group. 'Ok, what I'm about to say may sound odd.'

'Believe me' said Elliot. 'All we've had for the last few days is odd. We can handle it.'

'The man that kidnapped you... he's uh, he's not a police officer.'

'We guessed that' replied Helen. 'Then who is he?'

Jean Claude leaned in. 'His name... his name is Teo. Teo Brecher. Israeli born and one nasty piece of work.'

'How do you know him' asked Chris.

'Good question' he said, lowering his voice and looking around to make sure no one was paying attention. 'I've been searching for something. Something top secret... an ancient treasure...'

'Left by Alexander the Great' Elliot interjected.

'Yes' replied Jean Claude, looking confused. 'How did you...'

'We've been looking for it too' said Helen.

Elliot was surprised that they weren't the only normal people looking for the treasure. Surprised, but happy. Jean Claude wasn't built for fighting, but he did even the numbers out a little. Plus, Jean Claude could help prove that they were innocent. With his word, the police would realise they had nothing to do with the murders.

'The treasure is said to be hidden in a temple the size of a football pitch' said Jean Claude. 'Filled to the top with gold, precious gems and rare metals. But it's not the treasure I'm seeking. Legend tells us that there is something far more valuable.'

'The Philosopher's Stone' said Helen.

'Oh...so you know about that too' said Jean Claude, looking at Helen and Elliot who both nodded. 'I'm guessing if you've met Teo, then you've also met his muscle, David and Marco.'

'The tattooed skin-head and his companion' said Elliot.

Jean Claude nodded. 'Teo's family were killed a few years back. A terrible accident' he said, staring down at his glass of water on the table. 'Palestinian insurgents carried out a guerrilla warfare attack. They believed they were attacking the highly trained tactical forces known as Mossad.'

'Mossad' said Elliot.

'You've heard of them' said Helen.

'Who hasn't' replied Elliot. 'They're as dangerous as the SAS or the Navy Seals.'

'Well Teo was a member of Mossad and I can tell you... he is very dangerous' said Jean Claude. 'The Palestinian insurgents thought they were attacking a cell of Mossad set up to deal with Palestinian rebels.'

'What happened' asked Chris.

'They blew up the wrong building. It housed Mossad families. Teo's wife and child were killed. He swore they'd pay for what they did, but they never have.'

Jean Claude explained that he'd been working with his brother on a top secret project. His brother, an archaeologist and Freemason, learned about the treasure and the philosopher's stone. The Israeli government agreed to fund an expedition to find the stone and even paid for an exploration boat to assist Jean Claude's brother, the same boat Jean Claude came to France in. Unfortunately, Teo was assigned as security. When he discovered what the stone was capable of, Teo went rogue and decided to take over the search.

'You think Teo wants revenge and plans to use the stone to kill' asked Chris.

Jean Claude nodded. 'He lost sight of right and wrong a long time ago. Blinded by his anger, I fear he'll stop at nothing until he gets what he wants.'

'If he's so dangerous, why are you going after him' said Elliot.

'I'm not. I'm after the stone. My brother… he was the archaeologist and I'm here to pick up on his trail. I'm a scientist… haematologist to be precise. I focus on finding commonalities in different blood groups. You may've heard about the discovery by my university…it's been on the news.'

Elliot nodded. 'Yes, scientists discovered a haematological link in the gene pool of people that are more susceptible to disease and disability than others.'

'Exactly' said Jean Claude. 'By altering this pattern, we could wipe out disability, prevent disease and stop the spread of viruses. This is why I've been brought on board. If I can get to the stone before Teo, we can stop him, but perhaps more importantly, help the world from disability and illness. Not to mention save trillions of pounds in government funds worldwide. My path is one of salvation, rather than greed.'

They stopped talking as the shop attendant brought over their drinks. Two skinny lattes, a macchiato and a hot chocolate. The attendant gave the table a quick wipe, put the drinks down and gave them the bill. Chris picked up this one and gave the man twenty Euros. The guy walked off to get change. Elliot could only begin to imagine what the world would be like if everyone was physically and mentally free from disability. The impact it had on the world would be huge. Especially in developing countries, where they are not yet equipped to deal with certain disabilities and illnesses. He turned his attention back to Jean Claude, who he was beginning to feel inspired by. He had a bruise on his head from where Helen and Chris jumped on him in the Cathedral.

'Where's your brother' asked Elliot.

Jean Claude put his hands around his coffee cup and used one finger to make a circular motion around its edge. He didn't look up and just paused for a few seconds. 'When Teo found out about what the stone could do, he tried to take my brother's research. There was a struggle and…' he paused, stopped playing with his cup and looked up at Elliot. 'Teo killed him.'

'I'm sorry' said Helen, putting her hand on his shoulder. 'Could it be possible that Teo wants to use the stone to bring back his family?'

'I don't know that the stone is real. My brother swore it was. In any case, legend tells us that the stone can destroy or extend life, not resurrect it.'

'Does Teo know this' asked Elliot.

'Yes.'

'So he wants to destroy the people that murdered his family' said Elliot.

'I fear it's worse than that' said Jean Claude. 'Teo deeply believed it was the Palestinian people that were the cause of it all. Cut off the head of the snake…'

'And the body will follow' said Chris.

'That's genocide' said Helen.

Jean Claude nodded. 'Whenever anyone gets close to his trail, he just kills them. If it gets into his hands, Teo could cause death and destruction. He must be stopped.'

'Why hasn't he killed us then' asked Helen.

'I know why' said Elliot. 'We've been doing his job for him…all this time. Think about it. First his men tried to take the map in the British Museum, then he followed us to St Paul's where the tour guide was killed. He framed us so that we had to go on the run. We'd have no choice, but to continue forward to prove our innocence. They found us in Washington and again here. If we continue, we'll only help Teo and end up dead ourselves. Do the authorities know?'

Jean Claude shook his head. 'Due to the sensitive nature of it all, the government and Mossad want to deal with this themselves, without making it a public affair' said Jean Claude. 'Will you help me? Please. If not for national security, do it for the discovery of a lifetime.'

Elliot felt sick. The idea that they were all being played by a dangerous criminal was beyond overwhelming. The pressure was too much. First the deaths of innocent people, then a warrant out for his arrest and now his brother's foster parents were applying for permanent adoption. He may never get to see his brother again, especially if the foster parents thought he was some kind of dangerous offender. And to top it all off, he'd been leading Teo Brecher to the philosopher's stone so he could wipe out the Palestinian people. The worst part was that he'd been aiding and abetting mass genocide, without actually realising it.

'No' said Elliot. 'I can't do it.'

Elliot, Chris and Jean Claude looked at Elliot. Jean Claude looked surprised.

'Why not' asked Jean Claude.

'All my life, I've been trying to do the "right thing." I keep getting people and myself in trouble. Always. I've hurt my family, the woman in St Pauls is dead because of me and so are the other two. I've had enough. I don't know about you, but I'm going to turn myself into the police and explain everything to them. We have to come clean. The truth will set us free. Once they investigate this, they'll realise we've done nothing wrong. I will not lose my younger brother.'

Helen looked at Elliot, put her hand on his back and nodded. 'I agree. I'm sorry Jean Claude. This has gone too far and become too dangerous. Let's go to the police and clear this up.'

62

France – Present Day + 8 (Friday)

Elliot made his way by taxi to the Fourth Arrondissement. Helen joined him, but the others didn't. The gunshot wound still need to be dealt with. He hoped the police would have a medical kit. He was nervous about going to the police, and prayed they would believe him. It was the only way he could clear things up with the social worker and stop Toby from being adopted. The idea of never being able to see his brother again gave a knot in his stomach. Although it was the early hours of the morning, he tried calling Angela. She answered after a few rings.

'Angela, hi. Before you say anything, I can completely explain. Helen and I...'

'Elliot, how can you explain? You're wanted in connection with several murders. I've tried, God knows I've tried. There's no helping you. What am I supposed to do?'

'Just stop Toby from being adopted. Please. I'm coming back to take care of it' said Elliot, close to being tearful. 'It is not my fault. People have been chasing after us.'

'Sorry, Elliot. It's out of my hands. It is never your fault. You need to take responsibility and running from the police is not exactly being responsible.'

He hadn't slept and his brain wasn't functioning particularly well. However, the stress of helplessness and sleep deprivation made him boil in anger.

'No! I'm not going to let them' he shouted, kicking a public bench on the footpath. 'I'll do whatever it takes... whatever it takes.'

'Elliot, please calm down. I've told you, you need to control your aggression if you want to help yourself.'

'Please Angela... ' he pleaded. 'There must be something you can do.'

'I'll do my best, but first you need to sort out your mess. Look at it from the judge's position. A family that can look after him, give him the emotional and financial stability he needs, or Toby could live with a young man who's unable to hold down a job and currently wanted by the police in connection with murder. The odds are against us. I'm sorry.'

Elliot hung up the call and cursed. Helen looked at him, but refrained from saying anything and carried on walking in silence. He wanted to smash his mobile on the floor. Kick, shout or punch. Despite his urge to act out, he needed to stay out of trouble, especially if he wanted to sort out this mess. He could see the police station getting closer. They reached twenty-seven, Boulevard Bourdon and stood outside the police station. *This is it,* he thought and took in a deep breath to mentally prepare himself. Elliot stepped up to the automatic door and it slid wide open, inviting him in to come clean.

The entrance opened up to a small reception room with a desk, semi-protecting the officer behind it by a mid-height transparent screen. There were a few chairs along one side that seemed better suited to being in a school than a police station. Behind the desk, a plump officer sat in his chair, feet up on the table, with his head lent to one side as he slept. Elliot assumed from the officer's noisy breathing that he had a cold.

'Excuse moi' said Elliot.

The sleeping officer's eyes opened up suddenly and put his legs to the floor, trying to give the impression that he was just "resting his eyes", but it was obvious from his dazed look that he'd been asleep.

'We're here to report a crime' said Helen.

The officer looked up to see two tired foreigners. He lent forward and gave a lung filled yawn, half covered by one of his hands. He shuffled some papers that didn't need to be shuffled, then looked back at them.

'Bon soir. What seems to be le problem.'

Elliot spoke this time. He cleared his throat, although he was very nervous. 'There have been three murders, including one just now at the Notre Dame Cathedral. We've um, stumbled across something massive and need your help.'

Elliot and Helen told the policeman what they knew. The officer's English wasn't great, but understood the word murder and Notre Dame. He asked for their names and entered their details onto his computer. The officer told them to wait and he scuttled off. Elliot's gunshot wound had not healed and he was feeling faint. The office returned with another policeman. The taller of the two grabbed Elliot and pushed him up against the wall. He then proceeded to put Elliot in handcuffs.

'What are you doing' demanded Helen. 'We're here to report a murder. You've...you've got it all wrong.'

The other officer approached Helen and put her in cuffs too. At first she stepped back, but there was little she could do, but concede to being detained. Elliot tried to wriggle in protest, but it was no use.

'We're trying to help you catch a criminal' said Elliot, who tried to shout the words, but they came out as a murmur. He was struggling to stand.

'We av our hourders' replied the officer.

They started pushing Elliot towards another section of the station, when his legs lost balance, bringing him tumbling to the floor like a falling tree. He lay there unconscious.

63

France – Present Day + 8 (Friday)

Elliot awoke to find himself in a white holding cell, no bigger than a box room. No windows. No chairs. Just a bright light on the ceiling protected by chicken wire to stop it from being damaged by the cell's prisoners and a urine stained bed. Too solid to be passed off as orthopaedic. But then, he wasn't exactly staying at the Marriot and he didn't expect much. There was no sign of Helen. The last he could remember was her being handcuffed by the police. He assumed he was still in the police station and that Helen was also being held there.

His eyes were gritty and dry. As he sat up, he felt a pain in his lower back. He rubbed his hand over it to feel a thin layer of fabric, taped to him. *A bandage?* As he moved his arm back, he noticed a plaster in the middle of his arm. He pulled it off to see a small piercing. The police doctor must've stopped the bleeding and replaced the lost blood. He still felt weak, but as he came to, a million thoughts began to rush through his mind. Will Toby be ok? What if the police don't find Teo and his henchmen, will Elliot get the blame? He was the one in St Pauls at the time of the murder and again in the Notre Dame Cathedral. Where was Jean Claude, the only person who could vindicate him and Helen? Even if he didn't get charged, Teo and his men knew all about him and Helen. With Teo's tracking skills, would they ever be truly safe again? He doubted it very much, and just hoped the police would see reason. In a way, he was glad to be in the safe custody of the police. It was the first bit of peaceful sleep he'd had in a while.

He heard some footsteps on the solid floor outside his cell. The electric metal door to his cell him made a clunking sound and it started to open.

'Monsieur Hope, telephone call' said an officer.

Elliot didn't recognise the officer. He assumed the morning shift has started and, judging by the officer's tired eyes, it must still be early in the day.

'Who is it?'

'It is your lawyer.'

'My lawyer?'

'Oui.'

'I don't have a lawyer.'

'Shall I tell them you do not want to speak?'

Elliot wondered whether Helen or the British Museum had organised legal representation for him. It was unlikely, but any help would be appreciated.

'No, I'll come' he said, sitting up.

He swung his legs around the side of the bed, rubbed his eyes and stood up. The officer took him out of his cell and around the corner where a phone hung on the wall. The phone was off the dial and resting on top of a thin shelf that had pictures of missing and wanted people above it. Elliot drew the phone to his ear. He could hear some light breathing.

'Hello' he said.

'Help me' said a young sobbing voice.

He knew that voice from anywhere. But why would Toby be calling here and how did he know where Elliot was? His social worker wouldn't yet know. Pain surged through his body like an electrical current as he feared the worst and only possible logical conclusion.

'Where are you, Toby?'

He heard a shuffle as someone else came on the phone. 'You and your partner have proved to be quite a useful asset. It's a shame you've decided to give yourself in' said a deep male voice.

The voice was familiar. The taller man from Washington. It certainly sounded like him. Elliot thought back to the name Jean Claude mentioned. *David*!

'I didn't give myself in… I'm innocent. You know this. I came to clear up the truth. If you touch my brother, I'll, I'll kill you.'

'Mr Hope, you are not in a position to give orders' he said, laughing. 'As you've been so helpful on this journey, we can't let you stop now. If you play ball, your brother will be back safely, in the warm loving arms of his new family.'

'Why are you doing this?'

'We have our orders' replied David.

'Teo…your boss. You don't have to do this.'

David paused. 'Seems I am not the only one with intel. Not that it changes anything. You need to get back on track or else.'

'I can't' said Elliot. 'I'm in a police cell. It's not like they'll just let me go.'

'Pay attention to your senses, Mr Hope. You'll work something out. You're a resourceful boy.'

He hated being called a boy. *Condescending arse.* He wanted to punch David in the face. Despite his rage, he tried to remain calm.

David continued. 'Now for your own good, you need to pay attention. You'll be paid a visit by a Detective from London. If you or Helen tell him anything, Toby will be taking a swim in the river Seine. I hope he can float. We have arm bands made of brick, especially for him. You escaped us twice, Mr Hope. We promise we will not harm you, Toby or Helen, if and only if, you do as we say. Do I need to tell you what will happen if you don't?'

'No.'

'Good boy. Now go back to your cell and have some rest. You'll need it.'

The phone clicked and the dial tone went dead. Elliot stared at the wall of missing children. He didn't believe in God, but he was praying. Praying for a miracle that would undo all of this mess. If there was a way he could turn back time and make everything go away, he'd do it. He'd give his life for it. Because of his actions, his brother's life was in danger. He'd almost forgotten everything he'd been through...he just wanted Toby to be ok.

He was marched back to his matchbox of a cell. There was not much he could do. In a locked police cell and no way to escape. *Make a run for it now. No, bad idea.* Helen was still held in her cell. If he left, she would still tell them everything, as they had agreed. Unless the man on the phone had also spoken with her. He didn't know and couldn't take that risk. He had little time and lots to do. A plan was needed.

64

France – Present Day + 8 (Friday)

At lunchtime, the letter-box to Elliot's cell door slowly opened followed by the delivery of a less than edible meal on a less than hygienic plastic tray. Overcooked scrambled eggs, burnt toast and water, fresh from a warm tap. The sustenance was unfortunately needed. He played with his food, mentally preparing himself before taking each bite until it was finished. After his plate was empty, he got back to the day's entertainment of staring at a white washed wall with a few marks on it.

Faint footsteps came from behind the metal door again. They grew louder with every few steps, until the familiar clunking sound of the door caught Elliot's attention. He looked up to see the door slowly open followed by an officer standing in the doorway.

'Monsieur Hope...' said an officer. 'Someone is ere to see yieu.'

Elliot wondered whether his "lawyer" had come to help him escape. His nervous system went immediately into overdrive. He'd hoped it was a real lawyer, appointed by the state. The officer's English wasn't great and Elliot still wasn't entirely sure what he was doing there or who was waiting for him. Whoever it is, he couldn't say anything. Not now that Toby's life was in danger.

The officer escorted him into another white room, only moderately bigger than his cell. Its décor comprised a table, four chairs and recording equipment that looked more like a nineteen eighty's stereo player. He sat in a chair in the furthest corner and leant forward into the table, head in hand, apprehensively awaiting his visitor. The officer closed the door, leaving the only sound in the room to the persistent tick of a clock fixed to the wall.

Elliot's mind started following the tick of the clock like a metronome. Five minutes later came the sound of footsteps and a click of the electric door. Detective Henry Wrightman walked in, dressed as though he didn't have a mirror that morning. From his stubbled face and tired eyes, he looked like he'd slept in the spare cell next to Elliot. He wanted to tell him everything, just so that someone, someone on the right side of the law, would have his back. Unfortunately, he had to stay silent and had no choice. Initially, the detective didn't say anything. The silence was almost awkward. Henry just pulled out a chair, turned it around and sat on it backwards like a rebellious teenager or a jockey riding a horse. He wasn't sure if the approach was to try and relate to Elliot's youth. If it was the intention, it certainly had the opposite effect.

'Mr Elliot Hope' he said. 'You've caused quite a bit of trouble for us down at the Yard.'

'Detective, I assure you…'

'Wait, I haven't finished'… Henry said, hitting his fist on the table.

The detective's aggression was powerful, unexpected and intimidating. Elliot jumped back in his seat. *Definitely not trying to relate.*

'You're making my investigation very difficult, not to mention obstructing the course of justice. I told you and Helen not to venture far! Not only have you done the exact opposite, but you were at the scene of three murders, including one of my closest friends and partner.' He slammed his hand on the table again. 'I know you're involved. What are you hiding?'

Elliot could almost see steam emanating from Detective Wrightman's head. The detective's anger filled Elliot with anxious discomfort. There was no way of winning. If he told the truth, his brother would end up dead. If he stayed silent, he'd almost certainly be charged with murder and locked up, unable to save his brother who would still end up dead. The fatigue added to the mounting pressure. Arms shaking, lungs heavy, palms sweaty.

He took in a deep breath. He paused, unsure as to whether to say anything or not, then opened his mouth. 'It's not what you think. Helen and I... we, we're trying to help.'

'That's crap' said Henry, throwing a picture on the table of the shot victim spread out on the floor of St Paul's Cathedral, surrounded by a pool of blood. 'Why? Why do this? What's to gain?'

Elliot's eyes got a glimpse of the dead victim and his body convulsed in uncontrollable disgust. He quickly turned his head to face the wall. 'I... I didn't do anything. I swear.'

'That's not true. Blood with your DNA was found by a hidden vault... not far from the victim's body in St Pauls. How do you explain that? You weren't just in St Pauls. You were at the scene of the crime, the room where it all happened, despite what you said and I know...' Henry said pointing at him aggressively. 'I know you were there!'

He thought back to when he was in the underground crypt in St Pauls. *How could they have my blood?* Then he remembered he'd cut himself on the broken tile as he was on his knees, searching for the hidden safe. He closed his eyes as he realised he'd slipped up, but opened them again quickly in the hope that the Detective wouldn't notice his change in body language. The end result made him look as though he was blinking awkwardly. He was caught and he knew it. He couldn't think of anything that would help.

No reasonable explanation, other than the truth, which would get him out of prison. It was either tell the truth or stay silent. Elliot shrugged his shoulders.

Henry put another photo in front of him. He looked down to see a picture of a police officer covered in blood, stretched out in a dark stairway.

'What is this' asked Elliot.

'You tell me. My partner responded to a call out that you made for my attention' said Henry looking down at the table. 'It should've been me.'

'Officer Catchwell?'

'God damn right it is! I need answers, and you'd better start talking now' he shouted.

Elliot pushed his hands against his legs to try and stop them from shaking. His mind went into overdrive, but still had nothing to say that would get him out of this mess. He was desperate to speak, but just couldn't.

'I'm waiting' said Henry.

'I can't explain it. Not now. But, I will. I promise. Just give me time.'

'My guess… you and Helen found something in the vault. Something that you didn't want anyone to know about. When the tour guide found you, you killed her to stop anyone from discovering what you were up to. But why my partner?'

'That's not true' Elliot shot back. 'We didn't kill anyone.'

'If you can't help me, I can't help you. These crimes are all pointing at you. You're a murderer or an accomplice. If you weren't involved, you could've come clean when first questioned. All of this could've been avoided. Either way, it's your fault that my partner is dead! I'll find out exactly what's going on, believe me. In the meantime, I'm charging you with obstruction of justice and detaining you as a suspect in connection with multiple homicides' said Henry, who went on to read him his rights.

'You can't do this!'

'You don't give me much of a choice. I'm arranging for your immediate transfer back to the UK where you'll be tried for obstruction and a case will be made against you for the deaths. If you're found guilty, I will bury you. That's a promise.'

Elliot was speechless. Powerless. Hopeless. Stuck in a dark tunnel with no light at the end. Not even a glimmer. Nothing he could say would make a difference. He watched helplessly as Detective Wrightman stood up and left the interview room. He was escorted out and back to his cell. The door closed behind him, making its familiar clicking sound. He made his way along the corridor and noticed a small window on one of the holding cells. Helen was inside, holding her head with both hands. He felt guilty for her. He'd been strong up until now, but was losing control and didn't know what to do. A tear escaped from the corner of his eye. Fate had been decided for him.

65

France – Present Day + 8 (Friday)

Back in his cell, Elliot's mind was rushing like the air from a Boeing 747 jet turbine. He laid back on the firm narrow bed, kicking himself for not making up a story to the Detective in time. He still had no ideas that could realistically allow him to walk, without implicating Teo and David. *Those criminal, cold-hearted, bastards.* He felt anger, rage, fear. A culmination of intense emotions that made him want to hurt those that took his brother. He lashed out against the wall with his fist. A welcome anaesthetic to his overwhelming guilt.

A clunking sound came from the electric door. He looked up. He didn't hear any approaching footsteps and so whoever it was, must've walked quietly to the door. Elliot waited for someone to come in. Nothing. For a moment he thought he was imagining things. He made his way off the bed and approached the exit. He wondered whether it was Teo. Teo and his men were highly trained and probably capable of breaking into and taking over a small station like this. He touched the door gently with the tips of his fingers and opened it, bit at a time, trying to avoid making any creaking noises. He peered his head through the door way like a mouse checking for predators. No one. It didn't make sense. Elliot was unsure whether to make a run for it or not. It's unlikely that he could just walk out the front door. No doubt there were security cameras and policemen that would catch him. Plus, running would certainly implicate him further. His mind and body were so overwhelmed it made him second guess every thought.

An intermittent, high-pitch ring came from the corridor. The noise would get the attention of any nearby officers. Elliot knew the window of opportunity to leave his cell would reduce the longer the ring continued. He decided to investigate and stop the noise. If anyone was there, he could always run back to the room. *What's the worst that could happen?* If caught, he'd just explain the cell door was broken. It was the truth, after all and it wasn't as if things could get any worse. He put his head through the doorway again. *Clear.* He stepped through, one foot first, then the other. With his fingertips against the smooth white washed wall, he guided himself down the corridor. Feeling the solid wall in unfamiliar territory gave him a feeling of support.

The ringing grew louder. It was a telephone. He tiptoed around the L-shaped corridor, passing several cells. He peered into the cell that Helen had been in. Empty. He assumed she was being interviewed by Detective Wrightman. He prayed that she'd spoken with David on the phone and knew not to say anything. If she said anything, it could seriously harm his family. He needed to get her out too. Or at least contact her. *But how?* The humming sound coming from the corridor quickly brought his wandering mind back to the present moment and he continued on. On turning the corner, he saw the ringing phone, lifted it off the hook and left the phone on the side to stop the ringing. He was about to walk away when he thought the call could be his "lawyer" again. He needed to answer it, just in case. He held the phone up against his head, but said nothing.

'Mr Hope. Do exactly as we say and you'll get out of this police station unharmed' said an authoritative, but calm, female voice.

'Who is this?'

'No questions. There's no time. Just do as I say. At the end of the hallway is a door. Go into the room and open locker five on the right wall. Inside is a mobile phone. Go and get it.'

'Wait, what for?'

The phone line went dead. Faint footsteps made their way towards him. Someone was coming. No time to lose. He left the phone off the hook, then darted off to the door at the end of the hallway as quietly as possible. On approaching, it gave a clicking sound. Elliot looked up to see a camera staring at him in the face. *Whoever's doing this, must be using the security cameras.*

Elliot pushed the door open to be greeted by two benches in the middle of the room with a wall made of lockers on either side. He scanned across the right side...*locker 5, locker 5, locker 5*. 'Found it.' He opened the locker to see a wallet, mobile and some police clothes. The mobile lit up and moved along the surface as it vibrated. Number withheld. He drew the phone to his ear.

'Mr Hope. Welcome back' said the same female voice.

'What now?'

'Put on the police uniform. Quickly, you don't have much time. The shift change is going to happen in five minutes.'

Pressure. More pressure. If Elliot ever made it out of this mess, he'd make sure he had a holiday where the biggest pressure or decision was whether to swim in the outdoor pool, or go for a dip in the sea. He put on the uniform as quickly as he could. The woman on the phone may have been an expert at opening doors, but finding clothes that fit was not her forte. The navy trousers were way too big for him and the sleeves of his white shirt fell passed his hands. Fortunately, there was a belt to keep his trousers up, but he still looked like a kid in adult clothes.

He noticed a gun on the side and wondered whether he should bring it with him. *Bad idea.* He was pretty sure that carrying a gun was illegal and would just add to the growing list of reasons for sending him to prison. He put the phone to his ear.

'Done, now what?'

'Go back out the door. Take the first door on your left. It'll take you to the reception area. Keep your hat on, head down and walk slowly out the door. The officer in reception has just left to go to the toilet. Go now. A black car is outside waiting for you. Go.'

Elliot went to leave the locker-room, but stopped short when he remembered Helen was still in the station. The pressure and the pace of the last five minutes were all-consuming and he'd almost completely forgotten about her. He raised the phone to his ear.

'What about Helen?'

'Miss Phillips is being interviewed by Detective in charge. There's nothing we can do. Besides, we do not need her. You must come now.'

'No, I need her! I cannot do it without Helen. She has a vital knowledge of history which is has enabled us to get this far.'

Elliot thought for a moment whether it was a good idea to break Helen out of police custody. He was certain it was a criminal offense. However, he didn't want to do this alone and couldn't take the risk that she might tell the truth to the police. Toby's life was on the line. He needed to get her out.

'Listen, I'm not leaving without Helen. I can't do this by myself. I need her, you need her, and if she says anything to the police about you lot, it'll make everything much more difficult. Now fucking help me.'

There was a pause... If Elliot wasn't dealing with such psychos, social convention would almost make him feel awkward. The voice came back to the phone.

'Go back to locker 5. You'll see a gun. Pick it up. Quickly, you don't have much time.'

Elliot ran over to the locker and grabbed the pistol. 'What now?'

'Make your way back out to the corridor. When you turn the corner, take the third right. Do not move until I tell you. Understood?'

'Understood, but I'm not going to kill anyone.'

'You don't have to. Just do as I say.'

Elliot was shaking. If he was going to pull this off, he needed to calm down. Not that he knew what he was supposed to be doing, but he had a good guess. He stood by the locker-room door, awaiting the green light. He took a series of big, deep and much needed breaths of air. The door clicked open.

'Mr Hope, go through the door now. Quietly make your way to the end of the corridor and take a right. Go.'

He opened the door, much quicker this time, then jogged down the corridor with the phone by his side. He approached the corner.

'Wait' said the woman. 'There's someone coming.'

He didn't hear her speak. He turned right around the corner and carried on walking. Click. A door was opened in front of him. His body froze until he saw the navy blue blazer of an arm, protruding through the door way. He quickly back-stepped behind the corner of the corridor, desperate to avoid making any noise. A police officer stepped out of the door way and made his way towards Elliot. As each step grew louder, his heart pounded harder. He felt sick. He just wanted to throw the gun on the ground and run. He held onto a deep breath as though it was his last and froze, staying as still as he could. The officer stopped just before the turn of the corner, where Elliot's breath-holding face was beginning to turn red. He heard the swipe of a card and the click of a door opening. The officer stepped out of the corridor into a room just before the turn of the corner. As soon as the door closed, Elliot let out a big blow of used air and breathed heavily. He put the mobile back to his ear.

'Stay where you are' said the female voice. 'OK, the coast is clear. Go.'

Elliot turned right and jogged down the corridor. *Third door on the right.* He looked through the tiny porthole window on the metal door. Helen was in the interview room, being interrogated by Detective Wrightman.

66

France – Present Day + 8 (Friday)

'Miss Philips, you and Elliot have been on quite an adventure' said Henry.

Helen tried to gauge whether the Detective knew what they'd been up to. And, whether he'd already spoken to Elliot. Henry sat there staring at her. She could feel him observing her body language. His untrusting hazel eyes didn't move. Fixed onto her like a police dog fixes its teeth into its assailant.

'Why did you go to America, especially when I told you to stay put? You and Elliot are the only suspects.'

'It was my fault. Not Elliot's. We were on a big discovery for the Museum.'

'And so you found something, people got in your way so you decided to kill them?'

Helen shook her head. 'No, no that's not it at all.'

'No? Then why was your accomplice refusing to talk? Trying to protect you?'

Helen raised her eyebrows. She couldn't understand why Elliot had refused to co-operate. It was his decision to go to the police in the first place. It was him who wanted to come clean. She looked up at the security camera in the corner of the room, then leaned in.

'I assure you, it wasn't us. A man... he killed someone in Notre Dame Cathedral. A priest. There was nothing we could've done. Teo...'

An alarm interrupted her, ringing loudly in the interview room like a pulsing episode of tinnitus. Henry sat still, staring at her. After a minute of ringing, he stood up and looked through the small window. No one was around.

'Just a fire test or something ... don't move, I'll be back in a sec' said Henry.

The door locked shut as he left. Helen had no idea what was going on, but was relieved that she was no longer being grilled, even if it was temporary. Twenty seconds later, the metal door opened again. It wasn't Henry, but a police officer wearing baggy clothes. No, not an officer. Helen did a double take of him.

'Elliot, what the... what are you doing!?'

'Getting out of here.'

'You can't, you'll get in deep...'

Elliot interrupted. 'They have Toby. They have my brother and unless I get out of here and find the philosopher's stone, they'll kill him. I have no choice. If we say anything to the police, they'll kill him.'

'OK, let me think' she said.

'We don't have time to think. I understand if you want to stay here, but if you do, you can't say anything. Not a word, at least... at least until I have this thing sorted.'

'Elliot, they will kill you once you've finished helping them. You know who they are, what they look like and what they're capable of.'

'I know. I'll think of something. Right now, I don't have much of a choice. I have to try.'

Helen nodded. 'Dictum muem pactum.'

'Sorry?'

'I made a promise to look after you. I can't, in good conscience, let you do this on your own.'

She looked at him. He was shaky and sweating.

'I'm in' she said. 'There's only one problem. We're stuck in here and that persistent Detective's gonna come back any second!'

He put his hand on her shoulder. 'Leave that to me.'

Elliot walked up to the door, looked up and nodded at the camera in the corner of the room. The door clicked open. He did his usual peep and survey, then ran through the door way and into an adjoining cell. Helen followed. The door shut behind them and shortly after, the alarm stopped.

'Now what' asked Helen. 'We're stuck in this room. This is no better.'

'Just trust me' he said.

They waited behind the door, listening carefully to any sounds outside the room. Elliot kept the mobile close to his ear and awaited instructions. The tapping of footsteps passed the cell, then stopped outside the interview room. They heard the Detective swear, followed by the opening of the interview room door. A few seconds later, they heard the door shut, promptly followed by the loud banging of the Detective trying to get out of the locked room.

'Mr Hope' said the female voice from the phone. 'Take the hand cuffs from your jacket and put them on Miss Philips. Do it now, do it quickly.'

The camera in the room paid close attention as Elliot did as he was told.

'Good, now come out of the cell, take a right and go through the first door on your left. As I said before, you will be passing the reception area. The police officer is back at his desk. You will need to walk calmly, head down. Make sure Miss Philips' hands remain in front with the cuffs visible as you leave the building.'

He took a big, deep breath. 'Ok.'

He gestured for them to leave and to do so quietly. The corridor was clear. They reached the reception area where they were arrested last night. An officer was at the desk, reading his paper and not paying attention. A different guy from yesterday. Elliot walked as authoritatively as he could, back straight, with Helen in front. The exit was close. Three steps left, two...

'Attendez!' said the officer looking up from his desk and putting down his paper.

Elliot held his breath, as though staying silent and still would stop the officer from seeing them in plain sight. He wondered whether to run, or to carry on walking and pretend he never heard the officer. He stopped and stood still. He kept his face away from the officer for a couple of seconds longer than he should have, then turned around. Head down, trying to conceal himself under his hat. He cautiously walked up to the reception desk, in full flight or fight mode, ready to make a run for it if necessary. The officer gave him a "what are you doing" look. Elliot was about to run when the officer handed him a pen and tapped on a clip-board on the desk.

'Signer the register.'

Phew! Elliot acknowledged the officer with an emotionless smile, signed the register and nodded. He turned around and escorted Helen out of the building, walking as calmly as he could. A black BMW waited opposite the station at the side of the road. The backseat passenger door opened. Helen and Elliot jumped in and the car sped off as quick as it could.

67

France – Present Day + 9 (Saturday)

Henry swiped his electric pass several times, but the metal door just wouldn't open. From the outside, the thump of his fist was too quiet to alert the other police officers to come to his aid and so he kicked the metal door repeatedly. Even that was barely audible. *Bloody soundproofing.* Somehow Helen had disappeared. He prayed there'd been a mix up and that she was back in her cell. He stared through the door window. No one could hear him. No one was coming. He forgot he had his phone on him. He called the station. A few rings went by before someone answered.

'Bonjour' said a police officer.

'This is Detective Wrightman. I'm stuck in the interview room. I need you to get me out. Now!'

'One mineet, please detectife.'

A minute later, an officer marched over to the interview room, swiped his card and the door clicked open. The officer stared at his card, and gave a confused look as the door was working perfectly fine. Henry barged passed the officer and ran straight to Helen's cell. He looked though the small window on the heavy metal cell door, but couldn't see anyone. Henry had a small grain of hope that She was sitting in the corner of the cell, out of view from the window. He swiped his card, slung the door open and jumped inside. Empty. *Crap.* He ran over to Elliot's cell where he did the same thing. Empty.

'Sound the alarm' he shouted running through the corridor. 'Two people have escaped!'

Henry and the officers searched the station, but it was too late. They had disappeared. He finally had them, after all this time, energy and loss. And now, they'd managed to escape his grasp. Again. Angry was not the word to describe the fireball of energy that burned inside him. He lunged at a glass cabinet with his fist, leaving a trail of broken shards on the floor. The officer that helped him out of the interview room stood awkwardly, stiff as a board, with his back up against the wall, trying to avoid Henry's aggression.

He went to the bathroom, splashed some water on his face and stared at the aged man looking back at him in the mirror. *Too old for this.* He only had a couple of years until retirement, which he'd hoped would be much more quiet and peaceful than his earlier years. He may not get his wish, but he was damn sure he'd do everything he could to uphold the law and give peace to those he vowed to protect. He called the head office of the French police to speak with the inspector. Henry told him about the escape.

'Detective, I will ask my men to check the cameras and see how this happened.'

'Don't worry, I've already asked them to do it' said Henry. 'They're prepping the video feed as we speak.'

'Ok' replied the inspector, in a tone which made it obvious Henry should've sought his consent first. 'By the way, we found two bodies at the Notre Dame Cathedral. Not one, like the arresting officer said. It doesn't look good for your suspects.'

'Why?'

'They were seen going into the Cathedral. They weren't alone, but we don't yet know the people they were with. Not yet at least.'

'What happened?'

'A man of God was shot. Another priest was stabbed and left unclothed in a storage cupboard. Forensics are working on the details, but I will report back once I know more. We do know there were two footprints around the victim's body. One lady size six and a men's size ten… they match your suspects.'

'Thank you, inspector. I need everyone on high alert. It would be useful if I could use some of your men on this case.'

There was a pause for a few seconds. 'I will arrange what you need. These dangerous people need to be stopped.'

Henry was angry with himself. He was usually good at profiling a criminal. A skill acquired from his years on the force. But, he misjudged Elliot and Helen. He knew they were hiding something, but breaking out of police custody is big and didn't seem to fit their character. Trusting his gut had misguided his case and allowed further victims to die. If he hadn't trusted Helen and Elliot from the outset, maybe his partner would still be alive. He didn't understand why Helen said only one person was killed when the police found two victims. In any case, he knew now that they could not be trusted.

68

France – Present Day + 9 (Saturday)

As the car sped away from the Police Station, Elliot and Helen were relieved to see Chris driving and Jean Claude in the passenger's seat. Jean Claude explained how Teo's henchman, David, had contacted them and insisted they collect Elliot from outside the Police Station or Toby would never be seen again. Chris had no idea that they had been arrested and detained at the station.

'Well, thank you… both of you' said Elliot, staring out the window. 'It's nice to have support right now.'

Jean Claude leaned over and put his hand on Elliot. 'When I heard about it, I couldn't stand by and watch. Teo's misguided ways have caused more trouble than I can bear. My brother has died because of him, and I'll do everything I can to stop that from happening to someone else.'

Elliot was grateful to have his team back, but couldn't help thinking about the trouble he was now in. How could he not. After getting to grips with what had just happened, the first thing on Elliot's agenda was to get out of the oversized police uniform that made him look like a child in adult clothing. Apart from looking terrible, he stood out which was the last thing he needed. They drove several miles away from the police station and eventually pulled up outside a non-descript charity shop. Faded blue sign with worn timber around the door and windows. It looked pretty empty. They got out the car to see if they could find some clothes to help them blend in with the public. Chris picked up the bill, again. Elliot felt a bit guilty for allowing Chris to pay. He made a decision to pay Chris and Helen back for everything when he was more secure. Elliot hated money. Not because he didn't like to have it. But, because he wasn't good at saving and when he needed money for something and didn't have it, he felt disproportionately guilty for letting people down. Consequently, when people paid for him and he had no money, he felt shame and discomfort. He knew it was his problem and not a universal one, but it didn't stop it from hurting.

He changed straight into his second hand clothes. For a split second, he almost felt like a normal person again. He jumped back into the car to be greeted by a much needed hot chocolate. He welcomed the familiarity. It was about as much of it as he was going to get. The others were drinking their coffees that Jean Claude got from a nearby café.

'Thanks for the drink…I'll pay you back, I promise.'

Jean Claude raised an eye brow. 'Really, it's just a drink. Don't worry about it.'

He took a long gulp of his warm, sweet, chocolate and hazelnut liquid. The sugar worked its way through his body to give him the pick-me-up he so needed. As he leaned back into the car seat to get comfy, his ears tuned into the radio. It was in English. A Ted talk on the conflict in the Gaza Strip and the ongoing struggle between Palestine and Israel. The bloodshed that has taken place on those grounds in the name of the almighty.

'If Teo was able to, he'd destroy Palestine' said Elliot. 'Think about it. As Jean Claude's said, Teo has sworn revenge against the Palestinian people after what they did to his family. If he gets hold of the philosopher's stone, he'd be able to wipe them out. If we do his dirty work, we'd be aiding the death of thousands of innocent people.'

'I don't think that's right' said Helen. 'I doubt the philosopher's stone actually exists. I know of no scientific evidence to suggest it. Our priority needs to be to get your brother to safety.'

'I agree' said Chris. 'We need to make sure Toby's ok first. The philosopher's stone is nothing more than a spiritual placebo. But, it does have some place in history.'

Chris explained to Jean Claude how Aristotle, the teacher of Alexander the Great, was an alchemist and was believed to have created the philosopher's stone. Elliot thought it would certainly explain how Alexander the Great never lost a single battle, even though he took over the empire from the inexperienced age of sixteen.

It didn't take long until Elliot's attention was brought back to the present. He had no idea where Toby was kept and so any rescue attempt was pointless. It was not like he could call the police for help. The only way to save his brother was to find the philosopher's stone.

'Erm, guys' said Elliot. 'One small problem. The Marie Bell is no longer in the Notre Dame Cathedral. It was destroyed during the French Revolution in the seventeen hundreds. We've no way of knowing what the bell had to do with this. We're completely and utterly stuck.'

The car went silent for a few minutes as they searched the recesses of their minds for an answer. Jean Claude pulled his finger from over his mouth and then clicked his finger.

'I have an idea… the Bibliotheque Nationale de France is the country's biggest library, holding the repository of all that is published in France. It has rare and old accounts of Parisian history. Much of it isn't available anywhere else in the world. It's no guarantee, but worth a visit.'

'Agreed' said Chris. 'It could be a good place to start. You know they also hold one of the largest collections of Ancient Greek manuscripts.'

Elliot nodded with dampened enthusiasm. 'Did anyone bring their library card?'

He thought back to his graduate degree and his thesis on Ancient Greek philosophers. Aristotle, one of his favourites, wrote hundreds and hundreds of manuscripts, covering many intellectual subjects used and adapted by some of the greatest thinkers on the planet. And to think, scholars believe only twenty-five percent of his work survived. The rest, destroyed in the Great Library of Alexandria fire. If only the information was retained. Three quarters of the work of one of the brightest minds in the world, burnt in a careless accident in forty-eight BC. Elliot wondered what other advances would have been made if the world had access to all those manuscripts.

'Let's go check out the library then' said Elliot.

69

Bibliotheque Nationale de France – Present Day + 10 (Sunday)

Elliot, Helen, Chris and Jean Claude walked into the circular, Olympic-pool sized library room. Amongst the maze of desks were academics researching, students nervously preparing for exams and tourists trying to take photos without anyone noticing. Shelves surrounded the echoing room as tall as the Great Wall of China, each filled with books from top to bottom. They made their way to a desk in the middle, where the light was shining from a huge oval window in the middle of the ceiling of the dome shaped room. They each went off and searched for any books they could find on the Marie Bell or the Notre Dame Cathedral.

Elliot returned back to the desk and added to the already mounting pile of old books. He noticed a young man, two desks away, looking over at their table. The guy was awkwardly sat, wearing a tartan red shirt and stamping a pile of books. Ginger, glasses and unthreatening. Slightly nerdy. As soon as he saw Elliot staring back, the guy turned away and continued stamping his books. He dismissed it and sat down on a rigid wooden stool, picked up the first hardback in front of him and got stuck in. The others were already sitting down, consuming their books like a plate of unwanted brussel sprouts. A reluctant persistence. Helen and Chris worked their way through any English books they could find. Jean Claude spoke French fairly well and so he made a start on the French ones, which was the majority of them. Elliot scanned through his book, searching for anything to do with the bells in the Cathedral. There were a few references to the bell being destroyed, but nothing specific about what the Marie Bell looked like.

Elliot closed his book and dropped it to the floor. 'This is going to be like trying to find a needle in a haystack.'

'I agree, but we've got no other leads' replied Jean Claude, raising his head and pushing back the glasses from the tip of his nose.

Chris and Helen both nodded, then nestled their heads back into the pages in front of them. Elliot wasn't hopeful, but had to at least try to find something that would help him find the Philosopher's Stone. After a few hours of speed searching, the books on the desk reduced, but not by much. There was still a lot of information left to work through. Elliot's eyes were beginning to dry out. He rubbed them to spread what moisture he could, yawned, then stretched his arms out.

He saw the ginger guy from a few desks away, stand up. He walked towards them in his casual, non-offensive, attire then in a nervous sharp movement walked away. A few seconds later, he double backed on himself and continued to their desk. Elliot assumed from his look and name badge that he worked in the library. Whoever he was, the spectacled ginger-nut, was not one of Teo's men. He stood next to Helen.

'Erm, sorry to disturb you madam' he said in a broken English accent.

He looked straight at Helen who had her head deep into a thick book. She tilted her head up at the skinny man and just stared with an unfriendly frown.

'I heard you speaking English. I couldn't help but notice you seem to be looking for something' he said nervously smiling. 'Is there anything in particular... I mean erm, that you're looking for?'

It was obvious the librarian fancied Helen. He didn't attempt to make eye contact with anyone else. Helen looked back.

'No' she said curtly, then continued reading.

The guy quickly walked away. Elliot felt for him. Whilst he had his fair share of attention, it wasn't always that way and he knew how hard it can be to approach a random stranger. The first few times can be terrifying. Rejection is an inherent part of life, but that doesn't make it any easier. And for the unconfident, a knock is just another affirmation to the existing false belief that they're not good enough to be accepted, loved or worthy of the person they approach. Elliot knew it was rubbish. Of course it was. People tend to be attracted to confidence, even though it doesn't mean it would lead to a healthy relationship.

'Sorry guys' said Helen. 'As much as I didn't want to be rude, I don't have time for a library romance. Greater things are at stake!'

'The tone was a bit cold' replied Chris.

Elliot and Jean Claude shrugged their shoulders. Chris' mobile began to vibrate. Number withheld. He answered the call, paused for a few seconds, then held his hand out for Elliot to take the phone.

He pulled the phone to his ear. 'Who is this?'

'Questions are unimportant' said a deep male voice. 'All you need to know is that we have your brother, and if you don't continue to do as we tell you, his health will be at risk.'

The all familiar feeling of helplessness and rage re-emerged into the pit of his stomach. Despite wanting to shout a million profanities and threats, he bit his lip. 'What do you want?'

'Nothing more than you're already doing. For now, at least. Consider Toby as insurance. Just keep on the trail and update us every three hours. But Elliot... if you go off the grid or any of you try to cross me, Toby dies.'

The line went dead. Elliot slid the phone across the desk towards Chris and just stared into space, trying not to well up. He looked pale, as though he'd just caught the flu. Left with little choice, they all got back to work, sifting through the books, one by one.

As the sun fell, the light from the beautiful ceiling windows cascaded, leaving shadows around the sides of the room. There were still many books to search through and Elliot's brain was suffering. They turned the lamps on to help with their reading. Chris went away then came back with drinks and snacks. Elliot wasn't normally self-conscious when it came to eating, but he felt like everyone in the library was watching him every time he ate a crisp.

Jean Claude put a book down and sighed. 'This isn't working... there's nothing here. All these books were written after the bell was destroyed. We need something from the period.'

'I agree' said Helen. 'But none of these books are that old. Anything like that would need to be carefully preserved using specialist equipment. It wouldn't be on display for the public.'

Helen perked up after her coffee and went off to stretch her legs. She walked over to the religious studies section to see if she could find anything dating back to the pre-eighteen hundreds, before the bell was melted down and destroyed. There were hundreds of books, lining several floor to ceiling bookcases. She worked her way from the top shelf down to the bottom, scanning left to right and now bending down awkwardly. There was nothing that offered any assistance. Helen was beginning to lose hope. She stood up to see the geeky ginger librarian putting books away. As much as she felt bad for being curt, she needed his help. Helen approached him and asked him if the library had any books that might contain a description of the Marie Bell. The young man stepped back timidly, then gave a gawky smile.

'I doubt any books will contain a description of the bell' he said.

He noticed the immediate disappointment in Helen's face. 'But' he said, leaving a pause. 'We er, may have some old manuscripts that are kept in the preservation safe here. They are very old, but not open to the public.'

'Is there any way I can get access to them, please' she said, smiling. 'I work in a museum and am professionally trained at handling historical documents.'

'You can't. I can. I guess I could search the records. I'd need to submit a request form to make an inspection. It could be ready for inspection in a few days' he said.

'Please' replied Helen, putting her hand on his shoulder. 'Is there any way I could see them today. It's very urgent.'

The librarian giggled uncomfortably and rubbed the material on his shirt. 'Erm, well, I might be able to arrange a visit, but I'm not supposed to be there without proper authorisation and so we'll have to be quick... and quiet.'

'Thank you so much. That would be perfect.'

70

Paris – Present Day + 10 (Sunday)

Toby was kept prisoner in a dim, artificially lit, soundproof room. No furniture, no windows, no escape. He lay there frightened, in the foetal position on a dirty old mattress on the floor. His lungs were tired from distressed heavy breathing. Elliot's little brother had exhausted himself from crying so much, that he had no energy left to give other than a gentle sob. He didn't understand where he was or what was happening.

He could see a thin line of light under the door from the lit room behind it. He noticed a shadow moving along the white line until it centred itself at the door. A clank of a turning lock later and the door opened to reveal the shadow of a large man, more than twice the height of Toby. Not that it was difficult to be twice the size of an eight-year-old. The intimidating shadow stepped into the room. Toby's body seized up.

'You need to eat' said David, placing a tray of uninteresting food on the floor next to the mattress.

'I'm not hungry' said Toby. 'I wanna go home.'

'And you will. But you need to do exactly what I say, first. If you don't, you'll never go home.'

Toby sobbed. He held his hands over his head and arms in front of his face as he tried to hide from the unbearable fear in his prison cell. Shortly afterwards, David left the room and locked the door behind him, leaving Toby to himself.

In the next room, David joined Abrafo and Marco in the kitchen. They all sat there next to a battered faux mahogany table, covered in stains with an ashtray, a bottle of cheap whisky and glasses on its surface. Marco played with his knife, spinning its sharpest point on the table, leaving an indent with plastic and cork shavings on the table. He was bored of waiting and wanted to take out Elliot and Helen. Get it over with already. They'd been allowed to have a free reign for too long now.

'Ow long have we gotta wait' said Marco.

'Not long now' said David. 'Be patient. Not long and we'll be smoking cigars on a tropical island. For now, our employer wants us to keep track of Elliot and Helen. They're playing ball at the moment, but if they go astray, then you can do what you want with them.'

Marco grinned as he used his knife to carve a line in the table.

71

Bibliotheque Nationale de France – Present Day + 10 (Sunday)

The librarian took Helen into an air-controlled room on the eastern corner of the building. She sat down against one of the two microfiche computers pitched up by the wall. As the librarian went off behind her into a sea of bookshelves, she stared at the clock on the wall. Time was getting on and they'd have to update Toby's captors soon. She felt guilty for getting him involved in this mess. If she'd left the drawings for St Paul's Cathedral alone, Elliot and Toby would be far away from any danger.

The librarian came back with four parchments of rolled-up, tea stained, paper that were stored in transparent plastic bags. She could tell they were hundreds of years old. The librarian sat down and rolled one out. He held out his hand and introduced himself as Edward.

'Helen' she replied, extending her hand and shaking his.

'They didn't have publishing houses and printers in the sixteen hundreds. Instead, cathedrals and monasteries would have their own scribes copy documents. Some of these scribes had meticulous attention to detail, which has helped to retain much of our history from the medieval periods.'

'But not before then' said Helen.

'No. During the medieval period, the Church made a point of destroying any records from schools that were considered unholy. It's only because of the Arab world that we have records of the ancient Greek universities.'

They worked their way through the first three manuscripts, unravelling one at a time and placing each one under the light of the microfiche. The writing was blotchy on each parchment and difficult to read, even once projected onto the screen in front of them. The silence in the room made the whirring of the projector stand out which Helen found slightly distracting. They scanned through the first three documents, but found nothing. The librarian unravelled the last one. It was headed "Cloches Saintes de Notre Dame" which Helen translated as the Holy Bells of Notre Dame. Her hope was beginning to increase. The librarian laid the parchment out flat, again, careful not to cause any damage. It was barely legible, even worse than the others, dark brown and torn in places. Although parts of the script could not be read, it appeared to detail how repairs were carried out to the Notre Dame bells in the sixteen hundreds. At the bottom of the script was a description of the Marie Bell. The scribe had even copied the pattern from the bell with intricate detail. Helen noticed it was similar, if not the same, as the Emmanuelle Bell still in the Cathedral. This was definitely the Emmanuelle Bell's sibling. Helen could just about read the next paragraph.

'Is there any way we can make this clearer' she asked.

'Sure' said the librarian, adjusting the focus on the microfiche screen, revealing Latin script.

'This is it!'

She took a copy of the inscription, kissed Edward on the cheek and ran to the others.

72

Bibliotheque Nationale de France – Present Day + 10 (Sunday)

Helen rushed back to the main library hall. She found the rest of the team looking deflated, exhausted and surrounded by books. Elliot sat in his chair reading. His elbow was placed on the table, palm upwards, supporting his face and squishing his cheek as he used his arm for support. A small green lamp stood on the desk next to him, giving an unenthusiastic amount of light over his reading. He looked up to see Helen with a big smile on her face.

'Did you get lucky with that guy' asked Elliot.

'Erm, sort of' replied Helen.

Elliot raised his eyebrows and smirked.

'Not like that' she said, waving a piece of paper. 'I've got it. I've got an inscription from the Marie Bell.'

She placed the printed copy down on the desk, directly beneath the lamp. The Latin inscription read:

“**Pl**e**riq**ue **hom**in**es** per metum potius **quam** **re**v**e**r**enti**a**m** **aptum** na**t**um
m**o**ver**i** , et non f**a**ce**re** m**alu**m propter **p**oenam po**t**ius **q**uam pro**p**ter
a**ffert** foed**it**as

Facere **quod** in n**o**bi**s** est , **n**on **es**t **i**n pol**t**e**s**t**a**te nos**tr**a **ut** f**a**c**ia**m**us**n**a**."

'Any idea what it means' she asked, looking at Elliot.

Elliot read it over a few times. Some of the faded wording made it difficult to interpret. He wrote down the translation, then put it under the light. The others leaned in to read it:

"The generality of men are naturally suited to be swayed by fear rather than reverence, and to refrain from evil rather because of the punishment it brings than because of its own foulness

What lies in our power to do, lies in our power not to do."

'I know this from somewhere' said Chris.

'I'm not surprised' replied Elliot. 'It's an old and very famous principle from the Ancient Greek philosopher, Aristotle. The question is, why was it on the Marie Bell? Particularly as the church did everything it could to destroy the knowledge of the Ancient Greeks.'

'What does the principle mean' said Jean Claude.

'It means that people tend to do the right thing because bad behaviour has consequences. Not because they are naturally driven to be moral' said Elliot.

'An interesting point, but why was it on the bell? There must be more to it' said Helen.

Elliot was racking his brain. Although he was familiar with Aristotle's ideas, he couldn't piece together the clue in front of him. *What did it mean?* Maybe it didn't have a hidden meaning. If this wasn't the clue they were looking for, he had no idea where else to go. *The police perhaps? No, too dangerous. There has to be something else.* Chris picked up the photocopy of the Latin message.

'Why are some letters in one font, and some are in another' asked Chris.

'That's it' said Elliot. 'It's steganography.'
'What' said Jean Claude.
'You know. Hiding a message in plain sight.'

He explained that sometimes the Rosicrucian Order would send hidden messages using one of the earliest forms of cryptography. One where a secret code was incorporated into a seemingly innocent passage of words. Obvious and yet discrete. Every five letters would be highlighted in a certain way. Some letters would be written using one font type (font A), others would be written in another font (font B). Each five letter pattern would correspond to the letter that was being hidden. Elliot got out a pen and paper. He wrote the Latin alphabet, and underneath each letter, drew the pattern he used at school. It was a long shot, but he had no other ideas.

A	B	C	D	E	F	G	H
AAAAA	AAAAB	AAABA	AAABB	AABAA	AABAB	AABBA	AABBB
I-J	K	L	M	N	O	P	Q
ABAAA	ABAAB	ABABA	ABABB	ABBAA	ABBAB	ABBBA	ABBBB
R	S	T	U-V	W	X	Y	Z
BAAAA	BAAAB	BAABA	BAABB	BABAA	BABAB	BABBA	BABBB

Elliot looked at the first two words: **Pl**e**riq**ue **hominess**. The first five letters were ordered in font types BAABA. He looked at his chart and saw it was the letter "T." Elliot then did the same with the next five letters which were ordered in fonts BAABB, giving the letter "U."

'Elliot, I think you're onto something' said Helen, nudging her shoulder against his. 'Thank God you're here.'
'As if' he said. 'It is I who wouldn't be able to do this without all of you.'

It was late and the library was nearly empty. Elliot wrote out the remainder of the message. He smiled to himself, wrote the translation underneath the passage and gave it to Helen.

CHAPTER 72

"Tuta ab oculis Akhatan, Reginam Civitatum
Protected by the eyes of Akhatan, Queen of the Cities"

'Akhatan' said Jean Claude. 'I've heard of that.'

'Akhatan's the name for a monotheistic pharaoh, protector of a holy city in Egypt' said Chris. He scratched his chin and frowned. 'Holy crap.'

'What is it' asked Helen.

'This message' said Chris, rubbing his head. 'This is talking about the Copper Scroll.'

Elliot gave a blank expression. Chris told them that not far from Jerusalem, near the Dead Sea, ancient scripts where found during several excavations. These decayed historic records were known as the Dead Sea Scrolls. Many of the scriptures were copies of the Old Testament, although they were either incomplete or revised versions. Almost as if someone was trying to re-write the law of God. The most interesting scroll found was known as the Copper Scroll. A treasure map with coded instructions on how to find riches beyond comprehension. Based on research by scholars, it's believed the map shows the hiding place of around twenty-six tons of gold and sixty-five tons of silver worth over one and a half billion pounds. Not to mention all the other valuable artefacts which will be priceless. A wealth that has been sought after by many treasure hunters, archaeologists and historians.

'Some believe that the treasure was a collection of the Judaic wealth' said Chris. 'But this... this message is proof, proof that it's not the case.'

'I don't follow' said Elliot.

'The Copper Scroll was written in an ancient dialect. It's been an unsolved mystery amongst scholars, but at the end of each of the first ten sentences, there is an Ancient Greek letter. It can't be a coincidence that the first seven of these Greek letters spell the name of the pharaoh, Akhatan. I could be wrong, but I think the Copper Scroll leads to the treasure of Alexander the Great. When Alexander the Great died, it is rumoured that the reason his army disbanded was because his source of wealth disappeared. But this. The timing, language used and location fit. It all fits!'

'And the Copper Scroll has directions to the treasure… and presumably the philosopher's stone' said Jean Claude. 'Then we know how to get there. What are we waiting for…let's go.'

'Erm, I'm afraid it's not that simple' replied Chris. 'The clues on the scroll were personal to the writer. They're not easy to interpret. Many people have spent their entire lives looking for the treasure. No one has been successful.'

'Maybe this message can help us' said Elliot, feeling hopeful that they'd made progress. 'Someone deliberately left these clues behind. If the signs on the bell and the Copper Scroll are connected, then maybe both of them are needed together to locate the treasure. It must be obtainable.'

'True', said Helen. 'But let's not get a head of ourselves…we don't even know if the gold is still there. For all we know it could have been taken by bandits or grave robbers.'

Elliot wouldn't believe the treasure and the stone were lost. He couldn't. He needed the stone to rescue his brother. It was the only key to Toby's safe return. He noticed the lights go out in the corner of the room. The library was beginning to close and the few visitors left were making their way to the exit. He had an idea of where the treasure might be. But first, he needed somewhere quiet to continue working.

73

Paris – Present Day + 10 (Sunday)

As an escaped fugitive, Elliot needed to keep a low profile, away from the public eye. It was a warm night and they managed to find a local park to continue analysing their latest find. They walked to the centre of the public gardens, away from the active Parisian roads. Elliot stopped at a wooden picnic table directly underneath a lamppost. They all sat around the table, with the translation and cryptic steganographical message placed in the middle of them. The park was pretty quiet. The only movement was the slight wave of leafy trees around them. Elliot started tapping on the table to the rhythm of his favourite band, softly, but enough to annoy Helen so he stopped.

'So, according to the Copper Scroll, in which country is this gold supposed to be located' asked Helen.

'This is the point' said Chris. 'No one knows for sure. There are legends that say Akhatan was a keeper of a Holy City in Jordan. However, some scholars believe the treasure is in Jerusalum.'

'If the Copper Scroll was found in Jerusalum, surely that's the place to start' said Helen.

'I don't know about that. What do we know about history' said Elliot. 'Alexander the Great was a ruler of Egypt as well as most of the known world. If he hid his accumulated wealth, it could be in a number of places.'

'Yes, but this hidden message tells us it's with Akhatan, the Queen of the Cities' said Jean Claude.

'Actually, it doesn't' said Elliot.

'Er, what do you mean? Yes it does.'

'I think, what it's trying to say, is that Akhatan is protector of the Queen of the Cities. Not that Akhatan is the Queen of the Cities. Besides, Akhatan was a king, not a queen.'

'and Queen of the Cities' said Chris. 'is another name for...'

'Byzantium' said Elliot, jumping in. 'The Ancient Greek city and stronghold for almost a millennium.'

'Exactly' said Chris.

Elliot explained that Byzantium was an enormous Ancient Greek city. Taken over by the Romans and turned into Constantinople and then again by the Ottomman empire which was then turned into the Muslim city of Istanbul. They realise that they need to go to Turkey, but given how many times the great city has changed hands, there is a good chance the treasure will be gone.

Istanbul with all its ancient buildings, would have many places that Alexander the Great could hide his wealth. *But where to start?* Elliot thought about the police being after him and how border controls are going to be tight if not impossible to get through.

'So wait, let me get this straight' said Helen. 'You're saying the treasure is in Istanbul.'

Chris and Elliot both nodded.

'Guys' said Elliot. 'We have no way of getting to Istanbul. Helen and I have just escaped from a police station. The police will have our details at every airport, border control and harbour. We'll get caught if we try to leave France.'

Jean Claude gave a self-confident, self-satisfied smile. 'Leave that to me.'

74

France – Present Day + 11 (Monday)

Within a few hours, Elliot was speeding down the motorway to Cannes where Jean Claude's exploration boat was in port. It wasn't the quickest method of travelling, but it would get them to Turkey and it was the best chance of getting there under the police radar. He drove in the fast lane the entire journey. It was the first time he'd driven in France. A nerve wracking experience being on the opposite side of the road. Driving at night added to this anxiety. But with the police after him and Toby in danger, he had to face his fear and do it anyway.

Helen and Chris slept in the back of the car, both exhausted from being awake all night. Elliot put some relaxing music on, ensuring it wasn't too loud to wake them, but wasn't too quiet for him to enjoy. Jean Claude sat there, staring out the window with his arm up on the side. The only visibility was from the light from the lampposts zooming past them, one after the other.

'You're not sleeping' said Elliot.

Jean Claude took a long breath, scratched his nose, then looked at his watch and slowly let out the air from his lungs. 'No...lots to process.'

'Everything ok?'

'Yeah, just thinking about what happened in the Cathedral.'

'Teo is dangerous. Thank God you saved us' said Elliot.

'No, that's not what I meant. My epileptic fits have been getting more and more frequent. It scares me.'

'Is there a cure?'

'Medication and a healthy lifestyle can help a bit, but not when you're at my stage. Every time I have a seizure, it causes damage to my brain. Slowly, but surely. Before I know it…' he said, pausing… 'I'll be in a vegetative state, unable to string a sentence together.'

Elliot was indigenous to anxiety, but what Jean Claude was going through was a different breed of pain. Knowing he was dying and nothing he could do about it. Watching his body gradually eat itself away. It must be tough.

Jean Claude sighed. 'Could you imagine a world where there was no illness? Where hunger was non-existent. Poverty, a thing of the past.'

Elliot was conscious not to fantasize on the impossible. It made the unavoidable even more painful. Instead he just nodded and said 'if only.'

'Indeed' said Jean Claude. 'Governments try to help, but they only preserve the status quo.' Jean Claude laughed to himself. 'So much for survival of the fittest.'

'How so?'

'Charles Darwin's theory of evolution. The idea that the strongest are able to adapt to their surroundings. The weaker species cannot adapt and die out. The survival of the fittest. But most governments act as a nanny state, looking after everyone. Free hospitals or compulsory health insurance, government hand-outs and schemes to aid the helpless. The fit survive, but so do the weak.'

'That's a good thing, isn't it' said Elliot.

'Is it' Jean Claude shot back. 'The weaker are susceptible to viruses, illnesses and disabilities. If these weaker gene pools didn't exist, the strong would succeed the weaker. It would reduce, if not eliminate, most viruses.'

'Erm, with respect Jean Claude, but don't you have a condition.'

'I do' he said giving an emotionless smile. 'And I'd do anything to wipe it off the face of the earth.

Elliot could see the emotional and physical discomfort that Jean Claude was suffering from. It was understandable that he'd want to cure all illnesses. Anyone would if they could, but when you're in the middle of the trenches yourself, the idea of peace becomes desperate. An obsession, almost. Still, there was no way one could remove all illness, ailments and disabilities at the same time. It was impossible.

He brought his attention back to the car. Other than the relaxing music on the radio and the light noise of the car's engine, the car was silent. He checked the SatNav. It was French, but he could follow the arrow on the map. Two hours until they arrive. They were making good headway and should be in Cannes by sunrise.

75

Police Station, Paris – Present Day + 11 (Monday)

Henry checked his watch. Three am. He couldn't sleep. It wasn't his forte and with the killers of his partner on the loose, he'd rather sacrifice sleep for results. He knew it was counter-productive. He needed sleep to be more effective during the day. But, he wanted to continue working anyway.

After putting out a reward for information on Elliot and Helen, Henry searched the CCTV recordings of the police station cameras to see how they were able to escape from their cells. From the footage, it looked like they both just walked straight out. The recording showed Elliot had a phone with him at all times. It looked like someone was guiding him, giving him instructions. He knew when a room was clear and when it wasn't. *A mole in the police?* Henry couldn't explain how they managed to open the doors or avoid getting caught. No matter how they did it, they weren't doing it alone. The only information Helen gave was a name. Teo. *Who is Teo?*

A female officer walked into the security recording room. She put a file, a croissant and a coffee on the desk next to the recording equipment.

'What's this?'

'A croissant.'

'No, I mean the file.'

'Ah, the Inspector asked me to bring this to you' she said with a soft French accent.

Henry opened the file. The first page read "CLASSIFIED." He took a sip of his coffee and made a facial expression as though he'd bitten into a lemon. Strong coffee. Too strong. At least it should keep him awake. He was feeling very tired. He turned the next page. At the top was a picture of an olive skinned man with dark hair. Handsome, if not a little intimidating. Underneath the photo was the name, Teo Brecher. Forty-two year old, Israeli born combatant and wanted by his Government. Ex-Mossad special forces soldier. Trained in arm to arm combat, explosives, weaponry, espionage. With several medals in numerous wars, he was one hard ass. Henry read on to see that Teo was kicked out of the Mosad for killing an innocent civilian, Mr Nirek Aspinel. *This doesn't look good.* The file went on to explain that Teo was highly dangerous and should not be approached alone.

He sent an email to the research team at his station in England. He needed to find out what Helen and Elliot were up to, how Teo Brecher was involved and whether he was the reason they managed to escape their police cells. He asked for all known associates of each of them.

He got out of his chair and made his way to a glass cabinet in the corner, containing several bottles of whisky, vodka and cognac. His nerves were playing up. A drink would help. *Only a small one.* He lifted a bottle of whisky, twisted the cap off and sniffed it. A peated, single malt, eighteen years. He loved the smoky flavours. His hand was shaking. As he stared into the glass cabinet, he saw himself holding the bottle. Always fighting the demon. He put the bottle away, sat back down and leaned into the desk where his next report was laying. It was one he wanted to avoid. The report on the death of his partner, PC James Catchwell. Henry built an immunity to seeing violence, but when it was harm inflicted on those he cared about, he still very much felt the emotional pain. He counted in his head to three and digested the information in front of him. There was no evidence that Helen and Elliot were there. The only link connecting them to his friend was that Helen had asked him to come. But she didn't ask him to go. She asked Henry to go to London Bridge where his partner was killed. Maybe Helen, Elliot and Teo were conspiring to kill Henry, to get him off their tail.

His left thigh began to vibrate. *Who could be calling at this hour?* He pulled out his phone to see the first few digits. *Scotland Yard.* He pressed answer and held the phone to his ear.

'Wrightman speaking.'

'Henry, it's Louise.'

Louise Allan was one of the smartest researchers on the force. Too clever to be working where she was. There was a part of him that was attracted to her kindness and innocence, but he'd never make a move. It was too unprofessional and aside from the fear of being rejected, she was at least ten years his junior.

'Why aren't you sleeping? It's late' he said.

'Why aren't you?'

'Good point. I'm working on PC Catchwell's case…I'm looking, but I can't find anything that helps.'

'Well, you'll like me then. I've done a background check on people that Helen and Elliot visited recently.'

'What have you got?'

'They visited a man called Christopher James Seacrest. He works at the National Georgraphic Museum in Washington, specialising in Ancient Greece.'

'So that's where they were. Do we know what they were doing?'

'No, not yet' replied Louise. 'I'm still working on that. However, I've checked the online border control website and Mr Seacrest flew to Paris at the same time as our suspects.'

'They're not suspects anymore' said Henry. 'They escaped from police custody. They're fugitives and need to go to jail. Is there anything we can do to track any of their phones?'

'Not for Helen or Elliot. Their mobiles' are switched off. But Mr Seacrest' is on and we can track him. I'm sending a link to your phone now. It looks like they're on a motorway, heading towards Avignon, south of France. As long as his phone's switched on, you'll be able to trace him.'

Louise had found information on Teo. She explained that after he went rogue, he cut ties will all known associates. There was nobody. His family disappeared, presumably into hiding. A few whispers of his appearance in various countries. Never backed with solid evidence and always in areas of trouble.

'Thanks Lou. You get some rest. I'll take it from here.'

'Oh, Henry. There's one other thing.'

'What's that?'

'Elliot's younger brother's gone missing. His foster parents reported it a few hours ago.'

'What do you mean "missing?"'

'Just that' said Louise. 'He was playing in the garden whilst his foster parents were in the living room. They went to call him in for supper and within the space of an hour, he had disappeared.'

'Any leads?'

'Only one. Toby Hope's foster parents have recently applied for permanent parental control.'

'You mean adoption?'

'Yes. Apparently, Toby's social worker spoke with Elliot about it. He went flying off the handle and started making threats about getting his brother back. But Elliot's in France and so he has an alibi. Otherwise, we have little to go on.'

'I have reason to believe that Elliot and Helen are not working on their own. I think they got Teo to do their dirty work for them. Thanks, stay in touch.'

Henry called the inspector's office. No answer. He phoned the local police in Avignon. The nearest port was in Cannes. That must be where they are heading. He needed to get to the port before they did or Elliot and Helen would escape the country. Then it would be really difficult to catch them. He phoned border control to keep them on high alert. Henry sent them both the link tracking Chris and told them to do everything they could to detain Elliot and Helen. Failure was not an option. He emailed pictures of the fugitives so they knew who to look out for. Henry jumped in his car and drove south. *Got them.*

76

South of France – Present Day + 11 (Monday)

As early morning took form, Elliot could see the green meadows appear either side of the motorway. A flock of sleeping sheep stood still as he zoomed passed them. He had driven non-stop and was feeling pretty tired. The adrenaline had worn off and his sleepiness hit him like a punch of soft pillows in the face. A straight seven-hour drive. He saw the road sign for Cannes port, four miles ahead. A motorway garage was coming up on his right. The petrol tank was near empty and he needed a drink to keep him awake. He took a right turn, around the winding road until he reached the twenty-four-hour garage with a mini restaurant and gambling arcade. As he pulled up, Helen awoke, yawned and stretched her arms out, almost knocking Chris in the face.

'Where are we' asked Helen.

'Morning' said Elliot. 'Just outside Cannes…five minutes from the Port. Want anything from the garage?'

Helen leant forward and looked at the time on the dashboard of the car. Six am.

'Erm, no, I'm ok thanks.'

Elliot bought a cup of coffee and some sweets from the garage station. The place was pretty empty. No one was in the gambling arcade and only a couple of truckers were in the restaurant, eating their breakfast, or at least trying to. The truck drivers looked as tired as Elliot felt and seemed to be just staring at their food.

A small TV was fixed on the wall of the garage. For some reason an English news channel was on and Elliot assumed from the Polish employee's broken French that he must've understood English better than the local tongue. The news was reporting on a scientific breakthrough. Haematologists at Israel's Tel Aviv University had discovered a new link that could help cure cancer, other diseases and some disabilities. They found a pattern in certain blood groups that made some people more susceptible to viruses and disabilities. Governments worldwide had now agreed to contribute both scientists and funds to help focus on this haematological pattern in the hope that it could stop infections spreading through birth. Elliot thought that this must be what Jean Claude was working on. It sounded too good to be true. Maybe Jean Claude's comments about curing all illness could one day become true.

He got back into the car and attempted to wake himself. He put both hands against his face and stretched his skin back so he looked like a falling skydiver. It worked a little, but it was no substitute for sleep.

'Jean Claude, you said you studied in Israel right?'

'Yeah, at Tel Aviv Uni... why?'

'Tel Aviv university has discovered a pattern in blood that links people who are vulnerable to viruses and some disabilities. They think it could lead to a cure' said Elliot.

'Yes, we've been working on this for ages. I don't think it's going to go anywhere just yet' said Jean Claude.

They both sat in the car, facing forward. If they weren't so tired, the moment would be awkward. Elliot wasn't surprised that Jean Claude didn't have much hope, although he was sad for him. Hope can be a strong drug to carry people through difficult times.

'Where now' asked Elliot, turning to face Jean Claude.

'Park up near the Port' said Jean Claude, rubbing his eyes. 'There's a boat waiting for us. The Freedom Explorer. It's been a trusty friend on several of my brother's archaeological sites. It's most recent one was exploring the underwater area where the Antikythera Mechanism was found.'

Chris' ears pricked up and he lifted his head. He'd been working on the Antikythera Mechanism as part of his exhibition. He was too tired to engage in the conversation and so just lay his head back down against the side of the window.

'We need to be careful' said Helen.

'Agreed' said Elliot. 'If Detective Wrightman or the local police have an inkling that we'd try and leave the country, they'd have police around the Port looking for us. We need a plan.'

77

South of France – Present Day + 11 (Monday)

Elliot drove through the city of Cannes. Passing a big hill, surrounded by mansions with swimming pools and well-trimmed gardens. At the top of the hill he could see the rising sun, reflected over the glistening waters of the Mediterranean Sea, with the harbour jammed packed and getting ready for the world famous Cannes film festival. Elliot parked the car two hundred yards away from the harbour, in one of the only parking spaces that didn't require payment or a parking permit. They all got out and made their way down the promenade towards the sea.

They all agreed it would be safer for Chris and Jean Claude to scout ahead and make sure the coast was clear. Jean Claude pointed to his boat stationed in the harbour. From the hill they were on, it could be seen a hundred meters in the distance. He agreed to flash the boat's beacon if it was clear. Twice for them to come, three times for them to stay put.

Helen and Elliot sat outside a coffee shop, with the harbour and several high end fashion shops in their view. Chris and Jean Claude went off, passing an array of five star hotels, with their Lamborghinis, Ferraris and spotlessly dressed porters waiting outside. The harbour was stationed with yachts as big as houses, some as big as mini-cruise liners. The world's wealth gathered together to share in their exclusivity and enjoy the fruits of the ordinarily unattainable. Some of the yachts were more like ships with up to fifty employees. All crew were dressed in white. Chris thought they looked like some sort of over the top advert for a detergent brand.

As Chris and Jean Claude walked through the harbour, Chris saw two police officers and a German Shepherd. The dog was so big it's diet could've consisted of radioactive dog food with a side order of dangerous criminals. They stood just in front of Jean Claude's boat, the Freedom Explorer, talking to each other. It didn't look like they were discussing anything official, but they were still the police. Chris conceived it was possible they were looking for him and Jean Claude in connection with the known fugitives. *Perhaps they were just doing a routine inspection of the port.* From a distance the Freedom Explorer look pretty basic compared to its luxurious neighbours.

Chris and Jean Claude slowly walked towards the yacht, both on edge in case they had to turn around and make a run for it. One of the officers looked at Chris with an emotionless face, then turned his attention back to his colleague and carried on talking. Chris and Jean Claude passed the officers, praying they didn't get stopped. They climbed the gangplank and cautiously stepped up onto the Freedom Explorer.

'We'd better tell Elliot and Helen not to come just yet' whispered Jean Claude. 'At least, not until the police have left.'

Jean Claude started the yacht's engine and switched on a beacon located on the very top of the yacht. *Two flashes if it's safe, three to stay put.*

Outside the café, Helen ordered the cheapest coffee on the menu. It was still the most expensive one Elliot had ever seen. He asked for a diet coke. He didn't need to lose weight, just preferred the taste. They both kept their eyes on the harbour waiting for the beacon to flash. Elliot thought he knew which boat was the Freedom Explorer and fixed his eyes on the same point for ten minutes. Every so often, he lost his focus. He hadn't slept at all and was struggling. Plus, the sun was coming on strong which made it difficult to see the boat. As the sun was blinding Elliot's site, the light on the Freedom Explorer gave its first flash, going completely unnoticed by either of them.

He took a big gulp of his fizzy drink, then put it back on the table. He put his hand above his head to shade his sight from the sun. He saw a faint flash. Five seconds later, another flash occurred. He waited. There was no third flash. He thought it possible there could've been another flash which he didn't see, but unlikely. He had no way of contacting Chris or Jean Claude to double check and so had to assume the coast was clear.

'Time to go.'

'Are you sure' said Helen.

'I'm pretty sure the beacon flashed twice.'

'Pretty sure?'

Elliot shrugged his shoulders. He couldn't give any more assurance. They paid the bill and made their way to the harbour, passing the promenade of high end retail shops, where men in dark suits and ear pieces protected the aspirational brands like they were celebrities. He thought the security for these shops was a little over the top.

They paced quickly to the harbour's entrance. Helen put her hand on Elliot's shoulder and held him back.

'Wait.'

'What is it?'

'Police up ahead' she replied, looking at the two officers and their Alsatian.

'It can't be. Jean Claude gave us the go ahead.'

'Well, it looks like the police to me.'

Elliot looked at all the crew working on the boats, all dressed in white clothing. 'I have an idea.'

They both left the harbour and found one of the only cheap clothes shop in Cannes. Using Chris' credit card, they bought white t-shirts, trousers and two souvenir sailor hats. Elliot hoped the man in the shop didn't query the fact that he, a young looking man, was using an Amex Black exclusive credit-card. It made him nervous. But then, everything about this expedition made him nervous. The shop worker didn't bat an eyelid. It was Cannes after all. They changed their clothes and came back out looking like sailors.

Elliot approached the two police officers who were busy conversing with each other, right next to the gangplank of the Freedom Explorer. Their Alsatian sat next to them obediently. Even dressed up as crew, there was no way Elliot and Helen could get onto the boat without asking the police to move. *Way too risky.* He had an idea. They walked towards the large boat adjacent to the Freedom Explorer. It was a much bigger yacht. A big white thing with golden railings around its first and second deck and a spinning satellite on top that looked like it could receive messages from space. At ten yards away, the beast raised its head and stared in Elliot's direction. It stood up and started barking. Elliot could feel he was about to get arrested at any moment. He wanted to make a run for it, but running would alert the police that something was wrong. They slowed their pace and pulled their sailor caps down as much as they could to try and hide their faces. The police officer holding the dog lead, pulled on it to make the dog sit back down. The beast did as it was told and Elliot carried on walking with his head down.

When Elliot was five meters away, the dog started barking again. This time, it stood up and ran towards him. It pelted at him so fast the officer lost his grip of the lead. The dog charged without restraint. Elliot's heart gave way. Before he knew it, the dog was right next to him, mouth open and revealing its monstrous, criminal-hungry teeth. As he gasped, the dog leaped behind him and darted off. His anxiety shot up as he thought the Alsatian might attack him from behind. He turned around to see the dog barking at a member of crew from the ship next to them, carrying what seemed to be several bags of food. The police officers chased after their dog. Elliot's pounding heart began to relax a little, although the beads of sweet on his face were still there. As the police attended to the hungry dog, Elliot and Helen both walked across the mechanical gangplank and boarded the luxury yacht, next to Freedom Explorer. The police didn't pay any attention.

They climbed up the narrow ladder on the yacht to get to the upper deck. Elliot stopped as he heard someone talking just a few meters away. He signalled for Helen to stop and stay quiet. After a short conversation, he could hear the gentle footsteps of the soft rubber shoes fade away. He slowly and stealthily peered his head just above the steps. *No one in sight. Time to go.* They quietly made their way along the left side of the yacht, with the Freedom Explorer three meters across the water from them.

Elliot put his index finger against his mouth for Helen to be quiet. 'Follow me' he whispered.

He climbed over the rails, one leg after the other until both feet were standing on a thin support a few inches wide on the outside of the yacht. He held himself tightly against the rail. His view was restricted and so he couldn't see whether the police would see him jump or not. Helen leaned over the edge to see the police still next to the Freedom Explorer and talking to themselves with their backs turned. As soon as she gave him the green light, he leapt across the water, landing onto the side of Jean Claude's boat with a slight thud. His hands latched onto a white railing, as he clambered onto the boat. His feet landed firmly on one of the large tyres held in place to avoid the boat colliding with other yachts. He pulled himself up and onto Jean Claude's boat.

Helen's turn. She climbed over the rails and waited for Elliot to say when the police were not watching. He held his hand up, indicating for her to wait. Elliot leaned over the edge. The police still had their backs to them. It looked ok and so he waved for her jump. Helen moved her body forward and back, to gain momentum. She counted to herself. *Three...two...* One of the officers starting turning around, then turned back again. Elliot quickly held both hands up waving, telling her to stop. It was too late. Helen had already let go of the rails and when she saw Elliot, she tried to stop herself, but resulted in her plummeting down into the water with a big splash.

The police didn't see Helen fall, but one of them heard the splash. He looked over the edge to see what it was. Elliot quickly ducked to avoid being seen and stayed deathly quiet. As the officer looked into the rippled water, he sees a seagull splashing around, hunting for its breakfast. The officer turns back to his colleague and continues chatting. Elliot slowly looks over the edge of the boat. He can't see Helen anywhere. *Where is she?* He swears under his breath. In a fear that she may have bumped her head and be drowning, he ran to the loading deck of the Freedom Explorer. He was about to jump into the water, when he saw Helen climbing up the rear of the boat, completely wet and unimpressed. Jean Claude came over to the back of the yacht.

'Why are you wet?'

'Don't ask' she replied, leaving a trail of wet footprints as she walked along the deck.

Unlike the other boats in the harbour, the Freedom Explorer was not designed for comfort. It had the basics of a typical six birth yacht. Three bedrooms, kitchen/living room, captain's bridge, deck area and dive point. It was jam packed with machinery and archaeological equipment, all designed for underwater explorations and expeditions. A small submarine, held up by two mini cranes, latched onto the back of the yacht. It looked like a half-size petrol tanker, with the legs of a helicopter stuck on the bottom and head lights on the sides. Jean Claude had recently used the boat and sub to assist in the recovery of artefacts from the lost Port of Alexandria. Some items dating back from over two thousand years ago.

Chris started to untie the boat from the dock to leave, when they heard sirens going off in the distance. Elliot climbed to the top deck and looked around. Blue flashing lights made their way to the harbour.

'Guys, I think we've got company.'

78

South of France – Present Day + 11 (Monday)

The police sirens wailed down the streets of Cannes, as the force drove with great speed towards the harbour. The blue lights and noise were impossible to miss. Detective Henry Wrightman was up front, sitting in the passenger seat of a police car driven by the Inspector. Henry looked at the tracker on his mobile. His target was in the harbour. The piercing sirens made their way through the harbour and pulled to a stop when they reached the Freedom Explorer, wedged between two large yachts.

Elliot could see the flashing lights at the front of the boat. He cursed some unsavoury words in his head. He was too tired to think, too tired to run and had no idea how he was going to get out of this one. Jean Claude watched as Chris went to the front of the boat to unravel the rope keeping the Freedom Explorer tied to the harbour.

'Even if we make a getaway, the police will catch up with us at sea' said Jean Claude. 'Quick' whispered Jean Claude, pointing at mini-submarine. 'Climb in and wait until I come and get you.'

'Give me a break' said Elliot. 'This is not a good idea'

'I don't think we have much of a choice' Helen replied. 'It's that or be taken back into police custody.'

Jean Claude climbed up a metal ladder against the small submarine, pulled a handle and a small door clicked open, no bigger than the doorway of a dog kennel. He moved out of the way for Elliot and Helen to climb in. Elliot stepped onto the ladder, causing it to swing back a tad. He reached the top and stared through the door way.

'This isn't big enough for both of us' he said.

'You'll have to make it big enough…' said Jean Claude. 'There's no time to waste…just get in.'

Elliot awkwardly climbed in. Left foot first, then his right hand, making it difficult for his right leg to move in afterwards. As his head went inside, he ungracefully stumbled forward, letting his arm break his fall. He dragged his right leg in behind him, catching the back of his shoe on the side of the door.

'OK, Helen, your turn' said Jean Claude, offering her his hand.

Helen climbed up the ladder. 'Erm, where am I supposed to sit?'

'I'm not sure, just get in.'

'Sit on my lap' Elliot said, feeling slightly uncomfortable at the idea.

Helen gave him a funny look.

'Yes, I know. Let's not make it weird' he said. 'They'll be here any minute. Come on.'

Helen got in, one foot, then the other, using her arms on the side of the door to position her in. Her shoe stepped on Elliot's leg and just missed his crown jewels. He guided her leg to the side of him to stop himself from getting squashed. She sat uncomfortably, part on Elliot, part on the remainder of the seat. It was definitely not designed for two people, but they'd kind of managed to make it work.

'I'm going to lower this to the sea' said Jean Claude.

Helen frowned. 'What?'

'Trust me. See that buoyancy control lever' said Jean Claude, pointing.

Helen put her hand over it. 'This one?'

'Yes. When you touch the water, you need to push it down, all the way. Otherwise, when I lower you, you'll just stay afloat on the water.'

'Got it' said Helen.

Henry and his men came to an abrupt halt outside the Freedom Explorer. He swung the door open and jumped out. The inspector and eight officers marched behind him, armed to the teeth. When the police by the boat saw the army of police cars coming, they demanded Chris stop untying the rope and stay put.

At the rear of the boat, Elliot could hear the police were very near. Jean Claude pushed a green button on a control device. Two large cogs each turned releasing a thick metal wire that lowered the sub from two small cranes into the water. On impact, a few bubbles came from the edges of the submarine, but the only splash was the slight waves that hit against its sides. Elliot could hear marching footsteps over the gangplank. *The police are onboard.*

'Close the door and push the buoyancy lever' said Jean Claude. 'Oh and erm, don't forget to switch the-'

Helen pulled the handle on the hatch to close the door. Elliot had already pushed the buoyancy control lever button, and they immediately started to submerge.

'Wait' said Helen. 'What did he say?'

'It's too late! The police are already on the bloody boat. If we go back up now, we'll get caught. Whatever it was, it'll have to wait.'

In no time at all, the armed officers and Henry were all over the Freedom Explorer, like a pack of wolves on an antelope. They found Chris near the front and Jean Claude on the rear deck. There was no sight of Helen or Elliot. Henry stood next to Chris as the officers searched the boat from top to bottom.

'Where are they' demanded Henry.

'Where are who' said Chris.

'You know who. Helen Philips and Elliot Hope. They've been with you from Washington.'

Chris went bright red. He wasn't a very good liar and wasn't familiar with being on the wrong side of the law. 'Oh, we flew here together, but erm...' he said, looking at a side table with a pamphlet of the Cannes movie awards. 'We went our separate ways. I came to France for the film festival.'

Chris picked up the festival pamphlet from the side table and showed it to the Detective. Henry looked at it, then gave Chris a wide eyed stare that told showed he didn't trust Chris. Henry looked out from the bridge and over the harbour.

'So tell me, Mr Seacrest. When were you with Elliot and Helen last?'

Chris walked around the bridge of the Freedom Explorer and didn't respond. He stopped pacing next to the captain's chair in front of the steering wheel and cruising controls, accidentally knocking over a plastic bag carrying Helen's clothes. Henry was watching the police search the front of the boat and didn't pay attention. Chris quickly moved the bag under the cover of the steering wheel with his leg. Henry turned and faced Chris.

He stood up straight and tried to act normal. 'I was last with them in Paris. We arrived at Charles de Gaulle airport, freshened up, and then met for dinner. I haven't seen them since.'

Henry turned to an officer holding an assault rifle, then gave him the once over.

'Status?'

'We've searched the place inside out' said the officer. 'Bedrooms, living-room, even the engine room. It's clean.'

'Search around the boat, the other yachts, the whole god damn harbour if you must. They're hiding somewhere. I know it.'

The officer ran off and spread the word to the others. Within minutes all but two of the armed men had left the yacht to search the harbour.

The submarine sat motionless at the bottom of the seabed, only eight meters below the surface. Not deep, but low down enough to avoid being easily identified. From the surface it looked like a big grey rock. Inside Elliot and Helen were squashed together like Siamese twins. Elliot's leg was beginning to get pins and needles. Helen wasn't heavy, but she'd been on top of him for a few minutes now. Their body heat was making them warm. They were hot, unable to concentrate and both had headaches.

'They should invent air conditioning for these things' said Helen.

'Erm, don't you need access to outside air for air-conditioning' said Elliot.

'Oh yeah, maybe not.'

Elliot looked around to see if there was a fan. Nothing. He noticed Helen's face had turned slightly pale and her lips were becoming blue. His breathing was getting heavy, but with each lung-filled breath, his quench for air was left unsatisfied. He had a pounding headache.

'Er, Helen. I know what Jean Claude was trying to tell us. We need to switch the air supply on.'

Helen dragged her head, tilting it towards him, looking drunk. 'What?'
'Help me. We need to switch on the oxygen supply.'

He scanned the controls in front of him, but with the limited light and his loss of concentration, he wasn't having any luck. Helen started panicking. Her arms waved around the confined space, touching and pushing as many different controls and buttons as she could. Most of them appeared to do nothing, but one switch turned on the outside main beams.

An officer on the yacht, fixed a tracking locater in a big container on the lower deck of the Freedom Explorer. The container was filled with tools and supplies, making it less easy to find. He then searched around the lower deck area and noticed wet footprints on the floor near the rear of the boat. The officer walked to the edge to see if the fugitives were hiding in the water. Just before he knelt down, the beams from the submarine switched off. The officer looked over the side of the deck and into the water. He saw nothing, other than a big grey rock at the bottom of the sea which he stared at for a few seconds.

Back in the sub, Elliot had managed to release the oxygen valve causing bubbles to release into the water. Within a few seconds, Oxygen filled the submarine and they were able to breathe again.

The officer leaning over the edge saw the bubbles coming from the water. He looked closer at the big grey rock. The sun light from above caused something in the water to shine. He squinted his eyes as he tried to focus on the big grey rock and leaned closer to the water.

'Hey, what are you doing' said a male voice behind him.

The officer turned around to see a higher ranking policeman standing there with a large gun held with both hands.

'I think there's something in the water' replied the officer leaning on the floor.

'Leave it. We've received a call. A witness has just phoned in to say they've seen our suspects in Paris. False alarm.'

Back on the captain's deck, Chris was still glowing red. Henry had finished his questions and he could see that Chris was doing little to help.

Henry gave Chris a look of distrust. 'It's a coincidence that you were with Elliot and Helen in Washington and are all now in France.'

Chris shrugged his shoulders. 'I guess.'

Henry's experience taught him that coincidences tend to happen less than people think. If someone was a suspect, there was usually a good reason for it.

Chris leaned forward and offered a hand shake. 'If I see them officer-'

'It's Detective' said Henry, refusing to shake his hand.

'Detective… if I see them, I'll be certain to let you know.'

'Be sure that you do' said Henry, handing over his card.

Henry and his men left the yacht and drove away from the harbour to follow up on their Paris lead. The Freedom Explorer stayed there until the police were out of site. As soon as the police left, Jean Claude tied a large metal lock to a piece of rope, dangled it into the water and knocked on the submarine three times. Gradually, it came to the surface. He attached the submarine to the cranes and lifted it back up until it was safely locked in place. The door opened and out popped Helen's head.

'We'd better get out of here' said Jean Claude. 'Now.'

79

Mediterranean Sea – Present Day + 11 (Monday)

The Freedom Explorer made its way across the Mediterranean Sea, with Jean Claude at the captain's bridge, sailing full steam ahead. Despite the waves causing the yacht to move up and down like a bouncy castle, Elliot slept without trouble. As soon as his head hit the pillow, that was it. He was out for the count. The same could not be said of Helen who was suffering from a chronic case of sea sickness.

Seven hours later, Elliot awoke to the smell of cooking. Garlic and basil waft through his cabin. He swung his legs off the bed, sat up and just stared at the floor as he let his brain gather itself for a moment. He'd slept in his clothes, but still felt like a great sleep. He got up and made his way through the corridor. The waves hitting the yacht were so bumpy that he couldn't walk in a straight line. He put his hands against the walls of the narrow corridor and carefully walked to the kitchen/living-room area as it moved left to right like a fun house.

Chris was in the kitchen creating one of his signature dishes. Spaghetti bolognaise with garlic bread. Elliot was so ravenous he could barely wait for the grub to be dished up, staring at the food as though he'd not eaten in a week. Helen was sitting at the dinner table, looking at a tourist map of Istanbul and reading a translation of the Copper Scroll interpreted by

Oxford scholars.

'Welcome back to planet earth' said Helen. 'You've been asleep for hours.'

Elliot yawned, stretched his arms out, then sat down next to Helen. 'How are you holding up?'

'I'm ok. I'm trying not to think about what we've been through. I'll reflect on it once we've got your brother back. Until then, we need to focus on moving forward. You coping ok?'

'I'm fine' said Elliot.

I'm fine. The universal code used by the passive aggressive, avoidants and avid stone-wallers. Elliot was far from fine. He'd been arrested, broken out of a police cell and was now a wanted fugitive, his brother had been kidnapped, his own life and that of his friends were in danger. There was nothing about his situation that was fine. Helen put her arm on his shoulder. It didn't take a psychologist to see he was hurting.

'We'll get Toby back. We just need to stick together' she said.

'Thanks' said Elliot, unable to look her in the face without bursting into tears. 'So erm, what have we found so far' he said, leaning into the table and looking at her notes.

'I've had a look at the Copper Scroll translation. Whoever wrote it made the description very vague. I think it was meant to be more of a reminder to the scriber than to serve as a treasure map. I've not found any obvious landmarks yet, but I'm still working on it.'

Chris interrupted. 'Yes, but for now, dinner's ready.'

It didn't take much persuasion to change the subject. Elliot jumped in to devour his food. He tried to pace himself as he was in polite company, but the pasta on his plate still got sucked up like he was a vacuum cleaner. His last meal was a piece of slop from the prison cell, and so by comparison, he was now dining like a king. Chris went and took some food up to Jean Claude who was steering the yacht. Elliot stared at the tourist map. It had cartoon pictures of buildings and popular tourist sites. There were several temples and old buildings. There were churches that had been turned into mosques and an ancient underground cistern used to collect and store the city's water.

Chris returned to the living-room to see their empty plates. 'You were both hungry.'

'Mmm' said Helen with the last piece of food in her mouth. She swallowed, covering her mouth with her hand. 'It was delicious, thank you.'

'Yes, thanks Chris' said Elliot. 'Compliments to the chef.'

After dinner, Elliot and Helen washed the dishes and then joined Chris and Jean Claude upstairs in the captain's bridge. Jean Claude was steering the captain's wheel, navigating the seas. The winds were not bad, but for a small vessel, even light waves were felt by the crew. Elliot thought the wheel was much smaller than the ones they have in pirate movies. Not what he was expecting, although he wasn't sure what to expect. They spread the tourist map out in front of the wheel and rested it on top of the dash board.

'What are we looking for' asked Jean Claude.

'I don't know' said Elliot. 'But I thought we could do this all together. You've been a great help so far, and I wouldn't be here without you.'

Jean Claude nodded and gave a small smile as they all hobbled around the map. Helen put the translation of the Copper Scroll down next to the map.

"In the ruins which are in the Valley
under the steps which go eastward
In the big cistern in the court of
the peristyle, in a recess of its bottom which is
plugged up with sediment

CHAPTER 79

across from the upper opening"

They looked at the tourist map, but couldn't see a valley anywhere. At the time the Copper Scroll was first written, it was known as the great Greek city Byzantium, of the Byzantine empire. Since then it was taken over by the Romans for eleven hundred years where it was turned into Constantinople and then taken by Islam and turned into Istanbul. It had gone through a millennia of changes and there was no way of knowing where the "valley" would be now.

On the side of the map were pictures of the various different tourist attractions one could visit. Smoke a flavoured shisha, visit a temple, ride a bike around the city. Elliot noticed a picture of an underground lake with pillars supporting the roof above it.

'Peristyles' said Elliot, under his breath.

'What did you say' asked Helen.

'Peristyles. Look here' he said, pointing to the picture of the underground lake. 'See, these columns. They're also called peristyles.'

Elliot read the caption underneath the picture. It was the Basicila Cistern, one of the oldest cisterns known to man. Used to store the city's water supply. It dated back to the Ancient Greek period and was one of the only buildings to survive the city's capture by the Islamic world.

'I think you might have found something' said Chris.

'Let me see' said Helen. Elliot moved over so that she could read the caption. 'I think you could be right. It's not definite, but then, when is anything. In any case, it's the best we've got so far.'

Elliot searched the internet, using a computer set up in the corner of the room. He Googled several key words, including "valley", "cisterns" and "Istanbul" to see if there was any information that might help. Over four hundred thousand search results returned. Although the Basicilla Cistern was the main one still preserved, there were numerous ancient cisterns in Istanbul. Of those, some still exist today. Unfortunately, many of them have disintegrated or been forgotten over time.

It was nearly time to update Teo and his men. Elliot needed to give them a heads up that they were in Istanbul. But, if he told them the exact location of the treasure, they'd have no incentive to keep him or his brother alive. For now, he needed to keep his findings as vague as possible. *Keep the ball in the air*. He decided to check out each cistern first, find the treasure and then make the swap.

80

Istanbul – Present Day + 12 (Tuesday)

The Freedom Explorer docked at Istanbul Harbour in the middle of the night. The harbour was lit up by market stalls and outdoor eateries. The moon cast its reflection on the silent waters in the background. A floating restaurant, with more neon lights than a small disco, was anchored near their yacht. Blaring out Turkish music, which seemed to do the opposite of attracting customers to dine there.

Elliot walked down the gangplank and onto the harbour. It felt weird walking on land after being on a rocky boat for so long. His body was telling him that he was still moving. It would take a little adjustment. The others followed behind. The tellers and market workers spotted the tourists and, without hesitation, tried hard to sell them souvenirs and get them into their market store. The men took particular notice of Helen. Elliot wondered how long it would be before someone offered to buy her for a camel.

They soaked up the atmosphere, passing market stalls and busy streets, filled with people from all walks of life. Drinking herbal tea, Turkish coffee and smoking shishas. Stalls covered with dates, trinkets, souvenirs, braids, necklaces and carpet rugs. The area was called New Town, but to Elliot, it looked pretty old.

A small boy with fair skin and chestnut hair stood next to a market stall. He turned around quickly, then walked away. *Toby!* Elliot ran over to him and touched his arm. The boy stared up at Elliot. It wasn't Toby. From the pressure he was under, his mind was manifesting his most desperate wishes.

Jean Claude and Chris were discussing the ancient buildings in Istanbul and their origins. They took it in turns to give examples of buildings known to exist at certain times in history, together with some background information. Each time, they would try and say something more impressive. It sounded more like a phallic measuring competition than anything else. Elliot left them to it. Helen walked out in front with her map of the city, looking like a typical tourist. At every couple of junctions, she would stop, look around, tap on the map, talk to it, then move on. Elliot caught up with her.

'How ya getting on?'

'I'm not lost' she replied.

'I didn't say it or think it.'

'Good. Our place is just a few blocks around the corner.'

Unlike him, she hadn't slept since early that morning. She was cranky and her fatigue was showing.

'Sorry, I just want to get there and rest. We can start afresh tomorrow.'

'Here, let me help' he said, holding his hand out for the map.

'Thanks. I'm losing the will' said Helen.

'You're doing great. We'll get some rest and face this head on. It'll all be over soon. Before we know it, we'll be back in the British Museum, working on the exhibition.'

'I'm sorry I got you into this mess' she said. 'This is all my fault. I took you to St Pauls and Arizona. You're my responsibility.'

Elliot raised an eyebrow. 'Helen, none of this is your fault.' He looked on the floor and kicked a pebble into the curb. 'You know, since my parents died, I've struggled to open up. I guess there's been no one to open up to. Toby's too young to talk to. You're the only person that's truly stuck their neck out for me. You're the only one that's had any faith in me. I owe you so much.'

Helen put her arm on his shoulder. 'You owe me nothing. We're a team and I'll stick by you. No matter what.'

Elliot welled up inside, though his face expressed little emotion. A defensive mechanism acquired to help him appear strong for his little brother. He'd tell people he didn't need anyone or any help, but the exact opposite was true.

They arrived at a small two-bedroom apartment, not far from the Galata Tower, a giant spire that rose from the ground. The spire looked like something Rapunzel would be stuck in, awaiting a prince to save her. Elliot saw no prince around. Just old Turkish men in white socks and slippers, sitting outside cafés drinking herbal tea and playing board games.

Chris stood in front of the apartment door and stared at the lock. 'You know, in thirty years, locks have not changed that much. Electric ones have, but not these manual ones.'

'You were a locksmith' asked Elliot.

'Not me. My uncle used to have a shop. I'd help out as a teenager. I spent most of it behind the till studying for college, although I did pick up a trick or two.'

They all entered the badly decorated apartment. It looked as though it had not been cleared in a couple of years. Given Jean Claude had provided travel on a yacht, Elliot expected the place to be a little nicer. He didn't complain. He was happy to have a base. Somewhere that he could relax for the evening and not worry about being chased, shot at or arrested. He slung a bag on the bed, sat down on the side and took his shoes off. He felt the soft carpet underneath his toes. Any comfort he could get was welcome, no matter how small. Small comforts were all he could hope for.

Helen took the main bedroom, Chris and Elliot agreed to share the second. It only had one bed. They would have to make do. It was late and Elliot was more tired than he realised. With everything going on, he barely gave any thought to the fact that he was close to finding a treasure greater than anything ever discovered. If successful, archaeologists would have a field day. Not to mention all the scientists if they got their hands on the philosopher's stone. Elliot didn't believe in magic, but he did believe in science. He also believed that there were things way beyond his comprehension and so what may seem like magic, is really just logical, but beyond the understanding of the human mind. Elliot laid his head down on the pillow. As soon as he did, his body seemed to weigh twice as heavy and within minutes he was asleep.

81

France – Present Day + 12 (Tuesday)

Detective Wrightman finally got some much needed sleep, after arriving back in Paris. In the morning, the first thing on his agenda was to speak with the witness who saw Elliot and Helen in Paris. He rocked up at the police station ready for an interview, but was instead greeted with great disappointment. The witness who allegedly saw Elliot and Helen in Paris was a heroin addict, with a known history of fabricating "useful" information in exchange for reward money. The inspector had investigated the information in Henry's absence. As suspected, it didn't stack up and Henry was back to square one.

Henry instructed a team to keep track of Chris and Jean Claude. There was every chance that the fugitives would try and make contact with Chris again. Henry was used to reading people and Chris was definitely hiding something. For now, all he could do is go back to the crime scene and so he paid a visit to the Notre Dame Cathedral. Although forensics were good at their job, Henry liked to get a feel of a crime scene himself. The idea of pursuing a criminal without investigating the scene was like being in an art class and trying to draw a bowl of fruit blindfolded.

The cathedral no longer looked like a crime scene. The French authorities had worked around the clock to ensure its golden tourist attraction was cleared up and ready for the public. He was met by a senior member of the clergy who gave Henry a tour of the Cathedral, and showed him where the body was found. The once bloodied steps stank of bleach. Now spotless. It stood out compared to rest of the stairway, which showed how dirty the floor really was. Henry climbed up to the bell tower, walked around the room and made his way into a dark and cold storage room in the back. He shone his torch around. Nothing out of the ordinary.

Back in the tower, he walked over to a rusty old metal cage. Part of it had been broken off. He bent down to search the floor and saw two pieces of plastic zip-tags, both cut by the jagged edge of something. His mind went to work. The length of plastic zip-tags were different. One seemed big enough to hold someone's wrists together, and the other could have bound someone's legs. *Who was tied up, who did the tying and why?* He wondered whether the clergyman came to rescue and got killed for it. Something didn't add up.

The man of the cloth took Henry to the security room and showed him the footage of a security camera positioned at the front of the Cathedral.

'Do you have any security cameras from inside the Cathedral' asked Henry.

'No, I'm afraid not dear boy. We have cameras outside as we had a big problem with graffiti a few years ago. But, we never have any problems inside the Cathedral. God sees everything that happens inside these walls.'

Henry hadn't been called a boy in a long time. Still, compared to the man he was with, he probably was a boy. The man stood up like a twig. Bent out at the back and looked like a strong wind could blow him over. The TV screen of the external security footage showed several white lines as Henry rewound the tape to the estimated time of the murder. He paused when he saw four people leaving the cathedral. He played it over a few times. *Chris Seacrest and the other man from the Freedom Explorer.* Chris was with Elliot and Helen after he arrived in Paris. Chris had lied. Apart from the fact that he was aiding fugitives, he was present when the murder took place making him an accessory. Not to mention there was a strong chance he was with Elliot and Helen now. Henry turned to the old man.

'I'm sorry for your loss' said Henry. 'The man on the stairway must've been close to you.'

'What do you mean' said the clergyman.

'The men that was killed here. I'm told he was a member of the clergy.'

'He didn't work here' he said, giving Henry a confused look. 'I said this to the police.'

'What? What do you mean? Which Cathedral did he work for then' asked Henry.

'I have no idea. I've never seen him before.'

Henry called the inspector. Henry was pissed off that such an important piece of information was not brought to his attention. Every detail was needed, no matter how small. He wondered why a member from another Cathedral would be there, unauthorised and at such a later hour. And if they didn't work for another Cathedral, who were they and what were they doing? The inspector confirmed that his men were investigating the identity of the victim, but so far, they had nothing positive.

Henry asked for an update on the Freedom Explorer's location. Wherever the boat was, the chances are, Elliot and Helen would be there too. His smart phone beeped. An email from his boss, asking for a progress report. Henry didn't want to respond just yet. He'd just let Elliot and Helen escape, possibly out of the country. If his boss knew that they had escaped a police cell, it wouldn't look good on Henry, even if he wasn't in charge of the station. His tracker told him that the Freedom Explorer was in Istanbul, Turkey. The Turkish international treaties were not as tight as the French. Henry couldn't just ask for them to be brought in. He had no jurisdiction and would be without support. But he was close. For the sake of his murdered partner and everyone else, he had to go there by himself.

82

Istanbul – Present Day + 13 (Wednesday)

Elliot woke up at four am by the snoring of his fellow top-and-tailer. Chris was in a deep sleep. He contemplated trying to do something to stop the snoring. *Hold his nose. Roll him over. Pillow over the face?* Chris had been through a lot and so Elliot decided to leave him in peace. The lack of air-conditioning made the room feel like a Bikram yoga studio. He felt all sweaty and gross. His mouth was uncomfortably dry.

He saw a dim light coming from the corner of the bedroom. He lifted his head to see Chris' phone flashing. Someone was calling. *At this hour?* Initially, he decided to ignore it, but after the phone was called for the third time, Elliot got up to turn it off. As he picked up the mobile, his tired eyes adjusted to the light. Numbered withheld and eighteen missed calls. It was not his phone and so he was reluctant to answer. As Chris' mobile was the only form of communication with Teo's men, he decided to take the call. He took the mobile to the bathroom to avoid waking Chris.

'Hello' said Elliot.

'Why didn't you answer!' replied David. 'I said no funny business. You were supposed to stay in contact.'

'But we were exhausted and needed to sleep.'

'I said to update us every three hours. I did not give you permission to sleep. As of this moment, you will never see your brother again.'

'No wait!' 'We know where it is. I can get the stone for you. Just give me time. Please. I can do this. You don't need to hurt Toby.'

There was a ten second pause, which to Elliot seemed like it lasted for an eternity.

'Twenty-four hours' said David. 'I'm giving you twenty-four hours. If you don't have the stone, that's it, no second chances, no excuses. Toby dies.'

'Thank you' he said with a broken voice. 'Please. I'll get it, I will.'

The call ended. Elliot was left in a state of shock, feeling physically sick. His mind raced as he tried to plan his next steps. But there were so many different sites to investigate and he didn't know where to start.

The rest of the city was beginning to wake. Elliot could hear the sing of calls to prayer resonating from the Islamic temples of Istanbul. He went to take a shower. It was icy cold at first, but within a minute or so the splashing water turned steaming hot. For a shabby apartment, the shower head was powerful. He used the power of its spray to massage his head, moving it around in circles. It was nice to feel clean and wash off his body's natural oils and stale sweat, although all he could do was think about Toby and the mission. He towelled himself down and picked up his clean clothes that he'd washed in the bathroom sink. They'd been left on the balcony window and were mostly dried out. His shirt was still a little wet, but would soon dry out. It stuck against his toned torso.

He looked out the window to the see the sun rising over the buildings, that gave off a red-ish blue sky behind the Turkish mix of spires, domes and flat roofs of Istanbul. Elliot walked in to the living room to see Jean Claude wide awake and sitting on the sofa in a t-shirt, boxers and white socks. He had a gun in his hand. He jumped as he saw Elliot and quickly tried to hide it behind his back.

Elliot stepped forward. 'Why have you got a gun!'

Jean Claude let out a deep breath, sat up and put the gun on his lap. 'Elliot. I'm gonna level with you. Teo's a dangerous man. He shouldn't be allowed to live.'

'I agree, but carrying a gun in Turkey is not a great idea. You get arrested for minor immoral acts over here. I'm pretty sure you'll be put in prison and they'll throw away the key if you get caught carrying a gun.'

'What do you want me to say? He's already killed my brother. How many more people should he be allowed to kill. He needs to be stopped, and damn it, if I get half a chance I'm going to stop him.'

Elliot could relate one hundred percent. He was filled with absolute hatred for Teo and fear for little Tobes. If Teo or anyone of his men killed Toby, Elliot would do whatever it took to take Teo down, even if it meant sacrificing his own life in the process.

'Ok. I understand. But you can't go around Istanbul carrying a weapon like that. Leave it here, and if we find Teo, we'll come back and get it. Deal?'

They shook hands on it. Elliot placed his free hand on Jean Claude's shoulder. He understood his suffering. They were in the same boat. Or at least sailing in the same direction. He looked down and couldn't help but notice how hairy Jean Claude's legs were. He didn't say anything to ruin the moment, but he'd never seen such a ginger jungle of hair.

Helen and Chris eventually woke up. Elliot explained to them all what David had said on the phone and how they had twenty-four hours to save Toby. After showering, they grabbed a quick but hearty breakfast to set them up for the day. Elliot had the Mediterranean breakfast. Olives, grilled halloumi, toast, goats cheese and eggs. It looked more like a lunch to him. He tried to eat as much as he could, but the worry for his brother made eating uncomfortable.

'So I've been going over the research' said Elliot. 'There are eight cistern's known to exist. I can only pray that the philosopher's stone is not in one that's been lost in history.'

'Well' said Chris, finishing a mouthful of scrambled eggs. 'We should split up.'

'I agree' said Helen. 'We'll cover more ground.'

'No' said Elliot.

'Why not' replied Helen.

'Each cistern is massive. It will take ages to inspect each one, we have no way to stay in contact and I need you. We don't have enough time to visit every cistern, even if we split up. Besides, I'm ninety percent sure we need to go to this one' he said, putting the tourist map on the table with pictures of the well-known tourist attraction, the Basicila Cistern.

'But if we split up, surely we'll increase our chances of finding the stone' said Chris.

'Please guys. This is my brother. It needs to be my choice. I wouldn't insist if I didn't think it was the best option we had.'

Jean Claude decided not to get involved in the difficult debate. Chris and Helen thought it was a bad idea. Chris' found a link, albeit a weak one, that would indicate the stone and the treasure were at a different cistern. However, Elliot was insistent that they go to the Basicila Cistern. Given it was his brother's life on the line, they decided to go with Elliot's decision.

They finished their food, paid the bill and made their way to Galata Bridge towards the Old Town where the Basicila Cistern was located. They hadn't been able to appreciate it in the dark when they walked passed it last night, but in broad daylight, it was beautiful. Istanbul was beautiful. A mass of old and very old buildings hobbled together in white, light grey and pastel colours. Unlike London, it wasn't covered with advertisement boards and suits going to work. They passed over the shop-covered bridge. Cruise-liners were docking nearby for tourists to visit the many overwhelmingly large mosques and temples around them. The mosque in front of them reminded Elliot of a blue version of the Taj Mahal in India. It had several blue domes in the shape of ice gems or walnut whips.

They passed through the Grand Bazar, one of the oldest markets in the world, with over three thousand different shops. It was stuffed with people. Tourists being nosey and touching things, then getting dragged in the shops to make a purchase. Spices, nuts, lentils, baklava and of course, more varieties of Turkish delight than Elliot had ever seen. With the excess of human traffic, trying to walk in a straight line was no easy task. They eventually managed to weave their way through the crowd and followed the flow of tourists to the giant church converted mosque and its sister, the Hagia Sofia.

They reached the entrance of the Basicila Cistern. From the outside, it was a small, rectangular building that looked more like a large public lavatory than the entrance of an ancient wonder of Greek history. People were queuing to go inside. Elliot joined the ticket line. Within fifteen minutes they had got their tickets and made their way down the fifty odd stone steps into the depths of the Basicila Cistern. It opened into a vast ancient water storage area, the size and shape of a football pitch and capable of holding up to eighty thousand cubic meters of water. Elliot found it beautiful. Captivating. The cistern was supported by countless columns symmetrically placed in twelve rows going down the length of the dark monster of a room. The air was wet, which was not surprising given the whole floor was one foot deep in water. They walked along the Olympic size water storage facility on a series of wide wooden planks with support rails at either side to stop kids and the clumsy from falling in. There was no natural light. If it wasn't for some dim torches attached to pillars, Elliot would be unable to see. Every so often, Elliot would feel a drip of water land on his head from the vaulted ceiling above.

Helen got out the translation of the copper scroll.

'It says "Under the steps which go eastward." Check.'

'What next' asked Jean Claude.

'Erm' said Helen, looking at the next paragraph. 'In a recess of its bottom which is plugged up with sediment... across from the upper opening... in the ruin-heap.'

'OK. So we need to go across from the entrance then' said Chris, pointing. That's at the very end of the cistern.'

As they ventured further into the cistern, they were met by the growing calm sound of relaxing classical music. Vivaldi's Four Seasons. Elliot's parents used to play it at home. It breathed an air of nostalgia into his lungs. They reached the farthest edge of the wooden raised platform. It didn't go to the very end of the cistern and there was no way of going further without jumping off the platform and into the water.

Elliot checked the time. One pm. Seventeen hours until they had to come up with the stone. With all the tourists and staff around, it wasn't possible to jump into the water and investigate the rear wall. Instead, they agreed to get some equipment from their boat and come back at night when no one was about.

83

Istanbul – Present Day + 13 (Wednesday)

By the time Elliot left the Basicila Cistern it was already three pm. The day was moving fast. He was glad that he hadn't seen Teo or any of his henchmen today. He knew a meet was inevitable if they were to exchange Toby for the stone. If he found it, that is. He was dreading it after what happened last time. He could just about handle himself in a fight at school, but these men were trained killers. They fought dirty and there'd be no teachers or dinner ladies to break it up if things went sour.

The sun brought a sweat to his forehead, although the day was cooler than a couple of hours ago. Elliot, Helen, Chris and Jean Claude weaved their way through the streets and alleyways of the New Town, back to the Freedom Explorer to collect some supplies. Elliot could see the yacht in sight. They approached it with a steady pace. He froze and grabbed Helen's arm.

'What are you doing?'

'Teo' he said, looking forward. 'Eleven o'clock.'

Helen put her right hand over her head to block the sun out and scanned the harbour. It was covered in people, but none of them looked like Teo.

'I can't see him' she said.

'Me neither' said Chris.

'Just trust me. He's sitting on the bench on higher ground, by the tall brick wall. It's not on the harbour, but he can see everything, the whole harbour from there' said Elliot.

It didn't take long until Teo's hawk vision picked up on them. He saw Elliot looking straight at him.

'Crap, he's seen us. We need to leave now! Helen, you go with Chris. I'll stick with Jean Claude. If you're not followed, meet us back at the apartment. Go... come on.'

Although they agreed to go their separate ways, they all ran north away from the harbour and towards the Grand Bazar. Teo stood up, threw his newspaper on the bench and ran after them.

The large market was filled with clothes, carpets, spices, fruits and chickens in wooden cages that gave off a cluster of feathers. Elliot turned around, but couldn't see Teo. They dashed inside the maze of market stalls. Helen and Chris took the first left, into an alley of market stalls selling clothing and wooden carvings. Elliot and Jean Claude took a right, leading them through an alley of carpets and spices. Teo followed behind, just close enough to see Elliot take a right down an alleyway. He sprinted after them.

Helen and Chris hid behind a market stall. A shop keeper by the stall kept grabbing Helen's arm and trying to show her clothes to buy at "cheap cheap prices". She didn't want to cause a scene and so stayed polite, but on any other day she would have told the market teller and his boundary crossing hand where to go. Chris saw Teo reaching the junction of market ways, then turn right and run after Elliot and Jean Claude.

Elliot was fast, but Jean Claude was a little squidgy around the edges and slowed them down. At the end of the market way, they came out into an open space.

'Frack' said Elliot. 'We need to find cover.'

They searched for the nearest place to hide. Jean Claude squinted as the sun distorted his vision. Behind the cover of the sun's gaze was the Rumeli Fortress. 'Follow me.'

They ran towards the huge spread out stone ruins and up to its dilapidated entrance. Elliot saw a "closed" sign and cursed under his breath. They checked to see if they could find another entrance. They pelted around the corner of the ancient citadel, passing a scaffolding against the fortress that was being used to carry out repair works. Beyond that led to a giant nine story tower and a dead end.

'What now' said Jean Claude.

'Back this way.'

'Teo could come from that way.'

'Just trust me' said Elliot, running back the way they'd come.

They stopped next to the scaffolding and Elliot started to climb up it. Teo came around the corner, no more than a hundred meters away. They both ascended as quick as they could. Elliot was the first to reach the top and jumped onto a walkway on the other side of the fortress wall. Jean Claude followed behind with a red face and sweat dripping in sweat. He slipped his foot as he desperately clambered to the top of the climbing frame and nearly fell off the structure. Teo reached the bottom of the scaffolding just as Jean Claude reached the top. He fired his gun, luckily missing Jean Claude by a couple of inches.

'Quick' shouted Elliot.

The stress and pressure was showing on Jean Claude's face, and as he climbed onto the top plank of the scaffolding, he clumsily fell forward onto the fortress wall with his leg in the air. Teo was halfway up. Jean Claude pushed his dangling legs out as he tried to balance himself, causing the scaffolding to wobble.

'I have an idea' said Jean Claude.

He climbed onto the walkway and stood up. Teo was nearly at the top. Jean Claude quickly pushed the scaffolding away from him. It rocked, but not enough to fall over.

'Wait. Elliot. I need to tell you something' said Teo. 'You're in danger.'

'Yes, from you, you deranged psychopath' said Jean Claude, pushing the scaffolding even harder.

The scaffolding leant back and began toppling over. Teo jumped off just before it crashed to the ground, leaving a pile of wooden and metal planks spilling on the ground. Elliot looked down to see Teo on the floor, pulling out his gun and aiming it at them. They ducked for cover just before hearing a whooshing sound come from Teo's silencer. They ran along the stone narrow platform, careful not to fall down the long drop either side of them.

'What should we do' said Elliot.

'We'll have to hide.'

Elliot wasn't confident about his options. Granted the castle was big, but Teo was a heavily trained operative and the risk of capture was too great. Hide and seek worked well as a kid, but today, it wasn't his safest bet. They ran down some stone steps, across the fortress and along its crumbling steps, broken statues and overgrowing weeds. Elliot stopped and turned around. Teo was nowhere in sight. They carried on running. Up a flight of dangerously narrow steps which zigzagged their way to the top of a fortress wall, then south along the eastern wall pathway, with a ten-meter drop to their left and a perilous drop inside the fortress to their right. The stone walkway reached a dead end and they stopped in front of a big tower. The entrance was locked. A metal gate, eaten by rust, with a padlocked chain holding it in place.

Elliot looked back. The only other hiding area was a hundred meters back the way they came. He couldn't take the chance of being out in the open and so needed to move forward. He kicked the gate a few times, and the rusted metal gate finally gave way, snapping off. As he put his foot through the gate, the rust brushed against him, staining his trousers. Fortunately, it didn't cut through. With his haemophilia, another cut was the last thing he needed. The padlock and chain stayed in place on the wall of the tower, with the snapped part of the gate dangling down against the stone wall.

He stepped through the arched doorway and into an ancient room. The floor was made of rotten wood and the stone brick walls had several cloths with the sign of Islam on them. The remanence of what was once a stairway leading upwards lay scattered in the corner. Another stairway led down to the floor below and while it looked sturdy, Elliot didn't fancy his chances. After coming out of the bright sunlight, it was too difficult for their eyes to adjust to see what was downstairs without a torch.

There was no way of going upstairs. Apart from an old mirror that bared no reflection, a torn up rug and a full length cupboard with the door missing, the room was empty. The floor was an old, dusty platform of wooden planks that looked centuries old and very unsafe. Infested with wood-rot and covered in cracks. There were broken planks revealing a large drop to the floor below. As Elliot carefully trod over the wooden planks, each step made a creaking sound. His third step gave off an uncomfortable overbearing cracking sound and he was sure it was game over. He stood still until he knew it was safe to continue. Slowly, he put one foot in front of the other, eventually reaching the broken stairway at the end of the room. Jean Claude followed behind, walking over Elliot's dust-moved footprints. He was heavier than Elliot, but the wooden planks seemed to take his weight. Just. He stepped over the same part that caused an uncomfortable creak. He stood still, waited a few seconds, then let out a deep breath of relief.

'Thank God for tha-' he said as the rotten floor below him gave way, causing both of his feet to fall through the ground.

He desperately clawed at the floor with his arms, as his body and legs dangled through the broken floor. He was no athlete and his arms were unable to hold his weight. His body started slipping further and further, slowly making its way down before gravity took full swing. Elliot went ran over and grabbed onto Jean Claude's jacket sleeves with both hands. He completely forgot about his own safety. As he pulled him up, the wood beneath made a cracking noise. He spread his legs apart so his feet were standing on two separate planks, hoping it would better distribute his weight on the floor. He gave one more final pull. One, two, three...pull. Jean Claude slowly and ungracefully climbed out of the hole and rolled over onto the floor, panting like a dog and covered in broken bits of decayed wood.

'Are you ok?'

'I am...' he said breathing heavily. 'Thanks to you.'

They both nervously crawled along the floor and over to the broken stairway, well away from the death trap of a hole that Jean Claude's body had made. Jean Claude sat on the floor, panting away whilst Elliot tried to think about where to hide. Teo was coming after them and they needed to act quickly. He carefully climbed down the steps to see a series of old bars and worn stone slabs around the edges of the lower floor, but no exit. They were trapped.

Elliot looked at the hole that Jean Claude almost fell through. It was just in front of the arched doorway and extremely dangerous. *Idea.* He picked up the torn rug and tried to cover it over the hole. It wasn't working. It barely covered the gap and kept falling through.

'Try putting the mirror down first' said Jean Claude, pointing to the mirror against the wall.

'Good idea.'

Elliot carefully walked to the side of the tower and picked it up off the wall. He pulled his hand back in pain. *Splinter.* He drew his palm to his face to see the little bastard wedged into his finger, used his teeth to try and pull it out, but only half of it gave way. *I'll deal with you later.* He brought the mirror back to the hole. It didn't cover the length of the death trap, but just about sat across its width. It was enough to support the rug. He heard footsteps outside the tower. They were moving fast and there was no doubt it was Teo. Elliot pulled the rug over it gently, making sure his contraption didn't collapse through and onto the floor below. When he looked at his not-so-masterpiece, it was obvious that something was underneath. In any case, he had no other ideas. This was the best he could think of and hoped Teo wouldn't notice.

84

Istanbul – Present Day + 13 (Wednesday)

Teo broke into an entrance on the southern side of the Rumeli fortress. He left the broken gate wide open and it wouldn't be long before someone would notice. He checked all other exits. All locked. There was no way Elliot and Jean Claude could've got out unless they climbed down from one of the very tall walls, which would almost certainly injure them if not worse.

As the middle of the fortress had deteriorated over time, it was completely open space. The only places to hide were the remaining towers on each corner of the citadel. Teo ran up to the tower on the north east corner. The door was locked shut and there was no way of Elliot getting inside. He ran along the wall, pistol in hand and headed to the tower on the south-east side. The rusted gate of the tower was shut, but not locked. Teo lifted up the broken gate attached to a padlock and chain.

Elliot could hear a clank from outside, followed by the opening of the gate. They were shaking in nervous anticipation, crouching behind the full length cupboard in the tower. As Elliot heard Teo's footsteps creaking against the rotten floor, he froze and just wanted to be sick. Teo was only seven or so meters away, but it was close enough to hear him catching his breath after running around the fortress. The decaying wood made the familiar creaking sound as he took carefully placed steps towards them.

'Elliot, I know you're there. Come out' said Teo, cocking his gun. 'I promise I won't hurt you. I just want to talk.'

Elliot froze. He wasn't sure if Teo had actually seen them in the room, or whether he was just calling out in the hope they were there. After all, there was every possibility that they were downstairs or in another tower in the fortress. Either way, he wasn't moving from behind the cupboard. Even if his mind wanted to, his muscles wouldn't let him. Teo took another step forward. *He must be close to the boobytrap.* Teo stepped around the rug covered hole on the floor and walked closer to the cupboard. Elliot heard several steps too many and he knew his plan didn't work. Several profanities ran through his head and he closed his eyes, praying for a miracle.

'You need to work with me if you want your brother back' said Teo.

Jean Claude pushed himself up from the floor, stepped out in front of the cupboard and stared Teo straight in the eyes. 'You leave him alone. You'll not get past me.'

'Got ya' said Teo, aiming his gun at Jean Claude's head.

Teo shot in Jean Claude's direction. It just missed his head and caused a chunk of stone to spit out from the wall. Jean Claude jumped. Elliot couldn't handle the thought of his friend getting killed for him. He decided to face his demons and forced himself up. Fists shaking, he went and joined Jean Claude.

'Wait' said Elliot. 'Don't shoot. We'll do anything you want.'

Teo laughed. 'You've already done it. I really didn't want to hurt you Elliot, but you left me little option. You know you really should be careful with who you choose to have as allies.'

'I know right from wrong' said Elliot. 'You're a murderer and deserve to rot in hell.'

'Am I' said Teo, laughing and lowering his gun as he engaged the conversation. 'Right and wrong are not absolutes. As with black and white, there are always grey areas. Arguably some of your actions are morally questionable.'

'What do you mean?'

'Aren't you a fugitive?'

'Yes, but I'm innocent' Elliot shot back.

'My point exactly. As Hitler once said, no man in his own mind is evil. He believed with every fibre of his being that he was doing the right thing.'

To Elliot, Teo has just affirmed his intentions. Like Hitler's genocide of the Jews, he was planning to use the stone to kill Palestinians, possibly even all Muslims. He had to be stopped. Elliot noticed that his gun was no longer pointing at Jean Claude. If Elliot charged him, there was a risk Teo would react and shoot him. He didn't have much of a choice. The window of opportunity was shrivelling like a slug in a salt-bath and Elliot had to act fast. He ran at him with all his might. Teo saw him coming and hit Elliot in the face with his gun, sending him down to the floor.

He raised his gun at Elliot. 'You really shouldn't have done that' he said, stepping back and raising his gun at Elliot. 'Big mistake.'

There was a loud cracking noise beneath Teo as his foot broke through the rug and mirror covering the hole in the floor. Before he knew it, Teo's legs and body fell through the hole, causing him to drop his gun which landed a few feet away from him. He clung onto the edge of the broken wooden floor with both arms. As he tried to pull himself up, the rug caught underneath his grip began slipping.

'Help me' said Teo, gasping.

'Why should I' replied Elliot.

'This is not what it looks like' said Teo, as his arms were falling off the edge. 'You need to watch out-'

Teo fell through the hole before he was able to finish his sentence. He crashed down with such momentum that he fell two stories, smashing through the first wooden floor and landing with a deathly thud on the stone floor below. Elliot carefully looked through the gap. There was broken wood everywhere. Teo had cracked his head on the ground and blood was spilling out, making its way through the grooves of the stone tiles. His leg began shaking for a few seconds, then his body became lifeless. Elliot felt sick. He'd been around a lot the last week or so, but seeing a human being die in such a tragic way was beyond traumatic. He began to hyperventilate.

'It'll be ok' said Jean Claude.

'Will it' said Elliot, breathing uncontrollably. 'I've just killed someone and Teo's men have my brother.'

'You had no choice. It was that or be killed yourself. Look. We have some time before his men realise what's happened. We'll play it cool, stick to the plan and find the treasure. If we do this now, then by the time they realise what's happened, you'll already have your brother back.'

Elliot agreed with his proposal, but didn't like it. There was no guarantee they'd agree to keep Toby alive. Teo was dead and if Toby's captors found out their boss was dead, the deal would be off. What Elliot didn't understand was why Teo was coming after Elliot. He knew that he was searching for the stone and, as he had his brother as collateral, Elliot was sure to come to him. The attempted warning also made him nervous. It was already five pm. Eleven hours to save Toby. They agreed to go back to the apartment and re-group with the others before going to the Basicila Cistern. For the sake of Toby, they had to find that treasure and it had to be now.

85

Istanbul – Present Day + 13 (Wednesday)

Henry arrived in Istanbul after a less than comfortable flight with a budget airline. He got what he paid for, but it didn't make the noisy, unsanitary experience a pleasant one. According to the tracking device, the bug on the Freedom Explorer was in the local harbour less than ten miles away. He knew Chris was with Elliot at the Notre Dame when the murders occurred and so there was every chance Elliot and Helen were with him now.

Henry hailed a cab. The driver's English was better than expected and within thirty minutes he was at the harbour. It was beginning to get dark, but the air was still warm. Certainly warmer than Paris. He found the yacht next to a floating restaurant, covered in disco lights. Apart from a waiter who was leaning against a rail-guard and smoking a cigarette, the restaurant was empty.

He passed the restaurant and went up to the yacht. The lights were off. He looked around. No one was watching and so he boarded the Freedom Explorer. He searched as much as he could, but some of the rooms were locked. No one was there. He made his way to the ground floor deck. The large container of tools he'd seen in France was open and he noticed many of the excavation tools were no longer there. *What are you up to Elliot*. He called his researcher, Louise Allen.

'Louise. Now a good time?'

'Henry. Hello. Where are you?'

'Istanbul. Dead end. I need you to look over all of the information again. See if you can find anything that may help me find Elliot and Helen. I know they're here, I just don't know where to look.'

'Erm, ok. I'm working on the Chrysostomou enquiry at the moment.'

'That can wait. This is more important.'

'I have my orders, Henry.'

'I know, but trust me, this is more important. I'll take the rap for it. I promise.'

Louise let out a deep breath. 'Ok. But you owe me dinner.'

'Deal. Do you still keep that big bottle of soy sauce on your desk?'

'Er, yeah' replied Louise.

'You weirdo. Great, I'll bring you some sushi to go with it.'

He hung up the phone and went for a bite to eat nearby. Somewhere that he could keep an eye on the yacht in case anyone turned up. Anywhere but the floating restaurant with disco lights. He sat outside a restaurant on an uneven cobbled street, drinking a Turkish coffee that was so bitter, it made him pull a face every time he took a sip. His phone was vibrating. Headquarters.

'Louise, that was quick.'

'Not Louise. It's Claire. Why would Louise be calling?'

Henry trusted his boss, Claire Nelson, but as she reports to someone higher up, he needed to be careful not to get Louise in trouble.

'No reason. She was going to update me on the Chrysostomou file.'

'Right' she said, unconvincingly.

'Anyway, how can I help?'

Claire explained that she's been getting heat from the Chief of Police, asking why one of her officers has gone off to Istanbul. If it's found out that Henry's been enforcing the law outside his jurisdiction, it would have serious consequences for her team, not to mention the political issues with the Turkish government.

'Unofficially, you know I'm behind you on this' said Claire, pausing.

'But?'

'If the Chief finds out you're in Turkey carrying out illegal operations, you'll be arrested.'

'So be it.'

'You don't understand' said Claire. 'You'll be dishonourably dismissed from the service. No job, no pension.'

'So what do you want me to do?'

'Bring back the people who killed my nephew and don't get caught by the local authorities.'

86

Istanbul – Present Day + 13 (Thursday)

Helen and Chris were just about to call the police when Elliot showed up at the apartment. His face had a perfectly round bruise in the centre of his right cheek. His trousers were cut up, with brown rust stains on them.

'What on earth happened to you' said Helen.

'Long story. All you need to know is that Teo's dead. But we need to act fast before his men find out and do something to my little bro.'

'Here' said Jean Claude, handing Chris and Helen some excavation tools. 'We got these from the yacht before coming here. We have to go this evening, under cover of darkness. If we leave it until tomorrow, it will be too late.'

Elliot cleaned up and got into a change of clothes. His legs were aching from all the running today. All he wanted to do was sleep. All he was allowed to do was press on. It was nine pm and time was getting on. They ate some food that Jean Claude brought back from a local takeaway shop, got their equipment ready and made their way back to the Basicila Cistern.

Elliot's mind wandered as they walked towards their destination. He thought back to the start of all this mess. Not back to the British Museum, but back to the demise of his family. Or the start of it at least. One cheating father that spiralled into so much hurt, eventually leading to two parentless children. The damage caused could filter into the next generation, if not further. Transcended through trauma and dysfunction. Helen looked at Elliot's sombre face.

'It'll be ok. We'll get Toby back.'

'It's not that' replied Elliot.

'What is it?'

'Nothing. Just um. I'm just angry. Angry at my father for what he did to the family. If he was faithful, he wouldn't have drunk drove and crashed. Both my parents would still be alive. Directly or not, he caused the demise of my family. If he didn't cheat, Toby would be safe at home I'd still be at uni and none of this mess would've happened.'

Helen nodded. 'I understand. I can't begin to imagine how difficult it must've been. But I promise you, your dad was not that bad. I've only ever known him to be a decent human being.'

Elliot gave a pursed lips, insincere smile and raised his eyebrows. Chris caught up with Helen and Elliot.

'Besides' said Helen. 'If you and I never met, David and Teo would have their hands on the architect's drawing and maybe even the Philosopher's Stone. The world could already be in chaos by now.'

'Don't forget, Elliot' said Chris. 'Because of you, we've managed to get closer to the world's greatest treasure than anyone else. You did this. You know... I have two PHDs and more letters after my name than I can recall. I've spent nearly a decade researching the lost Greek temple of Artemis and have got nowhere. You've spent two weeks on a trail and have discovered more than most scholars could ever hope to achieve in a lifetime.'

The pep talk helped to cheer him up a bit. Or at least it changed the focus from his family.

'Temple of Artemis?'

Chris explained that the temple was one of the seven wonders of the ancient world. Dedicated to the goddess, Artemis. Daughter of Zeus and Mistress of Animals. A beacon of its time that drew people from all over the world. Unfortunately, it is believed to have been destroyed. Its location was lost in history. Chris has been searching for years for clues that could lead him to it, but every time he finds new material, it leads to a dead-end.

After a forty-minute walk they reached the Old Town of Istanbul. Away from the market stalls and near the old monuments that were now closed. It was fairly quiet. Elliot approached the entrance to the Basicila Cistern. The windows and wooden doors of the public toilet shaped entrance were locked shut.

Chris took a closer look at the door, while the others stood around him facing outwards and trying, without success, to look inconspicuous.

'This is a pin and tumbler lock' said Chris. 'We used to sell these at my uncle's shop. I think I can open this.

Chris found a pick and tension wrench in the excavation tool set. He fiddled around with the door lock until it gave a click. 'The amount of times customers would lose their keys and we'd have to help get into their homes without causing damage. More common than you'd think.'

He turned the handle and the door came open. Elliot was surprised it was that easy. Either that or Chris made it look easy.

Once inside, they turned on their torches and made their way downstairs.

All the lights were off and in the depths of the Basicila Cistern, it was pitch black. The torches helped, but the area was so vast there was too much that couldn't be seen. Helen saw a pillar on top of a creepy stone carving of Medusa's head resting on its side. Without the classical music playing and the tourist walking around, the place was eerie. So quiet they could hear the sound of water droplets splashing into the water from the ceiling above. A noise previously drowned out by the tourists' footsteps earlier that day.

They walked through the damp and dark cistern, along the wooden raised platforms above the water and headed towards the rear of the room. The platforms seemed to go on forever.

'I was reading up on this place' said Chris. 'You know it was buried for centuries. It was only in 1545 when an archaeologist of Byzantine antiquities heard reports of people collecting water by lowering buckets in dark holes from the ground above. On investigating, they discovered the underground cistern. There were even records of some people catching fish this way.'

'Funny way of fishing' said Elliot.

'Tell me about it. Since then, it's been cleaned up for tourists, but otherwise the structure remains untouched.'

The path of wooden platforms eventually came to an end. If they wanted to continue, they'd need to climb down into the water. Helen shone her torch, but the end of the cistern wall was too far away to be visible. She sat on the floor and started taking off her shoes.

'What are you doing' asked Chris.

'I don't like walking in wet shoes' said Helen. 'Better to take them off now.'

'Good idea' said Jean Claude.

The rest of them also took off their shoes. Elliot climbed down from the platform. The cold water sent a tingling sensation through his body. Fortunately, the water only came up to his knees. He helped Helen climb down. They picked up their excavation tools and shoes and headed forwards, with each stride giving a gentle wave to the otherwise still water. After a few minutes, they reached the edge of the underground cistern.

'OK, we'd better split up to make this quicker' said Elliot. 'The Copper Scroll said we need to look for a recess at the bottom of the water, which is plugged up with sediment.'

'It must be referring to the point that the water enters the cistern from the underground passageways' said Chris. 'I read that the water comes from a forest several miles away from here. I bet that would collect mud and other sediment.'

Elliot and Helen went in one direction, along the wall, following the edge of the floor with their torches. Chris and Jean Claude went the other way, shining their torches in the water with a zigzag motion. It wasn't brilliantly clear, but it was enough to make out the ground below.

'I guess we're looking for an entry point that's not covered up by stone' said Elliot.

'Sounds sensible' replied Helen.

Elliot and Helen weren't having much luck. Elliot's attention span was causing him to draw figure eights in the water with his torch. It didn't help him find anything, but made the experience a little more entertaining. Helen slipped as she put her foot down onto the floor, expecting it to be higher than it was. She splashed around and almost lost her balance. She stood up straight and pressed her feet into the floor.

'I think I've found something' said Helen.

Elliot shone a torch where she was standing. 'What is it?'

'The floor. It's soft. Could be nothing, but it feels different to the rest of the stone floor around here.'

'I don't see anything. It looks like stone' he replied.

'Trust, me I can feel it. Come over here and feel.'

Elliot walked over and trod his bare feet on the same ground. It was well camouflaged and looked just like the rest of the stone around them, but as his feet pushed down, it felt soft. Squidgy almost. He could feel a very slight current of water making its way up between his toes. *The water entry point.*

'I think you're right.'

Elliot waved his torch at the other two, indicating for them to come over. He tied his shoes to his bag using his shoe laces, got out a spade and began digging. A few minutes later, Chris and Jean Claude came over. Chris walked as quickly as he could, causing the water to splash around his waist for which he was less than pleased.

'Look what Helen's found guys' said Elliot. 'Quick, give us a hand.'

'We need to act fast' said Helen. 'If anyone finds the door upstairs has been played with, they might report a burglary. That's the last thing we need. Turkish prisons are not exactly the Four Seasons of comfort.'

Elliot checked his watch. Eight hours to go. The mounting pressure added to his fatigue. He felt exhausted. He prayed they'd found a hidden passageway, but didn't want to get his hopes up just yet. Jean Claude hung his lamp on a groove of the rear stone wall and picked up a spade. Chris and Jean Claude rolled up their sleeves and helped them digging out the sediment.

87

Byzantium – June 323 BC (one month before the death of Alexander the Great)

The great general, Apollodorus of Amphipolis, ordered the last of the surviving slaves to finish the construction work to the hidden temple. A location known only to the general himself and Alexander III, King of Macedonia. Of the four thousand builder slaves kept in isolation from the outside world, there were less than one hundred remaining. The rest died from either exhaustion, starvation, work injury, punishment or murder to prevent the slaves from talking about the temple and its secrets.

The slaves worked day and night, kept underground in damp and dark conditions. Where disease and fatal accidents were inevitable. Their whereabouts unknown to them. All prisoners of the limestone and marble structure they gave their life to create. Given the promise of freedom if they finish their task, the dwindling survivors continued on, but their hope for survival was itself dwindling.

Hiding the temple was the biggest project of its kind and keeping it secret was no easy task. Each group of builders were given sections to construct and then put on rotation. The result was that no one person, apart from Apollodorus, knew the temple, its layout or its secret. Those that did venture off, never returned.

The main structure, walls and decorative features were all complete. All that was left were the carvings to the limestone entrance. The remaining builders, starving and broken, chiselled away at the walls. The taste of freedom had never been so close.

As the last of the work came to a finish, there was one more thing left for Apollodorus to do. He pressed his hand against his pouch and felt a vile of hemlock. The ultimate test of loyalty. His destiny. For the empire.

Apollodorus looked down at the entrance. A rectangular hole in the ground that led to the first chamber. He said a small prayer, then closed the entrance with a heavy solid stone slab. It fell into place with a loud thud. He pulled a leaver to release the water kept in one of the city's cistern's.

A few of the slaves heard water rushing in from the entrance. They put down their tools and ran to the exit to see it covered with a large stone slab. Apollodorus could hear them scream and shout. It sent a shudder down his spin. Before anyone could move the weighty stone, he covered it with mud to weigh it down, burying everyone alive.

The slaves panicked uncontrollably, trying with all their might to move the stone, but it was too heavy. They needed more people. They went back to get help. The cold water rushed into the entrance at an incredible pace. By the time they had returned, the entire entrance was covered in water, top to bottom. They tried again, but the weight of the water above the stone to the entrance made it too heavy. It was no use. There was no way out. The obedient survivors were left there, buried alive in the graves of their own making.

Without giving himself time to think, Apollodorus pulled out the vile of hemlock and drank it in one gulp. He prayed to the gods for a painless death, then gave a salute in the name of the King.

88

Istanbul – Present Day + 13 (Wednesday)

David's expensive, but reliable intel told him that Elliot was in Turkey. He hadn't received contact from his employer for a few hours. He assumed he'd got held up on something, and decided it would be better to move his operations closer to Elliot and the others. Moving country wasn't normally difficult, but bringing a kidnapped child would increase risk and, as a result, increase the cost of their mission. Additional baggage that would eat into his underlying profit. An unfortunate necessity. David was holding most of the cards, although he didn't know the hand Elliot was dealt. He needed to be prepared.

David rented an apartment in Old Town, Istanbul, using a pseudonym to sign the rental contract. He paid in cash and the landlord didn't ask questions. A holding deposit was given, but it was unnecessary given the dilapidated state of the place. He wasn't sure he could do much more damage. It was built on top of a fish mongers and so opening the windows was an unpleasant experience. David was sure he could smell the stench of fish on his clothes. Still, it was cheap and met their basic needs. Somewhere to lay low and a room to keep Toby locked up.

David unlocked the second bedroom to see Toby asleep. He closed the door, put the latch back on and joined his brother and Abrafo in the living-room. His leg vibrated. He pulled out his phone. An update on Elliot. *Time to go hunting.*

'Abrafo, you stay here with the kid' said David. 'Whatever you do, don't let him out of your sight. I mean it. Don't even leave the apartment. We're going to meet our little friends who seem to have found something.'

Abrafo was stuffing his face with Turkish food. 'Got it, boss' he said with his mouth full.

There was something about Abrafo eating that annoyed David. He wasn't sure if it was the gluttony of the oversized beast or the noises he made. He always seemed to be eating.

'And Abrafo' said David.

'Take my phone. If we don't contact you in seven hours or less, something will have gone wrong. Take care of the kid. Permanently. And make sure you hide the evidence.'

Abrafo nodded and continued stuffing his face. The rest of them went to the Basicila Cistern, armed to the teeth. David didn't want to take any chances and so asked the Organisation to arrange backup. He needed two of their best, right away. The Organisation agreed to send men to help, but would need at least thirty minutes. David didn't want to lose any time and so they agreed to meet inside the Basicilla Cistern.

89

Istanbul – Present Day + 13 (Wednesday)

Henry staked out the harbour for hours waiting for any signs of Elliot and Helen, but without any results. It was dark and the weather was humid. His eyelids were heavy, and he struggled to keep them open. The jetlag didn't help. Every so often, a few locals, tourists and sailors would walk past, but none of them were faces he recognised, and none of them boarded the Freedom Explorer.

He scanned through photos of the crime scene of the victims inside the Notre Dame Cathedral. One of the priests, or whoever he really was, had numerous scars on his body and several numbers tattooed on his arm. *An army tag number?* Henry wasn't sure. His mobile rang. Given the late hour, he knew it could only be one person. He pulled it out of his pocked and raised it to his ear.

'Louise, working late I see.'

'Pot, kettle.'

'Crime doesn't sleep' said Henry.

'No, but I'm pretty sure criminals do.'

'What have you got for me' he said.

'A couple of things. You asked me to check Elliot and Helen's contacts to see if I can find anything.'

'Yep.'

'Well, I ran by some checks on Elliot's mobile. When he was in Washington, he received a call from an unregistered number.'

'How does that help us' he asked, unsure at what she was getting at.

'The same number made another call. They didn't have GPS and so I'm assuming they're using an old phone. However, I was able to triangulate the phone's approximate location.'

'And' said Henry.

'Whoever it is, is in Istanbul.'

'You're amazing. Have I ever told you that?'

'Just doing my job' she replied.

Louise was being modest, but really she knew she was good. She had a nose for finding information and analysing stats that other professionals would normally miss. She'd helped to put away more than her fair share of criminals.

'Go to the Old Town. I can't tell you exactly where the phone will be, but it's somewhere in the Hoca Giyasettin area.'

'Thank you. Try and get some sleep' he said.

'You too.'

'Oh, Louise...'

'Yeah?'

'What was the other thing' he asked.

'Oh yes. The victim that was murdered in the Notre Dame Cathedral.'

'You got an ID on the priest?'

'Yes, but he wasn't a priest. Rav Manek. Wanted in the UK in connection with several violent crimes, including an acid attack, gang fights and a rape charge. This guy was one nasty piece of work. I have to be honest. I won't lose sleep over his death.'

'Noted. Have you seen the numbering on his arm? Any idea what that is?'

'I'm working on it. I'm not sure, but think it could be some kind of prison camp number.'

'Thanks Louise.'

The stakeout didn't give him anything, but at least Henry had a new lead. What he didn't understand was why a criminal would dress up as a priest in the Cathedral. And the numbers on his arm. *What did they mean?* It didn't add up. He was starving and so picked up a falafel wrap from a takeaway stand. It was cheap, but tasted delicious. He was always wary when ordering falafel. The last one he had was so dry, it was like eating cotton wool. He jumped in a taxi and made his way to Old Town. He was getting closer. He could feel it.

90

Istanbul – Present Day + 13 (Wednesday)

Elliot and the others were digging at the sediment for over an hour. His arms were getting tired. It wasn't easy. Every time they'd lodge a spade into the watery mud and lifted up, the weight of the water would push half the dirt off the spade and back into the water. Elliot could feel his toes becoming wrinkled from the water. It reminded him of being on the beach and dipping his toes in the sea.

Helen gasped and jumped back, causing a ripple around them.

'What's wrong' asked Elliot, fearful that maybe someone accidentally stabbed her foot with the spade.

'There's something in the water' she replied.

Elliot shone his torch around the floor, but didn't see anything. It must have been some rubbish or something. Whatever it was, it had gone now and so they carried on digging.

Helen snapped her right leg out of the water. 'What the crap. There it is again. It touched me. There's definitely something moving in the water.'

Elliot shone his torch again. This time he saw a silver and gold scaled carp, no bigger than a loaf of bread, swimming around looking for food. It was startled by the torch and swam away.

'Relax' said Elliot. It's just a fish. There's nothing in this water that can hurt you.'

'I agree' said Jean Claude. 'The most hazardous thing in here is Chris' spade digging around my toes.'

'Sorry, point taken' said Chris, moving his spade further away and digging in another spot.

They continued pulling up the watery earth, slowly making headway. As exciting as it all was, Elliot was tired and wanted this to be all over. He wanted to be back home, back at work and most importantly, back with his brother.

'Oh my God' said Helen.

'Helen, the carp won't hurt you' said Chris. 'The worst they could do is suck on your toe.'

'Isn't that a type of pedicure treatment' said Elliot.

Elliot and Chris found it funny, but the others were too tired to laugh. Elliot pictured Helen in a beautician having the royal carp pedicure treatment. A fish on each toe. *Maybe Clinique should offer a range of carp treatments,* his inner child thought. He chuckled to himself.

'No, not that' she said. 'I've hit something hard.'

'Is it the treasure' asked Helen.

'I doubt it' replied Jean Claude. 'Not submerged in water like this. It would've eroded by now.'

They stopped digging. Elliot put his shovel against the cistern wall, bent down into the water until his hands were on the floor and his chest was wet. He felt around the dirt with both hands reaching something hard. It was stone. A stone slab beneath the sediment. His hand moved along the surface of the slab to try and find its edges. He couldn't find them as there was still too much mud. Thirty minutes later, they had cleared the sides of the stone slab. It had a groove big enough for a hand to fit in and pull it up, but was slimy and difficult to grip. Jean Claude and Chris wedged their spades into the edge of the stone slab and pushed down. It moved, making a gargled gritting sound. It lifted up, but only slightly. It was heavy. Very heavy.

Elliot placed his spade through the small opening and turned it so that it hooked on the bottom of the stone slab. It was certainly better than grabbing the slippery underside and risk losing his fingers. Chris and Elliot held onto the spade and lifted it with all their strength. Chris' face was red and his arms began shaking. The square stone cover raised an inch at a time until it was fully upright. Between them, they just about managed to lean it up against the wall.

They all hobbled together, shone their torches into the gap and peered down. They could see a rectangular space. Empty and no more than four feet wide. Elliot could only see three sides and a stone bottom. The forth edge was out of site and appeared to be beyond the wall of the cistern. He put his spade down and jumped inside the gap causing a splash. The water went up to his shoulders.

'Hand me that torch' he said, looking at Helen.

'Here you go.'

He shone the torch under the edge of the cistern wall. The underwater gap went on for at least a couple of meters, but it was difficult to say for certain without swimming underneath to investigate.

'I'm going under.'

'But you can't. Not without proper equipment' said Helen.

'We don't have time' said Elliot. 'Besides, I'm a good swimmer and I won't go far.'

Elliot dunked his head in the water to get used to the temperature. He came back up and counted. *One, two, three.* He took a deep breath, went underwater and kicked his legs out, then swam until he was beyond the cistern rear wall and out of site. Helen saw his torch light fade in the water until it was gone. The only light she could see bouncing from its edges were the light of Chris' torch over the entrance.

Over a minute went by and Elliot still hadn't returned. Helen was starting to panic. *What if he got stuck and drowned?* Another minute went by. Nothing.

'Right, I'm going in' she said, putting down her tools and rolling up her sleeves.

'No wait, look' said Chris, pointing at the waterway.

The entrance grew lighter, and a few seconds later she could see the waving light path of the torch, followed by Elliot's head and some bubbles. His head popped up and he took in a big breath of air, then shook his head like a wet dog.

'What the hell' said Helen.

'Sorry' said Elliot, wiping the water from his forehead. 'But I found the entrance on the other side. I had to check it out.'

'I thought you'd drowned or something. Don't do that again!'

It was the first time Helen had taken the parental tone with him. He didn't mind so much.

'I won't stray too far again' said Elliot. 'Promise.'

'What did you find' asked Jean Claude.

'There's a chamber… just behind the wall' said Elliot, wiping water from his mouth. 'It's only five meters through here.'

Chris frowned. 'Under water?'

'We can swim it' said Elliot. 'A heads up. You might get a nasty shock on the other side.'

'What do you mean' said Helen.

'You'll see.'

Helen climbed down into the gap with her torch and was the first to swim under. Chris went next, then Jean Claude. Elliot stayed back to make sure everyone got through ok.

91

Istanbul – Present Day + 13 (Wednesday)

David and Marco marched across Istanbul to the Basicila Cistern, fully armed and ready to take down Elliot and Helen. By the cistern, two police officers on the same side of the street, headed in their direction. Rather than looking conspicuous, David and Marco carried on walking, hoping the officers weren't here for the same place. One of the officers gave Marco a wide eyed stare. That was usually enough to provoke him and David prayed that he didn't react.

As the policemen walked passed them, David relaxed a little. They slowed down and turned around. They waited and watched the police officers pass the cistern and turn a corner. David and Marco double backed on themselves until they were at the entrance of the Basicila Cistern. David noticed the door was unlocked.

'They must already be here' said David, pulling out his gun and pushing the door open.

David felt a hand on the back of his shoulder. *The policemen.* He jumped, raised his gun and turned around, ready to attack. It was not the police officers, but two large muscle bound men stood in front of him, armed to the teeth. They wore black khakis and carried Glocks, hunting knives and a pistol which David had not seen before.

'We've been sent to help you' said the taller one with tattoos on his neck. Apart from a thin line of hair running through the centre of his skull, he had a shaved head.

'You're just in time. I'm David' he said, shaking his hand. 'This is my brother Marco.'

'No names' said the other mercenary, who was shorter, but stockier than Mohawk.

David thought he looked like a bull.

'Whatever' laughed Marco, waving his knife around.

'Ignore him' said David.

The mercenaries did just that. Unfazed by Marco's lack of respect or ill attempts at intimidation.

David saw two people come around the corner and start walking towards them. It was the police officers again, patrolling the area. They immediately clocked David staring at them. His stress levels elevated. He knew that if the police found them next to the Basicila Cistern with the door broken into, it would create trouble. He thought about making a run for it.

The two policemen marched over to David and the others and started speaking in Turkish. David had no idea what they were saying. One of the officers pushed David out of the way and inspected the door to the cistern. He saw it had been unlocked and started shouting, pointing to the floor and signalling for them to lay on the ground. Without hesitation, Mohawk punched the officer in the throat to stop him from speaking, then used his knife to silence him permanently. The other officer tried to intervene, but the Bull was on top of him and took him out in seconds, making it look effortless. David knew he had the right team with him.

CHAPTER 91

'We'd better hide the bodies and get out of site' said David.

They dragged the bodies into the entrance of the cistern and lined them up, just behind the door. They all stormed tactfully but quietly downstairs to the depths of the ancient building. At the bottom of the steps, David shone his torch around the light-less place.

'Keep on your guard' said David, holding a gun close to his chest. 'They could be expecting us.'

'Elliot aint nothing to worry about' replied Marco. 'Or his Scooby Doo group of O.A.Ps.'

Marco walked down the wooden platform, carrying his flick-knife in his right hand, blade facing backwards and a torch in his left. There was a faint light in the far distance.

'Up ahead' said David, pointing. 'Turn off your lights.'

Marco turned off his torch, leaving them in the pitch black darkness. If it wasn't for the rail guard on the platform to guide them, it would've been nearly impossible to navigate their way around.

'Do you think they spotted us' asked Marco.

'I dunno, but keep quiet just in case.'

'I don't like it in here' said Marco.

'The only thing to be scared of in here, is us' said David.

Mohawk and the Bull didn't say anything. They all followed the faint light, until the platform ended, then climbed into the water and continued onwards. When they reached the end of the cistern, they saw the light was a lamp resting on the wall. No one was there.

'What's this' said Marco, walking up to the hole in the ground.

David shone his torch into the watery entrance and could see the underwater passage went beyond the wall of the cistern.

'This must be where Elliot and Helen went' he said, jumping into the submerged passageway. 'Marco, jump in. You two…' he said, pointing and Mohawk and the smaller merc. 'If we don't come back in ten minutes, come and find us.'

92

Istanbul – Present Day + 13 (Wednesday)

Elliot took in a lung-filled breath of air as his head reached the surface of the waterway, which ran the length of a new room. An ancient chamber. Jean Claude was climbing out of the water, while Chris and Helen were staring gobsmacked at a disturbing pile of human remains scattered in the corner of the chamber. The chamber was rectangular. The underwater passage that they'd come out of, continued as a shallow stream and ran along the length of the room. The stream continued into a dark, slim and short tunnel, just big enough to fit one person at a time. Apart from the human remains and the waterway, the room was empty.

Elliot shone his torch at the dusty human remains. There were at least fifty bodies. Decayed to the bone, leaving fragments of skeletons, leather pouches, belts and blunt instruments which had been worked down to the nib. Helen stood in front of a stretched out body on the floor. Its jaw was wide open. Almost as if it was trying to scream for help.

Helen held her hand over her mouth in disbelief. 'What do you think happened to them?'

'My guess…' said Elliot. '…they were working here and someone decided that whatever they were doing had to be kept secret.'

'Buried alive' said Chris.

Elliot nodded. 'Look at their tools… they must have been workers here. If you had something of importance, the only way to keep its location private is to bury the people that created it.'

The room was covered in Ancient Greek symbols and pictures. Elliot had seen some of the symbols from Chemistry at school. Others he recognised from his reading on Aristotlian physics, but had no idea what they meant.

Elliot shone his torch into the watery tunnel in the corner of the chamber, but couldn't see anything. 'Where do you think this goes?'

'The temple of Alexander the Great' replied Chris, reading the Ancient Greek text that was carved into the stone above the tunnel. 'This doesn't look good.'

'What doesn't' said Elliot.

'This here' Chris said pointing to the inscription above the tunnel. 'It says "Beware the fate of the soul, all hail the philosopher king."'

'You're right, that doesn't sound good' said Helen.

'Plato' said Elliot.

'Sorry' said Jean Claude.

'Plato. In Plato's Republic, Plato believed that only a philosopher should be a ruler. A king who was not trained to think wisely could become a tyrant and only think of himself. To ensure that any state or city is run justly, Plato considered that only a philosopher should be king. The term became known as the philosopher king.'

'This makes total sense' said Helen.

'What does' said Elliot.

'Elliot, this is why you've been able to work out all the clues and puzzles' said Helen. 'They were designed to be found by a philosopher. A philosopher king.'

'I wouldn't go that far' he said, walking up to the tunnel. 'Guys, this sounds dangerous. I should do this alone. You've already done so much for me. If I make it out of here, I'll make sure whatever is found, is split fairly.

You wait here. Over and above any treasure, I just want my brother back.'

Helen and Chris both put their hand on his shoulder.

'We're coming with you' said Chris.

'And me' added Jean Claude.

'We're a team and we'll see this through to the end' said Helen.

Helen's cotton blouse over her shirt was soaked through and uncomfortable. She took it off, left it in the chamber, jumped back in the water and started making her way through the pitch black tunnel.

She turned around and looked at Elliot. 'We can do this.'

Elliot hopped back in the water, while Chris and Jean Claude climbed in with less agility and enthusiasm. A reflection of their difference in age. Helen was in front with her light whilst Chris was at the back. They waded through the tunnel with the water up to their chest. Elliot kept his arms up in the air as he slowly walked through the narrow water filled passage.

After ten minutes, they could see the end of the tunnel. On reaching the end, it opened up into a huge expanse, much bigger than the previous chamber. As with the previous chamber, the waterway continued in a slim straight stream to the end of the cavern. Elliot, Chris and Helen shone their torches around. It was a giant cave with the front of an Ancient Greek temple at the far end. To the left of the stream were five tall, thick marble columns standing in a line across some steps, just before the temple's entrance. A statue, twice the size of Elliot, was placed in between each column. At the top of the steps was a large doorway, three times taller than an average door. Elliot shone his light along the columns to see a stone carving of the Rosy Cross in the middle of each one. He knew they were on the right track.

Elliot walked up to a statue. 'I recognise this one. It's Socrates…the grandfather of philosophy.'

Chris read the text beneath a statue to the right of Elliot. 'This one is Plato.'

Chris inspected the others. 'This one is Aristotle and the last one…'

'Let me guess' said Elliot. 'Alexander the Great.'

'Yes.'

'Each statue is that of the teacher and pupil' said Elliot. 'Socrates taught Plato, Plato taught Aristotle and Aristotle in turn, taught Alexander the Great.'

'Guys, this is incredible' said Chris, carefully touching the smooth statue in ore. 'If I'm not mistaken, this is the lost temple of Artemis. Elliot. I think. I think you've found it.'

Chris had a gleaming smile on his face. Elliot was pleased for him. He had been researching the lost temple for many years. He was almost tearful. If nothing good came out of this mess, at least he would have this finding. They made their way through the columns and giant doorway. Passed the doorway, they reached a narrow stone bridge with a very steep drop below on either side. The bridge was ancient. Elliot could see parts of its underbelly had crumbled away, leaving a small and thin remnant of a crossing. *The result of erosion over millennia.* At the opposite end of the bridge was a stone platform and semi-circular wall with five tunnels going in different directions. A statue sat in the middle of the platform.

'There's no way I'm crossing that' said Chris.

'I wonder if there's another way in' said Helen. 'Let's check the other room.'

They backtracked into the previous area with the five pillars to see if there was another route forward. Not that they knew which way was forward. In the cave, Elliot heard a splashing noise coming from the watery tunnel that they had originally come from.

'Did you hear that?'

'Hear what' said Chris.

'A splashing sound' said Elliot, pointing to the tunnel.

'I didn't hear anything' said Jean Claude.

Another splashing sound, followed by slight waves of water from the watery tunnel.

'There it is again' said Helen. 'We'd better hide!'

They turned off their torches and hid. Chris quietly climbed back into the waterway, at the opposite end of the room. He could feel a gentle current pull the water towards the wall. There was a gap for him to hide, but only just. The ceiling was so low that there was an inch of space between the water and stone. He crouched as low as he could and climbed in the groove. Most of his head was submerged under water, except for his mouth and nose. His face was pressed against the stone cold ceiling. It was wet and slimy to touch.

Helen and Jean Claude hid in the room with the bridge, while Elliot stood quietly behind one of the large five columns. A torch-light came out of the tunnel, and a minute later David and Marco appeared, treading through the water. They jumped out of the waterway and made their way over to the pillars.

Elliot carefully looked over to see Marco carrying Helen's blouse. *Crap.* David and Marco knew they were there.

'I'm calling dibs on Helen' said Marco quietly.

'No' said David. 'I'm not tellin you again. No one's touching her until we've got what we want.'

Marco shone his torch along the floor, revealing wet footprints going into the temple. 'Look.'

Elliot listened to David and Marco's footsteps approaching the temple's entrance. Closing up on him. Elliot held his hand over his mouth as he waited behind the pillar. He could hear Marco chewing a piece of gum. David and Marco walked on passed the columns and through the large doorway. *Helen and Jean Claude are in there*. Elliot swore under his breath. Marco and David immediately spotted them.

'Ha. We've got you now' said David, pointing a gun at Helen. 'Don't move. Where's the rest of you?'

Helen froze. Panic smacked her in the face. Marco walked up and grabbed her by the neck, causing her to scream. He pressed the sharp edge of his knife against her chest, and moved it down to the clothing over her right breast. He slowly began to cut her vest. Helen closed her eyes and shuddered.

'Marco. What the frack did I say' said David, walking up to Marco and smacking him around the head with the back of David's gun.

'Argh' said Marco, holding his head and stumbling back. 'Piss off.'

'No, you piss off, you idiot! This is not how we are doing it!'

During the commotion, Elliot crept up to the large doorway. He poked his head around to see Marco had let go of Helen and joined David. David was holding a gun at Helen and Jean Claude. If Elliot was going to act, he needed to do it fast. Problem was, he had no idea what to do. He wasn't trained for this. Sure, he'd been in a few fights after his parents passed, but he was dealing with dangerous people and he'd be lucky to come out of it unharmed. Still, Helen and Jean Claude were in life or death trouble, and despite his paralysing fear, he had to find his legs and use them. Chris came out from hiding and Elliot gestured for him to come over quietly. Chris tip-toed to Elliot. Elliot signalled for him to take Marco and Elliot would jump David.

They crept up behind them as quickly as they could, then, when they were two meters away, ran and charged. David and Marco were caught by surprise and Helen and Jean Claude fled to the corner of the room. After tackling David's torso like a rugby player, Elliot knocked his gun to the floor and a struggle ensued. He got a couple of hits in, but it was no use. David was much stronger than him and knew how to handle himself. David blocked the last punch then landed a blow to Elliot's jaw, sending him with speed to the floor. Before Elliot had a chance to regain focus, he felt a gut wrenching pain in his stomach as David kicked him as he was down. He lay winded on the floor, barely able to breathe.

David looked over to Chris, to see Marco had him in a headlock. His knife was pressed into Chris's neck, just hard enough to break the skin, letting his neck seep a little blood. When he wasn't looking, Helen bent down, picked up a gun and shot it in the air. Everyone jumped.

'Stop it. Both of you stop it now, or I will shoot' she said, facing the gun at David.

David stopped hitting Elliot and stepped away. Marco kept Chris in a headlock with the knife up against his face. Another shot went off in Marco's direction, missing him by a few feet. It ricochet against the wall, causing limestone to spray out over him.

'You know I said both of you' said Helen.

He let go of Chris who wriggled away as fast as he could. He touched the cut on his face, then looked at his bloodied hand.

'You're an animal' said Chris.

Marco and David grouped together, away from Elliot and Chris.

'Now do as I say, and no one will get hurt!'

Behind Helen, Jean Claude quietly raised his gun and aimed it at her head. 'On the contrary. It is you who must do as we say.'

93

Istanbul – Present Day + 13 (Wednesday)

Detective Wrightman got a taxi to Hoca Giyasettin, a rundown part of Istanbul, made of concrete buildings and the odd solitary tree. The buildings were either half constructed or so badly damaged they looked uninhabitable. On the street that the unregistered phone was traced to, most of the buildings even had parts of their roofs missing. It was a dilapidations surveyor's dream.

It was late at night and apart from a market stall across the road, the place was quiet. Deathly quiet. The area smelt of spices infused with the stench of fish. He looked up to see a closed fish mongers. All the fish had been removed from the window display, leaving empty pallets and pictures of cartoon fish with happy faces on the windows. The ground outside was wet from where the shop keeper had been wiping the floor, pushing the fish remnants onto the road. It added to the already pungent smell and Henry tried hard not to gag. He quickly moved away to a less smelly spot.

Henry was tired. Not just physically, but emotionally too. He'd seen most things in his line of work, but losing a close friend and partner hurt. He wasn't good at showing it. On the inside it ate at away at him like a disease. And now Toby had been taken. Henry had a kid a year older. He'd love to live with his son, but in truth he knew his ex-wife was better equipped to help their child grow. He empathised with Elliot wanting to reunite the family. Even if it was illegal to take him away from his foster parents.

The method used to track the mobile was not exact and the phone could be anywhere within a hundred-meter radius. He wondered if Louise gave him the right location. *No, she knows what she's doing.* Even if it was the right area, chances are that everyone would be asleep and there'd be no way of knowing where to start looking. Plus, there was no guarantee that Elliot's contact, or whoever he was calling were still here. He would have a better chance if he came back in the morning. He decided to walk around the block, just in case.

94

Lost temple of Artemis, Istanbul – Present Day + 13 (Wednesday)

Jean Claude held the gun against the back of Helen's head. His face was expressionless. He cocked the gun, ready for use.

'Drop your weapon please, Helen. I'd prefer to not kill you, but if you leave me little choice, I will do what's necessary. And David...'

'Yeah.'

'Keep your brother on a leash. I will not have animals on this expedition.'

Helen dropped the gun, kicked it towards David and stood next to Elliot and Chris. David picked it up from the floor and aimed it at her.

'What the hell is going on' demanded Elliot, moving in front of Helen to try and shield her from the guns.

'You've been very helpful Elliot. I thank you. But now, I think I'll take over from here. You've brought us far enough.'

Adrenaline rushed through Elliot's body as though he'd just jumped out of an aeroplane. He felt like a fool. All this time he was being played. Jean Claude made sure they stayed on track. He thought back to the encounter with Teo at the Rumelli Fortess, where he tried to shoot them. No, he didn't. He was shooting at Jean Claude.

'All this time, you've been working with Teo' said Helen.

'He's not working with Teo' said Elliot.

'What' said Chris.

'We've been had' said Elliot. 'Teo was trying to stop Jean Claude. He was trying to warn us to stay away from Jean Claude and his men. To save us.'

Jean Claude gave an arrogant smile. Elliot couldn't understand why, if Teo was innocent, did he kill the priest in the Notre Dame cathedral. *Maybe he wasn't a real priest?* Either way, Elliot wanted to end Jean Claude. To pretend as though he was helping the entire time. Playing on each of their vulnerabilities. Using a young child's life as leverage. He clenched both of his fists.

'Why are you doing this' asked Elliot.

'Why do you think' said Chris. 'Greed.'

Jean Claude laughed. 'I assure you my intentions are good.'

'Killing innocent people is hardly a good intention' said Chris.

'Often great causes require great sacrifice' replied Jean Claude.

Elliot heard the marching of footsteps. A few seconds later, two large men came through the temple doorway. Dressed in black and heavily armed. It was the mercenaries, Mohawk and Bull. Elliot didn't think there could be anyone more intimidating than David, until they walked in.

'Welcome to the party' said Jean Claude.

The men both nodded and stayed silent. Elliot thought about his brother. Elliot's life was unlikely to see the end of day, but that didn't mean Toby couldn't survive. They were stuck with these criminals and he needed to make his brother safe.

'You have me now. You don't need my brother. Please... please let him go.'

'Sorry Elliot' said Jean Claude. 'Anything can happen until I have what I want. He's a safety precaution. Insurance, I guess you could call it. If we do not make a call in just over four hours, Toby will be bled dry, like a Halal chicken.'

'You bastard' said Elliot, launching towards Jean Claude.

Mohawk punched a winding blow to his stomach, causing Elliot to curl into the foetal position on the floor, unable to breathe. Helen got down on her knees to comfort him.

'You won't get away with this' said Chris.

'Enough talking' said Jean Claude. 'We need to find the vault.' He gestured with his gun for Chris to cross the decrepit narrow stone bridge. 'Walk.'

Chris stood there, shaking. He slowly walked towards the narrow bridge and peered over the edge. The area was dark, but even with light from their torches the crevice below was still black. A bottomless pit where the slightest noise made an echo. Elliot put his hand in front of Chris and held him back.

'Wait' said Elliot. 'I'll go.'

'I don't care who goes...just get a move on' replied Jean Claude.

'No Elliot' said Chris. 'I've got this.'

'It's fine. I'm lighter, and besides, you wouldn't be in this mess if it wasn't for me.'

'OK, I don't have time for this heart to heart crap' said David. 'Elliot, get moving now' he said, prodding Elliot in the back with his gun.'

Elliot stepped close to the edge. He didn't like heights so much, especially when there were no rails to hold onto. The narrow stone bridge was no wider than a foot and must have been around two thousand years old. It filled him with an overwhelming dread. The drop was so deep, he assumed it was the where tectonic plates of Asia and Europe met.

He looked across to the semi-circular platform where the straight edge faced the crevice. He put his first foot cautiously on the bridge. He kicked a small stone over the edge. He waited for it to make a sound as it hit the floor. And waited. There was nothing. He started feeling shaky and all he could think about was maintaining his balance. It was not exactly a balancing beam, but the consequences of failure were certain death. It made keeping his balance even worse.

The first few steps were fine. He took another step with his right foot. The fear of wanting to stay in the centre, counter-intuitively caused his foot to land in the middle of his path, as if he was walking on a tight rope. It created a lack of balance. He wobbled, quickly knelt down with his hands on the bridge, then stayed still for a few seconds until he regained his balance. He reached the middle of the bridge, where the stone had eroded to the point that the walkway was under a foot wide. He slowly stood up and the stone creaked. *Crap, crap, crap.* His life flashed before his mind's eye and he knew he had to act fast. He sprinted then took a giant leap as he neared the end, landing on the platform and rolling. He knelt down and held onto the statue in the middle of the platform to catch his breath. He stared at each of the five tunnels surrounding the statue. *Where now?*

Jean Claude opened his bag and pulled out some rope. 'Probably should have got this out earlier.'

'Arsehole' Elliot whispered under his breath.

Helen gave Jean Claude a look of disgust. He gave the rope to David who tied a torch to one end, held on tightly to the other, then threw the torch to Elliot. The rope unravelled itself all the way across the big crevice and reached the other side. Elliot caught the torch and tied the rope around the middle of the statue.

'Here' said David, handing the rope to Marco. 'Tie this as tight as you can to the column in the other room.'

'Got it' said Marco.

'And make sure the rope is taught' said David.

Marco ran back to the entrance of the temple. After a few seconds, the rope raised up from the floor until it was at chest height. It vibrated a bit as Marco tightened the knot.

'There' said Jean Claude. 'This should make things a little safer.'

They made their way over the bridge to join Elliot, one after the other. Jean Claude went first. Elliot thought about tackling him as soon as he got over the bridge, but with a gun held to Helen's head, he couldn't take the risk. That and he needed to keep him alive to call off Toby's death. The mercenaries went next, then Helen followed by David and Marco. As Marco walked along, he pushed the rope hard as support, rather than using his feet to balance himself on the bridge. The rope became slack and as Chris walked over, the rope did little to assist his balance.

At halfway, the bridge gave the same creaking sound. Chris looked up in horror and held on to the rope so tight that it made his hands turn pale. He faced the rope and started to side step across, but with every step he had to move his clenched hands along the rope, which slowed him down. Suddenly, the bridge gave way. Large chunks of stone came tumbling down into the never-ending pit below. Chris held on to the rope, swinging left to right, dangling in mid-air.

'Help me!'

'Crap, we have to do something' said Helen.

'Leave him' said Marco. 'Let's go.'

'Don't be inhumane' said Helen.

'Ok' said Elliot, walking over to the edge of the platform. 'Just try and move one hand in front of the other. You can do this.'

Chris' breathing became heavy and his face was completely red from exhaustion. He let go with one hand, leaving a blood stain on the rope behind him and moved along by a small distance. He let out a deep wail from the pain of his arms giving way. He did the same process again and again until he was a few feet away. There was a build-up of lactic acid in his body, causing him to shake. He was too tired to go any further. Elliot could see he was losing grip.

Elliot held onto the rope, leant forward and reached out. 'Give me your hand' he said, reaching out.

Chris held on tightly and struggled to look at Elliot. 'I can't. I can't hold on. Help.'

Chris tried to grab Elliot with his left hand, swooping at Elliot, like a cat trying to catch fish in a fishbowl. His weight was pulling him down too much to allow his free hand to get closer. The rope was thin and ripping into his skin.

'It's no use. Help.'

Chris' left arm was the first to give way, leaving him dangling from the rope with one arm. Elliot leaned forward as much as he could. Just as he did, Chris' right gave way. Elliot leaped forward from the platform, held onto the rope with his left hand and grabbed Chris with his right. Elliot groaned as the rope cut into his skin. He swung Chris back and forward, until he was close to the platform. On the third swing, Helen grabbed Chris and helped pull him to safety. Chris collapsed on the floor, breathing heavily. Elliot climbed back to the platform and leant down to check Chris was OK.

95

Istanbul – Present Day + 13 (Wednesday)

Elliot helped Chris up from the floor and rested him against the statue. His hands were bloodied from rope burns and shaking. Elliot looked around him to see if there was anything he could use to help stop the bleeding. Nothing. He gave a length of clothing from the bottom of his shirt, and used it to wrap around Chris' hands. Elliot contemplated running, but they were surrounded. The mercenaries on one side, David, Marco and Jean Claude on the other. With the bridge collapsed, the only way forward was through one of the five tunnels.

'It'll be ok' said Elliot, resting his hand on Chris.

Jean Claude pointed his gun towards Elliot. 'Enough. Time to move on.'

'Which tunnel' asked David.

Elliot noticed that each tunnel had a carving into the limestone above it. The first on the left was a winged figure that looked like an angel. The second tunnel had a stone carving of a Greek man being slain. The third was a Greek god, the fourth was a group of demi-gods and the fifth was a group of Greek warriors standing over what appeared to be a treasure chest.

'Which one takes us to the vault' said David, pushing Elliot.

The Mohawk walked towards the tunnel under the Greek warriors and treasure chest. 'This must be the one' he said, in a deep husky voice.

'Wait' said David. 'I want Elliot to tell me which one.'

Mohawk sounded eastern European. Elliot thought that maybe he was Romanian. He stared at each tunnel in turn, but none of it made sense to him. He'd never seen these pictures before. In his research, studies or otherwise.

'Elliot, over here' said Chris, who was staring at an inscription on the statue in the middle of the platform.

Elliot walked over and recognised the face on the statue. It was Aristotle, standing on a square plinth.

'What is it?'

'The plinth has Ancient Greek text on each side' said Chris. 'It says that all humans are...'

Mohawk interrupted. 'Enough of this time-vaysting, it's obviously the one with the treasure' he said, then walked over to the tunnel on the far right.

'Wait' said David.

'Nie. I don't need babysittin' replied Mohawk. 'We need to take action if we want results.'

Mohawk marched off down the tunnel. The sound of his footsteps faded into the distance. David looked at Elliot, then at Jean Claude.

'I guess he must be right' said David.

'We'll see. Let's wait' said Jean Claude.

Jean Claude paced around the platform, looking into each tunnel using his torch. It was difficult to make out anything as the tunnels went on for some distance.

'We've done a thorough background check on each of you' said Jean Claude. 'I must say Elliot, that I'm surprised you're happy to work for the person who destroyed your family.'

'You didn't give me much of a choice' said Elliot.

'That's not what I meant' said Jean Claude.

'That's enough' Helen interjected.

'Oh... you don't know' said Jean Claude, facing Helen. 'He doesn't know?'

'What are you talking about' said Elliot.

'Helen, you were close with Elliot's dad, weren't you?'

Helen stayed silent. She shook her head and faced the floor with a look of guilt. Elliot twigged.

'You're the woman' he said.

She didn't say anything. All this time, Helen had been the other woman is his father's life. The affair that came between his mum and dad. The alcohol infused argument that led to his dad's deathly car crash and his mother's decision to stop chemo and let her cancer take her. All of it. Everything. His life was ruined because of his supposed friend. To her, he was a charity case. That's why she had him moved from cleaning to working underneath her. A sick, self-gratifying ploy to make her feel better for the damage she caused.

'How could you' said Elliot.

'Elliot' she sobbed. 'It's not what you think.'

'You know what, I don't want to hear it. I don't care.'

He absolutely cared, just didn't know how to express it. It was all too raw. Despite the gut-stabbing discomfort, he needed to try and block it out. His focus had to be Toby. Nothing but Toby. He was the only surviving member of the family. It was more important than anything right now. He checked the time. Midnight. He had four hours to get the stone and get out of there to call off the kill order on his brother.

They heard a screaming sound echoing through the tunnel, followed by Mohawk running back, waiving his hands around. He was unable to walk in a straight line and kept bumping into the sides of the tunnel. The piercing scream of a fully grown man sent a chill down Elliot's spine. The man held his hands in front of his face as he approached them, screaming for help. As soon as he got out of the tunnel, he collapsed on the floor, revealing the skin burns on his face and hands. Helen leant down next to him. His skin was melting off.

'Don't touch him' said Elliot, grabbing Helen's hand. 'You might get burnt too.'

'We can't just leave him' she shouted.

The Mohawk made some deep, barely recognisable gargling groans, like he was trying to talk with a mouth full of water. He coughed up a fountain of blood that spilled out onto the floor. Helen turned away and covered her face with her hands.

After a few minutes, he stopped moaning. Slowly his shaking ceased until he was completely still and his breathing stopped. If Elliot felt in danger before, he certainly felt it now. Elliot, Helen and Chris all watched, standing as still as possible, without saying a word.

'You...' said David, signalling Elliot. 'Go through another tunnel.'

'Wait' replied Elliot.

'No more waiting' said David, raising his gun at Elliot.

Elliot walked back over to Chris, who was standing by the statue in between the five tunnels. 'What does the text say?'

'Erm' mumbled Chris, shaken up and losing focus. 'It er, it says'

All humans are mortals,
All Greeks are human

'All Greeks are mortals' said Elliot.

'What does it mean' asked Helen.

'Aristotle's Syllogism. It's a logical method to work out truths. A form of deductive reasoning and is the basis on which the world's entire computer system works.'

'Choose a tunnel now' said David, cocking his gun.

Elliot looked at the stone carvings above each tunnel. By painful deduction, he knew it wasn't the fifth tunnel with the carving of Greek warriors standing next to a treasure chest. He looked at the first stone carving. It was an angel. *No, this would be immortality.* He stared at the stone carving above the second tunnel. A Greek man being slain. *All Greeks are mortals,* he thought.

'This is it' said Elliot. 'All Greeks are mortal.'

'Are you sure' said Chris.

'It must be. The rest don't fit' he said.

Helen looked at the stone carving of the Greek person being killed. 'It doesn't look very inviting.'

'Trust me.'

'We don't need to' said David. 'You're going first. Now move already.'

Helen looked at the third and fourth carvings of a Greek god, and a group of demi-gods. She'd suggested trying these tunnels first, but Elliot was adamant. He picked up his torch, and shone the light down the tunnel. It was too deep to see through to the other side. He stepped inside with caution and slowly made his way through to the other side. The rest waited with trepid anticipation for Elliot and tried to listen out for any noises. A few minutes later, the waving light made its way out of the tunnel. Elliot had returned.

'I've found another room. It's safe.'

96

Istanbul – Present Day + 13 (Wednesday)

Henry circled the block a couple of times and was feeling exhausted. He saw nothing that helped… the area was dead. Everyone was asleep. Everyone except Henry it seemed. He reached back to his starting point, which identified by the all familiar strong fish smell from the fishmongers. A light was on, on the apartment above it. It was dim, but noticable.

He was about to head to a hotel, when he got a message from Louise Allan. The traced mobile was on the move again. He needed to get out of site and quickly hid behind an old car. He saw a bulky man come down an external stairway on the side of the fishmongers. He didn't recognise the man, but stayed still just in case.

The stocky man crossed the road and into the late night corner shop. He was maybe five meters away. Henry saw him buying some junk food and a couple cans of soda. He was a big guy. Overweight, but Henry could tell there was muscle under the hood of that engine. The man handed over some cash and took his shopping. Henry stayed quietly behind the car and continued staring through the car windows. The light from the shop would've made it difficult to see Henry. As the man walked away from the shop, Henry noticed a distinctive tattoo on his hand. It looked like writing.

No. A series of numbers. Henry instantly thought back to Rav Manek, who was found dead in Notre Dame Cathedral.

The bulky man crossed the road and made his way back up the external staircase to the apartment. Henry could hear the scratching of Abrafo's key against the lock as he tried to open the door. Henry waited until the door closed shut, then walked up the external stairway. There was only one apartment. He couldn't read the number on the door, but then he didn't need to. He was fairly certain that this man knew something. However, he needed more to go on before he could barge the door down. Henry decided to come back tomorrow during the day, once he had more intel.

97

Istanbul – Present Day + 13 (Wednesday)

As was habit, Elliot was up in front and lead the way. Through the tunnel as it went downhill. After a minute or so of walking, they arrived at the next chamber. From the distance, it looked like a small gladiators' arena with steps on either side and a big sculpture in the middle. Helen and Elliot walked together a few feet up front, with the rest behind. As Elliot walked through the passageway, he realised that there was not steps surrounding the room, but marble basins. Like small baths or large sinks. Helen followed him into the room.

As Elliot stepped forward, his foot pressed against a stone tile that moved inwards. It caught him off guard and he nearly tripped over. The room started making a noise. Elliot held onto a basin and looked at Helen.

'What is happening' she said.

'I don't know, but let's go back' said Elliot.

Elliot turned around to see a stone door begin rolling in front of the passageway. He ran to the entrance and tried to stop it, but it was too heavy. It must've weighed over a ton. He quickly let go before his hands got caught as it closed shut. He thumped against the hard cold stone, but it was no use. They were trapped.

Elliot and Helen shone their torches around to see if there was another entrance. They searched the chamber, but they could see no way out. Just a series of basins along each side of the rectangular room, staggered inwards like a stairway. At one end of the chamber was a sculpture made of cup-like chalices, facing upwards. All grouped together to make a pyramid shaped structure. At the other end of the chamber was a large circular mosaic on the floor, revealing a picture of the Rosy Cross.

'Crap, what do we do!'

'Erm, not sure' said Elliot. 'There must be a way out. I bet this room is a puzzle, just like the other room. What do we know. We now know that Alexander the Great only wanted a philosopher to find the treasure and the philosopher's stone. This is why we've found so many philosophical clues. There must be a clue around here. See if you can find anything.'

Elliot walked over to the sculpture of cups at the end of chamber. 'This must have something to do with it all.'

'To do with what?'

'I dunno. To get out of here, I guess'.'

Several drops of water fell from the ceiling and landed on the floor. Elliot looked around then back at Helen.

'Did you hear that?'

'Hear what?'

Within a few seconds, a flow of water started seeping into the chamber from the ceiling. It trickled down from an opening above the sculpture, pouring water into the first chalice at the top of the pyramid. Once filled, the cup toppled over, pouring water into a lower cup. The lower cup, when filled, toppled over filling another cup beneath it and so on. Once emptied, each chalice swung back in the upright position to enable it to collect more water. The cups were all made of different sizes. Eventually, some smaller cups at the bottom of the pyramid structure collected water then individually poured it onto the floor. The water was so light that they made a gentle, barely noticeable dripping sound.

'What is this' said Helen.

'I'm not sure but I bet we're supposed to do something with this mechanism' he said, touching the pyramid of chalices.

At each corner at the bottom of the pyramid was a large heavy chalice. They were much bigger than the rest and looked more like four bells turned upside down. Next to each of them was a vertical column, the length of which stopped at the base of the chalice.

Elliot noticed a plaque with Ancient Greek writing on it. 'I wish Chris was here. He'd know what this message was.'

'We'll have to make do. We have no choice.'

All of a sudden, water started pouring in from the sides of the room with great ferocity. First it filled the basins on the edge of the chamber, then the next ones filled. They continued spilling out until Elliot's feet were under water.

'Uhhh, Elliot. Any chance we could hurry up.'

'I'm thinking, I'm thinking.'

Elliot stood on the tips of his toes to reach the chalice at the top of the pyramid. He could just about touch it with his finger-tips. As he brushed it with his index finger, the cup turned slightly. Once it filled up with water, it leant forward in a different direction, pouring its contents into a different lower cup.

'I get it.'

'Get what' she shouted. Her voice was deadened by the loud sound of the water filling up the room.

'It's Aristotle's Paradox of the grain of sand.'

Helen gave a blank look. The cold water was now at knee height and sent a chill into Elliot that made him shudder.

'What is it, and be quick!'

'Why does a grain of sand being dropped on the floor make no noise, but a bag of sand being dropped makes a large sound?'

'Don't know. Larger surface area?'

'According to scholars, Aristotle believed that inaudible sounds added together can make audible sounds. It's not the most scientific of answers, but it's what we need to do. I bet that's what the Ancient Greek text says.'

'Make a sound?'

'Sort of. Change the flow of the water on this pyramid of cups. We need to fill the larger metal bell shaped ones on each corner. The bigger cups will make a bigger sound than the gentle splashing it's currently making.'

Elliot turned some of the chalices, moving them left and right so that when they poured over, they'd move closer to each of the four corners at the bottom of the pyramid structure. Each time he moved a cup it would head towards one corner, but not all four. The water around them was rising rapidly and was now at waist height.

'Crap, it's not working' said Helen. 'What do we do?'

'I don't know...we need more time.'

'We don't have more time.'

Before they knew it, the water had risen above the level of the lower chalices. Even if they had got it right, the lower cups would not go anywhere as the water had risen too high. After another minute of fiddling with the pyramid and the water was up to Elliot's chest.

'Ok, idea' said Helen. 'The water was supposed to trickle down into the four large metal cups right?'

'Right.'

'And these cups would then fall over and hit these columns down?'

'I think so.'

'Well, what if we push them down with our weight, instead of the metal cups doing it? We must weigh more than the cups filled with water.'

'It's worth a try' said Elliot.

They waded through the water to each find a corner of the pyramid. Elliot stopped at one corner where a large chalice stood next to a meter-tall column. Only one foot would fit on top of the column, but as he was floating in water, he was able to balance himself. He kicked it down a few times. It was difficult to get force behind him in water. The first time he kicked down, he missed causing it to scrape his ankle. He jumped a couple more times and it slowly moved downwards into the ground, before making a stone clicking sound. Helen did the same with her column.

'I've done one of them' said Elliot.

'Me too.'

'Two down, two to go.'

The water had risen to head height and they were both now panicking. They both swam to the remaining columns and repeated the process. The water continued pouring in.

'This one's not going down' she said, paddling in the water and trying to kick the column into the ground.

'Let me try.'

Helen moved out of the way and Elliot stood on the column, but the water was so high that he was unable to put any weight down on it.

'It's not working!'

The water filled the chamber to the point that they could no longer touch the floor. All they could see was the light of their torches slightly brightening the water filled room, with just a small gap between them and the ceiling.

'We don't have much time' said Helen. 'I'm sorry. It's my fault. I want you to know I would do anything for this to have turned out differently' she said, trying to speak and stay afloat at the same time.

'Save that for another time. We're not dead yet.'

The water splashed everywhere in their panicked state. It was cold and Elliot was freezing. Their torches underwater gave a little light, but it was only just enough for them to see each other. Not enough to navigate the room.

'I've got an idea' he said swimming towards her. 'I'll swim down, balance on the column and push up against your feet. You can push down against the ceiling. It should give us enough pressure to push this damn thing down.'

'Ok, please hurry.'

Elliot counted to three, held his breath and kicked down into the water. He opened his eyes, but it was too dark to see anything. He pulled himself down by holding onto the pyramid of cups and worked his way to the column. He looked up and could just about see Helen with her torch kicking water. The water had risen further and was half a foot from the ceiling. Only a short space for Helen to breathe. He placed his right foot onto the column. Helen stood on his shoulders and pushed down against the ceiling. With some effort, the third column went down. One left to go.

He went up to get his breath, but it was too late. The water had filled the room completely. He saw Helen up against the ceiling just above the fourth column. She was freaking out and waving her hands around. He desperately swam down and did the same again with the fourth column. Helen felt him push her feet and so put both hands on the ceiling, causing the torch to fall into the water and onto the floor. She pushed her arms out, but the pressure caused his foot to slip and their acrobatic stance fell apart. Neither of them could see anything. Helen tried to bob her head up for another gasp of air, almost kissing the ceiling, but it was no use. *This is it*, he thought. For both of them. Elliot grabbed her foot again and pushed her up. She pushed against the ceiling as hard as she could with both arms, putting pressure against Elliot's hands as he stood on the column. Nothing.

He was starting to feel dizzy and was losing focus. He was desperate for air and just wanted to inhale. His chest felt like it was going to implode. They both pushed again and the column moved down slightly. He changed his position so that he was facing the column with his hands, pushed with one hand and used the other to hold underneath the pyramid structure. The column moved further, then a little more. His form collapsed and went into a spasm, violently shaking. Helen screamed under the water. It was too dark to see how far the column had gone down. A few seconds later, the sound of grating stone travelled through the water, as the large circular mosaic of the Rosy Cross on the floor turned clockwise. It opened, sucking up the water from the room. Several seconds on and the top of the chamber was filled with air. Helen could breathe again. She took several large gasps of air and coughed out water. There was no sign of Elliot coming up. She swam down to the torch, picked it up and waved it around. She couldn't see him.

She held her breath and swam back down. She spotted something shining under the pyramid structure. It was Elliot's belt. She went down, grabbed underneath his arm and pushed him up. The water had flushed out quickly and Helen could almost stand up. Elliot wasn't moving. She tried to keep his head above water, but he was heavier than she could handle. She bobbed her head up to get a breath of air, which made Elliot's face to go back into the water. She went back under to hold him up for as long as possible. Thirty seconds later and Helen was able to stand and breathe at the same time.

'Elliot. Elliot' she said, shaking him and patting his cheek. 'Don't you die on me!'

Helen felt his neck. He still had a pulse, but there was no breathing. As the water drained out she laid him on the floor and positioned him so the water could come out. She tilted his head backwards, opening up his airway. Some water trickled out of his mouth, but there was still no sign of breathing.

'Crap. No, no, no' she said, crying.

Helen had seen CPR on plenty of hospital films, but had never been trained in it. She pushed down against his chest in pulsed intervals, then pinched his nose and blew air into his lungs. A tear rolled down her cheek.

'Come on Elliot. You can do this.'

She went back to pressing his chest down a few more times, then breathed air into his lungs. Halfway through an assisted breath, Elliot coughed and water sprayed out from his mouth and his legs kicked out. She turned him onto his side to let the rest spill from his lungs. He took in several panicked breaths of air.

'Oh thank God' she said, grabbing him and hugging tightly. 'I thought I'd lost you.'

'No…' he said, coughing. 'Not yet. Remind me never to free-dive.'

Helen let Elliot's circulation recover and stopped squeezing him. 'What are we going to do about Jean Claude and his scary friends? Once they've found the treasure, they'll have no need for us.'

'I don't know, but we need to keep going. I don't want to see what'll happen if we stop helping. Besides, I need Jean Claude to set my brother free.'

Apart from some puddles on the floor and a collection of water in the basins, the water had completely washed away into the circular hole at the other end of the chamber. Almost immediately, the stone door blocking the entrance rolled out of the way. Chris stepped into the room, careful not to step on the stone that triggered the door to shut. He looked at Helen and Elliot lying there on the floor, dripping wet.

'What happened' said Chris, running towards them.

'Not much' said Elliot. 'But I must brush up on my Ancient Greek.'

Helen looked down at her water soaked, prune-esk feet. They were covered in scratches and a couple of toe nails had broken.

'Remind me to get a pedicure if we ever get out of here.'

'Will do' said Elliot.

'Enough play time. We need to move on' said Jean Claude.

Elliot didn't want to be around Jean Claude and the others any more than he had to, but the additional light from their torches was useful. After Chris and Jean Claude spent a minute surveying the chamber, they walked over to the giant plug, where there was once a mosaic of the Rosy Cross. Inside the big hole was a spiral staircase leading downwards.

'Onwards and erm, downwards' said Elliot.

'Move' said David, pushing his gun into Elliot's chest.

Elliot was still angry at Helen for having an affair with his dad. It caused so much disruption. Despite the years of trauma and resultant dysfunction, deep down he knew she was a nice person and highly doubted she intended to cause any damage to the family.

Three hours to get the treasure and get out of there. He walked down the steep steps, carefully placing his feet on the slippery surface. There was nowhere to hold onto. Elliot got off the last step and walked into a new chamber. It was a weird shape. The first half went uphill, presumably to stop the travelling water from going into the next room. Along the wall adjoining the stairway was a series of potholes for the water to drain through. At the lowest point of the chamber, the floor was wet. The remainder of the room, which was on higher ground, was completely dry. They walked up the hill, like a row of ants following each other. Elliot saw a glimmer of gold in the distance.

98

Istanbul – Present Day + 13 (Wednesday)

David prodded Elliot in the back with his gun, pushing him up the hill of marble steps. Not that it was necessary. He was walking in that direction already. However, he was not about to argue with a dangerous killer.

At the top of the upward climb, the chamber opened up into a hexagonal room, no bigger than a small bungalow. Elliot tried to avoid the cobwebs as he walked under its dome shaped ceiling. The architecture was relatively simple, although for a two-thousand year old building, it would have been a work of brilliance in its day. He weaved through some oddly shaped, unrecognisable golden and marble sculptures. Each sculpture was separately attached to a pole that stood in a circular track on the floor. There were multiple circles and from a bird's eye view, the circle of tracks looked like the circles of a ten year old tree trunk, with a statue in the middle.

Elliot reached the middle of the hexagonal room and stood next to the marble statue of a muscular man carrying a giant bowl on his back. On the floor was a stone tablet with more Ancient Greek writing.

Helen followed Elliot and stood next to him. 'What do we do?'

'I don't know, but there is some good news' replied Elliot.
'Great. I'm desperate for good news. What is it?'
'There are spiders here.'
'I hate spiders. How is that good news?'

Elliot used his peripheral to make sure Jean Claude and his men were not listening to his conversation. Jean Claude was investigating a golden sculpture of a head shaped ball on a staff next to a wall. David was keeping an eye on Chris who was near the exit.

'There's no way that spiders could have got in the way we came' said Elliot.
'So...' replied Helen, pursing her lips together as she thought. 'It means there must be another exit somewhere.'
'Exactly' said Elliot, nodding.
'That doesn't matter too much. Not now' said Helen.
'What do you mean?'
'Whatever we do, we can't let Jean Claude get his hands on the philosopher's stone. If we do, he could do anything with it. We still don't know his intentions, but given he's prepared to kill for it, I'm not sure we can take the chance. Many people could die. This is big. Bigger than you and bigger than me. If it means Jean Claude isn't successful, I'll die if I have to.'
'Don't say that' said Elliot.
'It's true.'

Elliot looked around at the golden sculptures. If this was the treasure, it wasn't as big as he was expecting. *Maybe someone took most of it and left this.* The chamber was cold. Elliot took off his blue unbuttoned shirt, resting over his no longer white t-shirt, and handed it to Helen who was rubbing her arms to keep warm.

'I'm ok' said Helen.
'Just until you get your blouse back' he said, holding his shirt out.
Jean Claude marched up to Elliot. 'Where's the Rosy Cross. The

philosopher's stone. Where is it?'

'This is the last room' said Elliot. 'Look at all the gold sculptures.'

'Please...please let us go. We've done what you asked' asked Helen.

'This can't be it' said Jean Claude. 'There'd be much more treasure than this. Where's the philosopher's stone?'

'This temple has been here for millennia' said Elliot. 'There's every chance that the treasure, or most of it, has since been moved. Who knows where it could be now.'

Jean Claude gave Elliot a long hard stare. His eyes squinted, giving a look of distrust. He nodded at David and gestured for him to bring Chris over. David grabbed Chris and dragged him to Elliot.

'Read' said David, as he pointed to the Ancient Greek message on the statue.

'No' said Chris.

David lifted up the back of his gun and swung it down with momentum onto Chris' back, causing him to fall forward to his knees. He landed next to the message and bashed his cheek against the marble plinth. It cut his face leaving a red mark on the stone.

'Read' said David, cocking his gun and pushing it into Chris' temple.

Elliot suspected the message would give another clue to find a different room. If he could get Jean Claude to believe they'd reach a dead end, it would stop him from locating the philosopher's stone and causing havoc. But it would also mean he'd never see Toby again.

Chris spoke up. 'It says:

"Gold is the wealth of the shadowed mind.
The philosopher king is contented with the wealth of wisdom.
The treasure you see is the treasure you'll see."

Helen let out a deep breath. 'As Elliot said, this is all the treasure of Alexander the Great and this message proves it. The treasure you see is the treasure you'll see.'

'Fine' said David, raising his gun at Helen. 'Then I guess there's no need for you.'

'I guess not' she replied.

David held his gun to her head. 'You're going to tell me where the stone is or you're going to die. Three, two...'

'Wait' said Elliot. 'There's something else...'

Helen looked at Elliot and opened her eyes as wide as she could, signalling for him to stay quiet. He knew he couldn't let Jean Claude get his hands on the philosopher's stone. He also knew he couldn't let Helen die. There must be another way. He didn't know how yet, but letting Helen die was not the answer. For now, he just needed to buy time until the right moment arose.

Jean Claude put his hand on the nozzle of David's gun, and lowered it to the floor. 'Speak, and don't mess me around. I'm no fool and I can tell if you're lying.'

'This is the work from Plato's republic. You know, the records by Plato where his teacher Socrates discusses how to create order.'

Jean Claude frowned. He had no idea what Elliot was talking about.

'Plato believed that only philosophers should be kings to ensure any state is run ethically. He also believed that to sufficiently deter immoral acts, legislation was not enough. We need to create punishment in the afterlife.'

'What's this got to do with anything' said Jean Claude who was getting impatient.

'I'm getting to it' replied Elliot. 'At the start of the book, Plato talks about a cave. This... this room is Plato's cave' said Elliot.

'What is' said Jean Claude.

'This chamber' said Elliot.

'Explain. And remember, I'm not a philosophy buff so use plain words.'

'Erm, Plato tried to relate the theory of philosophy to an untrained human. How do we know what is real? He gave a famous example of a group of people who, for all of their life, have been shackled in a cave, stuck facing a wall. Behind them is a fire which creates a silhouette on the wall of their shadowed form. They cannot turn their heads to look around, and as a result, they grow up their entire lives thinking that this is what people look like.'

'That's stupid' said David.

'I haven't finished' said Elliot. 'It is the philosopher who helps the people out of the shackles, and leads them from the cave into the light of day where they can see the truth.'

'What truth' asked Jean Claude.

'That our perceptions can deceive us. And that by leaving the cave of our minds we can be enlightened by a knowledge of the real world.'

Jean Claude understood what Elliot was saying, but David just looked blankly.

'So where's the stone' said David.

'I don't know, but this chamber is the cave and we need to find a way into the light.'

Chris got up off the floor, holding his back in pain from where David had hit him. Elliot helped him up and gave an evil stare at the floor. He was too frightened to move his gaze to David's direction. It was not worth the risk of provocation.

Elliot explained that this message affirms why the treasure was kept secret. Plato believed that only philosophers should rule. As a result, only a philosopher should be able to find the power that would enable them to conquer.

'But Plato also believed that every Greek should have a slave' said Chris. 'He's hardly a paragon of virtue.'

'Yes, but at the time, he was' said Elliot. 'Slavery in those days was an important part of society. As disgusting as it was, most of the Greek economic developments would not have been made had it not been for the use of slaves.'

'My Jewish father would beg to differ. It was very common for Jews to be born into slavery. It didn't help their economy.'

Elliot knew he was right, but didn't respond. Jean Claude looked at the giant bowl that the statue of a man was holding and put his hand inside. He wiped the base of the bowl with his finger. A black sticky substance rubbed off.

'This stuff is titch' said Jean Claude. 'A fuel that can last for centuries.'

'Or millennia' said Elliot.

'This isn't a bowl' said Jean Claude. 'It's a torch. A very large one.'

David pulled out a box of matches and handed them to Jean Claude. Jean Claude struck one against the side of the box, letting off a small flame and a gentle line of smoke. He threw it into the marble torch and within a split second, a large fire roared into the air, lighting up the whole room. The only shadows in the chamber were from the people standing by the Olympic sized torch and the random sculptures dotted around.

'Now what' asked Jean Claude.

Elliot moved over to a gold statue. He looked at the shape it made on the wall. *Idea.* He tried to move the sculpture. With a bit of force, it slowly turned, causing the shadow on the wall to change shape. He moved over to another one that was shaped like an L. On turning the L-shaped sculpture, it created a silhouette on the wall that looked like an arm shackled to the floor.

'We need to move these sculptures into place to make a picture on the wall.'

They all pitched in, moving and twisting the sculptures around the circular tracks. Although they could move around, it wasn't clear which wall was supposed to have the shadow cast on it or what the silhouette was supposed to be. Elliot fiddled with the sculptures that moved around the track. Some were able to rotate. Others were stuck in one direction and could only move around the track. He reached one golden sculpture that looked like a torso. He tried to twist it, but it didn't move. He then tried moving it along the track, but it was stuck. It was the only one that wouldn't budge. *This must be it,* he thought. He moved the other pieces around to the torso shape and tried to marry them up.

They all helped to move the other sculptures. Within ten minutes, a form was starting to take place. Elliot put the last piece in place. The room shook and dust fell from the ceiling.

'Look' said Helen, pointed towards the shadow on the wall.

Elliot turned his head to see a shadow of three men crouching down. The marble skirting at the base of the wall was patterned so that it looked as if the three men were all shackled together by chains that were fixed to stone plinths on the ground. To the right of the three men was the silhouette of a Rosy Cross at chest height. Jean Claude walked up to the shadow and pushed down on the Rosy Cross. The wall pushed back to create an opening the size of a narrow doorway.

'You've outdone yourself again' said Jean Claude. 'Now move.'

Elliot checked the time. Two hours to find the stone and get them out of there. *We must be getting there by now,* he thought. He heard a fast rush of air. It made him jump. He wasn't sure where it came from. He turned around and saw the Bull fall to his knees. Blood started to spill out of his mouth and neck and the gunman fell forward onto his chest.

99

Istanbul – Present Day + 13 (Wednesday)

After seeing the gunman fall to the floor, David and Marco jumped into defensive positions and ducked behind the sculptures. They didn't know who was shooting or where they were hiding. A few seconds later, another rush of air flew into the room, followed by a large clang as a bullet hit one of the metal sculptures. The loud noise echoed across the chamber. Chris and Elliot ran to one corner to take cover. Helen and Jean Claude hid near the new opening by the silhouette on the wall.

'Who the hell is that' asked David.

'I don't know' said Jean Claude. 'No one else knew about this place.'

'Well, they obviously do.'

'Elliot run' said a male voice that came from the stairway.

David looked at the Bull lying on the floor in a pool of blood, then at Jean Claude.

'Teo? I thought you said you took care of him' said David.

'I did' replied Jean Claude. 'I have no idea how he's alive. He fell three floors to his death.'

'Well, he's definitely alive' said Jean Claude, running through the new opening in the wall. 'Bring Helen.'

David followed shortly behind Jean Claude. Marco went next dragging Helen by her arm as she kicked and shouted. As soon as the room was clear of Jean Claude and his men, Teo ran up to Chris and Elliot.

'Are you ok' asked Teo.

'Yes, but I…I don't understand. How are you alive' asked Elliot.

'You won't believe me if I told you. Besides, we don't have time for that. We have to stop Jean Claude.'

'Do you know what his intentions are' asked Chris.

'I do' said Teo, without any emotion. 'Jean Claude's a professor of haematology at Tel Aviv University. A devout evolutionist, with unorthodox beliefs. He published a paper three years ago, "Demise of our Growth." You may have heard of it.'

Elliot and Chris shook their heads. Elliot was surprised at how unthreatening Teo's manner was. His perception had been manipulated to fear Teo all this time. He felt like a fool.

'Jean Claude wrote in his paper that the world is carrying the weak. Spreading viruses, supporting disabilities and diluting stronger breeding. He argues that by carrying the weak, it is not just the strongest that survive, but everyone. Our species ceases to evolve. As messed up as it is, he truly believes that the evolution of the human race is prevented by our caring. He called it the decay of the human race.'

'What does that have to do with anything' said Elliot.

'I was working on a protection project for Jean Claude's brother… an archaeologist searching for the philosopher's stone. I thought nothing of it, until I learned of its ability to take life anywhere in the world.'

'Jean Claude's discovered a way of identifying blood groups susceptible to viruses and hereditary disabilities' said Elliot.

'Exactly. He wants to use the stone to wipe out a chunk of the population. Genocide on a scale that we've never seen before. It could be worse than the Holocaust, Soviet Famine and King Leopold's Congo massacre all together.

He thinks he's helping the world. Jean Claude's brother was just a puppet. He wouldn't... he couldn't see sense.'

'So you killed him?'

'A fight did break out when they learned I wanted to stop them. It was self-defence. I had to go on the run until I could be sure the stone would not get into Jean Claude's hands. Without his brother, he was stuck. Until he found you...Elliot.'

Teo explained how he killed one of David's men, Rav, who was disguised as a priest in the Notre Dame Cathedral. Rav had planned to kill Elliot and Helen, once in the tower in the Notre Dame Cathedral. Teo also stopped one of David's men in Washington from killing Elliot, by pushing him over the side of a building by the White House.

'I'm sorry' said Elliot. 'Really sorry. I didn't realise...'

'Don't worry' interjected Teo. 'We just need to stop Jean Claude. If he gets the stone, it will be too late.'

Elliot walked over to the dead mercenary lying on the floor. He felt sick when he saw the man's leg shaking. The merc had a gun in his right hand. Elliot bent down and picked off each individual finger until the fresh corpse let go of the weapon. He took the gun then ran over to the silhouette of the Rosy Cross and the new opening to get Helen. Teo stood in front, Chris was at the back.

David, Marco and Jean Claude ran through a short tunnel from the opening, dragging Helen in their stride. The short passage led to a much larger room, more like a grand hall than a chamber. It was too dark to see, but the echo was noticeably more prominent and the air was colder. Jean Claude's torch made sure they didn't bump into anything as they ran passed statues and artefacts.

'You and Marco go on' said David. He stopped running, cocked his gun and waited behind an Ancient Egyptian statue of a goddess, made of gold and onyx. He rested his gun against the shoulder of the statue. 'I'll take them out as soon as they come through the tunnel.'

Jean Claude nodded then marched on. Marco continued dragging Helen as she tried to wriggle out from his grip. As Jean Claude and his torch departed, the only light in the vast blackness was a dim light in the tunnel from where he'd come out from. He'd be able to see Teo and Elliot, but they wouldn't be able to see him. A perfect hunting spot.

In the previous room, Teo stepped up to go into the passageway and cautiously went after Jean Claude. He held his gun at shoulder height.

'Wait' said Elliot.

'We don't have time to wait' said Teo.

'They'll be ready for us to walk through that door' said Elliot. 'Wouldn't you? We need a plan.'

Teo looked through the passageway and waved his torch around. It was pitch black, although he could see several coins at the foot of the new room. Otherwise, he was unable to see anything. Teo ran over to the dead mercenary, grabbed his legs and dragged his body into the passageway. He lifted the body up against the wall of the entrance.

'Ok, here's the plan' said Teo. 'I'll hold this body up so it looks like we're peering through the entrance. As soon as you hear a break in the firing, I want you to run into the room and take cover.'

'Got it' said Elliot.

'No' said Chris. 'You can't let Elliot do this. It's not safe.'

Elliot and Teo both looked at each other, gave a small smile. It had to be done. Elliot knew it and Teo knew it.

'Chris… it's ok. I have to do this' said Elliot.

Chris nodded, gave Elliot a manly hug, then patted him on the back. 'Be safe.'

Elliot moved next to the entrance then bent down like he was about to start the one-hundred-meter sprint. He had no idea where he'd be running to. It was too dark. He just hoped there'd be somewhere to hide. Teo slowly moved the Bull's dead body out into the grand hall. The body was heavy, but he was strong enough to support the extra weight. He was ex-Mossad special forces, after all. First the merc's head peered out, then the rest of the body. A loud bang echoed through the room as David's bullet shot into the dead body, causing Teo to jolt back. It was shortly followed by another three bullets. One missed, but the others fell squarely in the dead man's chest.

'Now' said Teo.

Elliot heard the gunshot coming from the right side of the room and so he sprinted out of the passageway in a forward direction, keeping as low as he could and away from the line of gunfire. The hall was pitch black. He felt his way around with his hands, trying to avoid bumping into anything. All he could hear was gunfire and the crunch of precious metal coins under his feet. The chamber was big and after running ten or so metres, he'd still not reached the other end. He tripped over something and landed on the floor, bashing his knee. He laid down as low as possible with his arms on the ground, like a possum, pretending to be dead. When he turned around, he could see Teo had dropped the merc on the floor, although the gunfire was still going on.

Elliot's eyes eventually adjusted to the darkness and he could just about make out the room was covered with golden coins, statues, trinkets, papyrus scrolls, jade, medallions and other items of historic and intrinsic value. And that was only the items that he could see. The rest of the room was too dark to be visible. He soon realised he was at one end of the room. David was somewhere further in. He stayed as silent as he could behind a golden sarcophagus. He looked back at the dead merc on the floor by Teo. An unused flare had fallen out of his pocket and rolled onto the floor.

Elliot listened to see if he could hear anything. The room was now totally silent. He crawled like a snake as close as he could to the dead body, desperately trying to avoid being seen. He put his hand out of cover and reached for the flare. A bullet ricocheted against the floor and several coins went flying over Elliot's head. He snapped his hand back and waited. Before he knew it Teo came running through the opening, taking advantage of the fact that Elliot was the new target. David fired several bullets in Teo's direction, but missed and they crashed into the wall, spraying out bits of stone. Elliot quickly darted his hand forward, grabbed the light, then got back into cover. He could see Chris in the light of the previous room, hiding in the passageway. Chris had frozen and looked terrified.

'Good work, Elliot' said Teo.

'Thanks. I think my heart is going to give out if this carries on much longer.'

He handed the flare to Teo, who snapped it causing it to light up like a firework about to take off. He threw it in David's direction, leaving a red ball of light flying through the air. Elliot looked through an opening in the statue he was hiding behind. As the flare brightened the room, he could see that the chamber was huge. As big as a football pitch, if not bigger. Covered in treasure. The ceiling was at least four storeys high. There were weapons covered in jewels, armour made of gold and silver, jewels and treasures seized from tribes during Alexander the Great's conquest. It was massive, and for a split second, Elliot was in a trance like state from what they'd found. It was surreal. The shot of a bullet hitting a silver shield sent a loud vibration that brought him back into the reality of his danger.

The red flare landed no less than five meters away from David. Close enough to even the playing field. Teo and Elliot were not the only ones left in the dark. An exchange of bullets were made, causing Elliot's ears to ring.

Jean Claude, Marco and Helen had made their way towards the end of the gigantic vault. Helen had bruises on her arms from being dragged by Marco, who took pleasure out of her resistance. Jean Claude's torch weaved its way through the accumulated wealth of Alexander the Great, as he looked for the Philosopher's Stone.

'Where is it' said Jean Claude. 'It must be around here somewhere.'

As they reached the end of the giant hallway, the room narrowed significantly. The end of the room split horizontally to create a large balcony, overlooking the expanse and all its wonders. Jean Claude shone his torch at the balcony. It had no rail guards and all he could see was the top of a cylinder stand with something placed on it.

'This must be it' said Jean Claude.

'You can't do this' said Helen, grabbing onto his arm.

'Get off me' he said, yanking her hand off of him. 'I'm trying to save the world.'

Marco punched her in the stomach. She fell back into an old storage unit made of decayed wood. It broke apart as she landed on it, causing dust and splinters to fall around her. Jean Claude marched off towards the stair way and left Marco to deal with Helen.

The gun fight continued, but apart from the already dead mercenary and some statues of famous philosophers, no one had actually been shot. Elliot agreed to hold the ground and keep shooting while Teo snuck up on David. Teo moved like a whisper and Elliot almost immediately lost site of him. Teo worked his way from the furthest edge so that David wouldn't see him coming. Teo could see David's outline from the weak red glow of the dying flare. David was busy facing the other direction, shooting at Elliot. He tiptoed behind David until he was only a few feet away, raised his gun level with David's head. As he pulled the trigger, it clicked, but no bullet came out. The chamber was empty.

David heard the noise and turned to see Teo and raised his gun to shoot. Teo lunged forward and disarmed him using a military technique. David's gun fell to the floor. A split second later, Teo pulled back his arm, clenched his fist and threw it forward with a force that knocked David backwards, causing him to land into a monument with a thud. David jerked his head and neck forward from being winded, and before he could regain his stance, Teo went straight in with a round of jabs to the ribs. Teo was relentless. Like pistons in an engine, firing back and forth with full force.

David let out a groan of pain, then pulled his hands together like a boxer. Teo swung a punch towards his head. Instinctively, David blocked the punch and countered with an uppercut to Teo's neck. Teo fell back, unable to breathe from the hit and David jumped forward. Teo was keen to ensure David couldn't get much of a swing while he couldn't breathe and so huddled into David, pushing against him. Their locked bodies fell to the ground.

Elliot ran up to see them struggling on the floor, elbows locked into place and trying to use their strength to restrain the other. He aimed his gun at the spaghetti of limbs. Teo was on top of David and their arms flailed around like butterfly wings. He just wanted to wound David. He tried to aim the gun at David, waited until he had a clear shot, then pulled the trigger. Just as he did, Teo's arm moved down and the bullet went straight into his bicep. Teo groaned deeply. David pushed him off, stood up then kicked him in the stomach.

'Leave him alone' said Elliot, shaking as he held his gun at David.

'Or what.'

'Or I'll shoot you.'

'No you won't.'

Elliot faced the gun at David's chest. David walked towards him, snapped the gun out of his hand, punched him to the ground then kicked him in the head. His upper body bent backwards and his head crashed into a metal sculpture. His head went dizzy with pain. David cocked his gun.

'You should be more careful next time you see an opportunity to take me out' said David, aiming his gun at Elliot.

Elliot looked up and saw the barrel of a gun, followed by a thudding sound. David fell to his knees then collapsed forward onto Elliot. He pushed David off of him and looked up to see Chris holding a golden staff, bloodied at one end.

'Urgh' said Elliot, holding his jaw and sitting up to look at Chris. 'Thanks for that. You saved my bacon.'

Teo stood up, holding his arm and limping. 'You bastard. You shot me.'

'I'm so sorry. It looked like a clear shot.'

'Yeah, well next time leave the shooting to me.'

'Where's Helen' said Elliot. 'I can see a torch light up ahead. That must be them.'

Elliot heard the scream of a female voice. They looked at each other, turned on their torches and ran as fast as they could to the end of the vault, jumping over chests, dodging statues and trying not to fall over.

Whilst on the floor, Helen picked up a silver, jewel encrusted candle holder and whacked Marco around the head with it. He lost his balance for a few seconds, giving Helen enough time to run after Jean Claude to try and stop him reaching the philosopher's stone. She ran up the steps to get to the balcony, but Marco was too quick. He grabbed her left leg and dragged her down the stairs. She slipped and hit her head against a stone step. He jumped on her, half way up the steps and pinned her down. He was too heavy for Helen and despite her best efforts, she could not get away from his grip.

'You're mine now' said Marco, licking her neck as he held her down.

He dragged his knife across her top and across her neck, letting blood gently seep out. She managed to wriggle up a little, but there was no escape.

'No, please no' said Helen.

Marco grabbed her hands and smashed her wrists into the sharp edge of a solid stone step. She screamed. She kicked her feet down and they both moved up by one step. She did it again and the steps made a cracking sound. Marco realised what she was doing, jumped up a few steps so he was further up the stairway, but still on top of her. He slammed Helen's hands down again into the stone, even harder. Just at that moment, the steps gave way under their weight and crashed down. As Helen fell down to the floor below, she grabbed onto Marco. Marco's head was over part of the stairway that had not fallen and as she held onto him, he came tumbling down twisting his neck back. It let out a loud crack as it broke his spinal cord and they both fell two metres to the floor. Helen screamed as she hit a rock covered floor.

Elliot, Teo and Chris saw what happened and rushed over. Elliot pulled

Marco's lifeless body from on top of Helen. His head flopped to the side. Elliot had never seen a broken neck before, but the site of it made him squirm. He moved the bricks out of the way and tried to pull Helen up. She cried in pain.

'Be careful of my shoulder. I think I've dislocated it.'

'Chris, Teo, give me a hand' he said.

'No' said Helen. 'You need to stop Jean Claude now. He's up there with the stone.'

Elliot checked the time. Thirty minutes to get Jean Claude out of there in order to save Toby. He looked at the rubble of steps. The only steps that didn't collapse were three meters high. Teo and Helen were injured and would have to stay put.

'Chris, give me a boost' he said, standing next to the broken stairs.

Chris put his back against the wall, stood over the rubble of broken steps and locked his fingers together, palms up. Elliot put his right foot on his locked hands, held onto the wall and pushed up. He was just high enough to grab onto the lowest surviving step. As he pulled himself up, some rubble and dust fell down into Chris' silver hair and face. Chris closed his eyes, scrunched his face and spat out some of stone that had fallen in his mouth. Elliot climbed onto the second half of the stairway.

'Quick, chuck me a torch' he said.

Chris threw him a light. Elliot ran up the flight of steps as quickly as he could. On reaching the back of the balcony, he shone the torch around. The balcony was large and covered in holes from where the stone floor had eroded and caved in. There were holes everywhere. Elliot saw a figure on the background. It was Jean Claude, walking over to a cylinder stand at the front of the balcony. There was something on top of the stand. *The stone.*

100

Istanbul – Present Day + 13 (Wednesday)

Elliot stepped onto the decrepit balcony. He was painfully curious to see the philosopher's stone and yet he feared it so much that he wanted it buried away from the world, never to see the light of day. He shone his torch over the potholed floor and saw Jean Claude with his hand over a container lying on top of the cylinder plinth. He ran towards him, but with each step came a cracking noise and he soon realised the stone floor beneath him was incredibly unsafe and would have to walk slower. He could see through the potholes where the floor had collapsed into the ground below.

'Wait' said Elliot. 'You can't do this. Can't you see what you're doing?'

Jean Claude stopped, picked up the container and turned to Elliot. 'I know it is difficult to understand, but it is a necessary evil for the greater good.'

'How is killing innocent people for the greater good?!'

'As a philosopher, I'd thought you'd know. Darwinist thinking is that the strongest of the species survive. But, we live in a world where governments have turned to nanny states and carry the weak, the disabled and the ignorant. These lower forms of being, breeding with the strong. There can be no survival of the fittest as our species is held back. Our society is in a state of decay.'

'This is madness. You're misguided and need help. This is not humane.'

'Isn't it? Scientifically and economically it is the one logical conclusion that people want to ignore.'

'There's nothing to ignore...'

Jean Claude interrupted. 'Let me finish. Scientists have proved that some genes are more susceptible to viruses than others. They harness infection and through the use of medicine, the virus itself evolves into a stronger, resilient and more dangerous germ. By destroying the weaker gene pool, we can reduce humanity's exposure to illness in the long run.'

'I'm sorry' said Elliot, raising his gun at Jean Claude. 'But I can't let you.'

'Elliot, don't do this. The removal of the weaker gene pool would save governments worldwide trillions of pounds, every year.'

'You're epileptic. You'd be killing yourself.'

'I've suffered enough in this world. I'm in a prison of my own illness. And each time I have a fit, my prison gets smaller and smaller. If I can do one great for this world, it would be this.'

'Drop the stone' said Elliot, walking towards Jean Claude.

'No.'

'Then you leave me no choice.'

Hand shaking, Elliot aimed his gun at Jean Claude and took a step forward. As he did, the flooring gave way. He managed to balance himself with his left foot. He wobbled for a few seconds and then regained his balance. A second later, the floor under his left foot creaked. The pressure from standing on one foot became too much for the ancient ground and he fell through a new hole. His legs dangled under the floor, as his upper body desperately clawed above it to keep him alive. Bits of rock smashed against the floor below. When he had his grip, Elliot looked into the hole to see a dark room with several pillars attempting to hold up the balcony. Some of them had fallen down and were no longer supporting the floor he was on.

'Help me. It doesn't have to be like this.'

Jean Claude looked over to Elliot, gave him a look of sympathy. He carefully stepped over the broken stone flooring until he reached him and bent down. Elliot held out his hand.

'I'm sorry' said Jean Claude.

Jean Claude stamped down on the floor next to Elliot to try and make him fall to his death.

'What are you doing' shouted Elliot. 'No.'

After a few stamps, the ground cracked and the stonework tumbled down to the floor below, taking Elliot with it. Elliot hit the ground with a thud. He landed on his feet, but the momentum gained from falling at a height made him fall backwards onto the hard floor. His lower spine landed on a chunk of rock and he groaned in agony as it dug into him. A moment later, Jean Claude also fell through the floor, landing forward and hitting his head hard against a pillar, briefly knocking him unconscious.

The heavy stone pillars supporting the floor above no longer had anything holding them in place. They began to twist and turn before leaning to fall over. *Oh crap*, thought Elliot. He rolled over so that his back was no longer under the falling pillar, but he was not quick enough. The pillar crashed down, pinning his legs to the ground. Fortunately, the end of the beam got caught on the bottom of another column, narrowly preventing his bones from being shattered into pieces. There was a small amount of room and Elliot tried to wriggle his legs out. It was no use.

'Help me.'

Jean Claude sat up, rolled his head around as he came to. He saw Elliot trying to escape. Jean Claude walked over to Elliot and put his hands on the pillar.

'I'm sorry, but I need to do this and I cannot let you stop me.'

Jean Claude pushed the resting pillar away to try and crush Elliot's legs.

'What are you doing' said Elliot, dazed and shaken up.

The resting pillar rolled away from the standing column and got caught on some rubble, enabling Elliot to get free. He wriggled out as fast as he could away from the moving heavy stone. A grating sound came from the standing column as its bottom gave way. It came tumbling down on Jean Claude, squashing him down by the lower back. His body made a loud crunching noise as the bones in his back broke like a twig. Jean Claude screeched. A sound that Elliot had never heard of before in a human. Blood came out from all areas.

'I can't. I can't feel anything.'

More of the ceiling came crashing down, pinning Elliot to the floor. He couldn't move and just lay there stuck.

101

Istanbul – Present Day + 13 (Wednesday)

In the great hall, Teo heard screams from a small hole in the wall by beneath the stairway. He shone his torch through the hole to see lots of dust. He could just about make out two bodies and a small cobweb of fallen pillars. He picked up a golden statue and started hitting it against the wall. Bits of brick broke off and the hole became wider. He shone his flashlight again and saw Elliot pinned under a mound of stone.

'They're through here' said Teo. 'Elliot needs help.'

Chris gently sat Helen down, grabbed a small log shaped piece of stone and rammed the wall. It wasn't easy, but gradually parts of the wall came away like Lego being taken apart, piece by piece. A few minutes later and they had broken enough of the wall to climb through. He hopped over and rushed across to Elliot and tried to free him, but the stone was too heavy. Chris followed behind, climbed through, but caught his foot on the wall and fell forward. He saved himself by putting both hands forward, arms stretched out. Chris dusted himself off then joined Teo.

'Ready' said Teo, holding the underneath of the rock.

'Ish' replied Chris, holding it from the opposite side.

'On three' said Teo. 'One, two, three.'

They both lifted with all their might. Chris' face looked like he was about to explode from spontaneous combustion. The stone moved just enough for Elliot to wiggle his legs free. His legs were badly bruised with several cuts, but nothing was broken.

'Thanks guys' said Elliot, dusting himself off and holding his arm.

Elliot looked over to Jean Claude, who was lying there helpless, squashed like a bug under the huge supporting beam. His breaths were short and fast. Elliot wasn't sure if he was going to make it or not. Teo picked a gun off the floor, checked the chamber and held it to Jean Claude's head.

'Because of you, I lost my job. Because of you, I'm a wanted man. Because of you, innocent people have died' he said, pulling the clip back on his gun.

'Teo' said Elliot. 'Believe me, he deserves to be punished for what he's done and for he was about to do. But this is not the answer. He'll go to jail and pay for it.'

Teo stood there with the gun held against Jean Claude's head, dead centre between the eyes. He paused then lowered his gun. Jean Claude was giving panting shorten breaths.

Elliot saw something in the rubble. *The philosopher's stone?* It was a stone carving of the cross with a rose in the middle. He picked it up to take a closer look. Whatever it was, it didn't look like a magical stone. There were cracks between the rose and the cross. Elliot wondered whether the stone was inside. He carefully twisted the rose and it came off. Inside there was no stone, just some very old, very worn papyrus. He pulled it out and gently unravelled it. At the top was a picture of the Rosy Cross. The rest of it was in Ancient Greek.

'Chris, what does this say' asked Elliot, holding it up.

Chris moved over to Elliot with his torch. 'Let me see. There are a couple of words that I'm not familiar with, but it says something like:

"The generality of men are naturally suited to be swayed by fear rather than reverence, and to refrain from evil rather because of the punishment it brings than because of its own foulness"

'I know this' said Elliot. 'That's Aristotle's. This is an original piece of his work. His very own script. This has to be in a museum. It's priceless.'

'Erm, Elliot' said Chris. 'It's more priceless than you think.'

'What do you mean?'

'It goes on to say how the life of the soul lives beyond the life of the body. Because of this, people cannot be fully deterred from doing wrong in this life as they know they'll be free from persecution in the afterlife.'

'That's from Plato's Republic' said Elliot.

'I think you'll find this is Aristotle's Republic' replied Chris.

'Plato's account of Socrates is that to create the perfect order and the perfect world, we need to design gods so that people will behave. It's not like they had the legal system back then, like we have now.'

'That's exactly what this one says' said Chris, scanning through it and trying to make sense of the ancient scroll. 'Aristotle's Republic seems to suggest that there needs to be only one god, superior to all others and one messiah to walk this earth. Only then will people follow.'

'Erm, you mean Jesus?'

'Let's not get ahead of ourselves' replied Chris.

Elliot raised his eyebrows. 'This could be the origin of the New Testament!'

'You're talking about the bible' said Helen.

'Think about it' said Elliot. 'There's a bucket load of historical evidence to back this. I remember in one of my lectures that Xenophobes, one of Socrates students, considered Homer's existing mythological gods had too many humanistic flaws and many Greeks were losing faith in them. Control needed to be restored. Xenophobes considered a new order was needed.'

'That doesn't mean this is the creation of the New Testament' said Helen.

'Ok, fine, how about this' said Elliot. 'The Church spent most of the dark ages destroying all philosophy universities. Aristotle's principles and ideas were the only non-Christian philosophical ideas that the Church accepted. Coincidence? Even Saint Thomas Acquinas, the Christian philosopher, affirmed this. Not to mention that both Aristotle and the Church are big on ethics and share very similar view points.'

Chris put his hand on Elliot's shoulder. 'You've got a point.'

'See' Elliot said, looking at Helen. 'Scholars believe about seventy-five percent of Aristotle's works got destroyed when the Great Library of Alexandria caught fire in forty-eight BC. Maybe it didn't catch fire. Maybe this is but one piece of his works that's been preserved.'

Chris went on reading. He explained that the scroll contains instructions on how to create the perfect republic and to maintain the existing slave trade, by creating a new religion and blaming the Jews for the death of a Messiah. It dawned on Elliot. All these years of persecution of the Jews could have been as a direct result of this scroll.

Chris carefully put the scroll in his jacket pocket. Jean Claude made a sickly groan and Elliot turned his head to see the broken man lying pinned to the ground. He had pure hatred for what he had done. And yet, he could see all the pain Jean Claude had been through. So much so, that it manifested such a misguided view he was prepared to sacrifice his life to ensure others wouldn't suffer in the same way. It was sick, wrong, immoral and twisted. But Elliot still felt sorry for him.

'We can't leave him here to rot' said Elliot.

'Agreed' said Helen, holding her dislocated shoulder and hobbling over to them.

Chris, Elliot and Teo all spread out on each side of the pillar, held underneath and tugged as hard as they could. It was too heavy and as they moved it, they heard a snap followed by a loud cry from Jean Claude. It moved just enough for Elliot to pull him out from underneath the stone. He saw Jean Claude's lower half and gagged. It looked like a clothed pile of road kill. It churned his stomach and he had to look away. He was never great with blood, but this was just way too much for his eyes to handle.

Teo saw Helen holding her shoulder in agony and walked up to her.

'Sit down' he said, pointing to a pillar laying on its side.

'What for?'

'We need to sort out your shoulder.'

Helen frowned. 'Erm, I think I'll wait to see a doctor, thanks.'

'You want to climb back the way we came like that? Good luck.'

Helen sat down next to Teo. He gently placed her arm down by her side, held her hand and moved it so her arm was shaped like a boomerang. Helen let out a cry. Elliot could see the shoulder line looked out of place and it made him a bit queasy.

'Are you sure you know what you're doing' said Elliot.

'We'll see, won't we' he replied. 'Helen, I'm going to count to three and then you're going to feel a bit of pain.'

'Ok' she said.

'One...' he said, then quickly pushed the top of her arm forward and twisted in retaliation to the pain.

She shrieked as her arm fell into place, then slapped Teo's face. Her arm was sore, but much better than when it was out of its socket.

'Thanks, you arsehole.'

'Trust me' said Teo. 'If you know when it's about to come you tense up and it makes it more difficult to fix.'

Helen raised her eyebrows. She sat there, holding her arm and starring into the huge dark vault. There was just enough light from their torches to allow her to see another giant bowl, similar to that in the room with the silhouettes. She stood up, walked over to it and put her hand in. It was the same black stuff.

'Hey guys, come and check this out. Has anyone got a match?'

'I do' said Jean Claude, barely able to breathe. He put his hand in his bloodied trousers and threw them to Helen.

She struck the match. It didn't light at first and just let off a small line of smoke. A couple more strikes and it lit up with a small glow. She threw it in the Olympic style torch and a giant flame flew into the air, lighting up the hall. The room was huge. Even with the bright light of the roaring fire, the edges of the room were dark, but only now could they appreciate how big the treasure room really was. Bigger than a football pitch and shaped like a coffin for a giant. Small at the bottom end where the legs would be, widening in the middle and then narrowing again at the top.

Elliot had never seen anything so overwhelming. There were mounds of gold, silver, jewels, statues of philosophers, weapons made of valuable materials, necklaces, head pieces, shields and coins of varying origin. A room several stories high, decorated from top to bottom in gold leaf paint, trinkets and ornaments. Each storey had mini viewing platforms like box offices in a theatre, one above the other, all occupied by statues of philosophers and Alexander the Great's top ranking army officials. There was too much to take in. Mountains of papyrus scrolls were stored in an organised section of the vault.

'I'm glad we didn't throw the flare in that direction' said Teo, looking at the library of scrolls.

'There are so many scriptures here' said Helen.

Elliot nodded. All the piles of writing. The largest collection of information and knowledge of the world conquered by Alexander the Great. Elliot thought about how every Ancient Greek university was destroyed by the Church in the dark ages. Nearly all non-Christian information, apart from that kept by the Arabic world, was believed to have been destroyed. But it wasn't. It was just kept very well hidden. The treasure is one thing, but the library itself would be absolutely priceless.

'We're going to be rich' said Helen.

'If you can get it out of here' said Chris.

Elliot was unable to celebrate the success of his find. Not when his brother's life was in danger. He grabbed Jean Claude by his shirt. The movement caused him to let out another cry of pain.

'Where's my brother?'

Jean Claude splattered a gargled cough. 'I don't know.'

'What do you mean' shouted Elliot.

'David...' he said, unsuccessfully trying to take a breath of air. 'David... one of his men is holding him somewhere in Istanbul. I am sorry. I... I don't know where he is.'

Elliot freaked. He checked the time. *Ten minutes left!* The idea that there was no way of getting hold of his brother made him feel sick. He was helpless. Toby was going to die. He had failed. Overwhelmed with a power driving from his stomach that made him want to cry and throw up at the same time. He burst out into tears. He couldn't go back the way they'd come. Not after the bridge had collapsed. He needed to find another way out, although deep down he knew it was too late. Elliot turned his head and looked back into the room with the collapsed pillars. There was rubble everywhere.

'I have a thought' he said.

'What's that' asked Teo.

'There's no way all this stuff was hauled in here across that bridge and through those narrow tunnels.'

'Your point' said Helen.

'My point is that they must have come into this vault another way.'

Elliot picked up his torch, climbed through the broken wall and went off to investigate. A few minutes later he came back with a degree of hope.

'It goes on for a little while, but it's all up hill. I bet this is the entrance they used to carry all this treasure. They must've sealed it up' said Elliot.

'I'm not sure how we're going to get him out of here' said Elliot, looking down at Jean Claude.

'Chris' said Helen. 'Give me your jacket please?'

Chris took it off and handed it to her. She picked up two spear shaped golden poles and tied an arm of the jacket around each pole to create a makeshift stretcher. She lay it down on the floor and they all helped lift Jean Claude on to it. Jean Claude let out a groan. The floor was covered in blood from where his legs had been crushed. Teo carried the stretcher from the front, Elliot from the back and they worked their way through the sealed room, moving uphill.

102

Istanbul – Present Day + 13 (Wednesday)

Henry followed Abrafo up the concrete steps, along the side of the fishmongers. He checked the time. Three fifty-eight in the morning. As the lights were on, he could see through the window. His tired eyes watched as Abrafo walked into the kitchen, made himself a plate of food and left it on the counter by the window. Henry ducked, waited a few seconds then slowly raised his head back up.

He saw Abrafo move to the end of a kitchen, take the latch off a door, peer inside then locked it again. Abrafo looked at a clock on the wall. It read four am. He went into another room and after a few seconds, came back wearing blue plastic gloves and holding a cloth and bottle of chloroform. Henry's senses were tingling. He knew something was up. He needed to get in that apartment, but had to be careful. He was out of his jurisdiction and any action he took would almost certainly be breaking the law. It was so late that the birds were beginning to sing their morning songs. Not long and it would be light.

Henry knocked on the door. Gently at first, but it was so light and timid that no one could have heard it. He knocked again. This time he did it harder and with authority. A shadow moved in front of the textured glass covering the top half of the door. A few seconds later, Abrafo opened the door half way, revealing a stocky man and behind him was an old side table with ornaments of Turkish dancers. His left shoulder and arm were kept behind the cover of the door. It looked as though he may have been holding something. Abrafo looked at his watch, then back at Henry.

'Can I elp ya' said Abrafo.

'I'm very sorry for knocking so late. I erm. It's my wife. I was just in the area with my wife. I had a few beers and went to drain the lizard, but when I came back she was gone. She's not at my hotel and I can't get hold of her on my phone. Before I went to the toilet I saw you walking around the market across the road. It's a long shot, but you didn't see anything unusual did you?'

'Nah, sorry' said Abrafo as he started to close the door.

Henry put his hand on the door to stop it from closing. 'I'm sorry. I don't mean to be rude. You didn't see anyone, anyone at all? Anyone else that maybe I could ask?'

'Try the shop keeper across the road. Take your hand off the door.'

Henry nodded and took his hand off the door. Just then, Henry heard a child crying from inside the apartment. Henry gave Abrafo a suspicious look. Abrafo noticed, then quickly bent down slightly, as if he was trying to grab something behind the door. *A weapon?* Before he had a chance, Henry kicked the door with great force, causing it to smash open. The door flew backwards, bashing Abrafo hard against his head and body. He saw Abrafo had a gun in his hand. Henry charged into Abrafo and pinned him up against the wall. Abrafo was bigger than him. It didn't take long after regaining focus before Henry was overpowered. His gun came away from the wall and started moving in Henry's direction, closer and closer to his face. In the struggle, Abrafo pulled the trigger which sent a deafening shot right past Henry's ear. His ears physically hurt and he was left with a disorientating ringing sound. He felt dizzy, but had to stay with it if he wanted to stay alive. He kneed Abrafo in the groin, bringing his chest forward. Henry saw a metal ornament on the side table, picked it up and swung it across Abrafo's temple.

The stocky giant fell to the floor with a bloodied head and collapsed into unconsciousness. Henry made sure he was out cold, and turned his body over so he was lying chest upwards. He picked up Abrafo's gun and checked each room to make sure there were no other dangerous people there. The place was clear. He walked back into the kitchen with the locked door, lifted up the latch and opened it. He saw Toby, looking frightened and even more scared by the presence of a new face with a gun. He cowered in the corner of the room, unable to move.

'Toby' said Henry. 'I'm a policeman and I'm here to help you. It's ok. You're safe now.'

103

Istanbul – Present Day + 13 (Wednesday)

Elliot's arms were aching from carrying Jean Claude on the makeshift stretcher. Although they'd only been walking a kilometre or so, the additional weight made it feel like miles. Walking in bare feet was not helping. They reached the end of the tunnel, which was blocked by a heap of piled stones.

'What now' said Chris.

'I don't fancy carrying him all the way back' said Elliot.

'Right then' said Teo. 'Let's see what's on the other end of this.'

They put the stretcher carefully down, then began removing the rocks out of the way. They started at the top to make sure they didn't topple over and land on anyone's feet. Elliot took the first, who handed it to Teo, who handed it to Chris at the back and threw them on the floor behind them. It took a while, but an hour later and they had removed most of the stones. Elliot shone his torch through the gap to see a broom, mop and bucket and several cleaning products in a small room.

'Since when did the ancient Greeks use washing up liquid' said Elliot.

Chris laughed. 'What?'

CHAPTER 103

They cleared the last of the rocks and Elliot stepped into the small room. It was dark, but he could see a wooden door at the end of it. A faint light protruded through the door's keyhole. Helen stayed behind Elliot as he crept forward. After what had happened, he wanted to be prepared for anything. He opened the door to see tables and chairs, with neatly laid cutlery. Elliot soon realised he'd just come out of a storage area of an old cistern. An old cistern that had since been converted into a restaurant.

'I don't know about you, but I'm starving' said Chris.

'You'll have to wait a few hours until they're open' said Helen.

Helen picked up some bread from a side table and threw a piece to Elliot. He was caught off-guard, but just managed to catch it.

'Thanks' he said, tearing into his slightly stale meal and taking a small nibble.

Elliot's body needed the sustenance, but he felt too sick to eat over the thought of his brother. There was no way he could eat now. He left the table area and made his way upstairs to the exit. The door was locked, but could be opened from the inside. He turned the latch and opened the door to see the sun start to rise. A welcome feeling of freedom and fresh air. His senses became alive as he felt the gentle breeze on his face, the smell of civilisation and the warmth of the sun on his skin. None of which he expected to experience again. He stood outside the restaurant, on a street near a market that had not yet opened, although some of the market workers were setting up their stalls and stands. Laying out their spices and produce for the day's supply and demand. They stared at him. He must've looked odd with his torn clothes, bruised face and darkened bare feet. He didn't care. He was just grateful to be out and around normal people that weren't trying to kill him. But more importantly, there was a big hole. Toby. Poor Toby was gone.

'Elliot' said Helen, pointing across the road. 'A payphone.'

He ran over, pulled out a scrunched up and barely readable card with Detective Wrightman's number on it. He punched the numbers in. The phone rang then Henry answered.

'Detective, it's Elliot.'

'Elliot...I've been looking for you. You've been a pain in my backside.'

'I know. I'm really sorry. Look, I need to come clean. I'm in Istanbul. I had no choice. They took my brother. He's gone' said Elliot, sobbing.

'It's ok, I know everything' replied Henry.

'You do? How?'

'I'll tell you what I know and you can fill in the gaps' said Henry. 'Where are you?'

Elliot gave him his location and told him about Jean Claude and his men. He hung up the phone and sat on the side of the street. Helen used her womanly charm to get the market stall workers to help carry out Jean Claude from the restaurant and they waited for Henry. When Jean Claude came out, they put him on the sidewalk. She sat down next to Elliot, with her knees up and feet next to her bottom.

'I'm sorry I didn't tell you about your father earlier' said Helen, resting her head on her knees. 'The truth is, nothing actually happened.'

'It's ok, Helen. It's out now, you really don't need to cover it up.'

'No, you need to understand. I loved your father. Very much. And as much as I wanted it, it was not reciprocated.'

Elliot was confused. He must have reciprocated enough to want to leave Elliot's mum. He even said he loved her to the medic as he was dying after the car crash. It was in the police reports.

'What do you mean?'

'I was persistent' said Helen, looking down at the floor. 'Your dad made it clear that nothing was going to happen. The night that your father died. He… he was coming to see me. To tell me that nothing was going to happen between us. He loved your mother and there was nothing going to get between that. I left a love note in his bag. He called to say we had to stay friends. I told him that if he wanted nothing to happen, I insisted he told it to my face. That was the day he had the car crash. I don't know what I was thinking. What can I say…. I, I loved him. But your dad. He was a good man.'

Elliot realised he'd misjudged his father. The unnecessary hate he'd carried against his father and his mistress, supressing the pain until it exploded into dysfunction. If only his mum knew, she may still be alive. His father rejected Helen. Elliot now understood why his father told the paramedic "I don't love her, I love someone else." Elliot got it the wrong way around. He was not leaving his mother. It was the opposite. Elliot put his hand on Helen's.

'It's ok.'

Half an hour later an ambulance turned up. Only one paramedic got out. He was pretty built for a medic and had a faint scar along his neck. It looked like a burn mark, imprinted on his skin. Not the usual look for someone in the health and rescue profession. Elliot and Chris helped the medic load the stretcher and Jean Claude into the back of the vehicle.

'Wait' said Jean Claude.

They stopped the stretcher mid-load.

'I'm sorry, Elliot' said Jean Claude. 'Sorry, to all of you. I didn't mean to cause you any harm. I…I was trying to do the right thing.'

Elliot bit his lip. He tried to smile, but physically couldn't. He'd been on the run, wanted for murder and had his little brother kidnapped and killed all because this man was "trying to do the right thing." They moved the stretcher fully into the ambulance and jumped out.

'Oh wait' said Elliot, running back to the ambulance and getting Chris' jacket. 'You don't want to forget this.'

Chris gently pulled out the scroll written by Aristotle. It was creased a little from being in his jacket pocket, but otherwise it was in surprisingly good condition for its age. Chris put it back in his pocket. The medic came over to them, asked them about how they got here. The medic seemed to believe the story and even gave Chris and Elliot a warm pat on the back. Elliot found it an awkward invasion of his personal space, but was too tired and worn out to react. Elliot noticed the medic's scar was a burn mark shaped like a snake coiled around a sword. He was about to say something to Chris, then see Teo begin to walk away.

'Where are you going?'

'I have to go' he replied.

'What for? What if we need an alibi. What if more people come?'

'No one will come. There are three of you. You won't need me. If you do, believe me, I'll hear about it and I'll be there.'

Elliot extended his arm. 'Thanks for saving us.'

Teo shook his hand. 'No, thank you. Because of you, the world has discovered one of the greatest finds known to man. And if the philosopher's stone had been real, then...well crap, you would've saved millions of lives.'

'What are you going to do' asked Elliot.

'Go back home. Clear my name and try and get my life back. You?'

Chris looked down at his bare feet. 'No idea. Get some shoes probably.'

Teo walked down the street and disappeared into the distance. Helen came up to Elliot and tapped him on the shoulder. The ambulance was behind them. He could hear the medic close the back door to the ambulance behind him.

'Where's Teo going' she asked.
'Home.'

A loud explosion ripped through the air, as parts of the ambulance flew everywhere. The force shoved Elliot to the floor, the debris narrowly missing him. The ambulance was scattered all over the place, along the street and bits even went into market stalls. Passers-by hid until they were sure it was safe then came out to inspect.

'What the hell' said Elliot. 'Was the medic in the vehicle?'
'No' said Helen. 'He just shut the ambulance door, then ran off.'

Fumes covered the street as the ambulance lay there burning away. Debris was everywhere. People came out of their homes to see what the commotion was. A few minutes later, a taxi turned up. Henry climbed out of the car. Elliot saw him open the back door and a small person got out.

'Toby!!'

Elliot couldn't hold back his emotions and wept. He ran over to the cab, picked up his brother and gave him the biggest hug he could possibly give. Toby held on tightly and smiled as he felt the warmth and protection of his older brother.

'I'm here little bud. I've got you.'

Helen came over and started to well up. 'You must be Toby' she said in a soft tone.
'This is my good friend Helen' said Elliot.

Toby nodded, but was too shy to speak. Instead he just buried his face into Elliot's chest and hid.

'Thank you Detective Wrightman' said Elliot. 'I can explain everything.'

'Well, you've certainly caught the police's attention' said Henry. 'Fortunately for you, Toby's kidnapper didn't delete his phone messages. That and one threat of him taking the rap and he spilled everything.'

'Thank God for that' said Elliot.

'However, there is the small issue of you causing criminal damage to St Paul's Cathedral, not to mention the fact that you and Helen broke out of a police cell.'

Crap, thought Elliot. He knew a criminal record would seal the coffin on him ever getting custody to look after his little brother. Still, Toby was alive which was more than he could hope for.

'But, you know, there's an awful lot of information to report on. Some records are known to go missing and my memory of everything that's happened… Well, let's just say there are certain things I may forget ever happened.'

'Detective, that would be unfortunate' said Elliot, smiling.

'Please, call me Henry.'

'Henry, thank you.'

'So is it true? Did you find the philosopher's stone and the treasure of Alexander the Great' asked Henry.

'Yes and no' said Helen. 'Alexander the Great's accumulated wealth is in that restaurant.'

Henry scrunched up his face and gave a confused look.

'There's a tunnel in the storage room downstairs' said Elliot.

'Ah' replied Henry. 'And the stone?'

Chris put his hand inside his jacket pocket. 'What the…'

'What is it' said Elliot,

'The scroll.... it's...it's gone.'

'What do you mean, gone' said Helen.

'The paramedic' said Elliot. 'He must've taken it.'

'How' asked Helen.

Elliot thought back to when the dodgy looking medic gave them a close pat on the back. Whoever he was, he wasn't a medic, that was for sure. He must've pick-pocketed Chris. There was no other explanation. None of them knew who the paramedic was, but none of them wanted to know. They'd only just escaped a near death situation and if they had got out of it alive, that was enough for them.

104

Istanbul Airport – Present Day + 14 (Thursday)

An overhead announcement was made for the last call to Amsterdam at gate four. Helen sat at a coffee table watching the electronic notice board flicker down with flight departures. Chris and Elliot sat opposite her, talking Henry through everything that had happened from start to finish. There was a lot to talk about. Toby was deeply engaged in drawing a picture of him and Elliot. He was shaken up, but with the right support network, a bit of therapy and love, he'd be fine. Henry's phone rang… it was a UK number.

'Excuse me' he said. 'I just need to take this.'

Henry walked out of the coffee shop and sat on a group of chairs outside an empty boarding gate. Elliot turned to Chris.

'That scroll. What do you think we should do' asked Elliot, trying to take a sip of his hot chocolate that had so much cream, it looked like a white Christmas tree.

'I don't know about you, but I'm glad it's no longer with us' said Chris.

'Why?'

'Do you want to be the person who breaks up a core belief that millions of people hold? One that teaches morals and gives people hope. People fight and kill to protect their religion and I don't want to get involved in that. Plus people's interpretation of it has evolved over time to make it kinder to the world. It's not the same as when we were in the dark ages and the Church was destroying any literature that wasn't from the church.'

'I guess' said Elliot. 'You know the Christian philosopher, St Thomas Aquinas, helped with that. He changed the Christian belief system from there being good people and bad people to one where each individual is capable of being good and evil.'

'Yeah. I'm not religious...' said Helen. 'But I'm glad I don't have to make the decision for anyone else.'

Elliot leant in on the table. 'But if it's true, think about all the chaos it's caused in the past. Blaming the Jews for the death of Jesus. The influence it could've had on history. The dark ages where millions of people were killed for being non-believers, Charlemagne's Saxon wars and the massacre of Verden. Let's not forget Nasizm. Man, I mean, I know Aristotle's Republic was to create order, but at what price.'

'I like that' said Chris.

'What' replied Elliot, raising his eyebrows. 'The persecution of innocent people?'

'No. The name. Aristotle's Republic' said Chris.

Henry came back over. Although they'd all had a night's sleep, it didn't show on Henry. His brownish grey hair was scruffy and his eyes were tired. He had a gleaming self-satisfied smile on his face.

'Someone get promoted' said Helen.

'No. I've just got off the phone with the chief. I've explained almost everything. You're all in the clear. There'll be no charges against you. Against any of you.'

'That's great' said Elliot.

'Well, it gets better' said Henry. 'Your boss, David Heartman heard about what's happened and has been speaking with Toby's social worker. She's aware that because of Elliot, we've managed to stop a cell of dangerous criminals and find one of the world's greatest treasures.'

'And' said Chris.

'And she's spoken with Toby's foster parents. They've agreed to remove their application for permanent parental control.'

'What does that mean' said Helen.

'It means there is still hope for me to live together with Tobes' said Elliot, putting his hand on his brother's head, shuffling his hair.

Elliot smiled with such authenticity he couldn't remember when he last felt this positive.

'Thanks Helen. Thanks all of you.'

'I'm glad we stuck together… as a team' said Helen.

'Plus the social worker's said that you can go and visit Toby whenever you want' said Henry.

An announcement was made for the departure to Washington at departure gate twelve. Helen and Elliot gave Chris a warm, but sad look. They'd all been through so much together. Whilst Elliot was glad it was all over, he was sorry to see Chris go. Helen gave him a hug. Chris went to shake Elliot's hand, but Elliot wrapped his arms around him with a warm man-hug.

'Until next time' said Elliot.

'Ha. Let's hope there won't be a next time' said Chris.

Chris walked off to his gate leaving Helen, Elliot and Henry, with Toby. Elliot finished his hot chocolate. He saved the cherry for Toby.

'Here Tobes' he said, passing the glazed cherry to him.

Toby smiled, held out his tiny hand and wolfed it down. Elliot helped him with his colouring in. His drawing skills were not great and he thought that Toby was perhaps doing a better job by himself.

'What are you going to do when you get back' asked Henry.

'Me' said Helen. 'Well, legally the Turkish authorities get to keep everything we've found. But, there's nothing to say they won't lend it to the British Museum. I've spoken with our boss. He's said we can do an exhibition on Alexander the Great. I think it will be a smash hit. What about you, Elliot?'

'I've decided that I'm going to go back to what I was doing before this mess all started.'

The announcement for the flight to London's Heathrow was calling for gate five. They began to gather their bags and made their way back home. Helen remembered what happened to her friend's husband's estate when he made a will before their marriage. It turned out that it became void. She encouraged Elliot to challenge his parents' wills that were made before they'd even met each other. It was unfair that the children should go without any financial security, and for the distant well-off family member to get everything. Helen agreed to pay for the legal fees. Elliot couldn't be more grateful for such a wonderful friend. One way or another, he would find a way to repay her.

105

British Museum, London – + 12 months later

The grand hall of the British Museum was covered in Ancient Greek artefacts. Tourists walked up and down, all admiring the new items on display. The exhibition on Alexander the Great was a hit. The daily clean was taking place and the all familiar mop worked its way down the aisle, making brushing movements on the floor as it created patterns from the direction of its master. It wasn't the best job, but it paid ok and it played an important part in the Museum.

Elliot walked through the door, dressed in smart-casual clothes and wearing a satchel. He was happy to see the new treasures on display. He passed the cleaner and gave him a warm smile. He had only been in that same position a year ago and if it wasn't for the events that happened in that job, he wouldn't be where he was now.

In the entrance way, giant advertisements of the exhibition on Alexander the Great hung from the ceiling like humongous curtains. There was a picture at the bottom of the ad showing Helen, Elliot and Chris. The discoverers of the world's greatest treasure. A proud memory. He only wished he had kept a memento from the treasure vault. Elliot made his way to Helen's office. It was next to David Heartman's room and was just as big, if not bigger. It had a golden plaque written on it saying "H Philips

– Head Curator." Elliot knocked on the door.

'Come in' she said.

Elliot turned the door knob and pushed the door open to see his old friend, sitting there at her big desk. She gave him a gleaming smile and stood up.

'My dear Elliot' she said, giving him a hug. 'So lovely of you to stop by. How's uni?'

'It's going very well thanks. Since they accepted me back, thanks to you, my results are much better. I'm finishing off my final year. If you can believe it, I'm due to graduate in a month!'

'I'm so proud of you' she said, resting her hand on his shoulder. 'You know there will always be a place for you here. Just say the word.'

He was glad to hear it. Once he'd finished uni, he'd planned to follow in his father's footsteps and work his way up to be a curator at the Museum. Besides, the British Museum was his heart and his family. Helen explained that although the treasure was kept by the Turkish Government, they had agreed to give the British Museum unrestricted and unlimited use of all and any artefacts. Helen is head of the exhibition on the treasure of Alexander the Great and the Museum is doing exceptionally well. Helen has even found a publisher for her book on the subject and two publishers entered into a bidding war over it.

'How's Toby?'

'He's good. I'm taking him to Lego Land tomorrow. You know, I spent so much time trying to work out how I can get him to live with me that I lost sight of what's best for him. I love him more than anything and his best interest is of paramount importance. The truth is, he's being looked after by a caring family. One that can provide for him. Until I finish university, that's something I can't offer. Not yet at least.'

'Well, he's lucky to have you' said Helen.

Elliot smiled. He had come to terms with the fact that his parents were no longer around and it was just the two of them left. They didn't have parents, but they still had a family, plus the support and love of friends around them, which was worth its weight in gold. Elliot used Helen's lawyer and his late father's will was successfully challenged. As a result, Elliot no longer had to struggle financially and when he is out of university, he can look after his little brother.

'What did you decide to do about Aristotle's Republic? Did you mention it in the exhibition?'

'No' said Helen. 'I've decided that it's not my place to. Even if I did, there's no evidence to prove it.'

'There is somewhere' said Elliot.

They both thought about the suspicious looking paramedic who pick pocketed Chris' jacket and took the scroll. Neither of them knew who he was, where he was from or where he was now. All they knew was that they were still alive and assumed that they were not of any interest to him or whoever he was working for.

'Ooh, I almost forgot' said Helen. 'There's something I've been working on. Actually, it is something your father was working on and I've picked up where he left off.'

'What is it?'

'We found a live working version of the Antikythera Mechanism. Chris had been working on a re-constructed model, but it wasn't right. The one we found was intact and has been used in the past to navigate as well as ascertain astrological projections.'

Helen placed a picture of the mechanism on her desk. 'Notice the symbol on the side.'

Elliot picked up the picture and studied it. It was a snake wrapped around a sceptre. It made him think of the scar on the medic's neck in Istanbul.

'What is it?'

'It's the Ancient Greek symbol known as the Asclepius wand. It's been linked to astrology and other mythological powers.'

Helen handed him an old leather book.

'Where did you get this from?'

'It's your father's. Turn to page fourteen.'

Elliot opened the front page of his father's journal. A photo was stuck inside. It was of Elliot and his father on a holiday, both eating ice cream together. Elliot remembered the holiday. It was one of his fonder memories. He turned to page fourteen to see the same symbol next to some scribbling and references to the Great Library of Alexandria. He couldn't understand why the same symbol that was burnt into the medic's neck was in his father's journal.

'What does it mean' asked Elliot.

'I don't know yet. Fancy another adventure?'

'Ha. Maybe when I've finished uni' said Elliot. 'I've had enough adrenaline to last me a life time.'

They both stayed silent and thought back to all the events that happened. The near death experiences, the challenges overcome, the friendships made, discoveries found and people lost.

'There's something I don't get' said Helen.

'What's that?'

'You said that Teo fell several stories onto hard rock at the Rumeli Fortress and was lifeless. By all accounts, he should be dead. There's no way he could've survived. How is he alive?'

Elliot shrugged his shoulders. 'God knows.'

Printed in Great Britain
by Amazon

79597937R00258